The smile froze on the c[...] [...]
head as if a fly had buzzed [...] [...]ing to me, boy?"

Doan moved to intercede. But Lon was faster. He took a step away from the counter where they were standing. "I'm telling you to apologize—right now."

"Apologize!" The Texan let go a harsh bark of laughter. "You talk mighty big for a snot-nosed kid."

The cowhand clawed at the gun on his hip. Lon's arm dipped in fast shadowy movement and the Colt appeared in his hand. He extended the pistol, thumbing the hammer, as the Texan got off a hurried snapshot. A slug whizzed past the youngster at the exact instant he feathered the trigger. A bright red dot pocked the cowhand's shirtfront. . .

RIO HONDO

MATT BRAUN

St. Martin's Paperbacks

RIO HONDO

Copyright © 1987 by Matt Braun.

ISBN: 0-312-96161-8

Printed in the United States of America

Signet edition/November 1987
St. Martin's Paperbacks edition/April 1997

St. Martin's Paperbacks are published by St. Martin's Press, 175 Fifth Avenue, New York, NY 10010.

10 9 8 7 6 5 4 3

To Dutch
companion, loyal friend
and one helluva Rottweiler

1

William Bonney was convicted on April 12, 1881.

The charge was murder and the jury vote was unanimous. Judge Walter Bristol, who believed in swift and certain justice, saw no reason to delay passing sentence. He condemned Billy the Kid to be hanged and set the date for May 13. The designated place of execution was Lincoln, New Mexico Territory.

No one was surprised by the decision. After a change of venue, the trial had been held in the town of Mesilla. But the murder had occurred in Lincoln, some three years past. There, on a pleasant spring morning, Sheriff William Brady had been gunned down in coldblood. It seemed a fitting place to stretch the Kid's neck.

Late that afternoon, Clint Brannock emerged from the hotel. He crossed the street and walked toward the jailhouse, where the Kid was being held. While he had no authority in the case, he'd traveled to Mesilla purposely to observe the trial. He was widely known, and his position as special agent for the army had set the local gossips to buzzing. None of them suspected the true nature of his business.

Inside the jail, a lone deputy occupied the outer office. He looked up from a dog-eared copy of the *Police Gazette* as Clint moved through the door. They were on nodding terms, though they had never exchanged more than casual greetings. The deputy spread his magazine out flat on the desk.

" 'Afternoon, Mr. Brannock."

"Hodgens," Clint said, inclining his head. "Where's Sheriff Garrett?"

"Up to the café," Hodgens replied. "Him and the rest of the boys are catchin' an early supper. They're planning to transport the Kid to Lincoln first thing tomorrow."

"I'd like a word with the prisoner. You think Garrett would object?"

Hodgens considered a moment. "Guess it wouldn't hurt nothin'. I'll take you back."

"Much obliged."

Clint followed him through the door to the lockup. There were four cells, three of them standing empty. In the one nearest the door, Bonney was stretched out on the bunk, hands clasped behind his head. His legs were secured with ankle shackles and chains.

Hodgens stepped aside, allowing Clint to move into the corridor. Then, bobbing his head, the deputy turned toward the door. "Give a yell if you need anything."

Clint halted before the cell. He took the makings from his shirt pocket and creased a rolling paper. Bonney watched silently while he sprinkled tobacco into the paper and licked the edges to form a seal. He struck a match on his thumbnail.

"Hello, Kid," he said, exhaling smoke. "How's tricks?"

"Just dandy," Bonney said with a go-to-hell smile. "How about your own self?"

"You're awful chipper for somebody that's gonna be hung."

"Hung, hell!"

Bonney swung his legs over the side of the bunk. The shackle chain rattled as he stood and hobbled to the cell door. His mouth split in a lopsided grin.

"You wanna make some fast money, Brannock? Lay odds that I never set foot on the gallows."

The statement was not altogether braggadocio. Barely twenty-one now, Bonney had killed eight men in the last six years, and never once come close to facing the hangman's rope. His exploits had brought him the adulation of the common people and the respect of ruffians throughout the territory.

Contrary to popular belief, Clint knew the Kid was nothing more than a common murderer. Far from a gunfighter, the young outlaw had given none of his victims an even break. Of the men he'd killed, at least seven had been gunned down with no chance to defend themselves. He was one of those oddities of God's handiwork, a man purged of conscience.

Studying him through the bars, Clint was struck again by his deceptive appearance. Bonney was runt-sized, shorter than many women, with a lantern jaw and the look of a bantam gamecock. Only his eyes, which were the color of carpenter's chalk, gave him away. His gaze was steady and confident, more menacing than a bald-faced threat.

Until today, Clint had never had any dealings with the Kid. Their acquaintance was through Virgil Brannock, his older brother, who had settled in New Mexico in 1874. A cattleman who dabbled in politics, Virgil's spread was located on the Rio Hondo. His closest associate was John Chisum, the largest rancher in the territory. Their friendship stemmed from the bloodletting that had consumed Lincoln County since 1878.

Essentially a political struggle, the Lincoln County War involved two factions. On one side were Chisum and several ranchers, and a local storekeeper, Alexander McSween. Challenging them were L. G. Murphy and shadowy figures of the Santa Fe Ring, a Republican political machine that dominated territorial affairs. The Kid, whose loyalties lay with one of the ranchers, had ended up in Chisum's camp. Before it was over, more than twenty men had died in the fighting.

Old animosities still lingered, and the threat of violence seemed ever present. But Clint's interest in the Kid had nothing to do with the Lincoln County War. He'd come to

Mesilla, instead, hoping to settle an older score. He thought the Kid might be persuaded to talk.

"Got a favor to ask," he said now. "I'm looking for a man by the name of José Tafoya."

Bonney's voice was suddenly guarded. "Why come to me?"

Clint took a long drag on his cigarette. His expression was sphinxlike. "You've been on the dodge close to three years. I figured you might've heard something."

"Mebbe so," Bonney said sourly. "But that still don't answer the question. Why should I turn songbird?"

Clint gave him a straight hard look. "I'll put it to you another way. Why would you protect a *Comanchero*?"

Bonney stared at him for a long moment. On either side of the law, Clint Brannock was respected for his cool judgment and nervy quickness in a tight situation. He was a tall man, lean and tough, with smoky blue eyes and a thatch of sandy hair. His manner was deliberate and he never indulged in small talk or encouraged it in others. He was reported to have killed eleven men in gunfights.

In 1874, after serving as a cavalry scout, Clint had been appointed a special agent by the army. His orders were to root out and destroy the *Comancheros*, an organization of Mexicans and renegade Anglos who supplied firearms to the horseback tribes. The mission was something of a personal vendetta, for his middle brother, Earl, had been killed after becoming involved in the illicit trade. Since then, he had devoted himself to tracking down the *Comancheros*.

Early in 1875, the last of the Comanche bands had been forced onto the reservation. With their downfall, the firearms trade ceased and the *Comancheros* scattered to the winds. Clint nonetheless pursued them relentlessly, and more than a dozen had been captured and imprisoned. Yet the man he wanted most had eluded him for the past seven years.

José Tafoya, the first *Comanchero* he'd captured, had

been turned over to the army. Under highly suspect circumstances, Tafoya had escaped from the guardhouse at Fort Bascom. Clint still believed that the escape had required the collusion of the post commander. While Tafoya had vanished, he hadn't yet closed the books on the case. He thought today might be his lucky day.

At length, he ground his cigarette underfoot. He looked through the bars at Bonney. "What the hell, Kid. It's no skin off your nose."

Bonney's mouth crooked in a grotesque smile. "Ask a favor," he said, "and that means you owe a favor. I'm liable to call the marker sometime."

Clint opened his hands, shrugged. "Short of breaking you out of jail, I'm open to a deal."

"No worries there," Bonney told him. "I'll bust myself out of jail."

"All right," Clint said woodenly, "let's just say I'm in your debt. Where can I find Tafoya?"

"I'd judge it about a day's ride south of here."

"He's across the border—Old Mexico?"

"Nope," Bonney said almost idly. "Last I heard he was in El Paso."

"El Paso?" Clint repeated, genuinely surprised. "What's he doing there?"

Bonney laughed out loud. "I'd just imagine the poor sonovabitch is hidin' out from you."

Clint grinned despite himself. He left the sack of tobacco and rolling papers with the Kid and walked from the jail. On the way back to the hotel, he was forced to a grudging admiration for José Tafoya. El Paso was the last place he would have looked.

The road from Mesilla generally followed the Rio Grande. Some thirty miles south, where the river made a slow dogleg, the boundaries of New Mexico, Texas, and Old Mexico briefly converged. A few miles farther downstream lay El Paso.

Clint was mounted on a buckskin gelding. He departed Mesilla early the next morning and set a pace that would put him in El Paso before dark. His years as a cavalry scout had taught him to conserve horseflesh whenever possible, particularly in Indian country. A band of bronco Apache was loose and a man never knew when he might have to ride for his life. He held the gelding to a sedate trot.

Along the shoreline, the countryside was dotted with native jacales and patches of farmland. The road Clint followed was an ancient trace, once a link between the old world and the new. He was reminded that New Mexico was a land of troubled complexity, a blend of Indian, Spanish, and Anglo. The mix, like oil and water, formed an imperfect bond.

The *conquistadors* first crossed the Rio Grande in 1540. For nearly three centuries New Mexico was a Spanish viceroyalty, in which the church and the crown ruled overlapping domains. Trade flowed along the Camino Real between Mexico City and Santa Fe, and pueblos flourished along the river valleys. Then, in 1821, when Mexico declared independence, New Mexico became a frontier province.

While trade with Mexico continued, commerce along the Santa Fe Trail created a foothold for Anglo influence. In 1846, when the Mexican War exploded, the American army quickly occupied Santa Fe. Scarcely two years later New Mexico was formally ceded to the United States. Within a matter of three decades, the land had passed from the Spanish crown to the Anglo republic.

Nor were the days of blood and violence yet ended. The Apache conflict was only briefly interrupted by the Civil War. Texas volunteers stormed Santa Fe and the territory was declared an outpost of the Confederacy. By 1862 the Confederate campaign in the West floundered and New Mexico was once again in Union hands. The Apache, led by Geronimo and Victorio, came under scrutiny when the war finally ended. Peace was a fleeting thing in a land forged by the force of arms.

Anglo settlement, which mushroomed with the expansion of the railroads, brought still greater violence. In 1875, political corruption and land frauds turned northern New Mexico into a battleground. The Colfax County War pitted the Santa Fe Ring against ranchers and homesteaders who had settled on what they regarded as public domain. Assassination and murder, and midnight lynchings by the vigilantes, lasted for three years. An uneasy truce finally halted the killing.

The Lincoln County War attracted even wider attention. Embracing twenty-seven thousand square miles, the county occupied the entire southeastern quarter of New Mexico. Lawlessness reigned, and late in 1878 President Rutherford B. Hayes declared Lincoln County in a state of insurrection. At the urging of General Phil Sheridan, Clint was appointed to investigate the situation. His credentials were in no way tarnished by the fact that his brother was allied with John Chisum.

Early in 1879, Clint's report forced the removal of Governor Samuel Axtell and several territorial officials, most of them members of the Santa Fe Ring. Lew Wallace, the youngest major general in the Union army, was appointed governor and ordered to bring peace to Lincoln County. Still, after three years in office, he had yet to disperse the bands of outlaws and root out corrupt politicians. The incessant bloodshed prompted General Sherman to remark: "We should have another war with Old Mexico to make her take back New Mexico."

Clint was sometimes of a similar opinion. His investigation had resulted in several attempts on his life, and he'd been forced to kill three men who were clearly hired assassins. The Santa Fe Ring's involvement in Lincoln County was compounded by an older arrangement with the *Comancheros*, who paid princely sums for political protection. Yet, while he was often close to exposing the Ring's leaders, Clint was never able to produce a live witness. Anyone tempted to talk either vanished or was killed under mysterious circumstances. Which was yet another reason why he wanted José Tafoya. He thought the *Comanchero* might at last unravel the web of intrigue.

Years of living on the razor edge of danger had honed Clint's instinct for survival. He had few illusions left intact, and the dead men littering his backtrail had taught him that a cynic was seldom disappointed. These days he carried a Colt Peacemaker chambered for .45 caliber, with standard sights and a 4¾-inch barrel. The guts of the gun had been completely overhauled, with a specially tempered mainspring and a trigger pull of scarcely three pounds. The end product was a weapon of balance and silky-smooth action.

Unlike many lawmen, he never spoke of the men he'd killed. His reputation with a gun was common knowledge and he figured that spoke for itself. He considered it both a deterrent and a rough form of insurance. Other men thought twice before they provoked him.

José Tafoya, with luck, would prove to be such a man.

Dusk settled over El Paso as Clint rode into town. He crossed the plaza and reined to a halt before the marshal's office. Dismounting, he left the gelding switching flies at the hitch rack.

The town marshal was new to the job. Yet his name was already the subject of headlines across the West. Not quite a week past, Dallas Stoudenmire had pinned on the badge. A former Texas Ranger, he brooked no nonsense from El Paso's rougher element. Within the space of a few days, he had fought two gunfights and killed a total of four men. Newspapers had promptly dubbed him the "town-tamer."

Stoudenmire looked the part. He stood six-feet-four, with a thick neck and powerful shoulders. His eyes were alert and penetrating, and a soupstrainer mustache was framed by a square jaw. The hip pockets on his pants were leather-lined and served as holsters for a brace of Colt six-guns. He appeared immune to anything mortal.

By way of introduction, Clint produced the federal badge he carried inside his wallet. After a firm handshake, Stoudenmire motioned him to a chair. He came straight to the point, outlining the reason for his visit to El Paso. What he sought was information regarding the whereabouts of José Tafoya.

Stoudenmire heard him out. There was a moment of strained silence, then the marshal's face set in an oxlike expression. "I won't dance you around," he said. "Your man's here, but you'll play hell arresting him."

"How so?" Clint asked.

"For openers," Stoudenmire said dourly, "he's one of the town's more upstanding Mexicans. Got himself a nice little cantina down by the river. Nobody cares about his *Comanchero* days."

"I care," Clint said with a measured smile. "He sold guns to the hostiles and got a lot of people killed. I don't aim to leave town without him."

Stoudenmire's eyes narrowed. "You try it and you're liable to start a war. Every hotheaded greaser on both sides of the river will take his part."

Clint considered briefly, then nodded. "I reckon that's why he picked El Paso. He figured he was safe here."

"You got to remember we're a border town. Across the river it's *El Paso del Norte*—Mexico."

"Your point's taken, Marshal. I see where it could get a touch risky."

"Touch, hell!" Stoudenmire barked. "It's a goddamn powder keg."

"Suppose . . ." Clint paused, thoughtful a moment. "Let's suppose Tafoya just vanished—poof!—here one minute and gone the next. Who'd be the wiser?"

Stoudenmire smiled uneasily. "Are you talking about abducting him?"

"I'm talking about the magician's dove. Now you see it, now you don't."

"How would we pull that off?"

"Leave it to me, Marshal. So far as you're concerned, I'm just a pilgrim on his way to nowhere. We never met."

Clint heaved himself to his feet. They shook once, a hard up-and-down pump, and Clint walked out the door. Stoudenmire still had a puzzled frown plastered across his face. He wondered what sort of magic act would be worked on José Tafoya.

The sky was flecked through with stars. Faint light glittered on the muddy waters of the Rio Grande and on the opposite shore *El Paso del Norte* was dark. A dog howled mournfully somewhere in the distance.

The last customer emerged from the cantina and walked toward town. A moment later, one by one, the coal-oil lamps inside were extinguished. Then, whistling under his breath, José Tafoya stepped outside. He turned to lock the door.

A figure materialized from the darkness. The snout of a pistol barrel was jammed below Tafoya's right ear. Like the buzz of a rattlesnake, the metallic whir of a hammer being cocked sounded in the night. Tafoya froze stock-still.

"Pay attention, hombre," Clint said softly. "Your life depends on doing exactly as I say."

"*Quién es*?" Tafoya stammered. "Who are you?"

"We met once before, when you were a *Comanchero*. I've come to take you back."

"Back where?"

"Enough talk," Clint said. "There are two horses in those trees by the river. Walk ahead of me."

Tafoya suddenly stiffened. "Stop and think, *gringo*. One yell and you would be a dead man. We are among my people here."

"Go ahead," Clint warned with cold menace. "But when you yell, take a deep breath. It'll have to last a long time. Savvy?"

"*Sí*," Tafoya muttered, "*lo sé*."

"Let's go."

The pistol barrel prodded Tafoya toward the river. A step behind, Clint kept his finger lightly connected with the trigger. They walked off into the night.

2

The sun was a fiery ball lodged high in the sky. Virgil Brannock reined his horse onto a beaten track which sloped toward the river. He crossed the stream at a shallow ford and rode west.

Before him stretched the Hondo Valley. Located in the foothills of the Capitan Mountains, the valley began ten miles east of Lincoln, where the Rio Bonito flowed into the Rio Hondo. From there, the grassy basin meandered eastward, ending far downstream at an escarpment of broken hills. On the eastern flank of the escarpment, the terrain turned to rolling plains, steadily dropping off in elevation into the Pecos Valley. Farther on, the Rio Hondo eventually converged with the Pecos River.

Hondo Valley was surrounded by craggy foothills studded with brush and scrub oak. The river, which generally followed the south side of the basin, was bordered by stands of cottonwood and popular. Some twenty miles long, and roughly three miles wide, the floor of the valley was a lush grazeland. Watered the year round by rain and spring melt-off from the mountains, it was sheltered from the harsh blast of winter and verdant with grass during the summer. Hidden away, it seemed fashioned by nature for raising cattle.

Virgil looked upon the valley as his personal kingdom. Some seven years past, he had purchased a Spanish land grant totaling 100,000 acres. His holdings were situated in the center of the basin, and there he had established the

Spur Ranch. West and east of his land, the valley was still considered public domain. Yet he claimed all the Hondo as his own, and he held it by right of possession. Fifty cowhands worked his herds and more than thirty thousand longhorns wore the ✳ brand. Among New Mexican ranchers, his outfit was second only to John Chisum's Jinglebob.

A large man, Virgil exuded an air of magnetism. He was forty-six, but still trim and bursting with vitality. His ruddy features were set off by a brushy ginger mustache and a mane of hair sprinkled with gray. His lodestar was an image of himself as a man of power and influence. History taught that nothing extraordinary was achieved without ambition and vision and the audacity to dare greatly. Before he died, he meant to leave his mark on New Mexico Territory.

Some distance upstream, he reined his horse to a halt. Spring roundup got underway in mid-April and he'd spent the morning inspecting operations scattered throughout the valley. On a level grassland to the north, one of his crews had gathered several hundred head of cattle. Calves were being dragged from the herd to a small fire where a gang of five men swarmed over them. Within a matter of seconds they were branded and earmarked, and the bull calves castrated, their raw scrotums scabbed with fly dope. Afterward, somewhat altered in appearance, the calves were choused back to the herd.

Working longhorns was a tough, dangerous business. As a breed they were cantankerous, short-fused, and born man-haters, which was what kept the job from getting dull. Cornered in the brush, especially after roaming wild through the winter, a mossyhorn would often turn and fight like a Bengal tiger. The first time a cowhand roped an outlaw steer he discovered that the hardest part of catching a longhorn was in letting go. Unlike domestic cattle, these rangy creatures, with their massive horns, could never be tamed. Even the she-cows were not to be trusted.

Virgil watched the operation with more than casual interest. One of the hands working the gather was his fourteen-year-old son, Morg. The youngster was large for his age, whipcord tough, and filled with brash self-assurance. Yet he was already a skilled roper, able to forefoot a steer or heel a calf with a flick of his lariat. He made nothing of the fact that his name was Brannock, and he seemed forever intent on pulling his own weight. The other cowhands accepted him as one of their own, extending no special treatment. For a boy working among men, it was a rare compliment.

From the dust and commotion of the gather, Morg saw his father watching. He waved and Virgil motioned to him with an overhead signal. The boy spoke to the *segundo* who was bossing the operation, then gigged his cowpony and galloped forward. He slid to a halt in a flashy display of horsemanship.

"Hullo, Pa," he said, grinning. "Out looking things over?"

"Here and there," Virgil noted. "How's it going?"

"Not too bad. We ought to finish this bunch before sundown."

"You're moving right along, aren't you?"

Morg laughed a cocky laugh. "We're the best crew on the whole spread. Nobody teaches us tricks."

The youngster's enthusiasm was infectious. Virgil saw a good deal of himself in the boy, and something more. The Brannock bloodline passed along spirit and determination, and an inborn refusal to be whipped by men or events. His son gave every sign of carrying those traits into manhood.

"You'd better head back," he said. "I'll see you at supper."

"Whyn't you stick around, Pa? We gonna cook up some calf nuts at noontime."

Virgil shook his head. "Your mother's expecting me home. Besides, I have to ride into town this afternoon."

"You reckon Mom and Jen would like some oysters? I could bring 'em a fresh batch."

"You do and your mother will thrash you good."

Morg whooped laughter. The rowels on his spurs sang as he feathered his pony and took off at a lope. Virgil wagged his head, remembering what it was like to be a young hellion full of piss and vinegar. He reined about and rode north across the valley.

Some while later, he halted before a fenced pasture. The enclosure was one of three such holding pens on the ranch, constructed of stout posts and galvanized wire. Always a visionary, Virgil foresaw a need to upgrade the quality of his livestock. Longhorns were lean and hardy, but produced almost as much bone and gristle as edible beef.

Accordingly, he had imported ten Durham bulls and a hundred brood cows, then embarked on a program of crossbreeding. The Durhams were built wide and hefty, packing nearly twice the beef of a longhorn, and he hoped to create a strain with the best traits of both breeds. Thus far, his search had produced mixed results.

Durham cows, along with calves sired by longhorn bulls, grazed across the pastureland. In the second holding pen, farther upstream, longhorn cows topped by Durham bulls were nursing newborn calves. The crossbreed, by whatever combination, produced a chunkier animal, yet one that sometimes lost the hardiness of native longhorns. The long generation intervals with cattle, usually four years, meant that his breeding program would span a decade or longer.

Horses were another matter entirely. In the third pasture, located east of the ranch headquarters, he was crossbreeding imported Thoroughbreds with wild mustang stock. The result produced a better cowhorse, one that was already in demand by many ranchers. For more immediate profit, he was actively engaged in a program of capturing and breaking *mestenos*. By early fall, he would trail at least five hundred head to Wyoming. There, on the High

Plains, the mustangs would be sold as green-broke cow-ponies.

Off in the distance, he saw Odell Slater approaching. The Spur foreman was short and bowlegged, but a man of considerable stature astride a horse. He knew cattle and he understood how to get the most out of cowhands. His authority was absolute, and he'd been delegated responsibility for the entire spread. So far, Virgil had no reason to regret the decision.

Slater reined in beside the fenceline. "Mr. Brannock," he said, nodding. "How's things look over to the west?"

"I'd say it's shaping up, Odell."

"Pretty much the same over to the east. I took a swing through the camps this mornin'."

"Any idea on the increase?"

Slater worked his cud and spat a streak of tobacco juice. "Wouldn't hazard a guess just yet. But I've gotta hunch we'll beat last year."

The spring calf crop was a matter of vital interest. Before fall, Virgil planned to send three herds north along the Goodnight-Loving Trail. One herd would be sold in Colorado and the other two were contracted to a rancher on the High Plains. By rail, he intended to ship between four and five thousand head to eastern slaughterhouses. But the current calf crop determined what he would ship next season, and perhaps many seasons down the line. Some years were better than others.

"All right, Odell," he said now. "Let me know when you have something to report."

"Yessir, I shore will, Mr. Brannock."

Slater rode off toward the west. Virgil sat for a moment gazing at the Durham cows and their half-longhorn calves. Then he turned and set a southeasterly course for home.

Operations for all the Spur were conducted from a head-quarters compound in the center of the valley. The buildings were ranged along the north bank of the Rio Hondo and formed an irregular half-moon beyond the main house. Aside from corrals and sheds, there were outbuildings for blacksmithing, carpentry, and general storage. A large bunkhouse, flanked by a combination kitchen and dining hall, was situated opposite the supply commissary.

Shaded by cottonwoods, the main house overlooked the river. Built along the lines of a hacienda, it was a vast sprawl of adobe with thick walls and deep-set windows. Hewn rafters protruded from the flat roof and the front door, which was seven feet tall and four feet wide, stood like a fortress gate. A galleried veranda, deep in shade, ran the length of the front wall. The house was cool in the summer and warm in the winter, sheltered by the foothills to the south.

Shortly before noon the dining room became the center of activity. Mrs. Murphy, the housekeeper and cook, began carrying serving dishes in from the kitchen. A widow woman, stout and gray-haired, she had been with the Brannocks for many years. She bustled around the long, brightly polished table, fussing over the arrangements. At last, hands on her hips, she stood back for a final inspection.

"It looks very nice, Sarah."

Mrs. Murphy turned as Elizabeth entered from the vestibule. While twenty years older, and virtually a member of the family, she remained somewhat awed by the lady of the house. "Thank you, ma'am," she said quickly. "I wanted it just right for today. Are you still plannin' to speak to the mister?"

"Yes, indeed," Elizabeth said in a conspiratorial tone. "Let's hope he's in a good mood."

"Oh, you'll win him over. You always do."

With a sly wink and a chuckle, Mrs. Murphy returned to the kitchen. Elizabeth was checking the table when Jennifer appeared in the doorway. At fifteen, she was tall and willowy, and moved with coltish grace. Her eyes were large and questing, and her auburn hair hung loose on her shoulders. She had the promise of her mother's beauty.

"Honestly, Mother," she said brightly. "You look absolutely ready to pounce."

"Behave yourself, young lady," Elizabeth admonished. "None of your flippant remarks today. I won't have your father angered."

Jennifer made a face, but held her tongue. Like her mother, she was an ardent suffragette and a strong believer in women's rights. She thought it deceitful and undignified to practice feminine wiles on men. Still, however grudgingly, she enjoyed watching her mother operate.

On the stroke of twelve, hoofbeats sounded outside the house. A moment later Virgil walked through the door and Elizabeth went to meet him. She smiled warmly and kissed him lightly on the cheek. He beamed down on her with genuine affection.

After sixteen years of marriage, Virgil was still somewhat moonstruck. His wife was a tall, statuesque woman in her middle thirties, and elegantly beautiful. Her features were exquisite, and by watching her diet, she managed to retain a sumptuous figure. She wore her hair upswept, drawn back and pinned, with fluffed curls on her forehead. Her looks fooled a great many people.

Over the years, Virgil had developed an appreciation for the inner woman. Elizabeth was intelligent, quick-witted, and acutely perceptive. She was also an activist, outspoken in defense of oppressed people, the underdogs. Working with a local doctor, she had opened a free medical clinic for the poor. In Lincoln County, the poor were almost all *mexicano,* and they had quickly learned that she was a woman of resilience and great willpower. Their name for her was *La Mariposa de Hierro*—the Iron Butterfly.

Today, after being seated, Virgil sensed that something was afoot. While the steaming dishes were being passed around the table, he saw Elizabeth and Jennifer exchange a hidden look. Jennifer was a mirror image of her mother, and in her own way, equally conniving. Yet it was a trait that Virgil understood, and one he considered admirable. His was a family of fighters, not a faintheart in the bunch, and he saw nothing wrong with a woman using every resource at her command. Apart from keeping him on his toes, he actually enjoyed it.

Elizabeth took the oblique approach. "Have you heard?" she asked innocently. "Dr. Wood plans to expand the clinic."

"Does he?" Virgil said, spearing a bite of beefsteak. "I wouldn't think Lincoln was ready for a hospital."

"No, silly, not a hospital. He's considering training a nurse— a Mexican woman."

"High time," Virgil observed. "You're there too much, anyway. He could use some extra help."

Jennifer stifled a giggle. Elizabeth shot her a look, then smiled sweetly. "Actually," she said, "it was my idea. I want to move on to something else."

"Oh?" Virgil stopped chewing, glanced at her. "What's that?"

"Well, it would be a new sort of clinic. A legal-assistance service . . . for *mexicanos*."

"You're joking!"

"Not at all," she said reasonably. "We both know the Mexicans are being victimized by Anglo business interests. I intend to do something about the land frauds."

"*What* . . . ?" Virgil's bushy eyebrows seemed to hood his eyes. "You're talking about politics, territorial politics! Have you any notion of where that would lead?"

"To Stephen Benton," Elizabeth replied airily—"and the Santa Fe Ring."

Stephen Benton was the reputed kingmaker in territorial politics. His land company in Santa Fe was the one from which Virgil had purchased the old Spanish grant. Later, the land fraud came to light when Virgil discovered that *mexicanos*, who lived within the ranch boundaries, claimed farming rights by an ancient system known as the *villa* code. He investigated and found that Benton had circumvented the code by leasing farm plots to the *mexicanos* for twenty-five percent of their crops. At the time Virgil purchased the land, no mention had been made of the arrangement.

Threatening legal action, he had demanded some form of restitution. Stephen Benton claimed that valid title had been transferred and refused to discuss the matter. After consulting an attorney, Virgil realized that his legal position was hopeless. He had agreed, instead, to let the *mexicanos* farm their plots as long as they or their descendants wished to stay. He charged them nothing, and they in turn soon referred to him as the "*patrón*." His enmity with Benton had been further aggravated by the Lincoln County War. They were on opposite sides, and neither of them was willing to forgive. Nor would the Sant Fe Ring forget that he was still aligned with John Chisum.

"You're aware," he said now, "that Benton and his cronies play rough. No one hits them in the pocketbook without one helluva fight."

Elizabeth laughed and tossed her head. "Since when have the Brannocks backed off from a fight? Or would you prefer to kiss and make up with Stephen Benton?"

"Lord save us," Virgil said, rolling his eyes. "You're bound and determined to do it, aren't you?"

She mimicked his dour expression. "Don't be such a sobersides. Mexicans are being defrauded and forced into a life of peonage. Someone has to take their part, make a stand." She paused, her eyes dancing merrily. "Why not me?"

"Come on, Dad," Jennifer said with a beguiling grin, "admit it! You're whipped."

"Well, maybe . . ." Virgil said with a great shrug of resignation. "But don't try getting sassy about it. I can still handle you, little lady."

"Of course you can, Father." Jennifer batted her lashes

and gave him her sweetest rosebud smile. "Every girl knows it's a man's world."

A smothered laugh erupted behind the kitchen door. Then, with a straight face, Mrs. Murphy swept into the dining room and began clearing the table. Virgil caught the byplay among the three women and realized he'd been sandbagged from the start. Not for the first time, he was thankful he had a son.

Females, he told himself, were born schemers. One way or another, they got a man to make a monkey of himself.

A fortnight later Virgil rode into Lincoln. West of the town the Capitan Mountains rose like a line of sentinels, and farther still, the snowcapped peak of Sierra Blanca towered against the sky. Beyond the road, the Rio Bonito roared with the high-country runoff.

Across from the courthouse, Virgil dismounted in front of Curry's saloon. Over the past two weeks he had put out feelers with various contacts from the Lincoln County War. While a hired gun was never mentioned, his go-betweens understood the arrangement being discussed. The man recommended for the job was a Texan, unknown anywhere in the territory. He was waiting inside now.

His name was John Taylor. For ten years, he had fought in the Sutton-Taylor feud, reportedly the most savage blood-bath in Texas history. He was a distant relative of John Wesley Hardin and thought to be no less quick with a gun. For the past four years, he had drifted from one job to another, quietly disappearing when his work was done. He was a professional gunman, available for a price.

Virgil found him a genial sort, though somewhat distant. He was a man of saturnine good looks, with dark close-cropped hair and unyielding gray eyes. His face was smooth-shaven and there was a tough, curiously sinister aspect to his weathered features. He wore a well-oiled Colt in a crossdraw holster and he sat with his back to the wall. He seemed a man who took few chances.

Taylor listened without comment or interruption. Virgil told the story straight through, explaining who and why and the risks involved. When he finished, there was a long, thoughtful silence. Then Taylor slowly wagged his head.

"That's a new one," he said. "I never before hired out to bodyguard a woman."

Virgil studied him with a calm judicial gaze. "Don't take it lightly because it's a woman. These men will stop at nothing."

Taylor nodded, considering. "Your wife must be a real stem-winder. Not many females would risk getting themselves killed."

"That's part of the problem. She'll never believe they would go that far."

"But you do?"

"For a fact," Virgil said ominously. "Once she starts exposing land fraud, her life's in danger. There's just too much money involved—millions of dollars."

"No disrespect," Taylor said pleasantly, "but why don't you just keep her at home? Wouldn't that be the simplest solution?"

Virgil laughed shortly. "You'd have to meet my wife to understand. She's what some folks call headstrong."

"In that case," Taylor said with an odd smile, "I reckon I'd better take the job. Sounds like a lady I oughta know."

"One last thing," Virgil said in a low voice. "When the chips are down, I don't want any maybes about it. You're to shoot first and ask questions later. Understood?"

"No argument there, Mr. Brannock. We think alike on that score."

Virgil then asked his price. The amount was steep but not out of line, and they shook hands on it. John Taylor went on the Spur payroll that night.

3

Elizabeth was amused. She thought Virgil was sweet and considerate, but something of a worrywart. The very idea of a bodyguard seemed to her almost laughable.

For all that, she found John Taylor to be no laughing matter. Early next morning, he was waiting outside the house with a buckboard and team. He'd been informed of her schedule, and today was one of the two days a week she devoted to the clinic. He was polite, though somewhat reserved, greeting Elizabeth and Jennifer as he assisted them into the buckboard. His manner indicated that he took his job seriously.

On the way into town, Elizabeth attempted to engage him in conversation. Taylor's answers were pleasant though short, framed to satisfy her curiosity. He volunteered nothing about himself and avoided any reference to his unusual occupation. Still, Elizabeth was familiar with men whose livelihood entailed carrying a gun. Her brother-in-law was sometimes called a "shootist" and he was widely admired throughout the territory. John Taylor was no law officer, and she suspected he was a man with a checkered past. Yet, oddly enough, he reminded her of Clint.

Jennifer was only briefly intrigued. She considered Taylor good-looking and dangerous, perhaps a bit mysterious. But her attention quickly shifted to the clinic, and the day ahead. School emptied of boys when spring roundup got under way, and as a result the term had ended in mid-April. Since last fall, today was the first full day she would spend at the clinic. She was so excited her stomach was fluttery, and she couldn't wait to get into town. The clinic seemed to her a magical place, a place of healing and cures.

Some five years ago Elizabeth had organized the clinic. When she first moved to New Mexico, the townspeople had looked on her as something of a radical. She attempted to form a local chapter of the suffragette movement and was quickly rebuffed. Suffrage was linked to the Women's Christian Temperance Union, and hardly anyone in the territory, the ladies included, believed that whiskey should be outlawed. No teetotaler herself, Elizabeth personally saw nothing wrong with alcohol in moderation. She was fond of sherry and occasionally took a nip of brandy.

After a couple of years, she admitted that suffrage simply wasn't a burning issue in New Mexico. She was no less committed to the vote for women; but neither was she a martyr to a lost cause. It was then her attention had turned to the plight of the *mexicanos*. For the most part, the people of Mexican extraction were humble farmers, grubbing a bare existence from the earth. Trade and business, not to mention territorial politics, were controlled by Anglos, the *americanos*. The system virtually consigned *mexicanos* to a life of poverty.

However compassionate, Elizabeth was no starry-eyed reformer. The Mexicans had been oppressed and exploited for centuries, first by Spain, then by their own government, and finally by the *americanos*. The system was ancient, a legacy of the past, and therefore not susceptible to overnight change. The *mexicanos* themselves were part of the problem, for they clung to traditional ways and accepted their lot with a sense of fatalism. Nothing would change until they themselves broke with the past.

In the meantime, she decided that something could be done about the state of their health. There were no Mexican doctors anywhere in Lincoln County, and the only medicine practiced in the native pueblos was an ancient form of home remedies and folk cures. For colds and sore throat, a poultice of mustard and onion was tied around the throat. To cure the croup, a mother took a hair from the child's head and placed it in the bole of a tree. Old midwives still inserted snuff in a woman's nose to make her sneeze and bring on labor. The infant-mortality rate was frightening and *mexicano* women seldom lived to old age. Mexican men fared little better.

Elizabeth hit upon the idea of opening a free clinic. Her father, the most prominent banker in Denver, had died in 1876. After settling the estate, she found herself a woman of independent means. Virgil considered the money hers to do with as she saw fit and supported her concern for the *mexicanos*. Soon thereafter, she contacted Dr. Chester Wood, the only physician within a radius of a hundred miles. His office was located in Lincoln and his practice was limited almost exclusively to Anglos. He nonetheless agreed to her plan.

Their arrangement was forthright and simple. The clinic would be open two days a week, every Tuesday and Friday. No one would be turned away, nor would there by any charge for the services. Elizabeth funded the clinic, paying all expenses and a monthly stipend for the doctor's time. She insisted on the latter, for a frontier doctor rarely eked out more than a hand-to-mouth existence. In Dr. Wood's case, the fact was borne out by the last census count. There were less than two thousand people in Lincoln County, including Mexicans.

The clinic opened in early 1877. At first, the *mexicanos* were hesitant to trust themselves to an Anglo doctor. But the curious and the desperately ill were perhaps less wary, and the barrier was soon broken. With time, the doctor's reputation spread and people were no longer so dependent on folk remedies. On clinic days, the office was now swamped with patients, many of them having traveled great distances. They viewed Dr. Wood with unstinting respect, but Elizabeth was the object of quiet reverence.

To them she was *La Mariposa de Hierro*, their friend and protector.

The office was located on the north side of the street, occupying two rooms in the doctor's home. Toward the east end of town, the street was lined with homes and a large mercantile, as well as an adobe church. A short distance uptown was the hotel, flanked by a saloon and several shops. Across the road, catty-corner from the hotel, was the Lincoln County courthouse. The upper floor, which had an outside staircase, was used for the county jail. There, for the past two weeks, William Bonney had been held awaiting execution.

As the buckboard rolled into town, Elizabeth was reminded of the impending hanging. She had never met Billy the Kid and she bore him no personal ill will. Yet she regretted his link to John Chisum, and by association, to her own husband. She wished death on no man, but she thought the Kid's execution, scheduled for May 13, would represent a godsend. When he mounted the gallows, it would write a symbolic end to the Lincoln County War. She prayed it would end the political struggle as well.

Taylor hitched the team to a tie-iron. He assisted Elizabeth and Jennifer from the buckboard and followed them up a short walkway to the house. A large group of *mexicanos* was already gathered outside. The men doffed their sombreros and the women, many of them clutching children, shyly ducked their heads. Elizabeth smiled graciously, still vaguely uncomfortable with their reverent manner. She hurried through the door.

Chester Wood greeted them with bluff good humor. He was a stocky man, with a mouthful of teeth as square as sugar cubes, and bald as a tonsured monk. When Elizabeth introduced Taylor, the physician shook hands with a knowing look. Lincoln was a small town and the gossips were already abuzz with the news of her Texican bodyguard. Taylor took a seat near the window, where he could watch the street. His attitude toward the clinic was one of casual indifference.

Like most Western doctors, Wood was his own pharmacist. The front of the house was a combination waiting room and apothecary. On one wall was a medicine cabinet with jars of roots, herbs, and assorted drugs. Using the base elements, he mashed and pounded with a mortar and pestle to mix the proper formulation. After measuring, the powdered doses were then packaged in small squares of paper.

A door on the far wall opened onto Wood's office. There he examined patients, and when absolutely unavoidable, performed surgery. The furnishings consisted of a battered rolltop desk and a glass cabinet cluttered with instruments. His medical library amounted to three volumes: *Elements of Pathological Anatomy, A Treatise on the Practice of Medicine*, and *A System of Surgery*. A lithographed chart of the human body was tacked to one wall and directly opposite it was the operating table.

Until now, Elizabeth had functioned as Wood's nurse and surgical assistant. He was in the process of training a Mexican woman to replace her, but he wasn't altogether keen on the idea. He valued her composure at the operating table and her ability to calm a patient's nerves. To delay matters, he stubbornly refused to allow the Mexican woman to assist on clinic days. He declared the pace much too hectic for training sessions.

Jennifer wandered into the doctor's office. While her mother and Wood talked, she checked the surgical cabinet. On the bottom shelf were a can of ether and a bottle of carbolic-acid solution. The upper shelves were aligned with trays which contained a glittering array of instruments. She was always drawn to the surgical cabinet, and she loved to browse through the medical textbooks. She often fantasized about healing the sick, visualizing herself at the doctor's side when he operated. She wanted very much to take her mother's place.

For now, her job was somewhat more routine. Over the
past two summers she had worked at the clinic in what she
termed the "fetch-and-carry" position. She emptied pans
and fetched water from the well and kept the kitchen stove
stoked with wood. Her one meaningful chore was to boil
the surgical instruments and sterilize homemade dressings
by baking them in the oven. Sterilized gauze and packaged
dressings were available, but often in short supply. In that,
at least, she felt she made a contribution.

Apart from her father, Chester Wood was the only man
she truly admired. She saw him as a heroic figure and
dwelled on stories that seemed to her the stuff of legend.
Once, on a call to a distant ranch, he'd found a child
choking with diphtheria. Quickly improvising, he had opened
the windpipe with his scalpel and kept the hole from
closing with sterilized fishhooks. Another time, when he
was called to a faraway bunkhouse, his patient was a
cowhand with a strangulated hernia. Fresh out of anesthesia, he borrowed a wad of plug tobacco and inserted it into
the man's rectum. The nicotine acted as a relaxant and
enabled him to reduce the hernia.

Where gunshot wounds were concerned, Wood had few
peers. Over the years, particularly during the Lincoln County
War, he'd treated dozens of men. He found that a wound
in the abdomen invariably led to hemorrhage and death.
Even without damage to major organs, the victim usually
died within the hour unless an operation was performed.
Where death was practically instantaneous, autopsies revealed that the bullet had severed a large abdominal ves-
sel. A perforated intestine, barring surgical repair, brought
on death in roughly twenty minutes. Wood attributed the
mortality rate to the large-caliber weapons used by Westerners. A .45 revolver bullet or a .44-40 Winchester slug
inevitably left a fearsome wound.

On slow days, Wood often held Jennifer spellbound
with stories of old-time medicine. To the pioneer patient,
the lancet was a familiar, and dreaded, instrument. Bleed-

ing was considered the proper treatment for fevers, inflammation of the major organs, and beneficial as well for headaches, rheumatism, and apoplexy. Seldom was less than ten ounces taken, and for apoplexy, forty to fifty ounces of blood was withdrawn. All too frequently, the patient succumbed to the treatment rather than the disease.

A large part of the problem stemmed from slipshod medical training. In the old days, a young man "read medicine" with the local doctor, learning by observation. After a time, he was permitted to assist in diagnosis, and within two years he usually hung out his own shingle. Prior to the Civil War, three-fourths of all Western physicians were products of the apprentice system. Since then, the emphasis had shifted to formal training in established medical schools. Still, there were no examining boards, or licensing requirements, anywhere in the West. A quack was free to set up shop wherever he chose, and accountable to no one.

For all that, advancements in medicine were nonetheless improving the odds of survival. Lord Joseph Lister, an English surgeon, discovered that bacterial infection causes suppuration. His experiments were a direct offshoot of the germ theory developed by Louis Pasteur some years earlier. Further experiments led to the adoption of a water-and-carbolic-acid solution for cleansing a patient prior to surgery. By employing antiseptic methods in the preparation of instruments and dressings, Lister was able to perform operations without introducing infection into the surgical wound. His discovery marked a turning point in the world of medicine.

Yet another breakthrough was the elimination of pain. Before the discovery of anesthesia, the operating room was no less terrifying than a medieval torture chamber. Surgeons rushed through operations, often performing an amputation in three minutes, their patients strapped to the table in unendurable agony. Then, in the 1840s, a Boston dentist discovered that ether could put his patients below the threshold of consciousness. Surgeons at Massachusetts General Hospital shortly proved that ether could be safely used as an anesthetic during operations. Within a single decade, surgery advanced farther than it had in the previous thousand years.

Today, Chester Wood's last patient before noontime was a case in point. A leathery-skinned man, his eyes bandaged against the light, was led in by his wife. After a brief examination, his condition was diagnosed as Coachman's Disease, often seen in stagecoach drivers. As a natural protection against dust and blowing sand, a layer of skin grows over the eyes, covering the pupils, and leaves the individual almost totally blind. The *mexicano* had worked all his life in the wind-whipped dusty fields bordering the Rio Bonito. His vision was now reduced to shadowy, indistinct movements.

Twenty years ago the man would have been consigned to a world of darkness. Today, Chester Wood ordered him onto the operating table and shooed his wife out of the room. Elizabeth doused a sponge with ether, gentling the *mexicano* with her voice, and told him to breathe normally. While he was being anesthetized, the doctor moved to the washstand and scrubbed his hands with strong soap. After shaking the water from his hands, he returned to the table with forceps and a scalpel.

He nodded to Elizabeth. "Hold his eyelid open with your thumb and forefinger. Then get a good grip on his head with your other arm and hold him steady. We can't afford any slips at all."

"How long will it take?" she asked.

"Not long," Wood assured her. "We'll start with the right eye."

Standing behind the table, Elizabeth locked her left forearm under the man's chin. She then pried his right eyelid open and held it firmly. Wood leaned down, intent on the nasal corner of the eye, and slipped the point of his scalpel beneath the flap of conjunctival skin. With his left hand, he clamped the freed tip of skin between the forceps. Ever so gingerly, he slid the blade under the skin and sliced toward the outside corner. Once started, he cut with one continuous movement and the wing-shaped skin peeled away. Holding the loosened flap with the forceps, he neatly severed it at the base of the growth.

"Nothing to it," he said jovially. "Like peeling a grape."

Elizabeth merely nodded. She reversed her armlock and pried open the left eye. Wood deftly repeated the procedure and dropped the flap of skin into a waste bucket. Inspecting his handiwork, he found what was to be expected in such an operation. Slight adhesions were still intact, forming almost indiscernible ridges over the cornea. Vision would be faintly distorted, like wavy light in an old mirror. But the man's sight had been restored.

A short while later the *mexicano* emerged from the operating room. He needed no assistance and his expression was that of a man who had experienced a miracle. His wife screamed, hugging the doctor and kissing Elizabeth's hand. Those waiting outside thought it no less miraculous and they crowded around the man as he stepped proudly through the door. Their voices blended in a swift murmur of awestruck amazement.

Then, suddenly, a shotgun blast reverberated through town. Elizabeth, who was standing in the doorway, hurried outside. She saw Bob Olinger, a deputy sheriff, sprawled in the middle of the street. Across the way, William Bonney stood on the upper landing of the courthouse stairs. A sawed-off shotgun was cradled in his arms and his mouth was curled in a crooked grin. There was no sign of the second deputy assigned to guard him, J. W. Bell.

Elizabeth walked toward the road. Her action was unwitting, more reflex than conscious thought. Behind her, the door slammed and John Taylor hurried to her side. The Kid watched as they angled across the road and stopped where Olinger lay slumped on the ground. The deputy's head was puddled in blood and when Elizabeth rolled him over, she saw that he's taken the shotgun blast in the face and throat. There was no need to check for a pulse.

Still kneeling, she became aware that Taylor had positioned himself in front of her. His hand rested on his gunbelt and his stare was fixed on the Kid. She realized that he had made a shield of himself, protecting her. His stance was more a warning than a challenge, intended to convey a message. He wouldn't draw unless the Kid threatened her.

Bonney laughed out loud. He flipped them an offhand salute and hobbled back into the jail, his leg irons clanking. Elizabeth rose to her feet and moved to face Taylor. Her gaze was direct, and searching.

"That was very gallant of you, Mr. Taylor."

"Weren't nothin', ma'am," Taylor said, smiling. "Down in Texas, Billy the Kid wouldn't last ten minutes."

She saw then that she'd misjudged him. Behind his stoic manner, there was wry humor and a sense of personal honor. Once again, she was reminded of her brother-in-law. Clint, too, seldom revealed himself to others.

No one attempted to stop William Bonney. He chopped through his leg irons with an ax and clanked down the courthouse stairs. Armed with a pistol and rifle, he rode out of Lincoln on a stolen horse. The townspeople seemed relieved to see him go.

Later, the body of Deputy J. W. Bell was found in the courthouse. In reconstructing the escape, it became clear that the Kid had somehow gotten hold of a pistol and killed Bell. Bob Olinger, who was taking his noon meal at the hotel, heard the shot and started across the street. The Kid killed him with his own shotgun.

Dr. Wood interrupted clinic day to attend to the dead lawmen. While he was occupied, Elizabeth saw those patients who required routine medical care. All the time she worked, however, her mind was on William Bonney. His hanging, the symbolic end to the Lincoln County War, was no longer a factor. Nor would the struggle for political power be put to rest. Nothing was resolved, and men still died.

She wondered who would be killed next.

4

To the west, the sun went down in a great splash of orange and gold. The ragged hillcrests, studded with pine and spruce, were bathed in a fiery glow. Then, quickly, dusk settled over the land.

Clint rode into Fort Stanton shortly before full dark. José Tafoya, whose hands were bound with rope, rode beside him. Their journey from El Paso had been one of fits and starts. Several nights had been spent at Fort Selden, far to the south. The balance of the trip they had camped along the trail.

Tafoya had at last broken under interrogation. His confession implicated the former commander of Fort Bascom, now retired. The man's name was Jacob Ingram, and by all accounts, he'd bought a ranch in the Texas Panhandle. According to Tafoya, his dealings with the *Comancheros* had made him greedy. He was reported to be trading in stolen horses.

On balance, Tafoya had proved to be a goldmine. Some years ago he'd been present when the *Comancheros* made a political payoff in Santa Fe. The man who accepted the bribe was an assistant to the territorial attorney general. And while the attorney general had since been forced out of office, both men still resided in Santa Fe. Tafoya believed as well that the men could connect Jacob Ingram to the Santa Fe Ring.

After considerable thought, Clint had decided to take Tafoya to Santa Fe. There the former *Comanchero* would be turned over to the U.S. marshal and jailed in the territorial prison. With Tafoya under lock and key, he could then expand his investigation. Tonight, however, he planned to quarter the *Comanchero* in the post guardhouse. On the trail with a prisoner allowed him little more than catnaps and he was bone tired. He needed a good night's sleep.

Fort Stanton was situated in the mountains west of Lincoln. The garrison comprised a cavalry regiment and an infantry regiment, all the men seasoned Indian fighters. Their mission was to serve as watchdogs over the Mescalero Apache reservation, located some miles to the south. The post itself centered on a broad quadrangle, with the buildings formed in a boxlike square. Headquarters was positioned on the east side of the parade ground.

Clint identified himself to the Officer of the Day. The Sergeant of the Guard was summoned, and Clint tagged along while Tafoya was escorted to the guardhouse. After the *Comanchero* was safely locked in a cell, he retraced his steps to headquarters. Before feeding himself, he still had to arrange a stable for the horses. Only then could he start hunting a bed.

Pat Garrett was waiting beside the hitch rack. They were old acquaintances but hardly old friends. He wondered what the sheriff of Lincoln County was doing on an army post.

" 'Evenin', Clint," Garrett said, extending his hand. "The OD told me you just rode in."

Clint accepted his handshake. "Where'd you spring from?"

"I was talkin' with Colonel Moore. Figured his patrols could be on the lookout for the Kid."

"Bonney?" Clint said, surprised. "I thought you had him in jail."

Garrett frowned. "Guess you haven't heard."

"Heard what?"

"The Kid escaped yesterday. Killed both my deputies."

Garrett went on to relate the details. He'd been out of town when the jailbreak occurred and had returned late last night. Since then, he had organized three posses and sent them fanning out across the county. He thought the army wouldn't mind lending a hand, even though it was a civil matter. Where the Kid was concerned, he would take whatever help he could get.

Clint had never liked Garrett. Formerly a saloon owner, the sheriff was a rawboned man with angular features and a sweeping handlebar mustache. He was ambitious, something of an opportunist, and he'd gone out of his way to cultivate John Chisum. With the backing of the Jinglebob owner, he had won a landslide victory in the last election. His one campaign promise was to rid New Mexico of Billy the Kid.

The irony was that Garrett and Bonney had once been friends. So close, in fact, that they were known as "Big Casino" and "Little Casino," for at six-four Garrett was nearly a foot taller than the boy outlaw. Still, despite past friendship, Garrett was perfectly willing to use the Kid as a steppingstone into politics. Clint found it difficult to like a man who put ambition before all else.

"Tough luck," he said now. "Any idea where the Kid's headed?"

Garrett pursed his mouth as if his teeth hurt. "Billy's got lots of friends hereabouts. He won't be easy to run down."

"No, I reckon he won't."

"Understand you brought in a prisoner of your own."

"Yeah, I did," Clint said equably. "You might recall the name—José Tafoya."

"The *Comanchero*?"

"Nobody else."

"Well, I'll be damned," Garrett said, genuinely impressed. "How long you been chasin' the bastard?"

Clint shrugged. "Close to seven years."

"Maybe there's hope for me yet. I've been playin' tag with the Kid less'n a year."

"And I recollect you've already caught him once."

"Wish to hell I'd shot him, not caught him!"

On that note, they shook hands and parted. Garrett mounted his horse and began the long ride back to Lincoln. As Clint walked toward headquarters, he recalled his last conversation with William Bonney. The Kid had sworn he would never be hanged.

From the sound of it, he'd been as good as his word.

The road wound through high-timbered country. Ponderosa pines stretched skyward, and off to the south the Rio Bonito was molten with sunlight. Somewhere in the forest, a woodpecker hammered away in determined solitude.

Clint held the buckskin gelding to a walk. Earlier that morning he and Tafoya had departed Fort Stanton, headed west. Before long, the mountainous road would start dropping off, descending gradually into the lowlands. There they would turn north, skirting the Jicarilla Mountains, and angle northwesterly toward Albuquerque. He planned to catch the train for the last leg of the journey to Santa Fe.

Oddly enough, he'd grown comfortable with the *Comanchero's* company. Tafoya was an easy trail companion and never shirked chores around camp. Apart from the fact that he had to be watched closely, and bound tightly at night, he presented no great problem. Once he'd agreed to talk, he seemed to reconcile himself to the inevitable. For turning state's witness, he would escape the hangman's rope, though not a prison sentence. All he had to do was testify before a grand jury.

Clint suddenly alerted. Some visceral instinct had touched a nerve and for a moment he couldn't place the cause. Scanning the forest, he abruptly realized that the woodpecker had stopped hammering. Then, in the next instant, the double crack of two rifles shattered the stillness. The shots were scarcely a heartbeat apart.

The first slug caught Tafoya in the chest and the second drilled through his forehead. He raised his bound arms like a holy man warding off evil spirits, and pitched sideways off his horse. The back of his skull was blown out, and as he toppled downward, a spray of brain matter misted the air. He hit the ground in a lifeless heap.

The buckskin gelding spooked, bolting sideways. Clint kicked out of the saddle as a rifle cracked and a slug fried the air past his head. He landed on one shoulder, losing his hat, and rolled behind a tree at the side of the road. In the split second before he quit the saddle, he'd seen twin puffs of gunsmoke from a patch of brush and trees farther up the road. He pulled his Colt, thumbing the hammer, and rolled to the opposite side of the tree. Hidden in the forest shadow, he waited for the bushwhackers to show themselves.

Nothing moved and a deadened silence settled over the countryside. A sliver of eternity slipped past, and then, off in the distance, he heard the drum of hoofbeats. He cocked one ear and listened, waiting until the sound faded beyond hearing. At last he climbed to his feet and walked back to the road. He stood there a moment, staring down at José Tafoya. The *Comanchero* lay twisted and torn in a welter of blood.

Clint holstered his pistol. Far back along the road, he saw his buckskin and the other horse. Having run themselves out, they were grazing on a crop of bunch grass. He collected his hat and turned away from the dead man.

For the moment, he avoided the question of who had ambushed him. His mind went instead to Fort Stanton and a more immediate problem. He considered whether it was proper to bury a *Comanchero* in the post cemetery.

There seemed no harm in asking.

"You never got a look at them?"

"I was too busy ducking."

"Damnation!"

Virgil smacked a fist into his palm. He stumped across

to a window and stood looking out at the compound. Clint was seated in an overstuffed chair and Elizabeth was opposite him on the sofa, her hands folded in her lap. None of them spoke for a time.

Clint had ridden into the ranch late that afternoon. Earlier in the day, the military had agreed to take Tafoya off his hands. With no reason to hang around Fort Stanton, he'd turned the buckskin eastward, toward Hondo Valley. His recounting of the ambush had raised more questions than it answered. Virgil seemed particularly agitated.

"Think back," Virgil said now, turning from the window. "Besides Pat Garrett, who knew you'd taken Tafoya into custody?"

"Lots of people," Clint said, then shrugged. "Word gets around an army post pretty quick."

"Not the military," Virgil said sharply. "I'm talking about civilians."

A shadow crossed Clint's face. "What are you driving at, just exactly?"

"There's talk," Virgil said in a disgusted tone, "that Garrett may have switched sides. As we all know, he's an ambitious man."

"You're saying he sold out to the Santa Fe Ring?"

"Wouldn't that explain the ambush? Thunderation, somebody rigged it awful damn fast!"

Clint stared stonily ahead. "I'd hate to think Garrett tipped them off. That's mighty low, even for him."

"Maybe not," Virgil said. "We're at a standoff in Lincoln County, but the Ring still controls the legislature. Garrett might have his eyes on bigger things."

The statement reflected the turbulent nature of New Mexican politics. Following the Civil War, a group of Santa Fe Republicans had seized control of the political apparatus. The White House, in concert with Congress, had initiated a program designed to punish pro-Southern Democrats. Even now, almost twenty years later, the Democrats were still battling to restore a balance of power. But it was an uphill fight conducted largely against men who operated from the shadows.

The territorial legislature was dominated by the Santa Fe Ring. Essentially an alliance of lawyers, politicians, and land speculators, the Ring used the legislature to further its own business interests. Over the years a network of influence had been established throughout the territory, with particular emphasis on *mexicano* politicians. Operating through Anglo bosses, the Ring controlled the *jefes políticos* by the judicious use of rewards and threats. The common people, *los hombres pobres*, generally went along, fearing *gringo* reprisals. The *jefes políticos* delivered the vote and the Ring maintained its power base. So far, the new governor had been stymied in his attempts to stamp out the corruption and graft.

"What about Stephen Benton?" Elizabeth said, almost to herself. "Whatever Pat Garrett has done, he's just a flunky. It's Benton who gives the orders."

"Only one problem," Virgil said dully. "We've got no proof. Our star witness was killed this morning."

"Nonsense," she said in a firm voice. "From what Clint says, Tafoya named names. Why not go after them?"

Virgil frowned, shook his head. "What we have are allegations made by a dead man. No court would issue a warrant on that basis."

"Why should we worry about the legal niceties? Stephen Benton certainly doesn't observe the rules."

Clint marked again that his sister-in-law was a woman of some spirit. To her, an obstacle was merely an annoyance to be surmounted by the most expedient means. She was a fighter, and she never gave ground.

"Beth's right," he said, glancing at Virgil. "When the other side plays dirty pool, that makes it a whole different game. I think I'll pay a call on Ingram."

"The retired army officer?"

Clint nodded. "I suspect he's the key to getting at

Benton. Leastways, he could implicate some of Benton's cronies. That's a starting point.''

Virgil looked worried. ''Aren't you forgetting something? You've got no authority in the Texas Panhandle.''

''That didn't stop me in El Paso.''

''Yes, and you almost got yourself killed this morning.''

Clint permitted himself a grim smile. ''Virge, the only shot that counts is the one you don't hear. So far, I've heard 'em all.''

Elizabeth stifled a laugh. At times, she thought Clint was too cocksure for his own good. But she deeply admired his casual courage and his bold nature. She considered him a man of great personal character.

''Oh, I almost forgot,'' she said suddenly. ''I have a message for you.''

''Yeah, who from?''

''Sallie Chisum.'' Elizabeth paused, watching his reaction. ''She wonders why you've stayed away so long.''

Clint wagged his head. Sallie Chisum was the niece of the Jinglebob cattle baron. When business took him to the Peco Valley, he usually called on her. But he'd made it a point to steer clear of any lasting entanglement. He looked at Elizabeth now with a sardonic smile.

''You just don't quit, do you?''

''Why, whatever do you mean?''

''Come off it,'' Clint said jestfully. ''You know damn well what I mean. You're still playing matchmaker.''

''Well, someone has to,'' she told him. ''The way you're going, you'll end up in an old soldiers' home. It's disgraceful!''

''Pull her off, Virge,'' Clint hooted. ''She's like a bulldog with an old bone.''

Elizabeth screeched indignation. Virgil nodded absently, his attention fixed on something outside the window. A buggy rolled to a halt in front of the house and he recognized it as the hired rig from the livery stable in Lincoln. The driver was a young man in his early twenties, dressed in a rumpled sackcloth suit and dusty brogans. He was strikingly handsome, a strapping six-footer with wheat-colored hair and a square jaw. He jumped down from the buggy and walked toward the house.

Virgil met him at the door. There was a murmured conversation and Virgil suddenly whooped laughter. He led the youngster into the parlor.

"Beth! Clint!" he said loudly. "Look who dropped out of nowhere. It's Ellen's boy—Brad Dawson!"

The Brannock brothers were originally from Missouri. Their cousin Ellen was the daughter of Ezra and Angeline Brannock.. She had married a Dawson shortly after the outbreak of the Civil War. While Virgil had corresponded with her, neither he nor Clint had seen her since 1861. Nor had they ever laid eyes on her son.

Clint shook his hand warmly. "How's your mother and your grandfolks?"

Brad's smile faded. "Well, Mom's fine and Grandma Angeline is living with her now." He paused and his voice dropped. "Grandpa died just before Easter."

There was a stunned silence. Clint mumbled a curse and Virgil's face grew overcast. He put his hand on Brad's shoulders.

"We're mighty sorry to hear that," he said. "We thought the world of Uncle Ezra. He was a fine man."

"Yessir, he was," Brad agreed. "Just about the best friend I ever had. Matter of fact, he's why I'm here."

Virgil looked puzzled. "I don't follow you."

A note of pride came into Brad's voice. "Grandpa talked a lot about you and Cousin Clint. He called you the westering men of the family. Always wished he'd done the same himself."

"Uncle Ezra?" Virgil said, clearly amazed. "I thought he was a farmer born and bred."

"No, sir," Brad said soberly. "He left the farm to my folks and they'll likely work it the rest of their lives. But just before he died, he told me to come West where the Brannocks belong. You'll recollect I'm half Brannock."

"Well of course you are!"

"So here I am," Brad announced. "Grandpa told me to ask you for a job."

"A job?" Virgil repeated. "You want to be a cowboy?"

"No, sir," Brad said with grave courtesy. "I figure to start out as a cowhand and learn the business. One day, I aim to have a spread of my own."

"By jingo!" Virgil said expansively. "Spoken like a true Brannock, even if your name is Dawson. Consider yourself hired."

Elizabeth laughed happily. She moved forward and bussed Brad on the cheek. "We're delighted you're here," she said. "We'll try to make you feel at home."

"Thank you, ma'am," Brad said, suddenly flustered. "But I don't expect special treatment of any sort. You just point me in the direction of the bunkhouse—"

"No, by God!" Virgil declared sternly. "You're family and you'll live under the same roof with us. I won't hear another word on the subject."

"Yes, sir," Brad said, grinning. "All the same, I mean to earn my keep. I'll start first thing in the morning."

A flicker of humor showed in Clint's eye. He slowly looked the youngster up and down. "Virge, before you put him to work, you'd better get him some new duds. What he's wearin' is liable to spook a cowpony."

Brad flushed beet red. For a moment, everyone stood looking at his brogans and store-bought suit. Then Clint let go with a graveled chuckle and Virgil broke out in a rumbling belly laugh. Elizabeth took the youngster's arm and tucked it into her own.

"Welcome to Spur, Brad."

5

On the first day of May Virgil rode eastward out of the Hondo Valley. A narrow wagon track bordered the river and gradually wound upward through the foothills. Abruptly, where the foothills ended, the trail topped a high mesa.

The terrain dropped off sharply. Below, spread out in a sweeping panorama, was the Pecos Valley. Dusty plains, dotted with patches of short grass, were broken by canyons and occasional rolling meadows. The Pecos River, with its headwaters in the lofty snowcapped Sangre de Cristos, traced a southerly path to merge with the Rio Grande. Farther east, *Llano Estacado* stretched onward into the west Texas plains.

Virgil got an early start. He topped the low range of foothills not long after sunrise. From there, the Rio Hondo meandered eastward several miles and ultimately flowed into the Pecos. Near the juncture was a crossroads trading post called Roswell, established as a supply point for trail herds and outlying ranches. The small settlement consisted of one store and two saloons surrounded by a few ramshackle houses. Not yet a town, it served as an oasis for thirsty cowhands.

Some four miles to the southeast was the headquarters of the Jinglebob Ranch. The compound was located on South Spring River, an artesian stream which emptied into the Pecos. In 1872, after trailing a herd of longhorns from Texas, John Chisum had selected the spot as a base of operations. The springs provided water year round and the site was central to the Pecos Valley. For a cattleman with big ideas, it represented that once-in-a-lifetime opportunity. North and south along the Pecos, most of the land was still public domain.

Everything about the Jinglebob was mammoth in scope. Natural landmarks, such as rivers and mountains, were used to measure its boundary lines. Over 100,000 cows grazed its range, and a crew of one hundred fifty cowhands worked the spread. A decade past, John Chisum had laid claim to a sprawling empire, defending it against outlaws and marauding Apache. In a land where the nearest law was a day's ride away, he recognized no authority but his own. He ruled the Pecos like a feudal lord.

Chisum began by purchasing title to forty acres on the South Spring River. He then used relatives and loyal cowhands as a front, encouraging them to homestead one-hundred-and-sixty-acre tracts along a strip of the Pecos roughly sixty miles in length. The tracts were gradually deeded over to Chisum, and he extended his holdings, by right of possession, onto public-domain lands. By 1881, the Jinglebob stretched one hundred miles along the Pecos, from Bosque Grande in the north to Carlsbad in the south. Outlying cow camps, with crews of heavily armed men, stood watch over the scattered herds.

On South Spring, the *casa grande* was of a style befitting the King of the Pecos. It was one story, constructed of native adobe, with broad wings extending off the central living quarters. Beneath a tile roof, hewn beams protruded from walls four feet thick. The window casements gleamed of tallowed oak, and the double doors were wider than a man's outspanned arms. Shaded by cottonwoods, the house overlooked the spring-fed river.

The buildings of the ranch compound were grouped with a methodical symmetry. Four bunkhouses formed a quadrangle, with a dining hall the size of an army barracks in the center. Corrals and stables, flanked by a line of storage buildings, angled south along a bend in the river. A com-

missary and an open-sided blacksmith shed were situated
on a plot of open ground central to the entire compound.
The effect was that of a small but prosperous village
bustling with activity.

Chisum himself presided over the South Spring headquarters. His two brothers, James and Pitzer, bossed the
cow camps up and down the Pecos. During the trailing
season, from late spring to early fall, they were seldom
seen. From the outreaches of the ranch, they trailed contract herds to army posts and Indian reservations throughout New Mexico and Arizona. Still larger herds were
shipped by rail every fall to eastern slaughterhouses. The
operation was now so vast that Chisum had outstripped his
closest competitor, the King Ranch of Texas. He was the
largest cattleman in the West.

Virgil found him seated on the veranda of the main
house. Chisum looked anything but the fabled King of the
Pecos. A withered giant, he had the features of a fleshed
skeleton bound with gray, chalky skin. He was almost
bald, with bone-china teeth, and he spoke with the slurred
inflections of a man wasted by illness. Other contests
might end in a draw, but it was clear that he'd already lost
his struggle with the years. Only his eyes were alive, and
by exercise of sheer will he still ruled the Jinglebob.

Late yesterday, one of Chisum's hands had ridden into
Spur. The message for Virgil was somewhat cryptic, and
vaguely urgent. Chisum wanted to see him and suggested
that he drop by the Jinglebob within the next day or so.
But now, as Virgil stepped onto the veranda, his presentiment turned to outright concern. While the day was warm,
the old man was slumped in a rocker, a shawl draped over
his legs. The cancer that was killing him appeared to have
gained ground.

"Hello there, Virge," Chisum said, sitting straighter.
"Grab a chair and take a load off your feet."

"Don't mind if I do," Virgil said, lowering himself into
another cane-bottomed rocker. "How are you feeling, John?"

"Not worth a gawddamn," Chisum snorted. "Here lately, I plumb run out of starch."

"You could've fooled me. I was thinking you looked a mite better."

"Quit tryin' to humor me. You never was much of a liar."

"Well, one thing's for certain," Virgil said cheerfully. "You haven't lost your ornery disposition."

Chisum seemed to look through him. "Lemme tell you, it's a helluva note. Outlived Apache and stampedes and half the goddurned calamities known to man." He paused, slowly shook his head. "The Lord shore has a queer sense of humor."

There was a moment of strained silence. Then, with a wave of his hand, Chisum seemed to gather himself. "I didn't ask you over here to listen to me gripe. We got more important things to talk about."

"Oh?" Virgil inquired. "What's that?"

"Why, the gawddamned rustlers! What else?"

The statement required no elaboration. Every rancher in the territory suffered heavy losses in rustled stock. Gangs of thieves, both Anglo and *mexicano*, were constantly raiding unprotected herds. Virgil was doubly vulnerable because of his horse-breeding operation. Brands were easily altered, and good horseflesh brought top dollar in cattle country. He needed little coaxing to work himself into a temper.

"Sonsabitches!" he said angrily. "I've got night guards riding the whole valley and we're still getting hit. There's no end to it."

"We're all in the same fix," Chisum grated. "I lose a couple of hundred head a month, regular as clockwork. Christ knows how many of the bastards I'm supportin'."

Virgil nodded. "Same song, second verse. We've had this conversation before."

"So we have," Chisum agreed. "That's why I sent for you. The Association meeting's less than a week away."

The New Mexico Cattlemen's Association met four times a year in Santa Fe. At the last meeting, Chisum had been elected president for 1881. He'd taken office with the goal of bringing about a more cohesive organization. Large ranchers tended to shy away from collective action. For the most part, they stubbornly went their own way.

"Way it looks," Chisum said without inflection, "I won't be in any shape to make the trip. I'd like you to take my place."

"How do you mean?"

"I've drafted a letter to the members. Told 'em you speak for me and I appointed you to run the meeting. Nobody'll give you any guff when they hear the letter."

Virgil scratched his jaw with a thumb. "Lots of people could run a meeting. Why pick me?"

"Couple of reasons," Chisum said in a voice webby with phlegm. "First off, they respect you and they'll listen to you. On top of that, I trust you to knock their heads together and hammer out an agreement. We've got to stop talkin' and show the rustlers we mean business."

Virgil was in complete agreement. For all practical purposes, the Association existed in name only. The members looked upon the meetings as an excuse for a trip to Santa Fe. Hard drinkers, they all talked a big fight but refused to band together. No strategy had ever been approved for a full-scale war on rustlers.

"Well, John," Virgil said with conviction, "I'll try not to let you down. One way or another, I'll get their attention."

"I never doubted it for a minute. And when you do, tell 'em—"

Chisum abruptly stopped. His eyes went past Virgil and his features congealed into a scowl. Twisting around, Virgil followed the direction of his gaze. William Bonney, mounted on a coal-black horse, forded the stream. A pearl-handled Colt was holstered on his hip and an insolent grin was plastered on his face. The two men watched as he walked his horse toward the house.

Virgil was frankly astounded by the Kid's brazen manner. Pat Garrett and several posses were scouring the countryside for the young outlaw. Army patrols, as well as every peace officer in the territory, were on the alert. Having killed two deputies, there was every likelihood that the Kid would now be shot on sight. Yet, only four days after his escape, he was still sticking to his old haunts. Virgil thought somewhere south of the border would have been far safer.

Bonney reined to a halt before the veranda. He waited for an invitation to dismount, but Chisum merely stared at him. After a moment he nodded to both men. "Gents, how goes the battle?"

Chisum grunted sharply. "Suppose you tell us! You're the one being hunted."

"Don't worry yourself," Bonney said, still grinning. "I got plenty of friends hereabouts. Garrett won't take me again."

There was a grain of truth to the statement. Throughout the territory, *mexicanos* admired Bonney for his contempt of *gringo* laws. He was known to them as *El Chivato*, and wherever he rode, he was welcomed into their homes. They counted it a mark of honor to share a humble supper with the young *bandido*.

"What brings you here?" Chisum demanded. "We've got no business."

"Mebbe not," Bonney said lazily. "All the same, it's slim pickin's with Garrett on my tail. I figgered you might stake me."

"Why would I do a fool thing like that?"

"Let's just say it's for old times' sake. Five hundred and you'll see the last of me. *Adiós* and no hard feelings."

"No soap," Chisum said with a flare of annoyance. "We were quits a long time ago. That's the way it stays."

At the outset of the Lincoln County War, Bonney's

employer, a rancher named John Tunstall, had been killed.
Afterward, because Tunstall had been a staunch ally, Chisum
tolerated the Kid. Then, in a savage act of reprisal, Bonney
had murdered the sheriff who was behind Tunstall's death.
Chisum thereafter disavowed the Kid, branding him a
common outlaw. Their brief alliance had ended on that
note.

"Lookit here," Bonney said sullenly. "I figger you
owe me for times past. Who else would've done your dirty
work?"

"Get off my land!" Chisum thundered. "Whatever
you did, it was for your own reasons. I don't owe you a
gawddamn thing."

Bonney gave him a strange crooked smile. "Old man,
there's more'n one way to collect a debt. I might just help
myself to some of your stock."

Before Chisum could reply, Virgil jackknifed to his
feet. He moved to the edge of the veranda. "Listen close,
Bonney," he said in a low voice. "Stay the hell away from
the Jinglebob and the Spur. Otherwise I'll sic my brother
on you."

A ferocious grin suddenly lit the Kid's face. "Fat chance
of that, since Clint and me are old pards. Case you hadn't
heard, he owes me a big favor."

"Think about it," Virgil said in a flat monotone. "Whatever he owes you, he's still my brother. Who do you
reckon he'd side with?"

"You talk like that ought to scare me."

"Well, if it don't, you're plumb loco. No sane man
would want Clint on his trail."

Bonney peered at him, one eye cocked askew, like a
watchful animal. Finally, with an idle shrug, he nodded.
"Like it or not, the tally still ain't square. I'll see you
gents around."

Virgil let it drop there. He watched as Bonney reined
about and rode back across the stream. At length, when

horse and rider gained the far shore, he turned to Chisum. His features were somber.

"I doubt we've heard the last of him, John."

Chisum took a deep breath, blew it out heavily. "All the more reason for you to attend the Association meeting. The Kid might be just the excuse we needed."

"How so?"

"Never occurred to me before," Chisum said, "not till you mentioned Clint. But Gawdalmighty, wouldn't he make a fine stock detective! He's the one man the Association might hire."

Virgil looked doubtful. "Clint thinks he has a lead into the Santa Fe Ring. Knowing him, he won't be pulled off the trail."

"Hell's bells," Chisum grumbled, "he's just chasin' his tail. Nobody's gonna nail Stephen Benton."

"I've got a hunch Clint wouldn't agree."

"By Judas, you can try, can't you? Tell him we need his help—now!"

Chisum's strength seemed to desert him. He coughed raggedly and slumped lower in his chair. His chalky skin turned paler still.

The front door whipped open. Sallie Chisum hurried outside, nodding stiffly to Virgil. "Help me," she said. "When he starts coughing, he's overtaxed himself. We have to get him into bed."

"Confound it!" Chisum protested weakly. "Just lemme be, girl."

"Hush, Uncle John," she chastised him. "You know very well I'm right."

Virgil moved forward to assist her. Beneath his clothes, Chisum was gaunt and wasted, painfully frail. Supporting him under the arms, they all but carried him into the house and down a long corridor. Sallie led the way into a room with gun racks lining the walls and a stuffed bobcat mounted on a pedestal.

Too feeble to resist, Chisum allowed himself to be

lowered onto the bed. Sallie ignored what sounded like a
curse and went about pulling off his boots. She fussed over
him, fluffing his pillow, and cajoled him into crawling
under the covers. He was still protesting when Virgil
stepped out of the room.

A short time later Sallie returned to the veranda. She
had dark eyes and high cheekbones and raven hair wound
in coils atop her head. Her skin was soft and creamy,
untouched by wind or sun, and her mouth was a lovely
oval. She seemed to Virgil something out of a storybook,
ethereal and strangely out of place on Jinglebob. Yet she
was mistress of the house and clearly a match for her
uncle.

"Thank you," she said graciously. "I'm sorry you had
to see him that way. He simply refuses to admit he needs
rest."

Virgil shook his head ruefully. "What's Doc Wood say
about your uncle?"

"Nothing good," she said, her eyes grave. "He told us
it's only a matter of time. A year, perhaps less . . ."

"What about an operation?"

"Yes, we've discussed surgery. But Dr. Wood said it
would have to be performed back East. He doesn't feel
qualified to handle it himself."

Virgil studied her downcast face. "What was John's
reaction?"

She was quiet for several moments. When she spoke,
there was an echoing sadness in her voice. "Uncle John
believes he's needed here. He thinks Jinglebob couldn't
last without him."

"Horsefeathers!" Virgil said crisply. "Your father and
your Uncle Pitzer could look after things. John's just being
stubborn."

"No, not really," she murmured uneasily. "Uncle John
holds Jinglebob together by force of will. Once he's gone,
we'll lose the public-domain lands."

For a woman of twenty-two, she seemed to Virgil unusually mature. Her assessment of the situation dovetailed with his own reckoning. James and Pitzer Chisum were caretakers, not visionaries. Jinglebob would not long survive the death of its founder.

"Look here," Virgil said gently. "Don't try to shoulder the whole load yourself. Give a yell if you need help."

"You've already helped," Sallie confided, "perhaps more than you know. Uncle John believes someone has to assume the leadership in Lincoln County." She paused, her voice suddenly stronger. "He's picked you as his successor."

"I know," Virgil admitted. "When he told me about the Association meeting, I saw through it right away. He's priming me to take the plunge into politics."

"And you will—won't you?"

Virgil laughed. "You and Beth are birds of a feather. She'd like to see me in the governor's palace."

The talk turned to Virgil's family. Sallie inquired after Jennifer and Morgan, and listened raptly to the news of Brad's sudden appearance at Spur. All the while Virgil knew she was biting her tongue not to ask about Clint. She was a lady, and ladies weren't permitted to display indecorous interest in a man.

There were times when Virgil agreed with Elizabeth. He was proud of Clint and on occasion he even envied the younger man's footloose approach to life. Yet he was of the firm opinion that Clint would do well to marry Sallie Chisum. Nor was there any doubt that she would accept should Clint ever pop the question. She was not a woman given to guile and subterfuge. Her feelings were plain for all to see.

Virgil nonetheless prided himself on being a realist. The odds on his brother marrying anyone were somewhere between slim and none. Sallie Chisum deserved better and there seemed little reason to give her false hope. Still, he saw no harm in a white lie.

"Almost forgot," he said casually. "Clint asked to be

remembered and sent along a message. He'll ride over the first chance he gets.''

Sallie blushed, unable to hide her pleasure. She wanted desperately to believe it was true. "How is he?" she asked. "We heard about the shooting."

"You mean that *Comanchero*?" Virgil said, chuckling. "To hear Clint talk, it was just another day's work. He's got more lives than a cat."

Sallie was still standing on the veranda when Virgil rode out. He turned in the saddle and waved and the sight brought a lump to his throat. Her face was bright with happiness, and she looked for all the world like a young girl awaiting a gentleman caller. Just for an instant he regretted his white lie. Then, quickly, he made himself a promise.

He resolved to have a talk with Clint. Having nine lives and chasing around after outlaws was one thing. A girl like Sallie Chisum was another matter entirely. Her kind came along only once in a blue moon.

The last one he'd met was Elizabeth.

6

On Spur, the working day began before sunrise. The men were rousted out of their bunks by the *segundos* of the various crews. Scratching and yawning, they quickly dressed and stamped on their boots. The jangle of spurs soon filled the bunkhouse.

Outside, the hands generally separated into two groups. Those with weak kidneys beat a path to the five-holer privy. The others ganged around long tables arrayed with galvanized washbasins. Few of them shaved on a daily basis, and none of them bathed. On average, they managed two baths a year, spring and fall.

Their morning ritual seldom varied. They dabbed their eyes with cold water and briskly scrubbed their faces. Some cleaned their teeth, but most simply rinsed out their mouths. Almost without exception, they damped down their hair and slicked it back with combs. Then, ready to face a new day, they trooped off toward the cookhouse.

There they were joined by Morg and Brad. While the youngsters lived in the main house, they took their morning meal with the hands. Odell Slater, the foreman, had assigned Morg to act as Brad's guide and mentor. At first, because he was so obviously a greenhorn, the other men razzed Brad unmercifully. His spanking-new boots and range duds, topped off by a pristine Stetson, were the objects of considerable hilarity.

Brad took the ribbing with undaunted good humor. These were rough men, hardened by the life they led, but not spiteful. Even though he was the butt of their jokes, he realized it was sportive and meant in jest. Had he joined the cavalry, he would have undergone a similar rite of initiation. Seasoned veterans, whether in a bunkhouse or an army barracks, forever tested the tyro. A man who sulked or lost his temper was quickly written off and left alone. No one had any use for a poor sport.

The morning meal was the largest of the day. Four cooks turned out food that was hearty and meant to stick to a man's ribs. Gallons of Arbuckle coffee were used to wash down beefsteak and flapjacks, sourdough biscuits and gravy, and that staple of a cowhand's diet, pinto beans. Eggs were served only at Sunday breakfast, but beans were served twice a day, every day. The result was a constant and somewhat thunderous chorus as the beans followed nature's course.

After breakfast, the men saddled frisky cowponies and rode out for the day's work. There were several crews, each bossed by a *segundo*, and they scattered to the far corners of Spur. Some worked the old stuff, gathering barren cows and mature steers. Others beat the brush for cows with calves and worked the branding fires. Still another group was assigned to the breeding pastures, and a crew of six men tended to the horse herd. By sunup, every man on the spread was in the saddle.

Brad provided the morning's entertainment. Back in Missouri, on the family farm, he'd worked draft animals and plow horses. But climbing aboard a snorty cowpony was a new experience. The most highly prized of all range stock on Spur was a spirited crossbreed of mustang and Thoroughbred. At times, however, it seemed that the mustang temperament would never be quelled by an infusion of new blood. Cowponies, even after being broken, were still half-wild. One in a hundred was willing to start the day in a civilized manner. The others bucked.

For the past four mornings Brad had put on a display of determination and grit. He'd been thrown and stomped, and every muscle in his body ached. Yet he was willing to learn from his mistakes and he seemed possessed of an inexhaustible stamina. His morning workout always drew a crowd, for a tyro on a cowpony was a barrel of laughs. The *segundos* had a hard time pulling their men away from the corral.

Today Brad's mount was a chestnut gelding with a blaze on its forehead. The horse was not quite fifteen hands high and weighed out at about nine hundred pounds. He was stout and ornery, and fast as a cat. Like most cowponies, he allowed himself to be saddled without a fight. He stood absolutely still while Brad tied off the latigo.

Jennifer walked down from the main house. She took a spot beside Morg at the corral fence, watching intently. There was a gamine quality about her these days, something new since Brad's arrival on Spur. Whenever he was around, she suddenly materialized, and she looked eager as a sparrow. She was moonstruck, suffering a schoolgirl crush for an older man. She'd never seen a Greek god, but she thought Brad would surely qualify.

Brad put his foot in the stirrup and swung aboard. For a moment the cowpony stood as still as a bronzed statue. Then, like a firecracker bursting apart, he exploded in the middle. He crow-hopped across the corral, pounding the earth with all four hooves, and suddenly tossed his rump skyward. Brad sailed off, arms and legs akimbo, and hit the ground hard. The cowpony stopped a short distance away, eyeing him with a look of disdain.

The crowd of onlookers hooted and jeered, laughing uproariously. Not a man among them hadn't been dumped in much the same way, and they considered it something of a sporting event. They shouted encouragement, some of them offering raucous advice, as Brad climbed to his feet and slapped dust from his clothes. He squared himself up and walked across the corral.

The cowpony again stood immobile. He gathered the reins and stepped into the saddle. An instant of silence slipped past, then the gelding bounded skyward and sunfished. Brad stuck this time, and as though nailed to the saddle, he stayed aboard through the volcanic twisting and pitching that followed. He rode the cowhorse to a dead stop, then reined sharply about and halted in the center of the corral. Grinning broadly, he doffed his hat and took a bow.

All around the corral the hands whooped and shouted. They appreciated a man with a sense of humor, particularly one who could laugh at himself. Even more, they admired a man who took the jolting and hammering and always came back for more. Nothing was lower in their view than a quitter, and Brad had proved to them, and himself, that he wouldn't be whipped. He was skinned and bruised, but he'd ridden the spirited little cowpony into the ground. They decided he might make a hand after all.

Jennifer looked enthralled. When Brad rode to the fence and dismounted, her breath caught in her throat. She thought she'd never seen anyone so daring and bold, and certainly no one quite so handsome. Her eyes suddenly shone, and she laughed.

"Honestly, Brad," she said wonderingly. "You're a born horseman."

"Wasn't bad," Morg allowed, a devilish glint in his eye. " 'Course, one ride don't make a top hand."

"Don't listen to him," Jennifer said, staring calf-eyed at Brad. "You were just wonderful . . . absolutely wonderful!"

Brad fidgeted uncomfortably. "Well, it was better anyway," he said. "I only got thrown once today."

"And tomorrow," Jennifer bubbled, "you won't get thrown at all. I just know it!"

Morg rolled his eyes with a clownish grin. He looked across the fence at Brad. "You'll have to excuse my sister. She gets a little dopey sometimes."

Jennifer put on her best pout. "And you'll have to ignore my brother, Brad. He's just a trifle uncouth."

Her nose in the air, she turned and marched off toward the house. Brad appeared embarrassed, and somehow troubled. Morg gave him a sly wink.

"I think she's got a crush on you."

"I hope you're wrong," Brad said. "I don't want your folks to get any ideas."

"Leave it to me," Morg said, laughing. "I'll protect you from her."

Brad stared after her a moment. Then he brought the gelding through the corral gate and they walked to where Morg's horse was hitched. When they were mounted, they rode off toward the southwest. Neither of them said anything more about Jennifer.

The crew was working a bunch of old stuff. Under the brassy dome of the sky, the men dripped sweat and tried not to breathe dust. They were holding some three hundred head on a grassy swale near the southern foothills.

Outriders were stationed at the cardinal points of the compass. Their job was to contain the cows on the holding ground and haze bunch quitters back into the fold. The rest of the crew was busy doctoring blowfly sores with the standard range remedy. Bawling cows were lassoed and thrown, then the sore was cleaned and the proud flesh cut away. A man carrying a rag dauber and a wooden bucket quickly stepped in and coated the raw spot with axle grease. The cow was released and the next patient was hauled forward to have its sores doped.

Brad was acting as one of the outriders. The job required less skill than either the ropers or the men on the ground. For the most part, his horse did all the work, and a good deal of the thinking. When a bunch quitter started in his direction, he had only to touch the reins. The chestnut gelding would then spring forward and enter into a game of cat-and-mouse with the cow. No matter which way the cow swerved, the horse was always a step ahead, alert to the next move. A good cowpony, after being trained in the ways of longhorns, operated largely without command. The rider was often little more than a spectator.

Some of Brad's initial wonder had worn thin. In a mere four days he'd discovered that the dime novels had it all wrong. Far from the romantic heroics he had read about, the cattle business was mostly hard work. Granted, the work took skill and a reasonable amount of intelligence. Anyone short on brains could get skewered by a longhorn or crippled by a spooky horse. But a roundup, from what he'd seen so far, was equal parts drudgery and dust-soaked sweat. He got to where he wanted a cow to quit the bunch. Anything to break the tedium.

The worst part was sitting a saddle for ten hours a day. The old-timers assured him that his galled butt would soon toughen into whang leather. In the meantime, he was raw and sore as a boil, and found walking to be an exquisite form of torture. At night, Morg would rub his backsides with liniment, laughing every time he flinched. The boy had been riding horseback since he was three and his own backsides were as impervious as stone. None of which did anything to improve Brad's condition. He slept with his legs spread wide apart.

One thought triggered another. At first, he'd enjoyed being quartered in the main house. All the more so since the bunkhouse smelled like a wolf den and afforded a man no privacy. But a problem had developed, and he saw that it might pose trouble. Jennifer was infatuated with him, suffering from a severe case of puppy love. While he gave her no encouragement, the situation was steadily growing worse. She was a girl with a woman's body and a head full of fanciful notions. She was also headstrong, and damnably persistent.

Brad was no tyro when it came to women. On the farm, he'd taken several buxom young girls to the hayloft. He was flattered by Jennifer's attention and he felt the sap rising whenever she got too close. Yet the predicament was loaded with danger, more for him than for her. One misstep on his part—even the hint of hanky-panky—and Virgil would send him packing. Thinking on it now, he saw that the situation could jeopardize all his dreams, force him to leave Spur in disgrace. Somehow, without creating hard feelings, the girl had to be dissuaded. He began considering how it might be done.

"Hey, Brad!"

Morg rode up beside him. "C'mon," the boy yelled, grinning broadly. "Try your hand at ropin' one."

Over the past few days Morg had given him rudimentary instructions with a lariat. Directing his attention, the boy now pointed out a yearling bull at the edge of the herd. He explained that the bull had somehow escaped last year's roundup and needed to be fixed.

Working as a team, they walked their horses toward the bunched cattle. Morg took the lead, easing his cowpony into the herd and chousing the bull onto open ground. Brad missed on his first try, but got a loop over the yearling's horns the second time out. He dallied his lariat around the saddlehorn and dragged the bull toward the doctoring crew. Morg hindfooted the bull with a heel catch and dumped him on the ground.

The men swarmed over the yearling. While Morg and Brad kept their lines taut, one man grabbed a foreleg and planted his knee on the bull's neck to hold it steady. Another man wielding a short-bladed knife quickly notched the Spur earmark, a vee-shaped cut known as a swallow fork. He then moved to the rear and with deft strokes of his knife transformed the yearling from a bull to a steer. A third man daubed the raw scrotum with dope and they all stepped aside. Morg and Brad slacked off and flipped their loops clear.

The men on the ground grinned and bobbed their heads, nodding to Brad. A quick glance at the boy confirmed that Morg was equally proud of his ropework. The crew, despite their razzing, were pulling for him all along. They wanted him to make a hand.

Brad knew then he'd passed muster. He was now a Spur man, one of the crew.

An hour or so before sunset Clint moved out onto the veranda. He took a chair and began rolling himself a smoke. His expression was abstracted, somehow faraway.

Several matters weighed heavily on his mind. Foremost was the retired army officer, Jacob Ingram. He felt a nagging pressure to leave for the Panhandle and get on with the job. Yet he'd delayed the trip after Virgil's visit with John Chisum. Virgil wanted him along as an adviser at the Cattlemen's Association meeting. Horse thieves and rustlers were to head the agenda, and Virgil felt his presence would influence the outcome. He'd agreed to go along, albeit reluctantly.

His reluctance was underscored in part by a personal matter. The proposed trip to the Panhandle reminded him of other things left undone. In Indian Territory, across the line from the Panhandle, was the Comanche reservation. There, deep in the Wichita Mountains, lived his sister-in-law, Earl's widow, a Comanche woman. With her were Earl's sons, Lon and Hank, both Brannocks in name and blood. Since Earl's death, Clint had looked upon the boys as his responsibility. Yet he hadn't visited the reservation since late last fall.

The press of other matters robbed him of time. The *Comanchero*, and the Santa Fe Ring, and now the need to apprehend Ingram. There was always another lead, another trail to follow, something that demanded attention. He felt as though he'd shirked his duty to his nephews, and himself. And that bothered him.

Brad and Morg provided a distraction. They rode in from the day's work, still frisky as a couple of bulldog pups. One thing led to another, and Morg started bragging on his uncle's renown with a six-gun. The youngster then insisted that Clint prove his point with a demonstration. He argued, as well, that Brad was overdue for a shooting lesson. Clint allowed himself to be persuaded.

Morg scrounged an armload of empty tin cans from the cookhouse. They then walked down to the river and found a spot where the bank rose sharply from the water. The empty cans were arranged in a line, with the bank providing a solid backstop. Clint stepped off ten paces and turned to face the cans. He told the boys to stand behind him.

While they listened, he explained the basics of handling a pistol. He covered the correct stance and the proper grip, and sighting, which with the Peacemaker was largely a matter of aligning the front sight with the center of the target. He advised them that the Colt was a natural pointer, with excellent balance, and could be brought on target in much the same way a man points his finger. Last, he stressed the importance of a steady, uninterrupted trigger squeeze. Nothing, he informed them, took the place of accuracy. Speed was meaningless unless combined with an instant of deliberate aim.

One at a time, he coached the boys in firing the Colt. Morg was no stranger to pistols, having had lessons before. He made the cans jump, missing only when he hurried his shot. Brad was older, and somewhat more serious, and he took the instructions to heart. He concentrated on the front sight, slowly squeezing the trigger, and every shot sent a can flying. While he'd hunted with a shotgun, he had never before fired a pistol, and it was an impressive first effort. Clint thought he showed a natural talent for shooting.

The boys watched each time Clint reloaded. He thumbed the hammer to half-cock, flipped open the loading gate, and shucked empties with the ejector rod. His hands worked with practiced speed, never pausing, never skipping a beat. He stuffed fresh cartridges into the cylinder, stopping on the count of five, and lowered the hammer on an empty chamber. To Brad's question, he explained that a Colt was unsafe with the hammer resting on a live round. The chance of an accidental discharge dictated that it be carried as a five-shooter.

Morg wasn't satisfied with a lesson in marksmanship. He'd seen his uncle practice on past occasions and he wanted a repeat demonstration. He said Brad ought to know what a gun could do in the hands of an expert shootist. Clint never encouraged fancy gunwork, for it was no casual skill. But the boy badgered him into it and he finally turned to face the target. Brad watched him like someone waiting for a magician to perform a trick.

Clint's arm moved in one fluid motion. The Colt appeared in his hand and spat a sheet of flame. His arm was extended slightly below shoulder level and his eyes seemed to be fixed on the row of cans. There was scarcely a pulsebeat between shots and he emptied the Peacemaker in a deafening roar of gunfire. The first can was still rolling when the last slug sent a can spinning into the air. He lowered the pistol and began shucking empties.

Morg whistled softly under his breath. Brad stared transfixed as the last can dropped to the ground. His gaze shifted to Clint, who was calmly reloading. He suddenly realized that the dime novels hadn't got it all wrong. A cowboy's life wasn't what it was cracked up to be, not by a damnsight. But there really were shootists and gunfighters, steely-eyed mankillers. A breed apart, and deadly beyond belief.

He was looking at one now.

7

Early next morning Virgil and Clint departed for the Association meeting. An hour before sunrise, one of the hands drove them into town in a buckboard. They had a steak-and-eggs breakfast at the hotel.

Clint disliked leaving his buckskin gelding at the ranch. Yet the detour through Santa Fe made it impractical to take the horse along. He nonetheless lugged his saddle and his Winchester carbine into the stage-line office. He planned to buy a spare mount when he headed for the Panhandle.

From Lincoln, they took the stage across the Capitan Mountains and through a fifty-mile stretch of desert known as *Jornada del Muerto*. West of the desert, the stage line connected with the railroad in the mining camp of Socorro, located on the banks of the upper Rio Grande. With forty-four saloons, Socorro was the latest and the wildest—boomtown in the territory. The discovering of a silver lode had transformed it into a rip-roaring round-the-clock den of iniquity. On average, two men were killed every night in shootouts and busthead brawls. Socorro's boot-hill was overcrowded and gaining in population daily.

After a night in Socorro, they boarded a passenger train which chuffed northward toward Albuquerque. Scarcely two years past, the Atchison, Topeka & Santa Fe had crossed the Colorado border through Raton Pass. From there, the line meandered southward until it reached the foothills of the Sangre de Cristos. Building westward, the railroad bypassed Santa Fe with its main line and laid track down the Rio Grande valley. Later in the year, a division point would be established at Rincon, with one branch extending to El Paso and the other to Deming. There a transcontinental link would be forged with the Southern Pacific, which was building eastward from California.

Some forty miles northwest of Albuquerque, Virgil and Clint switched trains at Lamy. At that point, the main roadbed curved around the Sangre de Cristos and angled northward toward Colorado. A trunk line spiraled upward from Lamy through Glorieta Pass and on into Santa Fe. The traffic was principally boxcars and flatbeds loaded with freight and trade goods. One passenger coach was usually coupled onto the last boxcar, with a caboose hitched to the rear. High in the mountains, Santa Fe had few visitors besides politicians and those seeking favors from the territorial government. Some people referred to the lone passenger coach as the "gravy train."

Santa Fe was situated along a stream that flowed southwesterly from the Sangre de Cristos. Surrounded by mountain ranges, the town was at an altitude of seven thousand feet. From the train station, it was a short walk uptown to the plaza. A broad square dominated by the governor's palace, the plaza was the town's center of activity. Built on commerce and politics, the territorial capital was the major trade center between Mexico and the United States. The plaza was crowded with shops and businesses and several open-air markets. The architecture was predominantly adobe, and the scene had a quaint atmosphere. For all its growth, Santa Fe still retained much of its native charm.

The Exchange Hotel was located on the southeast corner of the plaza. There, in a hall normally reserved for banquets and formal balls, the Cattlemen's Association held its meeting. The men who congregated in the hall were mostly large ranchers, and they were old acquaintances. Their politics tended toward the conservative, and they looked upon homesteaders and sheepmen as mortal ene-

mies. Yet, for all their wealth, they carried little clout with
the territorial legislature. Almost to a man, they were
opposed to an even more powerful organization, the Santa
Fe Ring. Few of them expected the meeting to result in
any profound changes.

On the fifth day of May, Virgil called the session to
order. Certain influential ranchers had already been allowed to read the letter appointing him John Chisum's
spokesman. Word had circulated among the others, and no
one objected to his running the meeting. Yet he had no
illusions about the thirty or so men gathered there. They
were a stubborn lot, fiercely independent, and seldom
swayed by logic. Never before had there been unanimous
accord except where it concerned sodbusters and sheepherders. Even then, they always fell to squabbling about
the solution.

Virgil made it a practice never to display inner doubt.
By nature he was an optimist, and he'd learned early in
life that confidence counted far more than the odds. A man
assured of himself bred that same conviction in other men,
and therefore gained an edge. It was a belief that had
served him well, and today he addressed the cattlemen
with a solemn air of authority. His eyes burned with
intensity and his voice was strong, filling the hall. He
hammered the lectern for emphasis.

The ranchers appeared lukewarm to his proposal. While
they agreed that rustling had to be stopped, they were
hesitant to invest power in any one man. None of them
were comfortable with the thought of Virgil—or anyone
else—directing affairs on their home range. A war on
rustlers sounded good, but nobody thought the campaign
should be directed by a single commander. Virgil argued
that their individual efforts had achieved nothing in the
past. To succeed, a campaign would have to be coordi-
nated throughout the territory, and organized along the
lines of a military command. He offered to step aside for a
man of their choice.

Not a man among them wanted the job. Virgil saw then that further discussion was useless. His patience strained, he steered the meeting onto another topic. He pointed out the need for a stock detective, someone accountable solely to the Association. Such a man, he explained, would be able to work the entire territory, tracking rustlers wherever the trail led. He then introduced Clint, noting that his brother had already refused consideration for the post. He stressed, however, that Clint was a lawman of wide experience. He asked them to listen with an open mind.

The hall fell silent as Clint walked to the lectern. Among themselves, the ranchers considered him a man who was prodded by strange devils. He had no ideology, no political ties, and no ambition for power. He was, instead, a private man, cold and remote and curiously detached. He had the look of one who holds himself apart from the crowd, not out of contempt but rather out of preference. The look of a loner.

Unversed in public speaking, Clint addressed the issue in blunt terms. His voice was quiet and dry as dust, and those at the back of the room had to strain to hear. What they heard was dispassionate and hard, and straight to the point. He told them that stockgrowers' associations throughout the West employed what were loosely termed "detectives." For the most part, the purpose of such men was not to recover stolen cows or bring rustlers to trial. Their job was to drive the thieves out, or kill them.

"What we're talking about," he concluded, "is organized extermination. You have to convince the rustlers that their lives are at stake. Once you do, they'll head elsewhere."

The cattlemen shifted in their chairs. At length, a weatherbeaten man with sparse black hair rose to his feet. His name was Bud Wilson and he operated a spread on the lower Rio Grande. His face was a prunelike mask of skepticism.

"Lemme ask you," he said. "Would you consider the job if we doubled what you're makin' now?"

"No," Clint said in a flat voice.

"Why not?"

"I don't kill men for hire."

"Thought so!" Wilson cackled. "We ain't talkin' about stock detectives, are we? We're talkin' about stranglers and backshooters."

Clint's eyes were impersonal. "Virgil told you one way to stop rustlers. I've just told you another. So far as I know, there's no third way."

"What about the law?" Wilson demanded. "Ain't we got a right to expect the law to stop 'em?"

"You'd need an army of lawmen to get the job done. A sheriff here and there just won't cut it."

"Then answer me this," Wilson said slyly. "How could *one* stock detective manage it?"

Clint's mouth curled. "A stock detective leaves his calling card wherever he rides. Word generally gets around."

"So you're telling us to hire ourselves a bounty hunter—an assassin!"

"Mister, if it was me, I'd kill my own snakes. 'Course, some people prefer to have it done, and there's men willin' to do it. That's all I'm telling you."

"And I suppose you know where we could hire just such a man?"

"Yeah, I know a couple," Clint said without expression. "Either one would solve your problem real quick."

As usual, the Association members argued themselves into a dead end. When they failed to reach a concensus, one of the ranchers suggested a compromise. The idea was quickly seconded and the resolution passed without a dissenting vote. Virgil was authorized to speak to the governor and request official action. Failing that, they would then consider hiring a bounty hunter.

The meeting adjourned to the hotel barroom.

Late that afternoon Virgil emerged from the hotel. He paused to light a cigar and stood for a moment surveying the plaza. Then, the cigar wedged in the corner of his mouth, he crossed San Francisco Street.

Over the years the plaza had changed in appearance. The streets bordering the square were still dirt, lined with buggies and horses and delivery wagons. But the Anglo influence was evident everywhere, oddly intermixed with the town's *mexicano* legacy. Three decades of territorial status had altered an ancient trading ground.

A white picket fence now bordered the plaza. Tall elm trees lined the four sides and the enclosed square was a grassy park crisscrossed with pathways. In the center, towering thirty feet high, was a granite memorial commemorating the dead of the Civil War. On the southeast corner was a large circular bandstand with a conical roof rising to a peak. At first glance, the visual effect was that of a Victorian park transplanted from Baltimore.

Other things had changed as well. Before the railroad, the town had been the terminus of the Santa Fe Trail. Only a year past, freight wagons from Missouri jammed the plaza from early summer to late fall. Trade goods were off-loaded there and stored for transshipment to all points of the compass. But now the parklike square was a meeting ground for land speculators and entrepreneurs, government officials and fast-talking promoters. There were few *mexicanos* in sight, except those tending the grass. A handful of tame Indians, most Pueblos, hawked their wares on street corners.

To Virgil, it was merely a sign of the times. He possessed that curious blend of pragmatism and compassion. He regretted the erosion of cultures that had thrived here for more than two centuries. Yet he was realist enough to understand that progress was like a great juggernaut. History taught that the old inexorably gave way before the new, that nothing lasted forever. The process was sometimes distasteful, but it was a bitter pill eventually swallowed by every culture. The *mexicanos*, though far from Anglicized, were witnessing still another history lesson.

The Palace of Governors was on the north side of the plaza. Built in the year 1610, it had served as the seat of government under Spanish and Mexican rule. A low adobe structure with massive walls, the palace occupied one entire side of the square. On one end were the federal district court and chambers for the territorial legislature. On the other were the office of the U.S. marshal and the territorial prison. In between were a dozen rooms set aside for the attorney general and government offices. Toward the rear, the governor's living quarters overlooked a flagstone patio shaded by tall trees.

Approaching the palace, Virgil was reminded again of the comic incongruities wrought by progress. A Victorian balustrade had been erected along the entire front of the building. The balustrade, as well as square pillars supporting the overhang, were freshly whitewashed. The impression was that of a proud adobe structure somehow mongrelized by an Eastern architect. Still, there was no doubt as to who ruled what was once a Spanish province. An American flag hung from a whitewashed staff atop the palace.

The main entrance was in the center of the building. Virgil moved along a corridor and entered a low-ceilinged reception room. His appointment was for four o'clock and a male secretary quickly ushered him into the governor's sanctum sanctorum. The walls of the office were lined with books and a broad window afforded a view of the patio outside. Lew Wallace rose from behind his desk with an outstretched hand.

The governor was a large man, with a leonine head and a deep, resonant voice. His face was covered by a square well-trimmed beard and his eyes were stern as any deacon's. He wore a dark conservative suit and a high starched collar, snugged tight by a four-in-hand tie. He stood stiff and straight-backed, in a posture of austere self-assurance.

Virgil considered him a most unlikely politician. By trade a soldier, he was a scholarly man and something of a philosopher. He spent a good deal of his time writing, and had recently published the lengthy historical novel *Ben Hur: A Tale of the Christ*. Virgil thought it an odd mix, politics on the one hand and religion on the other. Yet Wallace had allowed nothing to thwart his efforts in halting the Lincoln County War. Nor had he dirtied his hands by forming an alliance with the Santa Fe Ring. He was his own man, indebted to no one.

"Good to see you," Wallace said, indicating a chair. "How are things in Lincoln County?"

Virgil seated himself before the desk. "Nothing much to report, Governor. John Chisum's still in bad health and Billy the Kid is on the loose again. But I suppose you heard about that."

"Most regrettable," Wallace intoned. "Let us hope Sheriff Garrett recaptures him quickly."

"I doubt that Billy will let himself be taken a second time. He'll most likely go down fighting."

"Well, on to more pleasant subjects, Mr. Brannock. What can I do for you today?"

Virgil puffed his cigar. "I'm here at the request of the Cattlemen's Association. We need your help."

"Indeed?" Wallace said in an avuncular voice. "How may I be of assistance?"

Briefly, touching on the salient points, Virgil recounted the morning meeting. He concluded with a tactful demand, stating that ranchers accounted for a large share of New Mexico's economy. He asked that the U.S. Marshal be ordered onto the case.

Wallace nodded, thoughtful a moment. "You have a legitimate grievance," he said rather formally. "However, the marshal and his deputies are kept busy enforcing federal law. I suggest the ranchers look to their own county sheriffs."

"We already have," Virgil reminded him. "I'm here because that's gotten us nowhere. A sheriff's jurisdiction stops at the county line, and the rustlers know it." He paused, gestured with his cigar. "We need somebody with wider latitude."

"I appreciate that," Wallace temporized. "But to quote the old homily, every tub must stand on its own bottom. Territorial government has its limitations, Mr. Brannock."

"You intervened before," Virgil insisted. "Without your help, we'd still be fighting the Lincoln County War. Where's the difference?"

Wallace let his gaze drift out the window. "Anarchy and rustlers are hardly comparable. You're talking to me now of cows—" his eyes snapped back to Virgil—"I acted then to save the lives of men."

Virgil gave him a lightning frown. "Governor, we're on the verge of anarchy again. Unless you act, cattlemen will be forced to take the law into their own hands. I'm talking about Judge Lynch and a swift hanging—or worse."

"What could be worse than lynch law?"

"A stock detective who works on the bounty system. For every rustler he kills, he gets a flat fee. No questions asked."

Wallace appraised him through narrowed eyes. "I've always considered you a civilized man, Mr. Brannock. Are you advocating coldblooded murder?"

"No, sir," Virgil said indignantly. "I'm trying to prevent bloodshed and six-shooter justice. Otherwise I wouldn't be sitting here."

"I see." Wallace nodded sagely, silent for a time. "On occasion, even the highest authority cannot respond to every need. We seem to be at an impasse, don't we?"

Virgil smiled bitterly. "When a man's cows are being rustled, he can't afford to be philosophical. I doubt the impasse will last too long."

"Then we've both failed," Wallace said, his voice suddenly drained of humor. "Take a message back to your Association members, Mr. Brannock. Tell them to exercise caution in this endeavor, or rue the consequences."

He stared straight at Virgil. "As governor, I cannot condone vigilantes."

Virgil stood and walked to the door. With his hand on the knob, he looked back. "Clint asked me to relay a message. He thinks he's got a lead that'll bust the Santa Fe Ring. He wanted to keep you posted."

"Give him my regards," Wallace said amiably. "Your brother has few peers, Mr. Brannock."

"Yessir, he's one of a kind, and that's a fact."

Outside the palace, Virgil paused to light a fresh cigar. He told himself he'd done his best and no man could ask more. Still, he was in a disgruntled mood and none too pleased with the prospects ahead. He found the idea of a bounty hunter personally, and morally, repugnant.

" 'Afternoon, Brannock."

Stephen Benton halted beside him. Whenever they met, Virgil was always amazed by the man's civility. The antagonism between them was visceral as a festering wound, raw and deep. He kept his voice neutral.

"Long time no see, Benton."

"Too long," Benton said cordially. "You ought to visit the capital more often."

"Not worth the trip," Virgil said, forcing a smile. "I'm more at home on the Rio Hondo."

"Well, there's much to be said for the outdoor life."

Benton possessed an oily, serpentine charm. He was a man of formidable intellect and overwhelming presence, with the bearing that powerful men exude. Neither tall nor short, he was in his early forties and looked ten years younger. His features were pleasant, tanned and smooth-shaven, and his dark hair was expertly barbered. A widower, he was said to be something of a ladies' man.

His companion provided a study in contrasts. Wherever Benton went, the shadow of Wilbur Latham was not far behind. Landgrabbing schemes, abetted by political skulduggery, had created a legion of men who would like to see Benton dead. Latham was a mercenary, quick with his fists and reportedly chain lightning with a gun. A man with lean hips and a massive chest, he seemed forever poised for trouble. His job was to keep Benton alive.

"How's the cattle business?" Benton asked now. "I understand beef prices are holding steady."

Virgil shrugged. "All things considered, it looks to be a pretty good year."

"Your Cattlemen's Association has the rumor mill working overtime. There's talk you plan to make it open season on rustlers."

"A stiff rope and a short drop solves a lot of problems."

"So I've heard," Benton said equably. "How does the governor feel about that? Or were you just paying a social call?"

"Never hurts to observe the formalities. Even cattlemen have to mind their politics."

Benton looked at him strangely. "Well, good seeing you again, Brannock. Say hello to John Chisum."

"John will appreciate you asking after him."

Benton strolled off, followed closely by Latham. Virgil had to admire the man's gall, for no greater enemies existed than Stephen Benton and the King of the Pecos. To send greetings, and do it with a straight face, took real brass.

He thought it would give Chisum a good laugh.

8

Lightning flickered on the far horizon. A sough of wind brought with it the distant smell of rain, and dark clouds tinged the sky farther north. The storm appeared to be moving on an easterly course.

Clint reined to a halt. The roan gelding he'd bought in Santa Fe nervously eyed the thunderstorm. Nearly a week has passed since he parted with Virgil and in that time he'd covered almost three hundred miles. His path took him straight into the heart of *Llano Estacado*.

The Staked Plains was a vast tableland. Flat and featureless, it stretched from eastern New Mexico into the Texas Panhandle. A brooding loneliness hung over *Llano Estacado* and the barren terrain marched onward to the horizon. Nothing grew there and no landmarks existed to record man's passage. Instead, like an emerald ocean, buffalo and mesquite grass rippled on forever.

Here and there the plains were broken by canyons. Clint sat staring into one now, an abyss that abruptly dropped off into space. Palo Duro Canyon was a colossal fissure gouged from the earth throughout aeons of time. A hundred miles long and a thousand feet deep, the broad gorge was walled north and south by sheer palisades. Far below, a winding river traced the floor of the canyon.

Along the south wall, an ancient path dropped downward into Palo Duro. Clint nudged his horse over the rimrock and began a slow descent on the narrow, rocky trail. In 1874, serving as an army scout, he had led the 4th

Cavalry Regiment down this same craggy escarpment. On the floor of the canyon, the troops had engaged the fiercest warriors of the Comanche nation, the Quahadi band. There, in a running fight, the lords of all the horseback tribes had been defeated. The battle of Palo Duro Canyon effectively brought peace to the Southern Plains.

Earl Brannock had fallen in the same battle. A misguided adventurer, he had joined the *Comancheros* in the illicit Indian trade. Trapped in the surprise attack by the cavalry, Earl had nonetheless absolved himself at the end. In an instant of raw courage, he had sacrificed himself to save Clint from certain death. After the battle, Clint had buried him beneath a tree along the stream. Only later would Clint discover that Earl's wife and two sons had escaped over the north wall.

On many occasions since then Clint had visited the gravesite. Today he forded the river and dismounted beside a towering cottonwood. A cairn of rocks marked the grave, weathered now by seven years of rain and snow. Clint stooped down, pulling weeds from the flinty soil, sobered by the knowledge that his brother lay at rest there. Somewhere the scolding of a blue jay was answered by the plaintive cry of a mourning dove. A squirrel chattered and then an eerie silence settled over the treeline.

For a moment, it seemed that time froze. A vivid picture of gunfire and death suddenly flashed before Clint's eyes. He saw again that last instant, when Earl rose from the boulders along the north wall. Heedless of the danger to himself, Earl fired on a *Comanchero* who had drawn a bead on Clint. In the exchange of shots that followed, both Earl and the *Comanchero* were killed. The battle ended only minutes later, with troops swarming through the Quahadi encampment. Fighting a valiant rearguard action, the Comanche warriors disappeared over the top of the canyon.

Some months later the Quahadi band had finally surrendered. They were the last of the Comanche nation to be herded onto the reservation, and with them went Earl's wife and sons. Today, thinking back on the aftermath of the battle, Clint remembered it as a bleak period in his life. Yet he believed that no man should die an insignificant death, and the sentiment was doubly meaningful for his brother. He had resolved then that Earl's sons would be as his own sons, even though they lived among the Comanche. Nothing had happened to alter his resolve.

Standing at the grave, he silently reaffirmed the promise. He thought perhaps Earl's spirit would hear, and rest easier, knowing the boys would not be forsaken. Whenever he came here, it was an oath he reaffirmed to himself as well. An oath strengthened by the kinship of blood.

He mounted and rode west along the river.

Palo Duro Canyon was the domain of Charles Goodnight. Like Chisum in New Mexico, Goodnight was the cattle king of the Texas Panhandle. He was, as well, a legend among westering men.

Several times a year Clint stopped by the headquarters of Goodnight's ranch. The JA spread was on a direct line with the Comanche reservation, and Clint usually spent the night before riding on to the Nations. He found Charlie Goodnight to be irascible good company, and one of the few men he genuinely admired. He considered the old trailblazer one of a dying breed.

A Texican frontiersman, Goodnight had served with the Ranger batallion during the early days. When the Civil War broke out, he signed on as an army scout and distinguished himself in several engagements. After the war, he formed a partnership with Oliver Loving and established a cattle outfit. In 1866 they blazed a 700-mile trail from Texas into the Pecos country of New Mexico. There they turned westward along the Rio Hondo to Fort Stanton, where the government was purchasing beef for the Mescalero reservation. Their trail drive opened the way for a generation of cattlemen.

Oliver Loving was killed by Comanche the following year. Undaunted, Goodnight went on to extend the trail through Colorado and onto the high plains of Wyoming. Long before the advent of the Kansas cowtowns, great herds of longhorns were being driven northward along what became known as the Goodnight-Loving Trail. At one time Goodnight was partners with John Chisum, and to a large extent helped found the Jinglebob. Later, he operated a cattle outfit in Colorado, only to be wiped out by the financial panic of 1873.

Three years of hard times followed. Then, early in 1876, Goodnight found a new partner. John Adair was a landed Irish aristocrat, heir to a vast fortune. Investment in Western cattle ranches was a popular sideline for Eastern businessmen and foreign entrepreneurs. Goodnight provided the experience and the expertise, and Adair provided the money. Honorable men, they signed no formal partnership agreement before organizing the venture. A handshake decided an equitable split of the profits.

In John Adair's honor, the ranch was dubbed the JA. With a half-million dollars in investment funds, Goodnight quickly acquired control of the whole of Palo Duro Canyon. His method was one employed by almost all cattle barons where public-domain lands were up for grab. He purchased 24,000 acres in a crazy-quilt pattern that gave him ownership of the canyon's water supply, thereby discouraging other ranchers. After leasing still more land, he controlled nearly a million acres. By 1880 the JA was running eighty thousand head of cattle.

The payroll of the JA exceeded a hundred cowhands. A score of lineshacks and distant cowcamps were strung out along the length of Palo Duro Canyon. The ranch headquarters itself resembled a settlement, with the compound overlooking a wide stretch of river. Goodnight and his family occupied a two-story log house, while the mess hall and bunkhouses and storage buildings were spread along the shoreline. Across the way, a stone residence was re-

served for John Adair and his wife on their infrequent
visits to the ranch. With a home in Denver and another in
New York, the Irish financier seldom traveled to the wilds
of the Panhandle. He wisely entrusted the cattle operation
to his Texican partner.

Clint found Charlie Goodnight down at the breeding
pens. Over the years the rancher had crossed longhorns
with blooded shorthorn stock. Yet, in his search for the
perfect range animal, he had gone a step further. He
started with the native buffalo, a beast that had survived
countless centuries of drought and blizzards and sparse
grazeland. What he sought was a new strain, one that
would forage and grow fat even in the harshest of times.
The first step was to domesticate the buffalo, which was
virtually impossible to rope and brand without being gored
or trampled to death. He topped a longhorn cow with a
buffalo bull and called the offspring a cattalo.

The experiment produced the strangest hybrid ever seen
on the Western plains. A cattalo came complete with a
goatlike beard, the woolly hide and meaty hump of its sire,
and a voice remarkably similiar to a pig grunt. Appearances aside, the new strain was nonetheless hardier than an
ox and considerably beefier than a longhorn. The beast's
tough hide could be converted into shoe leather or tanned
for luxuriant fur robes, which added even greater profit.
And compared to either of its forebears, it was docile as a
housecat.

Goodnight was staring glumly at a bunch of cattalo cows.
He turned from the breeding pen as Clint stepped down
from the saddle. His troubled expression dissolved into a
broad smile. He grabbed Clint's hand with a firm grip.

"By the saints," he said jovially. "Aren't you a sight
for sore eyes!"

"Hello, Charlie," Clint replied, grinning. "How's the
cattalo business?"

"Now you've gone and done it! Why the hell'd you
have to ask a thing like that?"

"Why shouldn't I ask? Last time I was here you chewed my ear off with your bragging."

"Well, I'm not braggin' no more. The dirty bastards have made me the laughingstock of Texas!"

Goodnight went on to explain. His experiment had progressed to a generation of cattalo suitable for a breeding. He'd bred selected heifers to prime bulls, and the results were the same in every instance. His cattalo bulls were sterile, incapable of producing offspring. Not one cow had dropped a calf.

"Goddamn ingrates," he grumped sourly. "No more seed than a common steer!"

Clint looked properly sympathetic. "Well, you can always breed buffalo to your longhorn cows. That seems to work pretty good."

"Yeah, about half the time," Goodnight said testily. "The other half, I get a stillborn calf or the cow dies. Goddamnedest mess I ever saw."

"Sounds like you're betwixt and between."

"Well, enough of my troubles," Goodnight said with a brusque wave. "What brings you out this way? Headed over to see the boys, are you?"

"All depends," Clint remarked. "I've got some business to tend to first."

"What sort of business?"

"I'm looking for a man named Ingram. Heard he was in your neighborhood."

Goodnight was on the sundown side of forty. His hair was prematurely gray, and brushy white eyebrows bridged his forehead. He had lived a rough, dangerous life, and he'd known many hardcases. Yet he had never crossed trails with any man who was a match for Clint Brannock. An expert tracker, relentless in the pursuit, Clint was deadlier than the outlaws he hunted. Either they were caught and imprisoned, or he killed them.

"Ingram?" Goodnight repeated. "Would that be Jacob Ingram?"

"Former army officer," Clint said. "Commander at Fort Bascom till he retired in seventy-five."

"That's him," Goodnight acknowledged. "Never met him, but I've heard stories. Word's around that he deals in horses—mostly stolen."

"I heard it the same way."

"What's your interest in a horse thief?"

Clint quickly recounted the last few weeks. He told how José Tafoya's confession had led him to Ingram. His plan was to use the former officer as a wedge in cracking the Sant Fe Ring. All that remained was taking Ingram into custody.

"Great God in the mornin'!" Goodnight rumbled. "I hope you're not plannin' on trying it by yourself."

"Why not?" Clint said stolidly. "He's only one man."

"Then you heard it wrong. He's got four or five men workin' for him. A regular bunch of toughnuts."

"Who told you that?"

"Storekeeper over in Tascosa."

"You saying Ingram trades there?"

Goodnight nodded. "He's got a half-assed ranch up on the Canadian. I'd judge it's about twenty miles east of Tascosa."

An isolated trading post, Tascosa was situated along the headwaters of the Canadian River. Apart from a few adobes, there was one saloon and a general store. To the west was *Llano Estacado* and eastward lay unsettled lands bordering the Nations. The town had no streets, only a handful of permanent residents, and no law. It was the perfect haven for outlaws, on the edge of nowhere.

Clint was silent for a time. "Guess it figures," he said absently. "Ingram picked a spot where nobody would get nosy. Just right for a horse-stealin' operation."

Goodnight regarded him somberly. "'How'd you like some help with Ingram and his bunch?"

"You got a personal bone to pick?"

"After a fashion," Goodnight admitted. "I've been

tryin' to form a stockgrowers' association hereabouts. So far, nobody seems much interested.''

"What's that got to do with Ingram?"

"Well, you might call it an object lesson. Nothin' better than horse thieves to convince cowmen they've got problems. Ingram's just what I need to show 'em the light.''

"Sounds reasonable," Clint observed. ''What've you got in mind?''

Goodnight looked at him. "Suppose me and some of my boys back your play. We could hit Ingram's place first thing in the morning.''

"Charlie, you've got yourself a deal. I'll even swear you in as my posse.''

"What the hell you talkin' about? Your jurisdiction don't extend to the Panhandle.''

Clint smiled. "Any badge is better than no badge at all.''

Goodnight laughed a loud, booming laugh. His penned cattalo now forgotten, he led Clint toward the log house. Their discussion turned to tactics and the element of surprise.

The pewtered sky of false dawn slowly lightened. To the east, the horizon was streaked with rays of orange flame. The leaves of the cottonwoods caught the sunlight like shiny silver coins.

There were nine men. Heads bent low, they crept forward in single file, shielded by the creek bank. Downstream, where the creek emptied into the Canadian, they had left the horses hidden in a stand of trees. Stealthily, disturbing nothing in their passage, they had slowly worked their way upstream. Off to their right, hardly a stone's throw away, stood a cabin constructed of rough-sawn lumber. Some thirty head of horses were penned in a log corral.

Clint held up his hand and the men halted. Except for Goodnight, who carried a double-barreled shotgun, every man in the party was armed with a Winchester. Still

crouched low, Clint slowly eased himself to eye level at
the top of the bank. Quickly, with the gaze of a veteran
scout, he subjected the house and the corral to intense
scrutiny. There was no smoke from the chimney and no
sign of anyone about. He spotted Goodnight's JA brand on
several cowponies in the corral.

The door of the cabin abruptly opened. Clint whistled
softly between his teeth, and motioned toward the clearing. Goodnight and his cowhands were still strung out in
single file. The rancher nodded and gently eared back the
hammers on his scattergun. The other men gripped their
saddle carbines and turned, like soldiers in a trench, to
face the cabin. On signal from Clint they rose in unison,
peering over the creek bank. Buttstocks tucked into their
shoulders, they waited.

One by one, four men stepped outside the cabin. They
stood for a moment, yawning and stretching, rubbing sleep
from their eyes. A tendril of smoke drifted from the chimney as they straggled down to the river. A heavily whisk-
ered member of the group muttered something and the
others laughed. At the shoreline they halted, some twenty
yards downstream from where the creek emptied into the
Canadian. Unbuttoning their pants, they proceeded to relieve themselves in the running water.

Clint hesitated, one eye on the house. His instincts told
him there was someone inside, tending the fires. Finally,
unable to delay longer, he raised his voice in a whipcrack
command. "Don't move! We've got you covered!"

The tinkling sound suddenly stopped. For an instant the
four men were immobile, their hands at the crotch of their
trousers. Then, almost as one, they whirled and clawed at
the pistols holstered on their belts. Clint fired first, and a
beat behind, the double roar of Goodnight's shotgun reverberated across the clearing. The cowhands' Winchesters
barked in a ragged volley.

A hail of buckshot and lead slugs sizzled toward the
river. One man stumbled sideways, dropping to the ground,

and another pitched backward into the stream. The bearded outlaw clutched at his stomach, slowly sank to his knees, and toppled over, staining the earth a rich, muddy brown. Untouched, the fourth man tossed his gun aside and hastily raised his hands. His features were etched with a look of terror.

The cabin door slammed shut. Clint turned toward the house, levering a fresh cartridge into his carbine. He sighted quickly and drilled a slug through the center of the door. To his rear, he was aware of Goodnight breaking open the shotgun and reloading. He jacked another shell into the chamber and kept his sights trained on the house.

"You're trapped!" he shouted. "Come out or get burned out. What do you say?"

"Hold your fire! I'm comin' out."

The door creaked open. A man dressed only in long johns and mule-eared boots stepped outside. His hands were raised high overhead and he was unarmed. He moved several paces into the clearing, then halted. He stared at them with a dazed expression.

"Anybody else in there?" Clint demanded.

"Just me," the man said hollowly. "Who the hell are you fellers, anyway?"

Clint rapped out an order. While Goodnight kept the man at the river covered, the cowhands scrambled over the creek bank. Walking forward, they cautiously approached the house. One of them took charge of the man in the long johns and the others swiftly searched the cabin. They found it empty, a coffeepot bubbling away on the stove.

With Goodnight at his side, Clint walked down to the river. A quick check revealed that the three men sprawled on the ground were dead. Cursing softly, Goodnight shook his head. He nodded to the bearded outlaw.

"Hate to say it," he mumbled, "but that's Jake Ingram."

Clint stared down at the dead man. His mouth compressed in a tight, bloodless line. A long moment passed; then he grunted harshly. "Helluva note," he said. "I can't seem to come away with a live witness. One way or another, the bastards get themselves shot.''

"Don't blame yourself, Clint. You gave him every chance.''

"Yeah, I suppose so.''

Goodnight jerked a thumb over his shoulder. "What about them?'' he said, indicating the other two rustlers. "You aim to take 'em on to Fort Sill?''

"Horse stealin' isn't a federal crime, Charlie.''

"Well, I'm damn sure not gonna let 'em go. They've got some of my stock in that corral.''

Clint stared at him. "What do you suggest?''

"Leave it to me,'' Goodnight said quietly. "You just ride out and forget you were here. That way it's none of your doing and nobody's the wiser—especially since you wear a badge.''

Some ten minutes later Clint forded the Canadian. He reined to a halt and twisted around in the saddle, looking back upstream. The rustlers were mounted, hands tied behind their backs, their horses positioned beneath the stout limb of a cottonwood. He watched as nooses were slipped over their heads and cinched tight around their necks. The one in long johns seemed to be praying.

Clint turned and rode toward the Nations.

9

The morning northbound pulled out of Socorro. Smoke and soot drifted back over the coaches, occasionally sparked by fiery cinders. Most passengers wisely kept their windows closed.

Westward, the mountains were bathed in early-morning sunlight. Elizabeth stared out the window, seemingly lost in thought. Yet she was all too aware of John Taylor, who was seated beside her. Until this trip, she and her bodyguard had not been away from Spur overnight. Their destination now was Santa Fe.

Traveling by stage, they had arrived in Socorro late yesterday. The last northbound train had already departed and there was no choice but to spend the night. Taylor had arranged separate rooms, requesting that they be across the hall from one another. He was merely performing his job, ensuring that she would never be too far out of his sight. Still, the loafers in the hotel lobby had traded knowing looks. None of them appeared convinced by the separate rooms.

Elizabeth had spent a restless night. She suddenly realized that her reputation was almost certain to be compromised. A married woman traveling alone with another man was fodder for the gossip mill. All the more so when her husband was a figure of esteem and prominence throughout the territory. Nor was she able to stick a sign on Taylor identifying him as her bodyguard. Wherever they went, there was bound to be talk. None of it flattering.

After tossing and turning, Elizabeth had finally resolved the matter in her own mind. Virgil was much too busy to travel with her and he himself was absent a good deal of the time. After the Cattlemen's Association meeting, he'd entrained for Kansas, where business affairs demanded his attention. So she could either travel with John Taylor, thereby exposing herself to gossip, or limit her activities to the town of Lincoln. She refused to be governed by the narrow-minded attitudes of others, and her choice was simple. She would travel where she pleased, whenever it suited her. People would just have to talk.

Today, however, she was nagged by second thoughts. Having confronted the issue, she was somehow more sensitive to Taylor's presence. While he was taciturn, and curiously withdrawn, he was nonetheless a man of saturnine good looks. Beneath his hard exterior there was an occasional hint of humor and wry, intelligent wit. She suspected he was the type of man who intrigued women but could never be beguiled by their feminine stratagems. He gave the uncanny impression of seeing everything while pretending to see nothing. His eyes seemed to glint with hidden amusement.

What little she knew of his background was oddly unsettling. Virgil had alluded to some long-ago trouble in Texas and several years spent as a professional gunman. How many men Taylor had killed, and under what conditions he had killed them, was not the subject of polite conversation. Nor would she presume to ask him anything of a personal nature, particularly as related to his work. Among Westerners, questions about a man's past were one of the great cardinal sins. No sensible person asked more than a man was willing to tell.

For all that, Elizabeth had no qualms about her Texican watchdog. Some three weeks past, when Clint stopped over at the ranch, she had observed his reaction with considerable interest. After hearing Virgil's explanation, Clint had then talked with John Taylor himself. Nothing of

their conversation was repeated, but Clint appeared satisfied with what he'd heard. So far as Elizabeth was concerned, that in itself was sufficient. She trusted Clint's
judgment in such matters.

There was only one reason for concern. She saw John
Taylor as a symptom of a larger problem. After sixteen
years of marriage, she and Virgil had settled into a pattern.
He pursued his vision, which centered on the ranch and
growing involvement in politics. She, in turn, devoted
herself to social causes. First the suffrage movement and
then the medical clinic. The upshot was that their marriage
often got short shrift. She loved him no less dearly, and
there was no question that he still worshiped her. But their
interests had diverged onto separate paths.

Her trip to Santa Fe was all part of the pattern. She
planned to take the first step in organizing a legal-assistance
service for *mexicanos*. Once again, she meant to hurl
herself into the struggle against injustice and oppression.
Yet she was fully aware that social causes were to some
extent a substitute. In large measure, Virgil shut her out of
his activities, whether business or political. He shared his
dreams with her, but the attainment of those dreams was
his own personal quest. So she followed a star that took
her far afield, searching for her own lodestone. She sometimes wished she weren't so independent and that Virgil
was less understanding. Perhaps they would then have
followed a single star.

"You look awful serious, Miz Brannock."

Taylor's voice intruded on her reverie. She glanced
around at him, startled. "I'm sorry," she apologized.
"What did you say?"

"Well, you look like somebody with worries. That
tends to make me worried."

"You needn't," Elizabeth replied, smiling. "I haven't
stepped on anyone's toes—yet."

Taylor studied her. "When you do, your husband thinks
it'll cause a real dustup. How do you feel about it?"

"Are you asking for professional reasons?"

"Let's say I like to know what I'm up against. Way I got the story, this Stephen Benton's nobody to mess with."

Elizabeth appeared unconcerned. "The Stephen Bentons of this world come and go, Mr. Taylor. What we must fear is the thing they represent."

"Maybe so," Taylor said with no great conviction. " 'Course, you don't often solve the problem till you've dealt with the man. Leastways that's been my experience."

"Would you care to hear how I view the situation?"

"I've been told I'm a good listener. Why not try me?"

Elizabeth quickly warmed to her subject. Following the war with Mexico, all land in the northern provinces had been ceded to the United States. By the Treaty of Guadalupe Hidalgo, the American government agreed to respect the holdings of Mexican landowners. Yet the title to all property in New Mexico Territory had evolved from ancient land grants. The issue of who owned what was clouded by a convoluted maze of documents. At various times, land grants had been awarded by the King of Spain, the Republic of Mexico, and the provincial governor. Ownership was often nine points physical possession and having the force to back the claim.

To compound the problem, many of the grants overlapped one another. Fraudulent land surveys further added to the confusion, and long legal battles seemingly resolved nothing. In one instance, Stephen Benton's land company persuaded the U.S. Land Commissioner to establish an extraordinary precedent. Henceforth, a court decision based on an official survey would determine the validity of a claim. Shortly thereafter, a favorable court ruling magically converted Benton's original 97,000-acre grant into a 2,000,000-acre claim. With one stroke, he had perfected a method by which New Mexico could be profitably, and legally, exploited.

By the same process, Benton's Santa Fe Land & Development Company acquired other huge tracts throughout the territory. Overall these holdings gave the company a form of business leverage in every county in New Mexico. While Benton was the owner of record, the company was widely thought to be a front for the Santa Fe Ring. The clique operated behind the scenes, but the land grants provided the base for them to move into an array of business enterprises. The members, even though they shunned publicity, were known to include bankers, lawyers, and prominent civic leaders. Like feudal lords of ancient times, they controlled the economic lifeblood of an entire territory.

Politics was part and parcel of the economic stranglehold. Flexible in structure, the Ring adapted to the realities of the electoral process. *Mexicanos* constituted a majority of voters, and therefore provided the key to control of the territorial legislature. In every county a prominent Anglo, loyal to the Ring, was appointed the political underboss. These men, employing graft and business influence, easily corrupted the local *jefes políticos*. For the most part, native New Mexicans were apathetic about territorial government, except as it affected their village. Thus they were fragmented, never a cohesive force, and unable to form organized opposition. They listened to their *jefes políticos*, who were tools of the Ring, and voted accordingly. The ballot, in any election, was preordained by a small group of Anglos in Santa Fe.

"As you can see,' Elizabeth concluded, "Stephen Benton is merely the overlord. Were we to remove him, someone else would take his place."

Taylor appeared skeptical. "To kill a snake you chop off its head. With Benton gone, wouldn't the whole thing fall apart?"

"No," Elizabeth said firmly. "The system is corrupt from top to bottom. Unless we change that, we'll have achieved nothing."

"All the same," Taylor commented, "when the Ring falls, Benton will fall. That still makes it personal."

"Only in a roundabout way."

"No, ma'am," Taylor corrected her. "When you monkey with a man's affairs, he don't make allowances. He takes it real personal, real sudden."

Elizabeth was silent, considering. "You believe my husband was right, then? Stephen Benton might attempt to . . . harm me."

"Depends on how much trouble you cause him. 'Course, he'd think twice, what with you being a woman."

"You're saying something without saying it, Mr. Taylor. Please be frank."

"Well—" Taylor hesitated, searching for words. "Suppose Benton figured you're untouchable. I mean, it'd be political suicide to hurt a woman. Who do you think he'd go after instead?"

"Virgil?" Elizabeth said blankly. "Are you saying he would harm my husband?"

"In his boots, that's how I'd see it."

"Do you think my husband knows that?"

Taylor slowly nodded. "Yes, ma'am, I just suspect he does."

Elizabeth had never been more impressed with Virgil. He had allowed her to proceed, knowing all the while that it might place him in danger. She was reminded that she had married a most remarkable man.

A thought occurred, one she'd had many times in the past sixteen years. She was proud to call herself a Brannock.

The train arrived in Santa Fe late that afternoon. Elizabeth led the way from the depot, a frilly parasol shading her from the sun. Taylor followed along with his warbag in one hand and her valise in the other.

The desk clerk at the hotel was studiously discreet. Though he recognized the name, he made no reference to the fact that Virgil had stayed there only last week. He gave Elizabeth a small suite and put Taylor in a room down the hall. His cordial manner in no way relieved

Elizabeth's concern. She knew tongues would start wagging before nightfall.

After freshening up, she met Taylor in the lobby. Outside the hotel they skirted the plaza and proceeded north on a side street. Halfway along the block, Elizabeth turned into a storefront office. The interior was cramped and utilitarian, sparsely furnished with a rolltop desk, two wooden armchairs, and a solitary file cabinet. A picture of Abraham Lincoln hung over the desk.

They were greeted by Ira Hecht. Young and idealistic, he had graduated only last year from Princeton's law school. He abhorred politics and generally refused criminal cases and therefore had few clients. His practice barely paid the rent on the cubbyhole office.

On occasion, Hecht had performed minor legal tasks for Virgil. Elizabeth knew everything about him, though they had never met. His father owned a mercantile store on the plaza, and for that reason alone, he had returned to Santa Fe. Among the town's legal fraternity, he was one of the few lawyers without political aspirations. Elizabeth thought he was perfect for what she planned.

After a round of introductions, Taylor posted himself near the door. Hecht seated Elizabeth in one of the armchairs and then sat down at his rolltop desk. He was small and slightly built, with thick-lensed glasses that gave him an owlish appearance. He smiled tentatively.

"Your letter aroused my curiosity, Mrs. Brannock. Although I must confess, it left me a bit in the dark."

"Sorry to be so vague," Elizabeth said. "What I have to say simply didn't lend itself to a letter. I preferred to speak with you in person."

"Quite understandable," Hecht said tactfully. "How may I serve you?"

"I plan to fund a legal-assistance service for the poor. Specifically, I refer to the *mexicanos*."

"An admirable endeavor, Mrs. Brannock. Not to say unique for this part of the country."

"Yes, I know," Elizabeth agreed. "I've read about such things back East, services designed to assist immigrants. I believe it's's time we organized something similar in New Mexico."

Hecht nodded approval. "You're to be commended for your progressive views. I, for one, endorse the humanitarian doctrine."

"I hoped you would say that, Mr. Hecht. In fact, that's precisely why I'm here. I want to retain you as counsel for the project."

"Indeed?" Hecht inquired. "May I ask your purpose in establishing a legal service?"

"I wish to expose—and redress—the land frauds throughout the territory."

Hecht was genuinely stunned. He looked at her with a baffled expression. "I must say you aim high, Mrs. Brannock. Where would you begin?"

Elizabeth had done her homework. By the Treaty of Guadalupe Hidalgo, native New Mexicans were awarded United States citizenship. However, the stroke of a pen did not result in social acceptance of *mexicanos*. Their language was Spanish, their religion was Catholic, and their traditions evolved from another culture. Anglos viewed them as quaint but inferior members of a peasant class. The prevailing attitude among *americanos* was that of conquerors.

In turn, the *mexicanos* saw all *gringos* as greedy invaders. Americans believed it was their "manifest destiny" to link the Pacific with the Atlantic, and to claim the land in between. Such nationalism was foreign to the traditions of native New Mexicans, almost incomprehensible. They looked upon the land as communal property, there to be farmed for the benefit of everyone. Anglos saw it as a commodity that could be bought and sold, a natural resource to be exploited. The *mexicanos* seemed to them ignorant and backward, *peones* grubbing a bare subsistence from the earth.

For three decades, the chasm separating Anglo and *mexicano* had grown wider. At the heart of the conflict was the land, and antagonisms ran deep. By ancient tradition, *mexicanos* had relied on three types of land grants. One was the community grant, given to a group of several households and distributed among the families by drawing lots. Another type, the town grant, was awarded to a *patrón* who settled thirty or more families on the tract. The third was a hacienda grant, normally allotted to aristocrats and utilized for vast ranching operations. Boundaries, regardless of the type of grant, were often vague and poorly defined.

Formal documents outlined general patterns of ownership. For it was tradition, not registered title, that determined who owned a plot of land. On town grants and hacienda grants, *peones* farmed their plots, paying homage to the *patrón*, and the land was theirs as though they held valid title. The Treaty of Guadalupe Hidalgo stipulated that property rights stemming from old land grants would be honored under American law. But *mexicano* customs meant nothing to Anglo entrepreneurs and land speculators. The idea of community-owned common land was simply ignored.

The largest single culprit was the Santa Fe Land & Development Company. Once an old land grant was bought, a crooked surveyor was hired to falsify the extent of the boundaries. The claim was then validated by a court and the company took ownership of the land. Shortly, the company would obtain an eviction order and have it served by the county sheriff. Few *mexicanos* had the money, or the knowledge of Anglo law, to challenge the action in court. Instead, falling back on ancient custom, they paid the new landlord a quarter of all their farms produced. Stephen Benton, in effect, had turned them into sharecroppers. And by court edict, he could sell the land out from under them. All he needed was a buyer.

When Elizabeth finished talking, Ira Hecht was silent

for a time. The implication of what she suggested was nothing short of revolutionary. Should her scheme prove successful, several Anglo businessmen would almost certainly be charged with fraud. The upshot would be the return of stolen land to the original *mexicano* owners. The audacity of it fired Hecht's imagination.

"If I agree," he asked, "what would you expect of me?"

"To begin," Elizabeth told him, "I want you to research the land grants and all these phony surveys. We have to establish fraud."

"In other words, you want me to create the basis for criminal charges."

"Yes, I see that as one goal. The greater objective is to return the land to the people."

"I'll need help," Hecht said thoughtfully. "We're talking about fraud on a grand scale. The whole of New Mexico Territory."

Elizabeth held his gaze. "In time, Mr. Hecht, I hope to enlist lawyers in every county. A legal network dedicated to the cause of justice."

"How would I fit into that network, Mrs. Brannock?"

"All records would be forwarded to your office. You would then coordinate the activities of the network and attempt to substantiate a pattern of conspiracy. We need evidence the attorney general simply can't ignore."

Hecht was young but hardly naive. He was aware of the power and the pervasive influence of the Santa Fe Ring. Even more, he was reminded of what happened to those who challenged Stephen Benton. As a boy, he had witnessed the twin bloodbaths of the Colfax County War and the Lincoln War. Nor was he unmindful of the potential for being drawn into a political quagmire. The woman seated before his desk was, after all, the wife of Virgil Brannock.

In the end, his idealism won out. He saw it as a crusade, the forces of good pitted against the forces of evil. The fact that he might get himself killed seemed almost inconsequential. No man could ask more of life than a just cause.

"Mrs. Brannock," he said with some pride, "I'm your man. When would you like to start?"

"Today, Mr. Hecht. This very moment."

Elizabeth extended her hand. It seemed to Hecht somehow unfeminine and he was momentarily flustered. But then he remembered who she was and why she was there. She was the woman who meant to lock horns with Stephen Benton.

He shook her hand with a beaming grin.

10

Not long after sunset the wind dropped off. The washed blue of the sky grew smoky as oncoming darkness settled over the land. In this brief interval, when dusk gave way to night, the plains lay shrouded in stillness.

Virgil had little thought for the solitude around him. The steady hoofbeats of his horse were something apart, unfelt and unheard. His mind had turned inward upon itself, rummaging through an assorted heap of problems. Tonight he would meet with some twenty ranchers, a meeting called at his own request, and what he told them would have far-reaching implications. He meant to defy the federal government and form an alliance with the Cherokee Nation.

Five years past Virgil had ridden into Indian Territory. His purpose was to expand his cattle operation, locating somewhere within a day's ride of the Kansas cowtowns. Through Clint, he'd heard stories of rolling grasslands south of the line separating Kansas and the Nations. There, in the Cherokee Outlet, he had established headquarters along the banks of the Cimarron. His herd of breeder cows had now grown to eight thousand head; before the summer was out, he planned to ship a mixed herd of three thousand head to Eastern slaughterhouses. The operation was profitable but not without problems. He was, in effect, a squatter on Indian lands.

By train, Virgil had departed from Santa Fe not quite a week ago. His trip had taken him through Denver, then

eastward across Kansas to the town of Caldwell. The latest
in a string of cowtowns, Caldwell was situated less than
three miles north of Indian Territory. Tonight, as Virgil
approached the border, he was reminded that ambition
sometimes exacted a heavy price. Within the hour, he
would have passed the point of no return in a venture
weighted with risk. All the worse, it was a venture mud-
dled by the complexities of a distant government.

The problem was essentially one of bureaucratic despo-
tism. The Department of Interior was charged with super-
vision of all Indian lands, and in Virgil's view it was
operated with godlike arrogance. Always leery of politicians, particularly those at the federal level, he was convinced that Washington bureaucracy had created the problem.
In the long run, he believed they would further compound
it with their high-handed tomfoolery.

Earlier in the century, when the Five Civilized Tribes
were resettled in Indian Territory, the Cherokee were granted
seven million acres bordering southern Kansas. As a further concession, they were granted a long corridor extending westward, which provided hunting parties with an
unimpeded gateway to the distant buffalo ranges. Some
one hundred and fifty miles in length and sixty miles in
width, comprising more than six million acres, it was
designated by treaty as the Cherokee Outlet. The legal
status of this strip was an exquisite bit of bureaucratic
convolution.

The Cherokee held title to the Outlet, but they were
forbidden by the government to dispose of it in any manner. Since their lands to the east were sufficient for the
entire tribe, the Cherokee rarely ventured into their western grant. It was a no-man's-land, unused and unwanted
and lying fallow. As a result, the huge landmass had
remained unoccupied and forgotten for nearly a half-century.
Like so many things originating in Washington, it lay
mired in the obfuscation of federal balderdash.

But if the Cherokee had no use for the Outlet, there

were others who did. The Chisholm Trail blazed straight through Indian Territory, and Texas cattlemen were quick to discover this lush stretch of graze. Watered by the Canadian and the Cimarron, it made a perfect holding ground for trail-weary longhorns. Through the 1870's, the Texans halted their herds for a week or longer in the Outlet, allowing the cows to fatten out before the final drive to a Kansas railhead. In late summer of 1876, Virgil stumbled upon this grassy paradise.

Ignoring both Washington and the Cherokee Nation, he trailed a herd of breeder cows into the Outlet. A foreman and crew were hired, and permanent quarters were established along the Cimarron. The Cherokee passively overlooked the intrusion and for three years the Spur operation flourished. But Virgil's boldness scarcely went unnoticed among Texican cattlemen. By late spring of 1880 some twenty ranchers had staked out similar claims, and the strip became a kingdom within a kingdom, swarming with longhorns.

That was more than the Cherokee could tolerate. Accompanied by a squad of Light Horse Police, Major D. W. Lipe, treasurer of the Cherokee Nation, rode into the Outlet in early June. In a most businesslike fashion, he levied taxes of forty cents a head on grown cattle and twenty-five cents a head on yearlings. When he returned to Tahlequah, the Cherokee capital, he had collected more than $40,000 and a good deal of ill will from his white tenants. Yet the real threat, as Virgil was quick to perceive, lay not in Tahlequah but in Washington.

The bureaucrats had been bypassed in a most cavalier manner. Should they become alerted to the situation and decide to vent their indignation, it could spoil a nice arrangement for everyone concerned. Over the winter, Virgil decided a formal accommodation would have to be struck with the Cherokee. Then, should the deal attract official attention, it might easily convince the Department of Interior to leave well enough alone. All the more so if the Cherokees became unruly about the loss of revenue from a chunk of land that had at last proved itself of value.

The meeting tonight, then, was of the utmost gravity. Unless he could organize the ranchers into a cohesive faction, there was every likelihood they would all be chased from the Outlet before summer's end. That the other outfits were smaller than his own, operating on a shoestring from season to season, seemed to him a distinct advantage. Where he could afford the loss, they stood to lose everything they owned. He thought that might make them more manageable, willing to listen to reason. For what he meant to propose would almost certainly provoke alarm.

There was yet another fly in the butter. Texicans were overly proud of themselves and tended to band together against outsiders. So they were doubly resentful of a New Mexican who had shown them the way into the Outlet. Somehow he would have to overcome their clannishness and their prickly pride. He figured the best way was the most direct way, no punches pulled. Even Texicans appreciated the truth.

Caldwell was dirty and dusty, a small blemish on an emerald prairie. But it had a vulgar lustiness that cattlemen found irresistible. All that was sordid and iniquitous about former cowtowns had been imported to this last outpost of rampant vice.

Whores and gamblers, thimbleriggers and grifters, gathered like jackals drawn by the scent of tainted meat. Killings were so commonplace that the undertaker worked nights, and a man's best chance for survival rested squarely on his gunbelt. The town marshal was a retired outlaw from New Mexico, the mayor a vagabond flesh merchant come recently to politics, and the city council a collection of rogues who made larceny something of a sport.

There had never been another cowtown like it. None so low or vile, and certainly none so deadly. Vice was its only industry, trailhands and cattlemen its only clientele, and those who called it home positively reveled in its infamy. Along Chisholm Street the season was in full swing, and cowhands out to hoorah the town staggered drunkenly from one dive to the next. The enticements were many and varied, some more exotic than others. No one departed for home without a new understanding of debauchery.

Outside every saloon and dance hall stood doll-faced women with painted cheeks and low-cut gowns and the Jezebel wink of a hussy practicing her trade. In one form or another, every business establishment in town was out to fleece the Texans. Apart from a clapboard hotel, a couple of cafés, and a scattering of stores, all of Caldwell was devoted to man's raunchier pursuits. Hitch racks were jammed with horses, the street seethed with trail crews out to see the elephant, and through the doors of every dive blared the raucous clamor of squealing women and laughing men. It was circus time at the end of the Chisholm Trail.

Dodge City and Caldwell were the last of the great Kansas cowtowns. Before long, as the railroads probed ever deeper toward Texas, these last remnants of a rowdy, tumultuous era would fade into obscurity. Like Abilene and Newton and Wichita, other trail towns which had sparkled briefly in the glory days, Dodge City and Caldwell would survive in the only way left to them. Sodbusters would come with their plows, gouging neat furrows across the grassy plains, and even as they seeded the earth a riotous epoch would have ended.

For now, however, Caldwell was known to cattlemen as the Border Queen. Only last summer the first train had steamed into town on a dusty ribbon of steel. The Santa Fe Railroad had arrived one step ahead of a coalition formed by grangers and shorthorn breeders. After intense lobbying, the legislature was poised to enact a statewide embargo against entry of tick-infested longhorns into Kansas. Upon reaching Caldwell, the Santa Fe shrewdly laid track to the border and erected its stockyards there. Texans were thus able to load and ship their cattle without regard for any future quarantine. By the close of the first trailing season, Caldwell's only remaining rival was Dodge City.

Shortly after dark, Virgil dismounted outside the Occidental Hotel. Tonight the hotel barroom was closed except to invited guests—cattlemen from the Outlet—and it came as no great surprise that they had heeded his summons. Overlooking the fact that he was a New Mexican, they grudgingly acknowledged the Spur as an outfit worthy of respect. They were here because common sense dictated that they couldn't stay away. From the hush that fell over the room as he came through the door, Virgil felt reasonably certain they would hear him out.

Something else he knew. These men wouldn't be persuaded by a glib line of chatter. They were tough and resourceful, and the only thing they would understand or accept, was straight talk. He strode directly to the bar and turned to face them, his bearing brusque and businesslike. His voice was pleasant but firm.

"Gentlemen, I appreciate your showing up tonight. I asked you here to thrash out some problems we've all got down in the Outlet."

The cattlemen stared back at him, attentive but reserving judgment till they had heard more. Virgil spoke first of the rustlers preying on their herds. The Outlet was a land without law or courts, and the cattle thieves were growing bolder. Unless the ranchers joined forces to stamp out this common threat, their losses would mount ever higher. That drew a murmur of assent, for unlike the ranchers in New Mexico, these men counted the loss of one cow a blow to their pocketbook. They waited for him to continue.

With the stage set, Virgil broached the greater problem— their shaky truce with the Cherokee Nation. Step by step, he led them through a sobering evaluation of the obstacles that lay ahead. Stressing certain points, he hammered away at the common danger. The Department of the Interior. Governmental restrictions on the Outlet. Petty bureaucrats with an inflated sense of self-importance and a very real power to banish all cattlemen from Indian lands. The truth, harsh as it seemed, was that they could not deal with the federal government.

Instead, he told them bluntly, they had no choice but to deal directly with the Indians. Which meant forming an organization of cattlemen and levying taxes upon themselves. In effect, leasing the land outright and paying the Cherokee enough so that it was worth their while to defy Washington. Otherwise, every cattleman in the Outlet would shortly be out of business. Boiled down to bare facts, unless they formed an alliance with the Cherokee, the bureaucrats were certain to skin them alive. There were no other options.

When he stopped talking, there was a marked silence. Nobody walked out, and for a while nobody said anything. Then a lanky Texan rose to his feet. "You're sayin' we've got to bribe the dirty bastards, ain't you?"

"After a fashion," Virgil acknowledged. "We have to sweeten the pot so that the Cherokee are willing to fight our fight."

"How much you figger to pay 'em?"

"I was thinking of ten cents an acre—on a five-year lease."

There was an instant of quick calculation. Someone muttered a rough curse, and the mood in the barroom abruptly turned tense. The Texan on his feet glared at Virgil. "Mister, you're mighty gawddamn generous with our money. That'd figger out to bettern'n a hundred thousand a year."

"So it does," Virgil agreed. "But the alternative is to trail your cows back to Texas. Or you could sell 'em and quit the business altogether."

"What makes you so all-fired certain the government will force us out?"

Virgil looked around the room. "I fought with the Confederacy, right to the very end. Unless I'm mistaken, everybody here tonight was a Johnny Reb." He paused, let the thought percolate a moment. "Who among you believes the Yankees won't jump at the chance to bust our butts?"

Heads around the room began nodding. Stubborn proud as they were, the Texans knew when they had heard the straight goods. The fact that the New Mexican was a former Confederate merely gave it an added ring of truth. They took a vote on it and decided to call their fledgling organization the Cherokee Cattlemen's Association. By acclamation, Virgil was elected president.

Texicans rarely needed an excuse to celebrate. Tonight, impressed by their own audacity, they crowded around the bar. Defying the federal government was heady stuff, and several toasts were proposed to those stalwarts of the Confederacy, Jeff Davis and Robert E. Lee. A sense of camaraderie engulfed them and the barroom soon vibrated with drunken rebel yells. After an hour or so, Virgil called it a night and shook hands all around. Over their protests, he made his way to the door.

On the street, he paused to light a cigar. Across the way he saw Marshal Hendry Brown outside the Longhorn Café. Cowtowns made a practice of hiring seasoned gunmen to enforce the law. Trailhands, not to mention the sporting crowd, were held in line by fear of summary justice. Hendry Brown, with the blessing of the town council, dispensed justice on a nightly basis. He'd been hired with the foreknowledge that he had ridden with Billy the Kid during the Lincoln County War. The governor had granted him amnesty on condition that he get out of New Mexico Territory.

Virgil knew Brown on sight. They had never had occasion to speak, and he went out of his way to avoid Caldwell's resident lawdog. He subscribed to the theory that leopards never change their spots, and Brown was the worst sort of outlaw. As a member of the Kid's gang, he had rustled cattle and taken part in coldblooded murder.

To compound matters, he had hired a man named Ben Wheeler as deputy marshal. There was talk that Wheeler had an equally unsavory record.

Walking toward the hitch rack, Virgil suddenly stopped. He saw Brown stiffen as an Indian, trailed by a squaw, rounded the corner. A town character, the red man was a Pawnee who drifted between the reservation and Caldwell. His name was Spotted Horse and his principal occupation was cadging whiskey from saloonkeepers. Tonight he was staggering drunk, but still possessed of his senses. Upon sighting the marshal, he slammed to a wobbly halt.

Brown approached to within a few feet. He said something to Spotted Horse and pointed off in the direction of the town jail. A brief argument ensued, and then, without warning, Spotted Horse grabbed for a six-gun stuffed in his waistband. The sight caught on the inside of his trousers, and he fumbled drunkenly, trying to free the gun. Brown was within arm's reach and could have easily buffaloed him with a pistol barrel upside the head. Instead, the marshal pulled his own gun and calmly shot Spotted Horse four times in the chest. The impact of the heavy slugs drove Spotted Horse backward in a haywire dance. His legs buckled and he rolled off the boardwalk into the street.

The squaw dropped to her knees beside the dead man. She raised her head in a keening wail that echoed off the buildings. Hendry Brown stared at her without a flicker of emotion, as though mildly curious. He shucked out the empty shells and reloaded, oblivious of the stares of trailhands crowding the boardwalk. Then he holstered his pistol and strolled off. No one moved to help the squaw.

Virgil knew what would follow. The local newspaper would laud Hendry Brown for keeping the streets of Caldwell safe. The town council would pass a resolution commending their marshal for his courage in the line of duty. Such was the way of things in the wild and woolly cowtowns. Abilene had Wild Bill Hickok. Newton had the notorious Bully Brooks. Dodge City boasted loudly of Bat Masterson.

In keeping with the times, Caldwell could do no less. Hendry Brown was merely the latest in a long line of such lawmen. He was a killer who wore a badge.

Late that night Virgil forded the Cimarron. On the south bank was a combination bunkhouse and mess hall, flanked by a large corral. A short distance away stood a stout log cabin.

After turning his horse into the corral, Virgil walked to the cabin. A lamp was still lit and he found Floyd Dunn, the foreman, seated at a rough table. Whenever he visited the ranch, they shared the cabin and took their meals with the hands. He nodded now, tossing his hat on an empty bunk.

"Glad you waited up, Floyd."

"How'd it go, Mr. Brannock? Everything work out?"

"Easier than I figured," Virgil said, seating himself at the table. "We're calling it the Cherokee Cattlemen's Association."

"No shit?" Dunn marveled. "And they agreed to ten cents an acre?"

"Unanimous vote."

"Well, I'll kiss your ass and bark like a fox!"

Dunn was a burly, bearded Texan. His ways were coarse and his language was foul, and he smelled vaguely of manure. But he was trustworthy and he knew the cow business. Of equal significance, he had an ironbound look about him, as though he ate nails for breakfast. He ran the wilderness ranch like a hard-eyed drill sergeant.

"What's next?" he asked. "You gonna pay a call on the gut-eaters?"

Virgil wagged his head. "Floyd, you know better than that. The Cherokee are more civilized than most white men."

"Well, now, I reckon it's like the fly said when he

walked across a mirror—it all depends on how you look at it.''

"What's that supposed to mean?''

"Why, hell, Mr. Brannock, an Injun's an Injun. Just because he talks good English don't make him any less a redstick.''

"In case you forgot," Virgil informed him, "those Injuns are our landlords. You'd do well to keep that in mind.''

"Yessir, you're right," Dunn said agreeably. "When they come around here, I treat 'em like high-ass royalty. But they're still a bunch—''

Virgil halted him with an upraised palm. "Spare me the sermon, Floyd. It's too late and I'm all wore out.''

"Yeah, you'd best get some shut-eye. Ain't no easy ride over to Tahlequah.''

"I'm not going," Virgil said with a slow smile. "An old horse trader taught me a valuable lesson, Floyd. You never dicker with a man on his homeground.''

Dunn searched his face. "How you aim to handle it?''

"Tomorrow morning I'll write a letter to their treasurer, Major Lipe. We'll let one of the boys deliver it.''

"What's the letter gonna say?''

Virgil grinned broadly. "The Cherokees are about to stumble onto a windfall—to the tune of five hundred thousand dollars.''

"Holy crucified Christ!" Dunn groaned. "You're gonna promise them that in writin'?''

"No, not just a promise. I plan to offer them an ironclad contract.''

"You got more balls than a brass bull, Mr. Brannock.''

"One thing's for sure," Virgil said almost to himself. "Major Lipe won't waste any time getting here. Not after he reads my letter.''

Dunn seemed at a loss for words. Virgil climbed stiffly to his feet and got undressed. He crawled into the bunk,

yawning widely as Dunn snuffed the lamp. He went to
sleep the moment his head hit the pillow.

His last waking thought was of the dead Pawnee, Spotted
Horse. He somehow wished it had been Hendry Brown
instead. Good riddance to bad rubbish. . . .

11

Fort Sill was located along the palisades of Medicine Bluff Creek. Three miles south were the agency buildings, headquarters for those charged with the welfare of the Comanche and the Kiowa. The horseback tribes, once the scourge of the Southern Plains, were now wards of the government.

West and north of the fort, the Wichita Mountains jutted skyward, wrapped in a purple haze. The red granite slopes were craggy and forebidding, dotted with scrub oak and cedar. Blackjack trees covered the foothills, while cottonwoods, and elm bordered the lowland streams.

The terrain sweeping away from the foothills was rolling prairie, lush with native grasses. Bounded on the north by the Washita River and on the south by the Red, the reservation spread westward toward the Texas Panhandle. By treaty, some 3,000,000 acres had been ceded to the warlike tribes. Not ten years past, their domain had extended from southern Colorado to the northern provinces of Old Mexico.

Clint rode in from the west. He dropped down out of the mountains and followed a rutted wagon road toward the fort. On the trail, he traveled light, with a bedroll, fixings for coffee, and vittles stuffed in his saddlebags. Four days earlier he'd parted with Charlie Goodnight on the Canadian. Today, with a warm May sun overhead, he pushed on with a sense of homecoming. Before nightfall, he would be with Little Raven and the boys.

For six years Clint had drifted between New Mexico and

Indian Territory. Apart from immediate family, few people were aware of the reason for his trips to the reservation. His brother Earl had married twice, once to a white
woman, who died of consumption, and the second time to
Little Raven. Hank, a seven-year-old, had been born to
Little Raven shortly before Earl's death. Lon, now fifteen,
was the product of the first marriage. Though white, he
chose to live among the Comanche, his adopted people.
He considered himself a member of the Quahadi band.

Whenever Clint neared the garrison, it stirred memories
of a long-ago time. On a bright June day in 1875, the
Quahadis had surrendered at Fort Sill. Led by Quanah,
their war chief, the band had roamed *Llano Estacado* for
ten months following the battle at Palo Duro Canyon.
Harassed by cavalry patrols, relentlessly pursued, their
ranks had been decimated by hunger and disease. To save
what remained of his people, Quanah had brought them at
last to the reservation. His band had been reduced to a
mere hundred warriors and less than three hundred women
and children.

Colonel Ranald Mackenzie accepted the Quahadis' surrender. His command had scattered the hostiles at Palo
Duro Canyon and ultimately hounded them into submission. In victory, however, Mackenzie had proved to be a
magnanimous conqueror. Other warrior chiefs, who had
signed and broken peace treaties, were imprisoned in the
Dry Tortugas, off the Florida coast. But Quanah had stead-
fastly refused to negotiate with the white man or put his
name on a treaty. He fought until his people could fight no
more, always in defense of his ancestral lands. Mackenzie,
who had come to admire the Quahadi leader, interceded on
his behalf. Quanah was allowed to remain with his people.

Clint and Ranald Mackenzie were old comrades. As
chief scout for the 4th Cavalry Regiment, Clint had distinguished himself in the campaign against the Comanche.
Afterward, with the warlike bands dispersed, Mackenzie
had arranged his appointment as special agent for the

army. They were friends, but more than that, they respected
one another. Whenever he visited the reservation, Clint's
first stop was a courtesy call on his former commander.
The years had served to deepen their mutual regard.

At post headquarters, an aide ushered Clint into the
colonel's office. Mackenzie was a man of medium height,
with chiseled features and eyes like ball bearings. His
temples were brushed with gray and his posture was ram-
rod straight. He greeted Clint with a warm handshake.

"By God!" he declared. "Where have you been keeping
yourself?"

"Here, there, and yonder, Colonel."

"Still chasing *Comancheros*, are you?"

"No, sir," Clint said, "I caught the last one. Our old
friend José Tafoya."

"And?" Mackenzie asked, his tone suddenly quite
military. "What happened?"

"We got ambushed west of Fort Stanton."

Clint went on to relate the details. He then recounted his
search for Jacob Ingram, the former army officer. While he
told of Ingram's death, he omitted any reference to the
hangings that followed. He saw no reason to mention a
civilian matter involving horse thieves.

"Too bad," Mackenzie said when he finished. "Ingram
would have made an excellent witness."

"There's a couple more I haven't got around to yet. I
aim to pay 'em a call when I get back to New Mexico."

Mackenzie leaned back in his chair. He steepled his
hands, tapped his forefingers together. "How long since
your last visit here—six months?"

Clint hesitated, then shrugged. "Closer to seven."

"You shouldn't stay away so long."

"Trouble?"

"Some serious, some not so serious."

"You're talkin' about Lon, aren't you?"

"I'm afraid so," Mackenzie remarked. "Your nephew

is a born hellion. He sets a bad example for the Indian youngsters.''

"What's he done now?"

"For one thing," Mackenzie said crisply, "he raided the chicken house. You may recall we kept a few laying hens for the officers' mess.''

Clint smiled in spite of himself. "How many did he rustle?"

"All of them," Mackenzie replied with weary tolerance. "We haven't had an egg in almost two months.''

"Guess I ought to have a talk with him.''

Mackenzie looked somber. "The hens are not my principal concern. He's involved in something more serious, Clint.''

"Oh?" Clint asked. "What's that?"

"Have you heard of the peyote religion?"

'Not that I recollect.''

Mackenzie briefly explained. The old Comanche religion was based on winning the aid of spirits found in nature. But white missionaries on the reservation actively worked to convert their red charges to "The Jesus Road." Quanah diplomatically approved, though he himself refused to convert. Instead, he imported a religious rite previously associated with the Mescalero Apache. The rituals involved the use of peyote, a mescaline drug that induced trancelike visions. The practice was slowly spreading throughout the reservation.

"I've done nothing about it," Mackenzie concluded, "because it offends no one but the missionaries. Insofar as Quanah and the Comanche are concerned, their religion is their own business.''

Clint brooded on it a moment. "You're telling me it's all right for the Comanche, but not for Lon. Is that it?"

"Yes," Mackenzie said in a measured tone. "This could be your last chance at reclaiming him, Clint. He's a white boy pretending to be a Comanche. Peyote could make the change real—and permanent.''

Clint absentmindedly rubbed his jawbone. Peyote, in his view, was merely part of a larger problem. Lon had refused all offers to join his kinfolk in New Mexico. He considered his stepmother and his stepbrother to be his family. Short of abducting the boy, there was no way to tear him away from the Comanche. Even then, the youngster would run off at the first opportunity and return to the reservation. Clint had long since resigned himself to a harsh fact of life: for all practical purposes, Lon was a white Comanche.

"I'll talk to him," Clint said now. "Maybe there's still time to make him see the light."

"May I offer a suggestion?"

"I'm always open to advice."

"Talk to the boy," Mackenzie cautioned, "but say nothing to Quanah. A wrong word would only aggravate matters."

Clint looked puzzled. "I don't follow you."

"To the Comanche, Quanah is a man without fault, almost godlike. And I needn't remind you that Lon considers himself one of the tribe."

"No," Clint said bitterly. "No need to remind me of that. I'm not likely to forget."

Mackenzie tactfully changed the subject. He asked about the Apache raids in Arizona and New Mexico, expressing concern that the army was unable to halt the depredations. Neither of them spoke again of Lon.

The reservation was operated by the Bureau of Indian Affairs. The agent was a man named Hazen, and his efforts were well-intentioned if somewhat misguided. He thought horseback warriors could be transformed into farmers.

Few Comanche were willing to labor in the fields. For countless generations the tribe had raided and plundered, striking terror across the Southern Plains. The men considered themselves hunters and warriors, and they took no pride in a well-hoed row of corn. Plows and harrows given to them by the government sat idle, gathering rust. Less than four thousand acres were under cultivation, and most of that had been planted by Agent Hazen's white employees. He hoped to show the Indians the wonders of modern agriculture.

Houses were another sore point. The older Comanche continued to live in hide lodges along the wooded streams. The government offered them sawn lumber, but they saw no reason to confine themselves within boarded structures. Nor were they willing to bind themselves in the white man's clothing. Coats were converted into vests by removing the sleeves, and trousers became leggings by cutting a hole in the seat. Among all the items issued, only the trade blankets went unaltered. As old buffalo robes wore thin, the Comanche adopted blankets for outer wear.

Some of the younger men were less resistant. A number of them took jobs in the sawmill and blacksmith shop operated by the agency. Others worked as teamsters, hauling freight bound for the reservation from distant railheads. Their purpose was to earn cash money, which could then be used at the civilian trader's store. For many, their entire earnings went to the illicit whiskey smugglers who set up shop in the remote wilderness. Liquor was seldom in short supply.

Oddly enough, Quanah attempted to guide his people along the white man's road. Having surrendered, he became as skilled at peace as he had been at making war. He was now known as Quanah Parker, for it came to light that his mother had been a white woman. In 1837, Cynthia Ann Parker, only nine years old at the time, had been taken captive in a raid on Texas. At the age of fourteen, she became the wife of Nacona, a young comanche warrior. Among their children was a boy, born in 1845. He was called Quanah.

After twenty-three years with the Comanche, Cynthia Ann was rescued in a raid by Texas Rangers. She was returned to her white family; but by then she considered herself one of the True People. She died a short time later, and some said her death was the result of a broken heart. Upon learning of Quanah's surrender, her family invited him to Texas and treated him with great dignity. He returned to the reservation with a new outlook toward whites, and a certain pride in his own white blood. Thereafter, like his kinsmen in Texas, he used the name Parker.

Quanah led his people by example. To show them the white man's road, he built a frame house near the foothills of the mountains. He also sent his children to the agency school, where they were taught to read and write English. Some Comanche ignored the school, unmoved by Quanah's arguments favoring education. But no one, young or old, question his authority in tribal matters. He acted as a magistrate in family disputes, and represented his people in dealings with the agency. He was still their chief, a warrior turned peacemaker. They believed he outwitted the whites at every turn.

Clint found him at the agency beef pens. By treaty, the Comanche had been awarded annuity goods for a period of thirty years. Part of the annuity was in cash, paid yearly, and the balance was in food, clothing, and implements. Once a week, on what was called Issue Day, flour and beans and other foodstuffs were distributed. The meat ration was in the form of cattle delivered on the hoof and held in large pens near agency headquarters. One or more families, depending on their size, were allotted a cow per week.

Quanah was tall for a Comanche. His features were hawklike and his manner was dignified, pleasant but somewhat aloof. His attitude toward Clint was scrupulously polite, and they shook hands firmly. He still thought of Clint as a scout, and between them was the respect of one warrior for another. Their talk was always inconsequential, like foreign emissaries at a social gathering. Today, exchanging pleasantries, they watched as the cattle were distributed.

Issue Day was a festive occasion. Families gathered from across the reservation with an air of celebration. There was feasting and gambling, and copious amounts of whiskey were consumed. But first, everyone attended to the cattle, slaughtering the beasts in the old way. The cows were released one at a time from the pens and pursued by men on horseback. Like a buffalo hunt of times past, the cattle were brought down with bow and arrow. As they fell, women and children swarmed over the beasts with flashing knives, butchering them on the spot. Soldiers and agency workers looked on with considerable amusement, like spectators at a bloody carnival. The field around the pens was soon littered with fallen cows.

Clint finally excused himself, turning away from Quanah. He spotted Little Raven in a crowd of women and moved toward her. She was in her early thirties, a mature woman, attractive rather than pretty. When he visited, Clint never failed to give her money. Hard cash was scarce on the reservation, and without a man she had no way to supplement the government rations. With the extra money, she was able to purchase staples at the trader's store. She always took it reluctantly, as though embarrassed by Clint's generosity.

Clint was genuinely fond of her. Their relationship was warm and friendly, though Comanche women seldom displayed affection. He nonetheless thought of her as a good woman and a good mother. All the more so because she treated Lon like her own son. Some women, under similar circumstances, would have been far less charitable. He admired her strength of character, her sense of family.

Little Raven greeted him shyly. Her eyes were happy but her manner was almost demure. They walked off a short distance from the other women and stood talking. After the usual pleasantries, Clint worked around to Lon. At first, she seemed hesitant, fearful of betraying the boy.

But then, all in a rush, she told the story of the past several months. None of it was good news.

Lon was now living in the mountains. At fifteen, he was already an accomplished woodsman and a skilled hunter. He'd built himself a rough cabin, and for the most part, he lived off the land. He refused to attend school or work at the agency, and he expressed contempt for those Comanche who had turned to farming. For all practical purposes, he rebelled at anything that smacked of the white man's road. Other youngsters considered him something of a hero.

On occasion, he brought Little Raven a haunch of venison. She accepted it gratefully, and she even allowed Hank to visit the mountain cabin. Lon was protective of the boy and she had no qualms about Hank's safety. Yet she had learned never to question Lon about his personal activities. She knew that he considered himself one of Quanah's disciples, and she'd heard that peyote rites were often performed at his mountain retreat. She worried about him, but she was powerless to influence his rebellious nature. He was a young renegade, and very much his own man.

The one time she could count on seeing him was Issue Day. The Comanche were inveterate gamblers, and horse racing was their passion. Lon was proud of his pinto pony and he invariably showed up for the races held once a week. As if to reinforce the thought, she nodded off into the crowd. Lon rode toward them on a chocolate-spotted pony, attired in buckskins and moccasins. Young Hank, mounted behind him, wore a proud grin.

The boys were a study in contrasts. Hank had inherited his mother's broad features and dark hair. Yet his eyes were blue and his skin was tawny, immediately pegging him as a half-breed. Lon, on the other hand, was a look-alike for his father. He had the promise of a six-footer, already full-spanned through the shoulders, with hair bleached copper by the sun. The resemblance to Earl was uncanny, and somehow haunting. Clint saw his dead brother reborn in the youngster.

After dismounting, the boys solemnly shook hands with their uncle. To Hank, who had never known his father, Clint was a mystical figure, authoritative and a bit scary. Lon secretly idolized his uncle. While he would never admit it, he saw Clint as one of the warrior breed. Not a Quahadi warrior, for the glory days of the Comanche were long past. But a man who nonetheless inspired fear in other men, and sometimes killed them. Still, these were feelings he revealed to no one, not even his stepbrother. He masked them instead with cocky indifference.

A while later Little Raven wandered off with Hank. Clint understood that she had purposely left him alone with the older boy. Yet he was uncomfortable playing uncle and he hardly knew where to start. He decided on the roundabout approach.

"Hear you've got yourself a cabin."

"Nothin' much," Lon said lazily. " 'Course, you're welcome to stop around. I got an extra bunk."

"I'd like that." Clint kept his tone light. "Maybe we could do a little huntin' while I'm here. Understand you keep Little Raven supplied with meat."

"Somebody has to!" Lon blustered. "What the agency gives her wouldn't feed a cat. Lots of folks hereabouts go hungry."

"Guess that makes you the man of the family."

"Well, I wouldn't say that. I just kill more than I need, that's all."

"Way I hear it," Clint said casually, "you must hunt near about every day. Or don't you feed all them people?"

"What people?"

"The ones that hang around your cabin. All those peyote eaters."

Lon eyed him with narrow suspicion. "Little Raven wouldn't've told you that. Who you been talkin' to?"

Clint shrugged. "Not many secrets on a reservation. You're a choice topic these days."

"Don't say?" There was something close to mockery in

the boy's voice. "I suppose folks gotta have something to gossip about. Looks like I got tagged."

Clint studied him with a thoughtful frown. "Way I heard it, you've gone hogwild. Holed up in the mountains with a bunch of peyote eaters. Sounds like you're askin' for trouble."

"No such thing," Lon said hotly. "And you oughtn't be so quick to judge. Quanah says it's a holy thing, like a church. That's good enough for me."

"Hell, boy, I'm not judging Quanah or anyone else. I'm just telling you to go slow—watch your step."

"I'm old enough to look after myself. Nobody needs to wipe my nose."

Clint shook his head with stern disapproval. "You've got an awful high opinion of yourself. A boy your age ought to be thinking about an education. How'll you make anything of yourself if you don't go to school?"

Full of himself, Lon laughed. "How far'd you go in school?"

"Well . . ." Clint hesitated, caught off guard. "How far I went doesn't matter. We're talkin' about you."

"Quittin' school don't seem to have hurt you any. Likely it won't hurt me neither."

Clint realized it was futile to argue. He decided to try another tack. "School's one thing," he said, "stealing's an altogether different matter. I'm told you've turned chicken thief."

"That so?" Lon's eyes gave away nothing. "Guess you must've got an earful from the colonel. How's he fixed for proof?"

"That's not the point," Clint said sharply. "Once you start stealin' there's no end to it. Gets to be a habit."

Lon cocked his head, grinning. "Killed anybody since I seen you last?"

The remark left Clint dumbstruck. By some muzzy logic, the boy had lumped together chicken stealing and his work as a lawman. Before he could reply, Lon turned and vaulted aboard the pinto pony.

"Gotta go!" he called out. "The races are fixin' to start. Bet a bunch on me. I can't lose!"

Wheeling the pony about, Lon rode off. Some distance away, riders and their horses were gathered near a half-mile-long track on the prairie. Clint watched as the youngster gigged his pony into a prancing trot. He was reminded of the old axiom "like father, like son." He saw in Lon the same wild streak he'd once seen in his brother. Earl had been a gambler and an adventurer, and finally a *Comanchero*. He blithely wagered on anything, even life itself.

Until one day, in Palo Duro Canyon, all the luck ran out. His wild streak had gotten him killed.

12

The *mexicano* arrived shortly after dark. His horse was spent and he left it standing spraddle-legged before the house. He pounded on the door, snatching his sombrero off when the housekeeper apeared. He asked to see Elizabeth.

The message he carried was an urgent appeal for help. A midwife had been unable to deliver a woman's baby, and requested that Elizabeth come quickly. The mother had been in the birthing bed since early morning, but the baby was in the wrong position. Nothing the midwife tried had worked.

Elizabeth asked if Dr. Wood had been summoned. The *mexicano* bobbed his head, rattling off a volley of Spanish. The woman's husband had gone to fetch the doctor late that afternoon. But he had not returned, and they could only assume *el doctor* was off attending to another emergency. The midwife was desperate, fearing she would lose both mother and baby. She begged Elizabeth to come now.

Jennifer insisted on going along. John Taylor was alerted and within minutes he pulled up before the house in a buckboard and team. Elizabeth and Jennifer seated themselves beside him and the *mexicano* jumped in the rear. The woman lived in a small village some five miles west of the ranch compound. There, on the banks of the Hondo, was a crude collection of adobes, the homes of farmers who worked the bottomland. Taylor popped the reins smartly and drove west.

No call was more urgent than one involving a childbirth. The mortality rate among newborns in the valley was tragically high. Midwives practiced ancient techniques that were more superstition than medicine. Women in labor were placed in a squatting position on the floor and told to pull on a rope hung from the ceiling. The result, rather than an easy delivery, was often hemorrhage and loss of the baby.

Still another superstition held that a half-moon standing-upright in the sky forecast a simple birth. When the half-moon turned on its back, nervous midwives often drove their patients into hysterics. Far worse was the belief that a new mother should not venture outdoors for forty days after the child was born. By then, poor sanitation combined with lack of fresh air produced a pestilent mix. Young babies died never having seen the light of day.

Between 1875 and 1880 Dr. Wood had kept detailed medical records. He found that sixty percent of all natural deaths occurred among children under five years of age. Disease was rampant in the poorly ventilated, squalid adobes inhabited throughout Lincoln County. Goats and hogs were penned beside the dwellings, and since there were no window screens, flies brought all manner of filth indoors. Diphtheria was the greatest scourge, but diarrhea, cholera, and dysentery took a brutal toll. A six-year-old child was thought to be a miracle of God's mercy.

Elizabeth was all too aware of the problem. At the clinic, particularly to younger women, she preached the benefits of sanitation and commonsense preventive measures. A good part of the time she felt her words were wasted. At home, the women would be confronted by husbands and family elders who scoffed at *americano* notions. Yet, with painful slowness, she saw women here and there who had adopted her advice. She had no illusions about the immediate effect, but she remained hopeful. One day the children of the valley would be freed of disease and early death.

Not long after nine o'clock the buckboard halted before a one-room adobe. Taylor and the *mexicano* stayed outside while Elizabeth and Jennifer hurried into the house. The midwife, a woman in her late forties, met them at the door. She appeared frantic with worry and it took a moment to calm her down. Then, under Elizabeth's questioning, she explained the problem. Gesturing rapidly, she inverted her hands over her stomach, confirming Elizabeth's worst fears. The baby was in the breech position.

Elizabeth moved to the bed. A young girl, no more than sixteen or seventeen, lay outlined in the butter-colored light of a nearby lamp. Her forehead was beaded with perspiration and her eyes were alive with terror. The midwife, standing at Elizabeth's elbow, commented that it was her first baby. A sudden contraction shuddered through the girl and her face was etched with pain. When it was over, Elizabeth spoke to her in Spanish, soothing her. The girl seemed beyond speech, aware of nothing but the torment within her body.

Jennifer looked on intently. She was allowed to watch because her mother took the progressive view where birth was concerned. Elizabeth believed that girls of childbearing age should know how babies are made and how they are born. On occasion, she'd even permitted her daughter to assist in routine deliveries at the clinic. By now, few mysteries remained for Jennifer, though she had never before witnessed a breech birth. She edged closer to the bed.

Elizabeth called for soap and water and washed her hands. Finished, she returned and sat down at the foot of the bed. She lifted the girl's flimsy nightshift and laid it across the swollen abdomen. Gently she probed deep into the birth canal with her fingers. She encountered the baby's buttocks rather than its head, which would have been presented in a normal delivery. Ever so gingerly she attempted to rotate the baby, working to turn its shoulders. When that failed, she tried to maneuver the legs into a downward

position. At last she withdrew her hand and stood. Her
eyes were grim.

"Damn!" she said to no one in particular. "I can't
move the baby.'"

"What will you do?" Jennifer asked anxiously. "Surely
there's some way."

"I only know one other thing to try. I saw Dr. Wood
perform it on a woman at the clinic."

"And it worked?"

"Yes," Elizabeth said without conviction. "He called it
extreme . . . but it worked."

"Then let's try it!"

Elizabeth quickly outlined the procedure. She directed
Jennifer and the midwife to roll the girl over on her
stomach. Working together, they then managed to raise the
girl onto her knees and elbows. She groaned, fading in and
out of delirium, unable to hold the position. The midwife
supported her by the shoulders while Jennifer kept her
head lowered on the bed. From behind, Elizabeth stabilized
the girl's bent knees and elevated her buttocks. Straining
to maintain their holds, they kept the girl there for a full
ten minutes. Finally, at Elizabeth's command, they rolled
her once more onto her back.

The procedure was meant to rotate the baby as the
mother was turned. Before, when Elizabeth assisted Dr.
Wood, the baby had revolved sufficiently to allow a normal
delivery. But now, as she performed her second examination, nothing had changed. The baby was still locked in
the breech position.

She forced herself to stay calm. Her eyes were an-
guished when she glanced around, and she slowly shook
her head. The midwife drew a sharp breath, her face
stricken with a look of dread and uncertainty. Jennifer stared
down at the girl, unwilling to believe.

"It's hopeless," Elizabeth said, her expression wretched.
"I don't know what else to do."

Jennifer snapped out of her trance. "Well, we have to

do something, Mother! We can't just let her . . . *lie there*."

"Please, Jen," Elizabeth said softly. "Shouting won't change anything."

"Then what will?"

"I only wish I knew."

The door rattled open. Chester Wood stepped into the room, followed by a young *mexicano* who appeared gripped by fright. One look at the women's faces was all Wood needed. He spun the husband around, shoving him outside, and slammed the door. Tossing his hat on a chair, he crossed the room, nodding to Elizabeth.

"I got delayed on a ranch call. The husband finally tracked me down."

Elizabeth smiled wanly. "Thank God he found you."

"How serious is it?"

"Very serious," she said. "It's a breech baby and he won't turn."

"I'll have a look."

Wood removed his coat, rolling up the sleeves of his shirt. The midwife brought soap and water, and he washed his hands. Still dripping water, he moved to the bed and sat down. His examination was performed quickly and he muttered something to himself. The girl moaned as he spread her legs wider and forced his hand into the birth canal. For several minutes he attempted to maneuver the baby into a more favorable position. At length, uttering a low curse, he turned back to Elizabeth.

"Have you tried putting her on her knees?"

"Just before you arrived," Elizabeth said. "We kept her there for at least ten minutes, maybe more."

"Some days it goes from bad to worse.

Wood rummaged around in his medical bag. He took out a stethoscope and plugged it into his ears. Leaning forward, he listened first to the mother's heartbeat and then placed the stethoscope on her abdomen, checking the baby. He next examined the girl's eyes, noting that she had slipped into unconsciousness. After a moment's pause, he got to his feet.

"We have to act fast," he said gruffly. "Otherwise we'll lose both of them."

"You're not saying . . ."

Her voice trailed off and Wood nodded. "I've got no choice," he said. "I'll have to perform a cesarean."

Elizabeth's breath caught in her throat. On the frontier, a cesarean section was the last resort, a surgical procedure to be attempted only in the direst extremity. While the operation was ancient even in biblical times, physicians still knew little of its complications, and the mortality rate was mentioned only in whispers. Generally, the child was sacrificed to save the mother, and even then, fully three-quarters of the women who went under the scalpel failed to survive the operation. Given an option, however unorthodox, any physician would avoid the risk of a cesarean.

Tonight, there were no options. To make matters worse, Chester Wood had no alternative but to perform the operation in the sweat-soaked bed. There were no sheets in the house, clean or otherwise, and the bedcoverings consisted of thin blankets. Nor was the rough dining table large enough to support the girl and act as an operating table. The surgery, like most backcountry operations, would be performed under adverse circumstances. A doctor could only improvise, and hope for the best.

Wood put the women to work. Few *mexicanos* had stoves, for cooking was traditionally done in the fireplace. The midwife kindled a fire and boiled water in an ancient black kettle. Jennifer brought the surgical instruments and sterilized them in the boiling caldron. At bedside, Elizabeth took a roll of sterile rags from the doctor's bag. A strip of cloth was used to cover a low bench, which she positioned near the bed. She then placed a can of ether and a bottle of antiseptic alongside the absorbent rags.

Finally, all their preparations were complete. The wick on the lamp was turned high, casting pale light over the bed. Wood knelt on one side of the bench, positioning himself over the girl, who was now stripped naked. On the opposite side of the bench, Elizabeth laid out the instruments and readied herself to assist. Jennifer knelt at the head of the bed, prepared to administer light doses of anesthetic. Looking on, the midwife crossed herself and muttered a silent prayer.

Elizabeth swabbed the girl's abdomen with an antiseptic solution. Wood leaned forward, scalpel in hand, and made a long incision from the base of the ribs to the pubic bone. The flesh melted apart under the blade and Elizabeth dabbed away the trickle of blood. With his left hand, Wood pressed inward, locating the exact position of the baby. Carefully he inserted the tip of the scalpel and cut through the thick uterine wall. A geyser of blood jetted outward as the womb was exposed. Elizabeth quickly sopped it up with sterilized rags.

Wood dropped the scalpel and forced his hands into the opening. He took hold of the baby's legs, his forearms now bright with blood. Working swiftly, he lifted the baby from the womb, noting that it was a boychild. Holding the newborn infant upside down, he slapped its bottom to clear the windpipe. The baby sputtered and let go a loud, angry screech. Elizabeth snipped the umbilical cord with scissors and the doctor tied it off. He handed the baby to the waiting midwife, addressing her in Spanish.

"Wash him off and wrap him in something clean."

As the midwife moved away, Wood turned his attention to the girl. Her breathing was shallow and labored, and her color was chalky. He removed the afterbirth, and then, working intently, he set about repairing the surgical damage. At last, with needle and catgut, he sewed the gaping wound closed. Elizabeth handed him a wad of rags and he wiped the blood off his arms. His eyes were still on the girl.

Her mouth opened in a delicate sigh. Then her features softened and she stopped breathing. Wood grabbed his stethoscope, leaning closer, and placed it over her breast. He listened for what seemed an eternity before settling back on his knees. His face was ashen and he stared down at the girl with a hollow gaze. When he spoke, his voice sounded parched.

"She's gone," he said. "Just couldn't hold out."

Elizabeth gently touched his arm. Unlike many doctors, he was not hardened to death and suffering. The loss of a patient was for him a wrenching emotional experience, and she quietly tried to comfort him. Jennifer seemed the least affected, curiously steady, her features composed. She pulled the thin blanket up from the foot of the bed and tucked it under the girl's chin. Stooping down, she smoothed the girl's dark hair, arranging it over the pillow. Hands clasped together, she then stepped back from the bed.

"What was her name?"

Elizabeth looked up. "Méndez. Rosa Méndez."

"She looks like she's sleeping, doesn't she?"

"Yes, she's at peace now."

Jennifer nodded, her eyes on the girl. *"Vaya con Dios, Rosa."*

Wood seemed to recover himself. He glanced around at Jennifer, then pushed himself to his feet and walked to the door. He opened it and beckoned into the darkness. "Señor Méndez," he called out in Spanish. "Will you come in now."

Elizabeth couldn't bear to watch. She brushed past the physician and hurried through the door. Méndez stepped aside, allowing her to pass, then entered the house. A streamer of light from the open doorway silhouetted her in an umber glow. She walked toward the buckboard.

"Por Dios, no!"

The scream echoed from inside the adobe. Héctor Méndez's tormented cry trailed off into racking sobs. The sound was finally too much for Elizabeth. Her composure deserted her and tears welled up in her eyes. For a moment in time, she was no longer *La Mariposa de Hierro*, the

Iron Butterfly. Her shoulders shook and she started to weep softly.

Taylor hopped down from the buckboard. He took her in his arms and she instinctively buried her head against his chest. Her tears spilled out in a great release of heart-break and sorrow, and she clung to him desperately. He held her close, lightly stroking her hair with his hand. A long moment passed before she cried herself out.

Her face pale and drawn, she slowly pulled herself together. He released her as she stepped back, letting his arms drop away. She dashed tears from her face, then pulled a handkerchief from the sleeve of her dress and wiped her eyes. She looked up at him and tried to smile, a tortured smile. She fought to keep her voice from trembling.

"I'm sorry," she said. "I don't know what came over me."

"No need to apologize," Taylor replied. "You've had a rough night."

"Still . . ." Elizabeth faltered, suddenly embarrassed. "I shouldn't have thrown myself on you. It's not like me."

"Well, I reckon it only goes to show you're human. Nothing wrong with that."

"You're very considerate, Mr. Taylor."

"With a lady like yourself, that's not hard. No, ma'am, not hard a'tall."

Elizabeth caught something unspoken in his voice. A week had passed since their return from Santa Fe and she'd been too busy for personal reflection. Yet now, thinking back, she recalled him watching her strangely. She remembered as well that he was always near, never far away. The moment she stepped out of the house, he was somehow there. Waiting.

A thought jolted her into sudden awareness. She real-ized that she'd unwittingly grown comfortable with his presence. He was solicitous and dependable and forever even-humored. Her concerns were his concerns, and he seemed genuinely involved in those things that interested her most. He was, in a word, constant. And she'd come to rely on him.

She suddenly wished Virgil would return, sweep her up in his arms, and hold her. She sensed she'd been alone too long.

Late that night Taylor let them off in front of the house. Jennifer thought her mother was acting strangely, but put it down to the death of the Méndez girl. The operation had been enough to unnerve anyone.

Elizabeth went straight to her room. Jennifer watched her disappear down the hall, vaguely troubled by something she couldn't identify. Then, noting lamplight from the parlor, she moved to the doorway. Brad rose from an easy chair as she entered the room. He had an open book in his hand.

"You're back late," he said matter-of-factly. "How'd things go?"

"Not very well," Jennifer said. "The baby lived, but the mother died. It was absolutely gruesome."

Brad shook his head. "Sounds pretty bad, all right. You must be wrung out."

"Oh, I'll survive. I am tired, though."

"Thing like that will do it to you."

Jennifer was still poised in the doorway. Her features were shadowed in lamplight, accentuating her slender throat and her sleek figure. She stretched voluptuously, staring at him with round, guileless eyes. Her mouth curved in a disarming smile.

"I think I'll run along to bed. Enjoy your book."

She turned out of the doorway. Brad stood there a moment, listening to her footsteps fade along the hall. He had the fleeting impression that he'd just seen a coquette plying her wiles. And yet, considering what she had been through tonight, that seemed highly improbable. The whole thing mystified him, but he dismissed it with an old bromide. No man ever fully understood the mind of a woman.

He wondered if it applied to nubile young girls as well.

13

Clint cut short his visit. Life on the reservation sapped his spirits and put him in a sour mood. He remembered the Quahadi when they were warriors, lords of the Southern Plains. Now, like all the horseback tribes, they were reduced to blanket Indians. It galled him to see proud men humbled.

There was a personal irony which further darkened his mood. He found it difficult to resolve his own role in having hounded the Comanche onto the reservation. Without their defeat, the settlers and settlements would never have advanced westward. Yet his days as a cavalry scout seemed oddly tarnished each time he visited the Quahadi. He felt as though he'd penned a wild thing, and the idea troubled him. He wanted to set them free.

Nor was his mood improved by family matters. While he enjoyed seeing Little Raven and Hank, he'd gotten nowhere with Lon. The youngster had behaved himself, and Clint had even spent a night at the mountain cabin. But any talk of schooling, or the peyote cult, had quickly degenerated into argument. Lon was willful and stubborn, and not to be dissuaded. He refused to listen to reason.

Clint departed with a sense of having failed. At one point, he had again debated hauling Lon off to New Mexico. He was the boy's legal guardian and therefore within his rights. But he'd quickly discarded the notion as unworkable. Short of placing Lon under guard, there was no way of holding him against his will. The youngster considered himself a Quahadi and despised the ways of the whites. He would always return to the reservation.

Upon leaving the agency, Clint rode north. He was considerably closer to the Cherokee Outlet than he was to New Mexico. He decided to stop over at Virgil's operation on the Cimarron and then catch the train out of Caldwell.

His horse could be sold easily enough, and it would shorten his return trip by several days. He was suddenly itchy to get back to work, resume doing what he did best. His thoughts turned once more to the Santa Fe Ring.

A couple of days later he rode into the Cimarron ranch. Virgil greeted him with some surprise, and immediately set him to work. Floyd Dunn and the hands were putting together the first trailherd of the season. The gather was all but complete and the drive would get underway within a day or so. Once the herd was sold, Virgil himself planned to return to New Mexico. Clint agreed to delay his departure until Virgil's business affairs were settled. Foremost on the list was the deal with the Cherokee Nation.

Only that morning a courier had arrived from Tahlequah. Dennis Bushyhead, principal chief of the tribe, had agreed to commence discussions on the matter. A diplomat, as well as an astute politician, Bushyhead realized the arrangement would have far-reaching implications. Any formal commitment by the Cherokee was certain to draw the wrath of the Interior Department. Still, he was receptive to the idea and willing for talks to go forward. The tribal treasurer was already on his way, scheduled to arrive a day after the courier. He was authorized to negotiate for the Cherokee.

Major D. W. Lipe rode into the ranch headquarters the following morning. A man of discrimination, he was trained in the law and affairs of state, and spoke flawless English. Like many Cherokee leaders, he had graduated from their male seminary and then gone on to Carlisle University in Pennsylvania. Over the years he had also put together comprehensive portfolios on the ranchers operating in the

Outlet. He had a storehouse of knowledge on the man who now spoke for the Association.

Virgil had prepared himself equally well. At first, his investigation into the Five Civilized Tribes had left him somewhat confounded. Though he knew the Cherokee had operated slave plantations before the war, he was unprepared for the extent of their cultural progress. He expected to find the usual blanket Indian, savages who had turned to farming after being whipped into submission by the government. Instead, he discovered dignified people who had taken the best from both worlds, and somehow made it work.

The Cherokee Nation was, for all practical purposes, an independent republic. Washington exerted minimal influence on the conduct of tribal affairs, and unlike the western Plains Indians, the Cherokee accepted no handouts from the federal government. They had made the best deal they could, upon being dispossessed of their ancestral lands in the South, and they retained their independence by being wholly self-sufficient. White men, except through intermarriage, were not allowed to own property within the Nation.

Yet, on the whole, the Cherokees were a democratic people. With slight variations, their form of government was patterned on that of the United States. A tribal chief acted as head of state, although with far less autonomy than a president. The legislative body, called the tribal council, comprised two houses, similar in structure to Congress. Except that the Cherokee, if anything, were more rabidly political than their counterparts in Washington. The two parties, the Union and the National, were bitterly hostile toward one another. They generally agreed only when the pressure of events forced a compromise.

Virgil's investigation left him with a profound sense of respect. These were people who wore swallowtail coats and top hats and conducted themselves with the aplomb of diplomats. From all appearances, they were as prosperous and industrious as the most advanced white community back East. They operated farms and businesses, and they had kept the federal government at bay for more than forty years. The Cherokee, quite plainly, were most uncommon Indians.

Negotiations got underway in the cabin. Virgil and Major Lipe seated themselves opposite each other at the dining table. Clint, who was solely an observer, took a seat on one of the bunks. Watching them, he thought his brother and the Cherokee were evenly matched. They were both men of craft and quiet cunning.

Lipe withdrew a sheet of paper from his inside coat pocket. He unfolded it and spread it before himself on the table. Even upside down, Virgil could recognize his own handwriting. It was the lease proposal he'd forwarded to Tahlequah.

"We reviewed your offer," Lipe said politely. "In its present form, Chief Bushyhead doesn't feel he could recommend it to the tribal council. He instructed me to tell you it is not acceptable."

Virgil looked at him without expression. "I assume you're prepared to make a counteroffer."

"Yes, we are."

Another document appeared from inside Lipe's pocket. Composed of several pages, it was written in precise longhand on expensive parchment. He spread it before Virgil on the table.

"We took the liberty of drafting a suitable lease agreement. I believe you will find everything in order."

Virgil quickly scanned the document. Then he read it through with deliberate speed, point by point. What the Cherokee had drafted was a five-year lease agreement covering 1,000,000 acres in the Outlet. The contract was airtight, an instrument of incontrovertible legality once signed. At length, Virgil folded it and idly tossed it across the table. A slight, ironic smile touched his mouth.

"We offered ten cents an acre," he said, "and you've

raised it to fifteen. I'm afraid we can't do business—not on those terms."

Lipe appraised him with a shrewd glance. "The matter is not negotiable, Mr. Brannock. Either you agree or we must insist that you and the other ranchers vacate the Outlet."

Virgil laughed out loud. "Careful, Major Lipe, or I'm liable to call your bluff. We could go on grazing our stock and not pay you a penny." He paused, underscoring the point. "By rights, you'd play hell even collecting a grazing tax."

"On the contrary," Lipe said. "We could report you to the Interior Department and claim you're trespassing on Indian land. Would you prefer to deal with the government?"

"Never happen," Virgil said confidently. "You call in the government and we'll all end up losers. No tax, no lease—no nothing."

Lipe regarded him with a dour look. "For the sake of argument, let's say you have a point. What would you suggest?"

"In here"—Virgil tapped the contract—"you stipulate that all improvements on the land would become the property of the Cherokee Nation at the expiration of the lease. Is that correct?"

"Essentially."

"Add a five-year renewal option to the lease and I'll go along. You'd eventually get the buildings and the corrals, everything."

"What about the fee per acre?"

"Ten cents," Virgil told him. "I won't dicker on that, Major. Take it or leave it."

Lipe fixed him with a curious stare. "How do you know I won't leave it?"

"Because you got what you came for—the improvements on the land."

There was a moment of weighing and calculation. Virgil held the Cherokee's gaze, as though defying him to dispute the statement. Finally, with an affable shrug, Lipe slowly nodded his head.

"Your terms are acceptable, Mr. Brannock. Subject, of course, to approval by the tribal council."

Virgil brought a pen and inkwell from a cupboard. Within minutes, the contract had been amended to reflect their accord. Lipe and Virgil initialed the changes, and then they both signed the document. The formalities completed, they solemnly shook hands.

Later, when Lipe was gone, Virgil hauled out a bottle of rye whiskey. He poured drinks for Clint and himself and hoisted his glass in celebration. The toast marked what he considered a personal triumph.

The Outlet cattlemen were now bona fide residents on Cherokee land.

The trail drive took two days. A herd of some fifteen hundred head swung east from the Cimarron and funneled onto the Chisholm Trail. From there, the longhorns plodded north toward the Kansas border.

Virgil got top dollar for his cows. He'd contracted in advance with a cattle buyer, guaranteeing delivery before the end of May. Herds from Texas were still a week or more down the trail, and Eastern slaughterhouses were clamoring for beef. Arrival of the Spur longhorns would officially open the season.

Virgil and Clint ranged ahead of the herd. Their talk, conducted on horseback, covered business as well as family matters. An item of considerable interest was a recounting of Clint's visit to the reservation. By the second day, they had about talked themselves out. Virgil at last turned the conversation to a sore spot.

"Need your advice," he said. "Every rancher in the Outlet is losing cows to rustlers. Not in dribs and drabs, either. It's a regular thing."

Clint looked at him. "What about this Association you put together? Hasn't that had some effect?"

"Not yet," Virgil answered. "We're just getting ourselves organized. Figures to take a little time."

"So what sort of advice are you after?"

"Well, it's different here than in New Mexico. The rustling doesn't appear to be a hit-or-miss operation. It's too damn systematic!"

"Are you saying it's a gang?"

"Let's say I've got a hunch."

Virgil went on to explain. Caldwell was overrun with cutthroats and outlaws, men on the dodge. Only two miles from the border, the town made a perfect haven for those with a price on their heads. At the first sign of trouble, they simply skipped across the line into Indian Territory. There, they were immune to arrest except by U.S. deputy marshals. No Kansas lawman had jurisdiction in the Nations.

By the same token, a crime committed in Indian Territory seldom resulted in arrest. Cattle rustling was not a federal offense, and therefore of no interest to federal marshals. Nor was the county sheriff all that concerned with thievery in the Nations. Once the rustlers got the cows across the Kansas line, they rarely ran afoul of the law. Unscrupulous cattle buyers were willing to ignore hastily altered brands and phony bills of sale. Cows were a commodity, money on the hoof.

"Way I see it," Virgil concluded, "it's too well planned. I've got a feelin' somebody's directing the whole shebang."

"You're talking about a gang leader?"

"No . . . not exactly."

Clint appeared puzzled. "What are you talkin' about, then?"

"An organizer of some sort. What you might call a boss."

"Has he got a name?"

"Unless I'm wrong, it's a grifter named George Hunt."

The roughest dive in Caldwell was the Red Light Saloon. A combination dance hall, gambling den and whorehouse, it was operated by a toughnut known as George

Hunt. The Red Light was headquarters for the town's criminal element, and several killings had taken place on the premises. Hunt and his customers were reputed to be birds of a feather.

"Got any proof?" Clint asked. "Anything that'd tie Hunt to the rustlers?"

"Not one iota."

"Sounds like you're between a rock and a hard place."

Virgil grunted angrily. "That's why I wanted your advice. What would you do in my spot?"

"Well, first off," Clint said with the barest hint of a smile, "I'd pay a call on Mr. Hunt. You might term it a social visit."

"A social visit—?"

Clint's mouth hardened. "What you've got to do is put him on warning. Either the rustling stops or you'll consider it a personal matter."

Virgil pondered it at length, eyes narrowed in concentration. "Maybe I ought to do that before we head home. It's not a thing to leave undone."

"No time like the present," Clint agreed. "Want some company to back your play?"

"Yeah, I wouldn't mind. The Red Light's not exactly my speed."

"Hell, Virge, there's nothin' to it. All you've got to do is talk the other fellow's language."

The remark had the ring of a jest. But Virgil knew his brother meant it in deadly earnest. Clint seldom joked about the law or lawbreakers. In that sense, he was like the wrath of Jehovah. He believed in the terrible swift sword.

Early next morning the herd was driven into the stockyards. Loading chutes were dropped into place, and the men began hazing cows up the ramp and into boxcars. It was hot and dirty business, mostly shouting and cursing and prodding, worse than the trail drive itself. The cows either balked at the head of the chute or spooked halfway up the ramp and started a stampede in the wrong direction.

As the morning wore on, the men gradually became grime-streaked and sweaty and thoroughly out of sorts. Their curses turned viler with each new mishap.

The last car was loaded shortly before the noon hour. It had taken two full trains to handle the herd, and Virgil felt immensely relieved to see the cows safely aboard and ready to pull out. He gave the crew an advance on their wages and told them to take the rest ōf the day off. Then, accompanied by Clint, he followed the cattle buyer into Caldwell. A bank draft exchanged hands and Virgil deposited it to his Kansas account. The herd had brought more than $40,000.

The cattle buyer treated them to dinner in a nearby café. After the meal, they parted outside with a round of handshakes. Virgil and Clint then crossed the street and walked toward the Red Light Saloon. Neither of them spoke as they went through the batwing doors.

A bartender pointed them in the right direction. At the rear of the saloon, Virgil rapped once on the door of a private office. He stepped inside, trailed closely by Clint, and found George Hunt seated at a battered desk. Clint closed the door and pulled out the makings. He began building himself a smoke.

Hunt was heavily built, with a square thick-jowled face. A fleeting look of puzzlement crossed his features; then his expression became flat and guarded. "What's the idea of bustin' in here, Brannock?"

Virgil halted, thumbs hooked in his vest. "I've got a message for you and your friends. I want the rustling stopped in the Outlet."

"You're daffy!" Hunt flared. "I don't know beans from bullshit about rustlers."

"Maybe you do and maybe you don't. I'm just saying, pass the word along."

"You got a goddamn nerve! Haul your ass outta here before I call some of my men."

Clint shifted away from the door. He struck a match

on the wall and lit his smoke. His eyes were hard as slate.

"Pay attention," he said evenly. "You've just been put on warning. Don't take it lightly."

Hunt glowered at him. "Who the hell are you?"

"Just another Brannock," Clint said, exhaling smoke. "Which one's not important."

"Well, whoever-the-hell you are, I'm gonna tell you something. I don't like people threatenin' me."

"No threat intended," Clint said quietly. "It's more on the order of a prophecy."

Hunt squinted querulously. "What d'ya mean, prophecy?"

"You rustle any more Spur cows and we'll hang you out to dry. Mark it down as gospel."

"That a fact?" Hunt bristled. "You talk like a muy tough hombre. Question is, are you as tough as you talk?"

"Ask your marshal about Clint Brannock. We met a few times down in New Mexico."

"You rode with Hendry Brown?"

"No," Clint said with a slow, dark smile. "Hendry and me worked on opposite sides of the fence."

"What's that mean?" Hunt demanded churlishly. "Are you a lawman or what?"

Clint dropped his cigarette on the floor. He ground it underfoot and looked up with a hard grin. "You and Hendry have yourselves a talk. He won't steer you wrong."

Hunt blinked, staring at him. Clint opened the door and motioned Virgil through. The saloon was full now, packed with the noontime crowd. They walked directly to the batwing doors.

Outside, Clint stopped on the boardwalk. His features were set in a thoughtful frown and his eyes were distant. Virgil studied him for a long moment before speaking. "Why so quiet?"

"Damnedest thing," Clint said, glancing around. "Were you watchin' his face when I mentioned Hendry Brown?"

"What about it?"

"Something queer in his eyes. I've seen that look before."

"What look?"

"Virge, I've got an idea we stumbled onto something. Wouldn't surprise me but what them two are thick as thieves."

"Hunt and Hendry Brown?"

"Nobody else."

Virgil recalled his own thoughts about the former gun-man. Hendry Brown, like a leopard, hadn't changed his spots. He'd merely changed his hunting ground.

Which explained many things. Outlaws flocked to Cald-well for the best of reasons. One of their brethren wore the marshal's badge.

14

Three breaking corrals were located a mile west of Spur headquarters. There, on the banks of the Hondo, a crew of broncbusters conducted daily battles with wild mustangs. They jokingly referred to it as the "riding academy."

On the first day of June, Virgil set out on an inspection of the ranch. He had returned from Kansas only yesterday, and over Elizabeth's objections, he'd refused to take any time off. She seemed to him unusually moody and yet joyously happy to have him home. Their reunion last night had been ardent and long.

With him this morning were Morg and Brad. While it was favoritism, he'd nonetheless excused the boys from their routine duties. He spent too little time with his son and he saw no reason not to indulge himself. Then too, Brad had never had a complete tour of the ranch. Today's inspection outing seemed a good way to accommodate both the youngsters and himself. Their first stop was the breaking corrals.

The center corral was the domain of Joe Stroud. He was the top broncbuster on the spread and a man who gloried in his work. Lean and wiry, he had a broken nose and one gold tooth and a sixth sense about horses. His specialty was training cowponies in the advanced skills of working cattle. But today was opening class for a bunch of mustangs fresh off the plains. He went at it like a barroom brawler in a one-on-one slugfest.

The mustangs were typical range stock. None of them

had yet felt a saddle or the weight of a man on their backs. The day's pupils were held on a stretch of grassland down near the river. There they could graze and water while awaiting their turn in the corrals. Several cowhands, mounted on their swiftest ponies, were stationed to keep a watch on the herd. An occasional hammerhead took a notion to head back to the wide-open spaces.

For the most part, however, the mustangs were content to crop grass. They had learned that a bunch quitter quickly came upon hard times. Shortly after being captured on the Staked Plains, each of the horses had been roped and thrown to the ground. When released, the horse discovered that one of its front feet had been tied to its tail with a length of rope. The rig kept the mustangs from running, and after dumping themselves a few times, the wiser ones seldom needed a second dose. Another day roped foot-to-tail convinced even the most stubborn that it was better to stick with the bunch.

With the herd grazing peacefully, the workday began. A rangy chestnut was hazed into the corral and the gate swung shut. Stroud hopped down from the fence with a lariat in his hand, shaking out a loop. He was joined by three other men and they slowly walked forward. Every man had his assigned job and there was little lost motion in their actions. What they were about required teamwork and lightning-fast reflexes. A man with lead in his pants was never assigned to the breaking corrals.

The chestnut bolted away as the men fanned out. Suddenly Stroud's arm moved and the lariat caught the mustang's front legs just as its hooves left the ground. Stroud hauled back, setting his weight into the rope, and the horse went down with a jarring thud. Working smoothly, every man to his own task, the other three swarmed over the chestnut in a cloud of dust and flailing arms.

One man wrapped himself around the horse's neck. He grabbed an ear in each hand and jerked the chestnut back to earth just as it started to rise. At the same time, another man took a length of braided rawhide and lashed the animal's back legs tight. The third man clamped hobbles around its front legs and slipped a hackamore over its head. Pushing and tugging, with the horse still on the ground, they managed to cinch a center-fire saddle in place. As the latigo was jerked taut, a blindfold was tied around the mustang's eyes.

The entire operation had taken less than a minute. Stroud shook the lariat loose from the chestnut's legs and it was allowed to regain its feet. Blinded and dazed, still winded from the fall, the horse stood absolutely motionless. The hobbles around its front legs kept it from rearing or jumping away, and the blindfold calmed it into a numbed stupor. However unwilling, the bronc was ready for its first lesson.

Stroud stepped into the saddle. One of the men unfastened the hobbles, front and rear, and quickly retreated with his partners to the top of the fence. They nodded to Virgil and the boys, who sat their horses outside the corral gate. Everyone watched quietly as Stroud jerked the blindfold loose and let it fall to the ground. For perhaps ten seconds the chestnut remained perfectly still, as though rooted to the ground. Then, with a faint smile, the broncbuster jammed his boots hard in the stirrups. The jinglebobs on his spurs sounded like chimes.

The mustang suddenly exploded at both ends. All four feet left the ground as the horse bowed its back and came unglued in a bone-jarring snap. Then it swapped ends in midair and sunfished across the corral in a series of bounding, catlike leaps. Stroud was all over the horse, bouncing from one side to the other, never twice in the same spot. Veering away from the fence, the chestnut whirled and kicked, slamming the broncbuster front to rear in the saddle. His hat spun skyward in a lazy arc.

Stroud let go a whooping shout. Lifting his boots high, he raked hard across the flanks with his spurs. The spiked rowels whirred and the mustang roared a great squeal of outrage. The bronc swallowed its head and humped its back, popping Stroud's neck like a bullwhip. As though berserk, the horse hit the ground and erupted in a pounding beeline for the corral fence. Stroud effortlessly swung out of the saddle at the exact instant the mustang collided with the cross timbers.

Staggered, the horse buckled at the knees and fell back on its rump. Stroud nimbly swung into the saddle as the mustang regained its feet. He rammed hard with his spurs but the bronc showed less fight, jolting away in stiff-legged crowhops that lacked punch. For the first time, Stroud hauled back on the hackamore, reining the horse around the corral in a simple turning maneuver. At last he eased to a halt and stepped down out of the saddle. The chestnut stood where he left it, walleyed and heaving for air.

Stroud retrieved his hat and dusted it off. Jamming it on his head, he walked to the fence and looked across at Virgil. He jerked his thumb back at the spent mustang.

"That's gonna be a good hoss, Mr. Brannock. Got plenty of starch."

Virgil laughed. "Think he'll run into that fence again, Joe?"

"Well, sir," Stroud said deadpan, "I'd tend to doubt it. One pile-up gen'rally does the trick."

Virgil motioned off toward the horse herd. "There's more where those came from. Let me know when you're ready for another bunch."

"Anytime a'tall will do, Mr. Brannock. You catch 'em and we'll break 'em."

Summer and fall were the broncbuster's work seasons. Wild horses were driven in from the Staked Plains and separated into herds. The mares and their spring foals were branded, and all the colts were gelded. Any stock four years or older was turned over to Stroud and his crew of broncbusters. Some were topped off with a couple of lessons and shipped out to distant horse markets. Cowponies for Spur were brought along at a slower pace, most being green-broke for saddlework. The cowhands then finished off their training.

The mustangs were direct descendants of the horses brought over from Spain by the *conquistadors*. Through the centuries, horses escaped into the limitless Southern Plains, where their numbers multiplied into hundreds of thousands. Early maps labeled vast areas of land simply as the "wild horse desert." The Staked Plains, particularly that stretch between Palo Duro Canyon and the Salt Fork of the Brazos, was the greatest breeding ground in the world. No one knew how many mustangs roamed *Llano Estacado*.

These wild herds were vital to the operation of Spur. Every cowhand worked a saddle string of ten mounts from spring roundup through fall roundup. As a rule, only two horses received advanced training, one for cutting cattle and the other for roping. The stock selected for these chores were usually crossbreeds, the offspring of mustang mares topped by a Thoroughbred stallion. The rest of a cowhand's string were green-broke geldings, products of the "riding academy." In the fall the older geldings, together with excess mares, were sold off on the horse market.

The demand for horses had enabled Virgil to build a thriving business. Throughout the West, there was a market for horses of every description. Stagecoach lines still operated across vast distances, with a fresh team needed every fifteen miles. The coaches were drawn by a six-horse hitch, and that number, multiplied by countless relay stations, created an unending source of demand. Still another market was found in towns and cities, where everything from streetcars to private buggies was horse-drawn. Demand in the larger Eastern cities forever outstripped supply.

Within the cattle industry, Virgil catered to several different markets. Some ranchers wanted only crossbred stock, suitable for cutting horses and roping. Others, particularly in the Southwest, preferred light, cat-footed mustangs broken to saddle. Farther north, in the mountainous ranching country, cattlemen favored a larger horse. To meet their demands, Virgil imported a Morgan stallion from New England and crossed it with range mares. When grown, the chunky offspring often weighed a thousand pounds and were perfect for working cattle through the heaviest snowfalls. Anywhere in the Southwest such a horse would have been harnessed between the shafts of a wagon.

Army remount stations were a steady, year-round market. The principal requirements for a cavalry horse were stamina, hardiness, and an even temperament. For these animals, Virgil developed a strain which was larger and heavier, with perhaps one-quarter mustang blood. Freight companies, which transported goods between railheads and interior sections, required a scaled-down draft horse. By crossing a Percheron stallion with oversized mares, Virgil supplies horses that stood sixteen hands and weighed fourteen hundred pounds. These same animals were a favorite among homesteaders and immigrants settling the Western prairies.

The horse-breeding operation on Spur had expanded far beyond Virgil's original design. Yet, with an eye to the future, he was sensitive to shifting market demand. From mustangs and blooded cowponies, he had gradually developed strains suitable for practically any kind of work. Throughout the summer, horse buyers from across the West traveled to Spur to look over the stock. At peak season, the various herds often totaled more than five thousand head. Annual sales for the upcoming season were expected to top $200,000, most of it attributable to the availability of mustang stock. For Spur, the wild-horse herds roaming *Llano Estacado* were a replenishable natural resource.

From the breaking corrals, Virgil and the boys rode over to one of the breeding pastures. On the opposite side of the fence a magnificent stallion charged toward them, suddenly pulled up short, and whinnied a shrill blast of challenge. He was a barrel-chested animal, all sinew and muscle, standing fifteen hands high and well over a thousand pounds in weight. A blood bay, with black mane and tail, his hide glistened in the sun like dark blood on polished redwood. He held his ground, watching them, and pawed the earth as though he spurned it and longed to fly.

Whatever Virgil's mood, it always improved when he came to inspect the mares and Coaldust. He had imported the stallion from Kentucky, five years ago, and begun a selective breeding program. A string of mustang brood mares was chosen from the ranch stock, picked for their conformation and speed. They had the spirit of their noble ancestors, the Barbs, and possessed an almost supernatural endurance. Yet, unlike Coaldust, the mares were essentially creatures of the wild, and no amount of breaking ever fully tamed a mustang. From this fusion, Virgil had bred the ultimate cowhorse, and the results were spectacular.

By culling the mares, continually breeding up, Coaldust's offspring now possessed all the qualities necessary for working cattle. They had stamina and catlike agility, intelligence and an even disposition, and blazing speed over the short stretch. Those who fell short of the requirements were nonetheless superb stock, and easily sold to horse dealers for blooded saddle mounts. Several colts sired by the stallion showed promise of further extending the bloodline.

As Virgil and the boys watched, Coaldust came on at a prancing walk, moving with the pride of power and lordship. Always protective of his mares, who had retreated to the center of the pasture, he halted a few yards short of the fence. Then he stood, nostrils flared, like an ebony statue bronzed by the sun.

"Goddurn!" Brad said, awestruck. "Would you look at that devil strut!"

Morg laughed. "You would too. He's got himself a lulu of a harem."

"Does he now?" Virgil said, subjecting the youngster to a speculative stare. "And how is it you know so much about harems?"

"C'mon, Dad," Morg drawled somewhat sheepishly. "I'm not wet behind the ears."

"All the same, you talk mighty wise for someone your age."

"I'm going on fifteen!" Morg said in a wounded voice. "Besides, I've been watchin' studs and herd bulls most of my life. What's the big mystery?"

Virgil was forced to an abrupt truth. His son was quickly edging toward manhood. The youngster's voice was deeper and he seemed somehow taller. Some night soon, he would sneak off and secretly meet one of the bold young señoritas from the village. Or perhaps he'd already done so and no one the wiser. Virgil was suddenly confronted with the thought that sooner or later haunts every father. He wondered where all the years had gone.

A faraway shout diverted his attention. He turned in the saddle and saw Odell Slater galloping toward them. The foreman was bellowing something, but his voice seemed unsteady and curiously garbled. He skidded his cowpony to a halt, slewing the reins harshly.

"Noonan!" he stormed. "They killed Chub Noonan!"

"Slow down," Virgil said sternly. "Get hold of yourself and make sense. Who killed Noonan?"

"Horse thieves," Slater said, gesturing wildly. "They raided one of the mustang herds just before dawn. Chub was ridin' nighthawk."

"Was he able to talk before he died?"

"No, sir, Mr. Brannock, they shot him deader'n hell. Poor bastard looked like a sieve."

"Any idea how many rustlers?"

"I checked the sign myself. Looks to be four, maybe

five men. They got off with better'n a hundred head. All geldings."

"Which direction?"

"On a beeline dead southwest."

"What do you think—Old Mexico?"

"Yessir, that'd be my guess. I figger they're gonna make a run for the border."

"Horses can't be run that far, Odell. Not without killing half the bunch."

Slater nodded agreement. "You're thinkin' they'll stop somewheres and give 'em a breather. That it?"

"I'm depending on it. Now, listen close, Odell. I want ten men ready to ride in an hour. Have the cook lay out rations for three days."

Morg shifted in his saddle. "You'll only need eight men," he said to his father. "Brad and me wanna go along. Don't we, Brad?"

"You damn bet'cha!" Brad said quickly. "Chub Noonan was aces high in my book."

Virgil stared at his son. He knew what Elizabeth would say and he silently overruled her arguments. One day the boy would inherit Spur, and some lessons were best learned firsthand. He looked back at Slater.

"You heard him, Odell. We'll only need eight men."

Morg suddenly sat taller. He grinned proudly, glancing around at Brad. Virgil gigged his horse and the others fell in alongside him. They rode off at a hard gallop.

A hunter's moon slipped from behind a cloud. Spectral light flooded the earth and the far mountains rose in dark silhouette against a starswept sky. The shelterbelt of the woods lay shadowed along a winding stream.

Virgil paused some thirty yards below the camp. Behind him were Brad and Morg and the eight cowhands, all armed with carbines. He motioned them to the ground and dropped to one knee beside a cottonwood. Scanning the area ahead, he slowly inspected the campsite. Four horses were picketed in the trees, and three forms wrapped in blankets were stretched out on the ground. A fourth man sat beside the ashes of a smoldering campfire, his head nodding. Off in the distance the horse herd browsed on an open patch of grassland.

Late yesterday morning Virgil and his men had ridden out of Spur. All afternoon and through most of the night they had trailed the rustlers on a southwesterly course. The tracks of a hundred horses were easily followed, even though the herd had been pushed along at a merciless pace. As the moon rose full, the trail had dipped through the bleak foothills separating the Sacramento Mountains from the Guadalupe range. By midnight, the herd had been driven some seventy miles and it became apparent that the pace had slowed. The rustlers would shortly have no choice but to call a halt.

An hour or so later Virgil had spotted sparks from a fire. Ordering his men to dismount, they had let their horses downstream and proceeded on foot. From the shelter of the trees, he saw now that his hunch had been borne out. The rustlers expected pursuit, but they never believed anyone would trail them through the night. Secure in that belief, they would have slept a few hours and then pulled out before dawn. Searching the camp one last time, Virgil told himself it would never happen. The trail ended here.

The plan he formulated was simple and direct. Orders were issued in a muffled whisper and the men spread out on a rough skirmish line. Virgil kept the boys on either side of him and signaled the men forward. Cautiously, ghosting through the cottonwoods, they walked into the camp. The night guard was fast asleep, his legs crossed, a carbine cradled across his arms. The cowhands fanned out around the blanketed forms, halting in the silvery moonglow. Virgil placed the muzzle of his Winchester behind the guard's head.

"Don't move!"

"What the—?"

The guard jerked awake, then froze. His startled yelp brought the other men upright in their blankets. Their eyes bugged and they too went immobile, staring at the ring of armed cowhands. One of them, a grizzled man in his forties, muttered a sharp curse. The others sat locked in strained silence.

"Hands on your heads," Virgil ordered. "Who's the leader here?"

A moment elapsed before the gaunt-faced man spoke. "I reckon that'd be me."

"I'm Virgil Brannock, owner of the Spur Ranch. I've come to collect the horses you stole."

"I don't suppose you'd settle for just that, would you?"

"No," Virgil said tightly. "You killed one of my men."

"You gonna hang us?"

Virgil seemed turned to stone. He felt Morg's eyes on him, watching him intently. When he spoke, his voice was hard, implacable. "Somebody kick up that fire. We'll give these gents a last cup of coffee."

By dawn, everything was in order. The four rustlers were mounted, hands bound behind their backs, their faces ashen. Their horses were positioned beneath the stout limb of a cottonwood and the nooses around their necks were snubbed to the base of the tree. Four cowhands were posted behind the horses, holding freshly cut switches. They stared up at the condemned men in cold silence, their features like bronze masks.

Virgil stepped forward. "Anyone got anything to say?"

The gang leader fixed him with a look of black hatred. "Quit jawin' and get on with it."

Virgil hesitated a moment, then raised his arm and dropped it. The switches cracked across the horses' rumps and the animals bolted forward. The rustlers were jerked clear of their saddles and swung back as the ropes hauled them up short. When the nooses snapped tight, their eyes seemed to burst from the sockets. Their gyrations spun them in frenzied circles and they danced frantically on air.

One by one their mouths opened and their tongues darted out like onyx snakes. A full three minutes passed while they vainly fought the ropes.

Without a word, Virgil walked to his horse and mounted. The others scrambled aboard their cowponies and trailed along as he rode toward the herd of mustangs. Beneath the cottonwood, the bodies hung limp, necks crooked, swaying gently in the dawn stillness. A faint spark of sunshine touched the distant mountains.

No one looked back.

15

The courtroom was packed. There was standing room only, every bench jammed with spectators. For the first time in memory, the majority of the crowd was *mexicano*. Anglos were outnumbered three to one.

The hearing was held on June 6. Ira Hecht represented a group of some thirty *mexicano* farmers. His petition was directed to the federal district court, Judge Alonzo Hammond presiding. At issue was a block of land outside a small village south of Santa Fe. The defendant was a local speculator named Horace Johnson.

Elizabeth sat in the front row. She was accompanied by Taylor and their seats were directly behind the plaintiff's table. For the hearing, she'd chosen to wear a tailored skirt and jacket, with a ruffled blouse and a jaunty hat topped by an ostrich feather. She looked surpassingly attractive and her presence in the courtroom hardly went unnoted. Her intent was a public statement of support for the young lawyer.

For his first case, Hecht had elected not to challenge the Santa Fe Ring. He had chosen instead an independent speculator, whose political connections were somewhat spotty. His purpose was to establish a precedent and thereby set the stage for larger actions. The block of land in question was less than a hundred acres, located on the fringe of an old Spanish grant. His clients claimed valid title to the small parcel.

The petition was deceptively simple. Hecht contended

162

that Horace Johnson, by means of an erroneous survey, had expanded the boundaries of the original grant. He further asserted that his clients' interests, by virtue of an ancient community grant, were protected under the Treaty of Guadalupe Hidalgo. He alleged that Johnson's survey illegally extended the Spanish grant to encompass the *mexicanos'* farmland. The federal government, he declared, had an obligation to investigate all matters involving treaty violations. He requested an injunction barring any sale of the disputed parcel.

Judge Hammond ruled for the plaintiffs. He issued a restraining order which blocked transfer of title for an indefinite period of time. He then formally requested that the attorney general's office investigate the validity of Horace Johnson's survey. He asked that the report, and all substantiating documents, be on his desk within thirty days. At that time, he would hand down a final ruling.

Hecht's victory was considered a masterstroke. By linking the case to a federal treaty he had effectively removed it from the arena of territorial politics. Never before had anyone petitioned the court on behalf of *mexicanos*, invoking their rights under the customs of ancient land practices. Apart from the injunction, there would now be an investigation into the matter of questionable surveys. A Pandora's box had been opened on the shadowy world of land fraud.

One of the more interested spectators was Max Flagg, publisher of the *New Mexican*. As the most vocal opposition to the Santa Fe Ring, Flagg used his newspaper to blast the Republican legislature. Yet his editorials were long on verbiage and short on substance. He wrote of cabals and conspiracies, but he offered nothing in the way of documentation. More than anything else, the *New Mexican* was a political organ for the Democrats. Thus far, however, the paper had done little to alter the balance of power.

When court was dismissed, Flagg approached the young

attorney. He wrung Hecht's hand, warmly congratulating
him on the victory. Then, as a group of *mexicanos* crowded
around, the publisher turned to Elizabeth. His manner was
openly cordial.

"A great day!" he said with cheery vigor. "You should
be proud of yourself, Mrs. Brannock."

"Yes, indeed," Elizabeth said, laughing triumphantly.
"Although the credit belongs to Mr. Hecht. He was positively brilliant."

"You're too modest," Flagg observed. "Everyone knows
the *mexicano* legal service was your idea. Except for you,
today wouldn't have happened."

"No, Mr. Flagg," Elizabeth protested. "An idea means
nothing unless it is acted upon. Ira Hecht deserves the
recognition, all of it."

"Well, anyway," Flagg said, sidestepping the point, "I
understand you're bringing other lawyers into the project.
Would you care to comment for the paper?"

Elizabeth chose her words carefully. Flagg was an avowed
enemy of the Santa Fe Ring, and therefore a potential ally.
His newspaper, moreover, could provide a public forum
for debate on the land frauds. Still, she was hesitant to
draw attention to herself rather than focus on the issues.
People weren't yet ready to grant a woman a voice in
political matters.

"Any quotes," she said thoughtfully, "should come
from Mr. Hecht. After all, he's the one responsible for
organizing everything. There wouldn't be a legal service
without him."

Max Flagg was an old hand at double-talk. His features
were pleasantly cynical and his eyes had the canny look of
a man who was surprised by nothing. "I admire discretion," he said, smiling. "All the same, making him your
spokesman doesn't change anything. We both know who's
calling the shots."

"Are you trying to put words in my mouth, Mr. Flagg?"

"Wouldn't think of it," Flagg said. "Off the record,

though, where would young Mr. Hecht be without you and your money?''

Elizabeth evaded a direct reply. A short time later she left the courtroom with Hecht and Taylor. The lawyer was jubilant, pleased with himself and his conduct of the case. On the way back to his office, he spoke with spirited eloquence about their future prospects. He looked like a cat spitting feathers.

For the next hour or so, Elizabeth and Hecht reviewed strategy. His own investigation of land records revealed widespread fraud, collusion between speculators and unscrupulous surveyors. He was confident of a favorable ruling by Judge Hammond and eager to broaden the scope of their activities. Elizabeth concurred, expressing optimism that it was time to move ahead. Their next target would be the Santa Fe Land & Development Company.

The mood of celebration abruptly ended. Stephen Benton walked through the door, accompanied by his bodyguard, Wilbur Latham. Taylor and Latham squared off, eyeing one another warily, like combatants entering an arena. Benton moved to the rear of the office, halting before the desk. He nodded to Hecht, then looked at Elizabeth.

"Mrs. Brannock," he said with perfect civility. "Good to see you again."

"Thank you, Mr. Benton."

Elizabeth stared at him and his gaze shifted to Hecht. "Nice work this morning, Ira. You made a strong argument."

Hecht cleared his throat. "Were you in the courtroom?"

"No," Benton said, "but I heard all about it. News of that sort travels fast."

There was a moment of strained silence. When no one spoke, Benton once more turned his attention to Elizabeth. "I wonder if you and I might talk, Mrs. Brannock?"

"Whatever you have to say can be said here, Mr. Benton. I have no secrets from Ira."

A shadow of irritation colored Benton's features. "In that case," he said, "I'll come straight to the point. Would you and your husband be interested in an accommodation?"

Elizabeth arched one eyebrow in question. "What is it you're suggesting, Mr. Benton?"

"A standoff," Benton said truthfully. "I'll concede Lincoln County to your husband and John Chisum. In return, you put an end to these land investigations. That seems equitable all around."

"I'm afraid you've been misinformed. My husband has nothing to do with the land investigations."

"Come now, Mrs. Brannock," Benton said with icy courtesy. "Your husband and I have been at odds for many years. Even your brother-in-law is nosing around in my affairs. Are you asking me to believe they have no part in your scheme?"

"Believe what you choose," Elizabeth said carefully. "I don't speak for my husband or my brother-in-law. I speak only for myself."

A veil seemed to drop over Benton's eyes. "Are you saying you won't call off the investigations?"

"Yes," Elizabeth told him, "that's exactly what I'm saying."

"Either we declare a truce," Benton said with chilling simplicity, "or it's no holds barred. Politics is a hard game, Mrs. Brannock."

Elizabeth regarded him with an odd steadfast look. "Politics isn't at issue," she said. "I'm only interested in returning the land to its rightful owners. Today we made a step in that direction."

Benton angled his head critically. "You'd do well to talk it over with your husband."

"You've had your answer, Mr. Benton. There's nothing more to be said on the matter."

Benton looked at her strangely. He seemed on the verge of saying something more, then appeared to change his mind. With a curt nod, he abruptly turned and walked from the office. Wilbur Latham trailed him out the door.

A moment passed, then Hecht laughed an exultant laugh. His eyes were bright with excitement. "We've got him!" the lawyer crowed. "Otherwise he would never have offered you a deal. He knows he's next!"

"Yes, he does," Elizabeth said in a musing voice. "And that worries me."

Her gaze moved to Taylor. She searched his eyes and read there what was uppermost in her own mind. Neither of them underestimated Stephen Benton. Once threatened, he would not stand idly by and await events. Nor would he allow them the next move.

Somehow, probably where it was least expected, he would retaliate. And it would be done quickly.

The trip south was a time of reflection. Elizabeth was anxious to speak with Virgil and urge upon him greater caution. Her every instinct told her to beware some unseen danger.

From Socorro, she and Taylor caught the eastbound night stage. They arrived in Lincoln shortly after sunrise the next morning. Over breakfast at the hotel Elizabeth suddenly remembered that it was clinic day. She decided to delay the trip to the ranch until that evening.

Chester Wood greeted her with gruff good humor. He was expecting Jennifer, but he welcomed an experienced assistant. Thus far, he'd done little by way of training the Mexican woman. His excuses were transparent, inventions designed to stall the inevitable. He simply had no desire to replace Elizabeth.

A few minutes before eight o'clock Jennifer arrived. From the office window, Elizabeth watched as Brad hopped out of the buckboard and hurried around the team. She wondered why he was driving the buckboard rather than working roundup. Then, without warning, her maternal instincts were alerted. She watched with sudden interest.

Brad handed Jennifer down from the buckboard. She wore her hair Grecian style, pulled back on top with ringlets falling on her neck. She was vivacious, full of verve and bubbling gaiety, compellingly attractive. She clung to Brad's hand an instant too long and vamped him with a smile. There was something brazen in her eyes, a look of bold invitation.

Laughing gaily, she turned and walked up the pathway. Brad stared after her, his mouth slightly ajar, hat still clutched in his hand. His expression was that of a tethered ram, part fascination and part lust. To Elizabeth, he looked somehow younger than his years, and her scrutiny suddenly sharpened. She saw in his face what she interpreted as the worst possible sign. He was a grown man bewitched by a sylph of a girl.

Elizabeth was no less aware of her daughter. Jennifer's hairstyle was far too fashionable for a day at the clinic. Her gingham dress was cinched tight at the waist and flared out over rounded hips. The swish of her skirt suggested long, lissome legs and her breasts were small, perfect mounds. She looked at once provocative and desirable, caught up in her own guile. A girl acting the part of a woman.

Jennifer was surprised to see her mother. She hadn't expected Elizabeth back from Santa Fe until later in the week. A fleeting look of guilt crossed her features, then quickly vanished. She smiled happily, greeting her mother with a hug and a soft kiss on the cheek. Neither of them paid any attention to Brad as he turned the buckboard and drove out of town. Instead, like any other clinic day, they went about their normal routine.

The first patient was an older man suffering from a severe case of rheumatism. Dr. Wood rummaged around in the medicine cabinet and returned with a bottle of liniment, a fiery mix of wintergreen and camphor. He ordered the man to apply the liniment at night and cover it with warm flannel cloth. The next patient was a heavyset woman almost prostrated by a bout of diarrhea. The physician prescribed flushing enemas of table salt, baking soda, and warm water. He took the woman off solid foods as well, ordering her to fast for forty-eight hours.

Complaints such as rheumatism and diarrhea often tried Wood's temper. All too frequently the ailment was in an advanced state before he was consulted. The patients relied instead on home remedies, or worse, one of the many patent medicines. These elixirs, extracts, and balms were the bane of a frontier doctor's existence. While they did nothing to treat the problem, virtually any patent medicine would relieve the symptoms. Some were laced with opiates and others contained sufficient alcohol to deaden nearly any pain. Among regular users, addiction to a particular brand of "bitters" was not unknown.

Thousands of such potions were sold across store counters. Bole's Worm Destroyer, Smith's Tonic Syrup, and Townsend's Sarsaparilla were guaranteed antidotes for any ailment, including a hangover. Far worse were the snakeoil pitchmen who hit town with a wagonload of nostrums and magic elixirs. These traveling "doctors" invariably drew a crowd with minstrel music or a buxom girl tricked out in an Indian costume. From the back of their wagons they hawked restoratives for ulcers, dyspepsia, pimples, bronchitis, female complaints, and every disorder known to man. The potions were generally equal parts creek water, grain alcohol, and cayenne pepper. One sip usually sufficed to make anyone forget his troubles.

For all that, a frontier doctor was accorded the respect normally reserved for holy men. People in Lincoln still told the story of Laura Sue Oxnard, the blacksmith's four-year-old daughter. Suffering from diphtheria, the child had not responded to any of the customary treatments. Finally, when she was on the verge of choking to death, Dr. Wood had incised her throat with a scalpel and opened the windpipe. With a linen handkerchief over the incision, he had then sucked the deadly secretions from the child's larynx. Laura Sue began breathing normally and soon recovered.

The folk tale surrounding the incident scarcely mentioned Laura Sue's recovery. Instead, it was told and retold how Chester Wood had endangered his own life by sucking the poisonous fluid from the girl's throat. Afterward, he had rinsed his mouth with whiskey and chewed an entire plug of tobacco to stop the infection from spreading into his own windpipe. The story, more than any other single factor, was responsible for the *mexicanos* finally entrusting themselves to the clinic. Throughout Lincoln County the physician was thought to be part saint and part shaman.

Today, there were no life-and-death crises requiring surgery. The people filing into the clinic were afflicted by the routine disorders that consumed a doctor's day. By late morning only a handful of patients remained to be seen. None of them were critical and Wood declared a halt for the noon hour. He walked uptown for a cool beer and a sandwich.

Elizabeth wasn't particularly hungry. She made tea for herself and Jennifer and they went outside, behind the clinic. There beneath the shade of an elm tree, was a small flagstone patio with wooden armchairs. A warm summer breeze drifted off the river and the faraway mountains shimmered under a haze of sunlight. The view was one of rugged grandeur.

Jennifer rattled on about the morning's patients. After seating herself, Elizabeth sipped her tea, merely nodding in response. She saw no way to avoid what was on her mind and yet the thought left her perplexed. She'd never before spoken to her daughter about men.

At length, the girl paused for a sip of tea. Elizabeth took a deep breath, steeling herself to the task. "Jen, listen to me," she said. "I think we need to have a talk."

"A talk about what?"

"You and Brad."

Jennifer feigned confusion. "What about us?"

"Please," Elizabeth admonished her. "There's no need to pretend innocence. I saw that little scene this morning."

"Scene?" Jennifer looked at her blankly. "I don't understand."

Elizabeth's tone was severe. "You understand all too well. You were playing the tease, and very artfully, I might add. You looked absolutely shameless."

"What a terrible thing to say!"

"I'm going to ask you something and I want the truth. Has it gone any further than that—teasing?"

"Oh, honestly, Mother!" Jennifer's face burned with a blush. "Brad's never so much as kissed me. He's a gentleman!"

"I'm relieved to hear it," Elizabeth said. "As of today, I want a stop put to it. You're too young to get involved with an older man."

"Brad's only twenty-three," Jennifer blurted. "And in case you've forgotten, I'll be sixteen next month. Lots of girls are already married at my age."

"Don't talk nonsense," Elizabeth scolded. "Besides, marrying Brad would be impossible. He's your cousin!"

"A *very* distant third cousin!"

Watching the girl, Elizabeth thought her heart would burst. She recalled her own first love and she felt a powerful tug of emotion for her daughter. Yet she was determined that the flirtatious infatuation would go no further. When she spoke, her voice was very low.

"Have you any idea what would happen if I told your father?"

Jennifer's eyes got big and round. "You won't . . . will you?"

"Nooo," Elizabeth said slowly. "Not unless you force me to. I'd hate to see Brad run off Spur."

"Me too," Jennifer replied with a sudden sad grin. "Especially since he hasn't done anything. He treats me like I was made of glass."

"Suppose we keep it that way," Elizabeth said gently. "Admire him from a distance and nothing more. All right?"

"Oh, all right." Jennifer's eyes grew faraway and dreamy. "He probably wouldn't have waited for me anyway."

"Waited for you?"

"Yes," Jennifer breathed wistfully. "Until I finish medical school. I've decided to become a doctor."

"A doctor!" Elizabeth said, genuinely surprised. "Whatever put that in your mind?"

"Dr. Wood," Jennifer said with soft wonder. "I want to be just like him, Mother. A healer . . ."

Her voice trailed off. She sat lost in her own daydream, staring at the distant mountains. She looked as if her eyes were on the moon.

Elizabeth curbed the temptation to state the obvious. She saw no reason to point out that lady doctors were frowned upon by the medical profession. Nor was there any need to mention the barrier of medical school. Few reputable colleges accepted women applicants.

She decided instead to say nothing. Girlish dreams, much like a first love, were passing things. A year from now any notion of a career in medicine would have fallen by the wayside. Still, as she reflected on it, Elizabeth thougt the idea itself had merit. Women should never be hindered by the limitations imposed on them by men.

She reminded herself to offer a word of encouragement— at the right time.

16

Summer lay across the land with fiery brilliance. Under a brassy haze, the sun seemed fixed forever in a cloudless sky. Waves of heat pulsed and vibrated, and left the valley bathed in a glow of illusion.

Virgil and Odell Slater sat their horses on a low rise. Below, spread across the northeastern corner of the valley, a herd of longhorns grazed on spotty grasses. There were some fifteen hundred head of cows gathered on the holding ground. Tomorrow, at sunrise, the herd boss would put them on the trail. The drive to railhead would take a week, skirting north around the Jicarilla Mountains. Already contracted, the cattle were destined for the Chicago stockyards.

For Virgil, it was a time of immense personal satisfaction. All through roundup he'd watched as herds were put together across Spur. The one on the holding ground below was the first to be driven to railhead. Over the ensuing months three more herds would be trailed out and shipped eastward. By September better than six thousand cows would have been sold off. The proceeds, roughly estimated at $200,000, would carry Spur through another year. Everything else, particularly the horse-breeding operation, represented undiluted profit.

Off in the distance, Virgil saw Brad hazing an old mossyhorn back into the herd. The youngster had developed into a passable cowhand, earning the respect of the other men. At his own request, he'd been assigned to the first trail herd of the season. Virgil thought it an admirable gesture, and at the dinner table one evening he had bragged on the boy's spunk. The look that passed between Elizabeth and Jennifer still had him bemused. But then, where women were concerned, he never knew what to expect. They were the most unpredictable of all God's creatures.

Elizabeth had returned home four days ago. He'd listened with growing pride as she related her encounter with Stephen Benton. One thing that never surprised him was her spirited determination, her inner strength of character. Whether or not she had correctly assessed the situation remained to be seen. He agreed Benton would retaliate, but he foresaw something shifty, perhaps of a political nature. An act of violence, on the heels of the court decision, would reflect badly on Benton and his cronies. Not that the likelihood of violence was to be completely ignored. The Santa Fe Ring looked upon killing as a routine business practice.

Oddly enough, there was a good side to the whole affair. Over the past month or so Virgil had sensed a strain between himself and Elizabeth. He'd always felt tongue-tied where personal matters were concerned, and he hadn't broached the subject. Nor had Elizabeth openly expressed herself, despite days of moody behavior. Virgil still had no idea what lay behind the tension and her brooding silences. But her encounter with Benton had once more brought them together, washing away any lingering strain. For that, he thought Benton deserved a vote of thanks.

Virgil was no great believer in hindsight. Still, in retrospect, he saw that he'd sometimes offended his wife. The hanging of the four horse thieves was a case in point. She was a sensitive woman, and she viewed such acts with deep personal repugnance. Her greater concern, however, was that he had taken Morg along on the manhunt. In her opinion, their son could only be brutalized by watching men put to death. Her objections had been expressed with sharp candor the day the horses were stolen. Since then, the rustlers had become a taboo topic in the Brannock household. No one dared raise the subject in Elizabeth's presence.

To Virgil, the amazing part was her absolute lack of fear. Any mother would be expected to pitch a fit when told her son was joining an armed posse. But Elizabeth possessed an unshakable faith in the Brannock men, including fourteen-year-old boys. She took no alarm that Morg might have been drawn into a gunfight with the horse thieves. As though protected by a lucky charm, she simply assumed no harm would befall her men. On occasion, Virgil wondered what secret witchery she practiced to make it come true. Any number of men would gladly dance on his grave. And Clint, with almost eerie regularity, survived still another shootout. So in the end, she hadn't worried about Morg either. She knew all along he would return safely.

"Any final orders, Mr. Brannock?"

Slater's question broke the spell. Virgil put his wool-gathering aside and got back to the business at hand. He looked at the foreman. "Are you satisfied, Odell?"

"Yessir, I am," Slater assured him. "We've got a top crew and Martin ain't no slouch as a trail boss. Ought to be a pretty routine drive."

"Fair enough," Virgil said. "Just be sure they get on the trail without any hitches. A good start sometimes makes the difference."

"I'll see to it personal."

Off to the west, a rider caught their attention. He was bent low over the saddle, flogging his horse with a short quirt. As he pounded closer, they saw that it was one of the older hands, Orville Duggin. His cowpony was lathered with sweat from a long run.

Duggin skidded to a halt, sawing on the reins. "Sheep!" he yelled. "There's sheep comin' into the valley!"

For a moment, Virgil was speechless. *"Sheep?"* he repeated, investing the word with scorn. "What the hell are you talking about, Orville?"

"Christ as my witness!" Duggin hollered. "Whole herd of the stinkin' woolly bastards. I saw 'em myself!"

"Where?"

"On the Rio Bonito. I was workin' them draws back up in the foothills. All of a sudden, here they come, big as life! Must've been a thousand of the sonsabitches."

Virgil stared at him. "How do you know they're headed into the valley?"

" 'Cause I got eyes," Duggin said testily. "Crew of greasers had 'em lined out straight as a string. No doubt about it, Mr. Brannock."

Among cattlemen, sheep were considered a dirty word. Tradition held that wherever sheep grazed, the country was ruined for cows. A flock of the woolly creatures was reported to crop the grass so short that the land afterward turned fallow. The only thing worse than sheep were the shepherds. Sheepmen were pegged a notch below rustlers and horse thieves.

With Slater at his side, Virgil rode off toward the western end of the valley. They left Orville Duggin behind, walking his horse to cool it down. Neither of them could believe that anyone would trail sheep onto Spur range. Nor were they prepared to let it happen.

Four *mexicano* shepherds worked the flock. The sheep moved slowly eastward, yapping dogs darting here and there around the flanks. A lone horseman, mounted on a high-stepping *grullo*, brought up the rear. His clothes marked him as an *hidalgo*, one of the landed aristocrats.

Virgil and Slater were awaiting where the Rio Bonito flowed into the Rio Hondo. Upon sighting them, the horseman cantered forward, outdistancing the sheep. As he approached, Virgil put a name to the face. Luis Varga. A *patrón* of the old school, Varga owned a large sheep operation west of Lincoln. He was also a *jefe político* for the Santa Fe Ring.

"*Buenos días*," Varga said, reining to a halt. "We meet again, Señor Brannock."

"Looks that way," Virgil said tersely. "Where are you headed with those sheep?"

"Where else, señor? I plan to graze them along the Rio Hondo."

"Think again," Virgil warned him. "I claim the Hondo Valley, end to end. Sheep aren't allowed there."

Varga shook his head with a sourly amused look. "I fear you have been misinformed, señor. A large part of the valley is public domain. *Verdad*?"

Anger mottled Virgil's features. "You're no fool, Varga. You know damn well the Hondo is Spur land. Nothing's happened to change that."

"All things change," Varga said with heavy sarcasm. "Yesterday the Hondo was yours alone. After today, we will share it."

"We will like hell!"

Virgil's face took on a sudden hard cast. He pulled the carbine from his saddle scabbard and jacked a shell into the chamber. His voice was edged with a quiet steel fury.

"Do yourself a favor," he said. "Don't cross the Hondo with those sheep. You try it and I'll kill the whole damn bunch."

Luis Varga was a gnarled, lynx-eyed man. He had a straight mouth and leathery features and a cold dark gaze. He studied Virgil without expression.

"Tell me, señor," he said flatly. "Are you prepared to kill me as well?"

Virgil fixed him with a baleful look. "Ask yourself the question, Varga. Are you prepared to die?"

Their eyes locked. Varga got the uneasy feeling that he'd just been told a truth. The *gringo* had the look of a man who would kill not in coldblood but as a matter of principle. At length, Varga spread his hands in an elaborate shrug.

"Another day, perhaps," he said. "For now, I will hold my sheep west of the Hondo."

"One other thing."

"*Sí*?"

Virgil's jawline tightened. "Tell Stephen Benton he's made a big mistake."

"*No entiendo*," Varga said with a faint smile. "Señor Benton has nothing to do with my sheep."

"Just tell him!"

Virgil wheeled his horse around. Slater was only a beat behind and they rode off along the banks of the Hondo. Varga stared after them, his brow wrinkled in a frown. One day was not a lifetime, he told himself, and one battle was hardly a war. There would be other days, bloodier days for the *gringo cabrón*.

He wondered when Benton would order it done.

Late that afternoon Virgil rode into the headquarters compound. When he dismounted at the corral, one of the wranglers took his horse. Head bowed in thought, he walked toward the house.

North of the compound, he'd told Slater to rejoin the trail herd. Other than ordering a watch placed on the sheep, he hadn't said much to the foreman. He wanted time to think it through before confiding in anyone. All the way home he had examined various courses of action, weighing one against the other. He'd arrived at only one conclusion. Sheep would never be allowed to enter the Hondo Valley.

Elizabeth was seated at a small rosewood desk in the parlor. Her afternoons were devoted to correspondence with a growing network of lawyers throughout the territory. But now, as Virgil walked through the door, she put pen and paper aside. She read his moods as though reading an open book. His expression today warned her that something was perilously wrong. He refused a chair and began pacing around the room. She took a seat on the sofa, listening.

Virgil told the story straight through. He faltered only once, when relating his threat to Varga. He seemed upset with himself for having lost control, allowing himself to be governed by temper. As he talked, a sudden cold dread spread through Elizabeth. She recalled the tone of voice and the fierce look in his eyes. Worse, she remembered all too well what happened when his iron control slipped and he lost his temper. The last time was almost sixteen years ago, in Denver. He'd killed a man in a bloody shootout.

At length, Virgil halted before the fireplace. He took a cigar from a humidor on the mantel and lit up in a cloud of smoke. A vein pulsed in his forehead.

"It won't end here," he said. "Today was just the opening move."

Elizabeth looked stunned. "There's no doubt in your mind?" she asked. "You're certain Benton is behind it?"

"Dead certain," Virgil affirmed. "Varga wouldn't pull a stunt like that on his own. Benton used him to send me a message."

"Actually, it's a message about me, isn't it?"

"Yeah," Virgil said, nodding. "Either you stop this land-grant business or he'll challenge me for control of the valley. That's it in a nutshell."

Elizabeth's voice dropped. "You know I couldn't stop now . . . don't you?"

"Stop?" Virgil said angrily. "Hell's fire, I want you to go at it hammer and tongs. No man tells me what to do."

"In that case, we have to expect another move by Varga. What happens then?"

"Just what I promised him. Any sheep that crosses the Hondo won't last the night."

A note of concern came into Elizabeth's voice. "Benton probably anticipates that. Wouldn't he simply have Varga file charges with the U.S. marshal? After all, part of the valley is public-domain land."

"Let him!" Virgil scoffed. "I'll put a bee in the governor's ear and that'll be the end of that. No need to trouble yourself about the federal marshal.''

"What do you mean," Elizabeth said—"a bee in his ear?"

"Beth, the last thing Lew Wallace wants is another Lincoln County War. But that's what he'll get if anybody claims this valley as public domain. I've got it and by the Lord God, I'll fight to hold it!"

"How strange," Elizabeth said quietly. "On the one hand, I'm trying to expose land frauds. And on the other, we hold Spur together by right of force. One seems to contradict the other, doesn't it?"

"Not by a damnsight," Virgil said with conviction. "You're working for the *mexicanos*, people who had their land stolen. The Hondo Valley will always belong to whoever's strong enough to draw the line.'' He paused, staring at her. "For now, that's me."

Elizabeth thought he'd rationalized it rather neatly. Yet it was a moot point, for he wasn't about to change. She addressed herself instead to the more immediate problem.

"Benton won't just quit," she said. "When one thing doesn't work, he'll try another. He may even try to have you killed."

"Well, if he does, it'll have to wait till I get back."

"Get back?'' Elizabeth repeated, "Where are you going?"

"Staked Plains," Virgil said, puffing his cigar. "I promised Morg he could come along next time we went huntin' mustangs. Tomorrow's the day."

"Aren't you concerned, leaving now? Benton might try something."

"I won't order my life around what Benton might or might not do. 'Course, when he does it, I'll make him damned sorry. He picked himself a fight with the wrong man."

Elizabeth stared straight ahead with a faintly stricken expression. Somewhere inside her a sense of foreboding took hold, and she knew it wouldn't let go. Her intuition told her that the time for talk and reason was past. A year of fragile peace was about to end.

And now, once again, the killing would begin.

Llano Estacado stretched endlessly to the horizon. It was a land of sun and solitude, evoking a sense of something lost forever. Flat and featureless, covered with a thick mat of buffalo grass, it swept onward toward the Texas Panhandle. A gentle wind rippled and moaned, disturbing nothing across the vast emptiness.

Here and there, the plains were broken by a latticework of wooded canyons. These rocky gorges were all but invisible from a distance, solitary space suddenly dropping off into a sheer precipice. Within the canyons was the breath of life—water—the only known streams in *Llano Estacado*. It was near these streams that the wild horses roamed.

Virgil and his crew of mustangers were hidden along the walls of a broad chasm. Morg was positioned nearby and the other men were spaced at quarter-mile intervals across from one another. All of them were concealed behind boulders and stunted trees, mounted on their fastest horses. They waited now, a band of silent hunters, surrounding a creek alive with hoofprints. Their eyes were fixed on the mouth of the canyon.

Earlier that day, they had constructed an elaborate trap. At the far end of the canyon, where the sheer palisades squeezed down to a narrow gorge, felled cottonwoods were used to build a corral. A half-mile-long fence was then erected on either side of the canyon, fanning out from the corral entrance in a V shape. The trick was to surprise a herd and drive them into the open throat of the funnel. Then, with any luck, the mustangs could be hazed along the narrowing fence and into the corral.

Sundown was but an hour away and deep shadows

slowly settled over the stream. One moment the mouth of the canyon stood empty, and in the next, like some ghostly apparition, the mustangs simply materialized. A barren old mare, the herd sentinel, was in the lead. She came on at a stiff-legged walk, ears cocked warily, eyeing the gorge for anything out of the ordinary. At last, satisfied, she broke into a trot and led the other mares and their foals toward the creek.

Behind the herd, a sorrel stallion advanced at a prancing walk. Larger than the mares, heavily muscled, he moved with noble pride. Yet he was skittish, nervously testing the wind, scanning the canyon floor with a fierce eye that missed not a rock or a blade of grass. He would water only at the very last, when the herd had taken its fill. Until then, protector as much as ruler, he would remain watchful and on guard. Halting, ears cocked and twitching, he stood alert to any sign of danger.

Virgil thumbed the hammer on his saddle carbine. He sighted and placed a shot in the dirt at the stallion's hooves. As the sorrel stud wheeled away, the men rode out from their hidden positions and barreled toward the herd. Their voices were raised in bloodcurdling screams and the blast of their six-guns echoed like thunder. Other men, shouting and firing guns, appeared on either flank.

Tails streaming in the wind, the mustangs took off in a thunderous wedge. Terrified, aware of nothing but the men behind, they entered the funnel without breaking stride. Suddenly the inverted V of the fence squeezed down to nothing, the only escape a narrow opening dead ahead. Never faltering, the herd pounded through the corral entrance at a full gallop. The barren old mare hit the far fence-line with a shuddering impact and toppled over backward.

The rest of the herd slid to a dust-smothered halt. Confused and frightened, they turned to retreat the way they had come. But the men were there, sliding long poles across the opening, and suddenly there was no escape. The mustangs milled about, wild-eyed and squealing, slamming against the corral. Gradually, after testing the fence, their panic faded and they huddled together in the center of the enclosure. Trembling, still alarmed by the man-scent, they stared watchfully at their captors.

Gathered before the corral gate, the men stared back at the mustangs. By rough count there were some forty mares and yearlings, and perhaps half that many foals. All in all, it was a good day's work, and an omen of things to come in the week they would spend on *Llano Estacado*. The men laughed and shouted, congratulating themselves on a job well done. Virgil looked on with justifiable pride.

Far away, a roar of outrage echoed along the canyon walls. The men turned, suddenly silent, shielding their eyes against the fiery sunset. Atop the westerly palisade they saw the stallion silhouetted along the rimrock. Snorting and whistling, he reared high and lashed the air with his front hooves. The mares whinnied their response, milling frantically inside the corral. Then, like a spirit horse, the sorrel stud vanished from sight. One instant he was there and the next he was gone.

Morg stood for a long moment staring at the canyon wall. Finally, his brow furrowed in a youthful frown, he turned to his father. "What'll the stallion do now, Dad?"

"Well," Virgil said with a broad smile, "I just suspect he'll find himself another harem. There's lots of mares out on those plains."

"Lucky devil," Morg said softly. "Wish it was that easy for two-legged critters."

"You're young yet, son. Don't rush it."

"Can I ask you something, Dad?"

"Fire away."

"How young were you—the first time?"

Virgil laughed a loud booming laugh. He put an arm around the boy's shoulders and turned back toward the corral. He marked again the passage of the years, the flight of time. His son, too soon, would be a man.

He pondered how he might delay the moment awhile longer.

17

Fort Sill lay dark and quiet. Stars were scattered like flecks of ice through an indigo sky and the garrison was bathed in silvery shadow. The hour was fast approaching midnight.

Lon and Hank were crouched in a shallow ravine. Not thirty yards to their immediate front was a large corral, directly opposite the hay yard. Some forty head of horses, standing drowsy and hip-shot, were penned within the enclosure. A lone sentry patrolled the area.

For the past hour, the boys had observed from the ravine. Apart from the corral, the sentry's post included the hay yard and the garrison wood yard. The area was somewhat isolated, located on the extreme southern perimeter of the fort. Farther north, the parade ground was faintly visible in the pale starlight.

The corral was a holding pen for untrained stock. There, over a period of weeks, remount horses were schooled in the ways of the cavalry. Drilled to instant obedience, the horses were considered fit for duty only after the most rigorous training. Having passed muster, the new mounts were then moved to the garrison stables, west of the parade ground. The horses in the corral tonight were green-broke saddle stock. All of them had been delivered late that afternoon.

At midnight, there was a change of guard. A sergeant appeared with fourteen troopers, formed in a column of twos. One of the troopers stepped out of formation and the old sentry took his place. On the sergeant's command, the

detail marched back toward the headquarters building. The
new sentry, much like the man he'd replaced, quickly fell
into a pattern. Stumping along, rifle angled across his
shoulder, he took almost a quarter-hour to complete a
circuit of his post. A good part of that time he was out of
sight, hidden by the mounds of hay and the mountain of
firewood. Ten minutes or more elapsed between each patrol around the corral.

Lon had spent a month planning the horse raid. As with
his raid on the officers' chicken coop, he had enlisted
Hank into the scheme. His young stepbrother was the one
person he trusted to keep a secret. Other Comanche boys
were prone to brag and tell the world of their exploits.
Hank, on the other hand, idolized his older kinsman and
obediently followed orders. He spoke to no one of their
nighttime sorties, not even his mother. She was unaware
of what they planned and would never know that he'd
slipped out of the lodge. He had waited until she was
sleeping soundly.

For all the secrecy, the raid would still be seen as Lon's
handiwork. The tribal elders, as well as the military, considered him a throwback of sorts. He was wild and ungovernable, constantly involved in mischief. His Comanche
name was Strikes-Both-Ways, a tribute to his talent for
fisticuffs. Hot-tempered, and easily offended, he'd whipped
any number of Indian youngsters in personal disputes. Yet,
despite his gift for the white man's way of fighting, he was
a Quahadi in spirit. He lived by an older code, one remi-
niscent of a long-ago time. He thought of himself as a
warrior.

In days past, skill at warfare was but one mark of
manhood. Hunting and a deft hand at stealing horses were
attributes of equal distinction. But now, with the Comanche
herded onto the reservation, there were no wars to fight.
So Lon had turned instead to the woodlands and the mountains, the life of a hunter. He followed the traditional path
of any boy who sought to know the ways of wild things.

For a time, he had listened to the older men, committed all they taught to memory. Then, not quite a year ago, he'd gone off alone into the wilderness.

High in the mountains, he had built himself a cabin. Yet part of every day was spent roaming the wooded slopes and lying in wait along game trails. He quickly learned that most essential of all truths: better a day spent in cautious stalking than a night spent in hunger. He taught himself to move with stealth and infinite patience, patterning his actions after those of the wild things. Alert to sound and wind, pausing often in a moment of frozen watchfulness, he became a shadow in a forest of shadows. Deer and bear, even the tawny lion, shortly fell before his *bois d'arc* hunting bow. By the end of that first winter, he was as one with the other predators of the wild.

With spring, his mind turned to the next step in the warrior's path. No longer was it possible to raid the *tejanos*, or follow the Comanche Trace into Mexico. But the army was close at hand, and he'd decided to test himself against those who had conquered the Quahadi. His first foray, with Hank standing lookout, was the officers' chicken coop. Not only a test of skill, it was also a way to bedevil the pony-soldier leaders. On a dark night, silent as a fox, he had filled a gunnysack with laying hens. Later, at his mountain retreat, he'd invited members of the peyote cult to a feast. The chickens had been consumed with gusto and considerable laughter.

Tonight marked still another step in his journey toward manhood. There was no place to sell the horses, and the whiskey smugglers, though greedy, would never trade in livestock stolen from the army. Nor was it worthwhile to secrete the horses in some hidden mountain valley. He had no use for them himself, and none of his friends would accept one as a gift. So his objective was not the horses, for he intended to scatter them to the winds. His sole purpose was the raid itself, an act of honor. He meant to make his mark as a horse thief.

The sentry disappeared on the far side of the hay yard. Scrambling out of the ravine, Lon and Hank catfooted across the open ground. At the corral gate, Hank paused, taking his position as lookout. Lon slipped through the fence rails and advanced slowly toward the horses. He spoke to them in a whispered, gentling murmur.

The horses stared at him, their ears alert. He selected a roan gelding, still soothing them with his voice. Step by step, he closed the distance until he stood beside the roan. Bending slightly, he put his mouth to the gelding's nostrils and breathed softly. The horse shuddered, its eyes half-closed, and nuzzled his arm. He eased a rawhide bridle over its head.

Grabbing a handful of mane, Lon vaulted aboard the horse. He was as comfortable bareback as in a saddle, and quickly reined the gelding to the far side of the corral. On his signal, Hank slipped the latch bar and swung open the gate. He booted the roan in the ribs and loosed a shrill war cry.

The herd stampeded out of the corral. Lon circled around their rear, urging them on with yipping shouts. As he went through the gate, he leaned to his left and extended his arm. Hank grabbed hold with both hands and swung up behind him on the roan. The boy wrapped his arms around Lon's waist and hung on tight. Triumphant, still barking war cries, they drove the horses south from the garrison.

Far to their rear, the sentry sprinted around the corner of the hay yard. He slammed to an unsteady halt, throwing the rifle to his shoulder. The Springfield roared, lighting the darkness with a fiery muzzle blast. The shot went wild and an instant later the horse herd vanished from sight. Lowering his rifle, the sentry uttered a sharp curse.

He hurried off to find the Sergeant of the Guard.

Early the next evening, everything was in readiness for the ceremony. A hide lodge had been erected in the clearing outside Lon's cabin. All the sacred trappings were positioned before a low stone altar.

The cult members began arriving shortly after dusk settled over the mountains. There were nine of them, the oldest not yet eighteen. While hundreds practiced the peyote rite, these nine were Lon's closest friends. He had invited them to mark the occasion of his manhood.

None of the youngsters mentioned the stolen horses. Throughout the day, army patrols had scoured the reservation. Finally, toward late afternoon, th herd had been found some miles south of the fort. The horses were grazing on a stretch of prairie along Cache Creek. One of them, a roan gelding, still wore a rawhide bridle.

There was talk of little else in the Comanche lodges. Word quickly spread that Strikes-Both-Ways had led the raid on the pony soldiers. His younger brother, the boy known as Bull Calf, was thought to have assisted. No one knew how these things were so, for young Bull Calf was reported to have slept the night in his mother's lodge. Yet all believed that Strikes-Both-Ways had covered himself with glory. His fame as a horse thief would be spoken of wherever men gathered.

As darkness fell, Lon led his guests into the ceremonial lodge. He took the seat of honor, at the rear of the lodge, facing the doorhole. The others positioned themselves on either side of him, forming the sacred circle. They were seated around the stone altar, symbolic of a mountain range in Old Mexico. There, according to legend, the spirit gods had made a gift of peyote to man.

For centuries the peyote rites were passed from tribe to tribe. The mythical Aztecs, ancient rulers of Mexico, were thought to have originated the ritual. Peyote, which was a mescaline button found on spineless cactus, produced visions of startling clarity and vivid color. Worshipers prayed and sang, with periods of silent meditation, chewing the buttons as a sacrament of the spirits. The ceremony, which began at nightfall, lasted until dawn.

From Mexico, the religion slowly spread northward. By the early 1870's the Mescalero Apache were seeking su-

pernatural power through peyotism. Shortly thereafter,
Quanah Parker became a convert, introducing the rites
among the Comanche and the Kiowa. He claimed to have
been cured of deep spiritual melancholy brought on by the
defeat of the Quahadi band. On one occasion he told a
group of followers: "The white man goes into his church
house and talks *about* Jesus. We go into our sacred lodge
and talk *to* the spirits."

Quanah often spoke to the younger men of the Jesus
Road. He was frank to admit that the nature of the white
man's god left him confounded. Every Sunday, church
services were held by the Methodist missionaries in the
agency schoolhouse. According to the minister, the all-
powerful Jehovah was both benevolent and vindictive. A
god of whims and moods, whose disposition seemed as
vagrant as the winds. If the Good Book was to be believed, he was a god who brought pestilence and famine,
flood and death nearly as often as he brought peace and the
joy of life.

Then there was the matter of heaven and hell. Somewhere, presumably down in the earth's bowels, there was
a chamber of fire and brimstone reserved for those who
had offended their God. Some burned in everlasting hell
and others floated throughout eternity on the feathery clouds
of heaven. For an Indian, it was simply too much. That a
god could tug and pull at a man's life was bad enough. But
that this same god could consign him to a pit of fire in the
hereafter was the ultimate indignity.

What the Comanche believed was perhaps as mystical
and fuzzy in its own way. Yet it nonetheless gave a man
the benefit of the doubt in his afterlife. When his shadow
soul crossed over to the other side, there was no judgment
one way or the other by the spirit beings. Instead, the land
beyond was a place of cool waters and green grass, fleet
ponies and immense buffalo herds. A land without hunger
or suffering, where all men, of whatever tribe, were brothers at last. To get there a man had only to die, whether in

battle or of old age. There were none to bar his path with threats of eternal damnation in a fiery hell.

In his present life, a Comanche need only seek the favor of the spirit beings through offerings and visions. True peace, the path of harmony, was to be found within the shadow souls of men. On earth men achieved such harmony when they realized their oneness with the universe and all its creatures. Inner peace came with the knowledge that the spirit beings were at the center of all things, and that this center was to be found within each man. Compared to the Jesus Road, it seemed somehow uncomplicated, and infinitely more reasonable. The spirit beings were a whimsical lot, but never capricious. A man always knew where he stood.

The ceremony tonight sought communion with the spirit beings. A small fire was kindled before the altar and Lon passed around a fringed buckskin pouch. From it, each youngster in turn took a peyote button and placed it in his mouth, chewing slowly. As the peyote took effect, one of the members began thumping a skin-covered kettledrum. Another took up a pebble-filled gourd, and they all began chanting in unison. Their eyes dulled, and within moments they were lost in the mysteries of their own visions. Yet, even as they drifted alone, there was a deep sense of brotherhood among them. A oneness along the path of harmony.

The chant and the rattle and the throb of the drum went on into the night. A feathered fan, symbolic of the birds linking man with the spirit beings, passed from hand to hand. As their visions flowered, the youngsters took more peyote buttons from the pouch, experiencing an inner union with their shadow souls. A ceremonial staff, representing observance of all the gods, was passed around the fire. From time to time, one of them would fall silent, momentarily lost in meditation. But their oneness was palpable, ever present, and their rhythmic chant never wavered.

Lon saw revealed before him a powerful sign. The image of a man, half white and half red, appeared from within the fire. Ever so gradually, the red half enveloped the white, burnished still brighter by the flames. He saw reaffirmed in the image what he'd always known within his shadow soul. Wherever he roamed, by whatever name men called him, he would remain more Comanche than white. Inside, no matter the passage of time or the turn of events, he would always be Strikes-Both-Ways. Only on the outside would he be the one known as Lon Brannock.

At dawn, a great light tinged the horizon, as if awakening from a pool of its own blood. Lon stared into the sunrise, slowly emerging from the depths of his vision. He saw now that there was no shame attached to his pale coloring and the blue of his eyes. For within his shadow soul he was a Comanche, one of the Quahadi.

A man of the True People.

Clint studied the telegram. The message was from Colonel Ranald Mackenzie, dated June 18. The point of origin was Fort Sill, Indian Territory.

Mackenzie wasted no words. He briefly recounted the raid on the garrison remount corral. Then, in no uncertain terms, he identified Lon as the culprit. He requested Clint's immediate return to the reservation.

For the past three weeks Clint had crisscrossed northern New Mexico. He was following a cold trail, tracking men who had seemingly vanished. One was Claude Gentry, the former attorney general. The other was Gentry's assistant, Fred Peterson, who had once acted as bagman for *Comanchero* payoffs. He'd found neither of them.

The trail began in Santa Fe. Upon his return from Kansas, Clint had combed the territorial capital. The men he sought were respected members of the community, with businesses and families. Yet he discovered that they had fallen from sight, their whereabouts unknown. By no small coincidence, both men had disappeared shortly after the death of Jacob Ingram, the retired army officer. All too clearly, they saw themselves as next on Clint's list.

After some hard digging, Clint finally got a lead. He learned that the men had boarded a stage for Cimarron, northern political stronghold of the Santa Fe Ring. From tnere the trail led westward, to a mining camp high in the Sangre de Cristos. Then, in an abrupt turnaround, the men had traveled by stage to Raton. The town was a major railhead, with daily trains operating north and south. At that point, the trail simply evaporated. The men vanished without a trace.

Stymied in his search, Clint returned to Santa Fe. He'd checked into the hotel and then spent the afternoon nosing around town. But now, standing in the hotel lobby, he stared at the telegram with a growing sense of disquiet. Mackenzie's request was more on the order of a demand, and not to be ignored. Still, apart from hauling Lon back to New Mexico, he saw nothing to be accomplished at the reservation. He suddenly needed a drink.

The hotel barroom was empty. He took a seat at the table and told the barkeep to leave the bottle. After building himself a smoke, he sipped rye and slowly reread the telegram. Mackenzie's rage was apparent in the choice of words, and despite himself, Clint was forced to smile. For an underage kid, Lon was fast developing a reputation. First chickens and now horses, both times nicking the army's pride. It was almost laughable.

Clint's every sense suddenly alerted. He set his glass down as Wilbur Latham entered the barroom and walked toward his table. He'd known Benton's gunhand for several years, and between them was a wary respect. Until today, they had exchanged nothing more than a passing nod.

Latham halted before the table. His eyes were friendly but sharp. "Hello, Clint," he said. "Mind if I join you?"

"Conversation or a drink?"

"Just conversation."

"All right," Clint said, motioning. "Have a seat."

Latham took a chair. "Understand, now, there's nothing personal in what I've got to say. I'm talkin' for Benton."

"Lemme guess," Clint said impassively. "Benton wants me to call off the dogs. Am I close?"

"Nope," Latham said with a wide peg-toothed grin. "You're no closer to Gentry and Peterson than when you started. Otherwise you wouldn't've come back here."

Clint flicked an ash off his cigarette. "Why'd Benton send you around, then?"

"Believe it or not," Lathan said, "he'd like to make peace with you and your brother. He's already sent one message along by Mrs. Brannock."

"Way I heard it," Clint replied, "he sent another one by Luis Varga. All them sheep caused quite a ruckus."

Latham's stare revealed nothing. "Why keep buttin' heads? Nobody wins that way."

Clint looked thoughtful. "You get paid to do it the hard way, not the easy way. How come he made you the go-between?"

"Well, in a manner of speaking, you and me are in the same line of work. I guess he figured we'd savvy one another."

"C'mon, Wilbur, let's get down to brass tacks. What's he want?"

Latham smiled, wolfish ridges at the corners of his mouth. "He wants you to drop this *Comanchero* business. As for your brother's wife, she ought to stay home where a woman belongs." He paused, spread his hands. "Mr. Benton's a reasonable man. All you gotta do is meet him halfway."

Clint laughed shortly. "How many times you reckon Benton has tried to have me killed?"

Latham shrugged noncommittally. "What's that got to do with anything?"

"Nobody's pulled it off yet," Clint said. "So why would I quit just because he sends you around?"

A moment elapsed while the two men stared at one

another. "Figure it out for yourself," Latham said. "You're not the only one we're talkin' about here. Other people could get hurt."

A stony look settled over Clint's face. "You know the truth when you hear it?"

"Try me."

"Tell Benton he's a dead man if anything happens to my family. No maybes about it."

"Christ!" Latham said with an unpleasant grunt. "That kind of talk won't settle nothin'. He's liable to send me after you—just to play it safe."

"Wilbur, if he sends you, don't come. Some things aren't worth dying for."

Latham uttered a low chuckle. "You figure you'd punch my ticket, huh?"

"Most likely," Clint said with a wry smile. "Hell, I'm damn near bulletproof. Or hadn't you heard?"

Latham stared across the table for a long, speculative moment. His eyes were marblelike, suddenly cold. "You're positive you won't change your mind? Never hurts to sleep on it."

"Put yourself in my boots, Wilbur. What would you do?"

"After today, I'd watch my step real close. You've bought yourself more'n you bargained for."

Latham shoved back his chair. He got to his feet, nodding abruptly, and walked from the barroom. As he watched him out the door, a thought popped unbidden into Clint's mind. He wondered whether he'd done the right thing by Virgil and Elizabeth. But then, just as quickly, he saw that nothing had changed.

In their own way, they'd already told Benton to go to hell. It seemed to run in the family.

18

The herd was strung out in a dusty mile-long column. Virgil rode out front, with the trail boss. Their course was due north, following the Pecos to old Fort Sumner. From there, they would take the Goodnight-Loving Trail into Colorado.

Virgil planned to stick with the drive until they passed Raton. The herd comprised two thousand longhorns and some three hundred head of green-broke mustangs. It was the first of two such herds that would be trailed to Wyoming by early September. The stock was contracted to the Swan Land & Cattle Company, the largest outfit on the High Plains. By cold weather, Virgil calculated he would have banked almost $200,000.

Their path northward was like a wilderness trace. The Goodnight-Loving Trail angled into Colorado outside the town of Trinidad. From there it skirted the banks of the Purgatoire until intersecting the Arkansas River. With the North Star as a beacon, the trail then zigzagged toward the headwaters of the Republican and on across the North Platte. The herd would be delivered another three days' drive northeast of Cheyenne. The distance from Hondo Valley to Wyoming was more than five hundred miles.

At Raton, just short of the Colorado border, Virgil would leave the drive. By train, he would travel from there to Caldwell and on to the Cherokee Outlet ranch. The Cattlemen's Association, as well as his own business affairs, required his presence. While the Outlet would never rival the Hondo, it was nonetheless a profitable operation. His purpose now was to upgrade the stock and make it even more so. Once his business was finished, he would then hop a train for Wyoming. He planned to meet the herd outside Cheyenne.

The situation at Spur was tense. His concern, if anything, had grown stronger in recent days. For the moment, Luis Varga and his sheep were still west of the Hondo. But there was every likelihood that Benton would attempt to provoke an incident. Clint had stopped over at Spur only three days past. He'd got a lead on Benton's former henchmen and was headed south. His recounting of the talk with Wilbur Latham was something of a last straw. There would be no more warnings, no further attempts to work a deal. Benton, when it suited his purpose, would strike where least expected.

Virgil was not a worrier by nature. He knew his absence from Spur might have come at a better time. Still, he'd left instructions with Odell Slater to cover most any situation. As for Elizabeth, he was reassured that her constant shadow, John Taylor, would protect her from harm. The fact that Clint was scouting around the Pecos Valley also relieved his mind. Should Benton strike in his absence, Clint would be there to take charge. All things considered, he'd left Spur in capable hands. He decided not to badger himself with second thoughts.

Life on the trail was a welcome diversion. Virgil enjoyed the rough camaraderie of a cowcamp, and the hands never failed to stir his admiration. Watching them at work, he was reminded that a trail drive was a young man's game. From the man at the point, to the drag rider at the rear, there was hardly a moment's rest once the herd got underway. With only a short noon break, they generally spent fourteen hours a day in the saddle. The choking dust kicked up by the longhorns, added to the blistering heat, took its toll. By sundown, every man in the crew was worn to a frazzle.

At night, the threat of a stampede brought still another burden. A sudden noise, even a shift in the wind, could spook the longhorns and set them off in blind flight. Working staggered shifts, the cowhands rode night guard, with at least two men in the saddle at all times. Thunderstorms, and silvery bolts of lightning, guaranteed that the entire crew would ride night herd. Stories of cowhands crippled and killed in stampedes put all of them on their mettle. No man wanted an unmarked grave alongside the trail.

Once the herd was bedded down, the men wearily collected around the chuck wagon. From a battery of charred Dutch ovens, the cook turned out beans and sourdough biscuits, and an occasional stew. After wolfing down supper, the hands swigged coffee and swapped tales around the fire for a while. Shortly after nightfall, as if by unspoken agreement, the talk ceased and the men crawled gratefully into their sugans. The camp would be up and fed and ready to move a full hour before sunrise. That left precious little time for sleep.

For all the drawbacks, there was no scarcity of men willing to go up the trail. Every spring, riders drifted into Spur, looking for work, eager to start another season. While the usual wage was a dollar a day and found, Virgil paid forty a month. That enabled him to get the pick of the crop and ensured that he was never short on trail crews. But even then, the wages hardly accounted for men being drawn to the grueling and oftentimes dangerous life of a cowhand.

Virgil believed the reason went deeper, touched on the matter of freedom and squareheaded independence. The typical cowhand believed himself the freest man alive, obligated to no one. Unlike ribbon clerks and other workingmen, there were no ties to hold him down. When he got a yen to move on, he collected his wages and rode out. It was the freedom of a horseback vagabond. No roots and no plans beyond tomorrow.

Halting on a low rise, Virgil let his gaze rove out over the herd. Leading them was a brindle steer who had appointed himself pacesetter for the scraggly column. It was one of the enduring curiosities that cowhands often rehashed around a campfire at night. Somehow, on every trail drive a certain steer would assume leadership of the herd. By what strange process he assumed the post was a mystery yet to be solved.

On the first day's march, the brindle had simply moved to the front of the herd and stayed there. The rest of the longhorns tagged along, content to follow in his path and let him set the pace. Whatever the reason for his behavior, the odd-colored steer had been worth his weight in gold since departing the Hondo. He was stringy and long-shanked, and he shuffled along at a ground-eating clip, which meant extra miles covered each day on the trail. Unless he gave out before Wyoming, it looked to be a fairly easy drive.

Virgil's thoughts turned to the Cherokee Outlet. For some time now he'd toyed with the idea of starting a crossbreeding program. What had worked on the Hondo would work equally well in the Outlet. The last obstacle had been removed when he'd signed the lease with the Cherokee Nation. No longer a temporary arrangement, the ranch had now assumed an aspect of permanence. He thought it time to start planning for the future.

A letter had arrived from Floyd Dunn only last week. In it the foreman stated that he'd happened across a blooded Durham bull. The owner was a small rancher who had decided to turn farmer. His place was located outside Medicine Lodge, some seventy miles northwest of Caldwell.

Dunn believed the bull could be bought for a reasonable price, and requested instructions. Virgil's reply advised that he would arrive in Caldwell by the end of June. And yet . . .

Somehow a sense of unease rode with Virgil. However much he looked ahead, a part of his mind was still back on the Hondo. He was too much the realist to think the standoff would last indefinitely. His streak of pragmatism told him it was only a matter of time. Which left the great imponderable.

Where and how would Benton strike? And even more worrisome, who would he try to kill?

Medicine Lodge was located on the banks of a river by the same name. The town's one claim to fame was that a great powwow had been held nearby with the Southern Plains tribes. In 1867, with a good deal of trickery, a peace commmission had established reservations for the Comanche, Kiowa, and Cheyenne. The army required another eight years to enforce the treaty and drive the tribes into Indian Territory. Quanah Parker's band had been the last to surrender.

Virgil and Floyd Dunn rode into town late in June. The foreman had met Virgil's train in Caldwell, leading an extra horse. After a day and a night on the road, they forded the river south of Medicine Lodge in the early forenoon. Compared to Caldwell, the community was slow-paced and conservative, surrounded by small farms. The rich prairie soil had convinced even the diehard ranchers that farming was the wave of the future.

Silas Urschel was waiting for them at the livery stable. A sturdy, thickset man, his beard was dappled with gray and his hair was thinning in a widow's peak. He had settled outside Medicine Lodge in the early 1870s, when cows were the economic mainstay of Kansas. But the steady influx of homesteaders and immigrants had finally convinced him to try farming. Today he hoped to sell his prize bull.

Virgil took to him right away. Urschel was genial and quiet-spoken, clearly reluctant to part with the last of his beef herd. He led the way to a large stall at the rear of the livery stable. Honest to a fault, he explained that he'd had the bull stabled there for the past two months. In that time he had received only one offer, so low that he'd taken it as an insult. He knew what the bull was worth and he wasn't about to be cheated. Times weren't that hard, he allowed, not yet anyway.

The Durham was blocky and massive. A length of rope stretched from a ring in its nose to a broad stanchion. Urschel forked a load of hay into the stall to keep the bull occupied. Virgil approved, for he'd learned that any bull, even domestic stock, was never to be trusted. He opened the stall door and warily circled the Durham. Only a brief inspection was needed to confirm Urschel's high opinion. The bull showed excellent bloodlines.

Outside the stall, Virgil stood for a moment longer studying the Durham. Finally he turned to Urschel. "How much are you asking?"

"Four hundred," Urschel said firmly. "Won't take a dime less."

"Done," Virgil agreed. "Let's draw up a bill of sale."

"Just like that? You're not gonna dicker me down?"

"Tell you the truth, I think I stole him."

"Jee-rusalem!" Urschel howled. "I knew I should've asked more!"

Virgil laughed. "I'll buy you a drink to ease the pain."

The livery stable was at the intersection of First and Main. The Merchants & Drovers Bank was catty-corner from the stable, and directly across the street was a saloon. Still muttering, Urschel led them into the saloon's dim interior. A bartender wearing red sleeve garters stood behind a row of brass beerpulls. Virgil and Dunn ordered beer and Urschel took a whiskey neat. he knew he'd skinned himself, and he seemed to accept it with good humor. He insisted on buying another round.

The talk turned to ranching. Urschel was familiar with affairs in the Outlet, for Indian Territory was only twenty miles south of town. He listened as Virgil explained how he'd formed the Cattlemen's Association and negotiated a lease with the Cherokees. By their third drink Urschel was all but ready to sell out in Kansas and move to the Outlet. His heart clearly wasn't in farming, and Virgil felt a twinge of sympathy. Cows, he observed with no attempt at irony, got into a man's blood.

Something over an hour later they emerged from the saloon. As they stepped through the door, a gunshot sounded from across the street. Outside the bank two men at the hitch rack mounted their horses and began brandishing pistols. Several passersby scurried for cover and suddenly two men with bandannas over their faces ran out of the bank. Waving six-guns, they jumped off the boardwalk and hurried toward their horses. One of them, in the process of mounting, somehow loosened his bandanna. His face was revealed in a glare of sunlight.

Virgil's features were arrested in shock. He watched with blank astonishment as Hendry Brown reined his horse away from the bank. The other robbers hauled their mounts around and fell in beside him. Four abreast, they galloped south along Main street.

A man stepped into the street outside Herrington's Mercantile. On his shirtfront there was the glint of a badge and his pistol was extended at arm's length. He snapped off three quick shots as the robbers hurtled past. None of them were hit and the one on the nearside returned fire. The mercantile's display window exploded in shards of glass.

The robbers thundered out of town. As they splashed through the river crossing, a man in a dark business suit stepped from the bank and hurried into the street. "George Geppert!" he shouted in a wavery voice. "They've killed George Geppert!"

Virgil intercepted the lawman. He quickly explained what he'd seen, identifying one of the robbers as Hendry Brown, town marshal of Caldwell. Floyd Dunn verified his story, and Sam Denn, marshal of Medicine Lodge, looked momentarily stunned. Then, collecting himself, he sounded the call for a posse.

Urschel and several townspeople, as well as Virgil and

Dunn. immediately volunteered. Not three minutes after the first gunshot, Marshal Denn led some twenty armed men in pursuit. Once across the river, they pounded south along a rutted wagon road. Some distance ahead they saw a plume of dust and assumed the robbers were making a run for Indian Territory. The men urged their mounts into a headlong gallop.

A few miles outside town the robbers abruptly veered off the wagon trace. Heading west, they rode toward a mass of hogback ridges known as the Gyp Hills. Their intent, clearly, was to lose the posse in the tangle of twisting arroyos and ravines. But none of them were familiar with the terrain and their luck suddenly turned sour. Hendry Brown led them into a box canyon.

By the time Brown realized his mistake, it was too late. The steep sandstone walls towered fifty feet high, blocking any thought of escape. As he turned back toward the mouth of the canyon, the posse rode into view. With the entrance sealed off, the robbers found themselves trapped, nowhere to turn. Brown ordered them to dismount and take cover.

A fierce gun battle erupted. Marshal Denn positioned half the posse at the canyon mouth, ordering them to keep the outlaws pinned down. The other half he split into two groups, waiting for them to scale the heights on either side of the canyon. From atop the sandstone walls, the men unleashed a withering crossfire. The canyon quickly became a death trap, slugs hissing and buzzing like a cloud of angry hornets. A dirty white handkerchief fluttered from behind the boulder where Hendry Brown had taken cover.

An hour after the holdup the posse rode back into town. Their prisoners included Brown as well as the deputy marshal of Caldwell, Ben Wheeler. The other two robbers gave their names as Bill Smith and John Wesley. Everyone in Medicine Lodge turned out to watch as they were paraded along Main Street. Marshal Denn hustled them into the jailhouse and locked them in separate cells. Outside a crowd of townspeople slowly began to form.

Denn bolted the door and took a pint bottle from the drawer of his desk. He poured himself a stiff drink.

Soon after dark that night the mob stormed the jail. George Geppert, the dead bank teller, had been widely respected throughout the community. His friends and neighbors were in no mood to await a lengthy court trial. Vigilante justice seemed to them more certain, and final.

Marshal Denn, backed by two deputies, offered only token resistance. He had a written confession from Brown, who admitted having faked a manhunt to cover his absence from Caldwell. The mob leaders released Brown and his confederates from their cells and marched them outside. Fully two hundred men, half of them carrying torches, were waiting in cold silence.

Virgil and Floyd Dunn stood on the opposite side of the street. As they watched, Hendry Brown suddenly broke loose from his captors and plunged through the crowd. He dodged clear of outstretched arms and made a run for the corner of the jail. A farmer in tattered overalls stepped forward with a shotgun and triggered both barrels. Brown stumbled, the back of his shirt peppered with red dots, and dropped to the ground. One of the vigilantes rolled him over, briefly searching his face, and nodded to the crowd.

Wheeler and the other robbers were quickly surrounded. Hangman's ropes appeared in the torchlight and the mob moved off toward a grove of trees along the river. Virgil waited until they were a distance away before stepping off the boardwalk. With Dunn a pace behind, he hurried across the street. He knelt down beside Brown, checking for a pulse. The outlaw's eyes slowly rolled open.

"Hendry, it's Virgil Brannock. Can you hear me?"

Brown's head moved in a barely perceptible nod. Virgil leaned closer. "Hendry, a man ought to die with a clear conscience. You've got nothing to lose now."

"What . . ." Brown labored to get his breath—"d'you want?"

"One answer," Virgil said. "Who's behind the rustling in the Outlet? Is it George Hunt?"

A trickle of blood seeped out of Brown's mouth. He smiled, nodding his head, and his eyes drooped shut. His mouth opened in a low sigh and his body went limp. His boot heel drummed the dirt in a spasm of afterdeath.

Virgil climbed to his feet. "Floyd, you stick around and look after that bull. Get him back to the ranch safe and sound."

Dunn stared at him. "Where you headed, Mr. Brannock?"

"Caldwell."

"Tonight?"

"Yeah, tonight."

Late the next morning Virgil rode into Caldwell. He went looking for cattlemen and cowhands from ranches in the Outlet. His thought was to form a citizens' posse and march on the Red Light Saloon. But what he found, instead, was an opportunity lost.

Early that morning a wire had come in from Medicine Lodge. It was sent by Marshal Sam Denn and intended for the mayor of Caldwell. The telegraph operator, who was something of a gadfly, spread the word on his way uptown. Within the hour, the whole town was abuzz with the news. Hendry Brown, caught red-handed robbing a bank, was dead.

An hour later, George Hunt had his buggy brought from the livery. His wife hopped in the front seat and he threw a couple of bags in the rear. Last seen heading north, they had disappeared across the plains. When asked, the bartender at the Red Light had only one comment. Hunt had cleaned out the office safe before taking off.

Virgil was at first confounded. But then, mulling it over, he saw a certain logic at work. Hunt couldn't take the chance that Hendry Brown had talked about the rustling operation. Faced with a hangman's noose, men often traded their darkest secrets in exchange for clemency. So he had run rather than risk what seemed long odds. There were other boomtowns, all ripe for the picking.

For Virgil, it was a moral victory of sorts. By no means would it put an end to rustling in the Outlet. Even a rope and a stout limb were but minor deterrents. Still, the departure of George Hunt was cause for celebration. As of today, he had one less reason to look over his shoulder.

One less enemy on a rather long list.

19

Morg and Brad rode east along the Rio Hondo. By mid-morning they topped the foothills at the end of the basin. Spread out before them was the Pecos Valley.

A chestnut brood mare trailed along behind. Morg had her lead rope tied securely to his saddlehorn, and both the youngsters kept glancing in her direction. As a favor to John Chisum, the mare had been bred to Coaldust, Spur's bloodbay stud. Brad and Morg were returning her now to Jinglebob.

Neither of them questioned the assignment. Odell Slater had singled them out for the job only last night. There was some good-natured grumbling from the other hands, but no one complained too loudly. As for the youngsters themselves, they looked upon it as a lark, two days away from their regular chores. One day over and one day back, with a night spent at Jinglebob.

Brad was particularly elated. He'd heard endless stories about the King of the Pecos and Chisum's mammoth cattle spread. To a former Missouri farmboy, Spur itself had seemed almost beyond comprehension. An outfit more than twice the size of Spur fairly boggled the imagination. He welcomed the opportunity to see it for himself.

A matter of two months had profoundly altered Brad's outlook. He was now a cowhand, the veteran of a trail drive, albeit one of short duration. He'd returned from the railhead with an air of newfound confidence and a Colt six-gun holstered on his hip. His features were weathered by the wind and sun, and he had put on ten pounds of solid muscle. The outward change was but a reflection of an inward attitude. He had begun to think of himself as a Westerner.

Other things had changed as well. Upon returning from the trail drive, he'd noted a curious difference in Jennifer. She was not avoiding him and she was no less personable than before. But she was no longer flirting openly, and she had stopped dogging his every step. Her mysterious turn-around left him bemused, though somewhat relieved. He knew he'd been on the verge of overstepping himself.

Even now, he felt like a man under a spell. Her presence alone was enough to set the blood ringing in his ears. Yet his feelings about her veered wildly, and he restrained himself with ruthless discipline. However much he was tempted, he never forgot that she was young and inexperienced, almost certainly a virgin. Worse, she was the daughter of a kinsman, a blood relation. All things considered, he hoped her change in manner would last, perhaps put even more distance between them. He thought he'd got off lucky.

Morg was no help. Seemingly overnight, the boy had become fixated on girls. Anything that wore skirts was a source of fascination, and he constantly bombarded Brad with questions. He understood the mechanics of what happened between men and women, for cowhands were notorious braggarts. But he was still at sea about the finer points of male conquest, precisely how girls were persuaded to "go all the way." Since he considered Brad his closest friend, as well as a man of the world, no detail was sacrosanct. He wanted to know everything.

For Brad, all the conversation about women was like a yoke. The questions as well as the answers, forced him to think about Jennifer. Which meant that she was rarely out of mind and therefore a continuing source of temptation. Then, too, he was further burdened by Morg's somewhat randy attitude toward the situation. The boy felt his sister was too much the tease for her own good and might one day try it on the wrong man. He thought Brad ought to teach her a lesson.

Today, much to Brad's relief, they finally exhausted the topic of women. Hardly skipping a beat, Morg switched to an altogether different subject. He had been into Lincoln while Brad was away on trail drive. The talk in town was that Sheriff Pat Garrett had boxed himself into a corner. The lawman had sworn to recapture Billy the Kid and he hadn't delivered. Some people were of the opinion that he never would.

"How come?" Brad asked. "He caught the Kid once before."

Morg shrugged. "Folks are sayin' it was outhouse luck. He just stumbled across the Kid that time."

"Who's to say he won't get lucky again?"

"Well, he'd better do it pretty goddarn fast. It's been more than two months since the Kid escaped."

"Yeah, you're right," Brad said thoughtfully. "Seems like someone would have spotted him by now. Hell, they've even got the army on the lookout."

"All the same," Morg said, "nobody's seen hide nor hair of him."

"Wonder where he could've got off to."

"Way I hear it, most everybody figures he skedaddled for Old Mexico. He could stay lost forever south of the border."

"Who'd want to?" Brad scoffed. "One of the fellows on the drive spent the winter down there once. He said it's nothin' but desert and scorpions."

Morg burst out laughing. "Even if it's so, that'd beat getting your neck stretched. Besides, there's all kinds of chili peppers down there."

"Chili peppers?"

"Señoritas!" Morg said, clicking his tongue. "Hot-blooded and hot to trot."

Brad wagged his head. "You ought to stop hangin'

around the bunkhouse so much. Those boys are all wind and no whistle.''

''I dunno about that,'' Morg said, grinning. ''There's them that claim to have seen the elephant. Not shy to talk about it, either . . . like some people I know.''

The goad almost worked. But then, on second thought, Brad decided to stick with outlaws. Their morning had been devoted to the subject of women.

''Tell you one thing,'' he said, straight-faced. ''Cousin Clint wouldn't monkey around the way Garrett's done. By now, he would've buried the Kid.''

At the mention of his uncle, Morg's preoccupation with girls was momentarily distracted. ''Goddang!'' he howled. ''Wouldn't that be something to see. Which one you reckon's the fastest?''

''Search me,'' Brad replied. ''But if they ever squared off, I'd bet money on who'd walk away. And it wouldn't be William Bonney, neither.''

''What makes you say that?''

''Just a hunch,'' Brad admitted. ''Some men weren't meant to be killed. I've got an idea Clint heads the list.''

Morg shared the sentiment. At the moment, his uncle was down around Seven Rivers, presumably hunting an outlaw. No one knew Clint's exact whereabouts, and there was an unwritten rule that the family never discussed his activities. Yet the boy took considerable comfort in the knowledge that his uncle was within riding distance of Spur.

While he rarely displayed it, there was a serious side to Morg's nature. He secretly worried that his father's trip to Kansas, and then on to Wyoming, was both ill-timed and potentially ruinous. The antagonism between his father and Stephen Benton was troublesome enough. But now, with his mother's involvement, it had assumed the overtones of a vendetta. He'd heard the talk in the bunkhouse, and he agreed with the hands. Spur, and the Rio Hondo, were about to become a battleground.

"Brad."

"Yeah?"

"Lemme ask you something on the square."

Brad gave him a sidelong look. "Fire away."

"I've been thinking about those sheep."

"What about 'em?"

Morg glanced around. "You reckon Varga intends to push 'em across the Hondo?"

Brad was silent for a time. He sensed something unspoken behind the question. "Why ask me?" he said finally. "What's your pa say about it?"

"He don't say nothin', leastways not to me. He still thinks I'm green as a gourd."

"But you've figured it out for youself—right?"

"Only about halfway," Morg said. "I'd like to hear what you've got to say."

"Well . . ." Brad hesitated, then went on. "Unless I miss my guess, Varga aims to do it. Otherwise, he would've trailed them sheep back to home ground."

"What's he waitin' on, then?"

"I wish I had a crystal ball. I'd like to know myself."

"Suppose you had to take a stab at it, though. What would you say?"

Brad frowned. "I'd say he's waitin' for your pa to come back. Takes two to make a shootin' war."

"Yeah, that's the way I figured it too."

Morg averted his gaze. His features were suddenly downcast, and a thick silence settled between them. Watching him, Brad saw the youngster age before his eyes. There seemed no need to state what was still unspoken. What they were both thinking.

Virgil Brannock had been marked for death.

Jinglebob was everything Brad had expected. He and Morg rode in with the mare shortly before sundown. They dismounted outside the large double doors of the stables.

An ancient *mexicano* hurried out to take charge of the

mare. He spoke to her in a low, affectionate voice and slipped her a cube of sugar from his pocket. The mare responded with a chuffing snort and gently nuzzled his chest. The old man grinned, rubbing her velvety muzzle.

Brad turned to survey the compound. His gaze swept the bunkhouses and outbuildings and the corral. A bunch of cowhands, laughing and joshing among themselves, trooped into the mess hall. Looking toward the main house, he unwittingly drew a mental comparison with Spur. There was a similarity in the layout, even though Jinglebob was built on a grander scale. He found himself suitably impressed.

A woman emerged from the house. As she walked toward the stables, Brad immediately identified her as Sallie Chisum. Earlier, while they were discussing women, Morg had explained that the Chisum girl was stuck on his Uncle Clint. He'd laughed about it, adding that Clint would never allow any woman to clip his wings. But now, looking her over closely, Brad told himself it was a terrible waste. She was svelte and graceful, one of the most attractive women he'd ever seen. He thought Clint ought to reconsider.

Morg performed the introductions. Sallie smiled graciously, welcoming Brad to Jinglebob. She inquired about the mare and Morg awkwardly replied that everything had worked out. Not for the first time, Brad noted that Western women exhibited no great embarrassment about the mating habits of livestock. He watched as Sallie inspected the mare with a critical eye. At length, she nodded to the old *mexicano*.

"*Gracias*, Miguel."

"*Sí, maestra*."

The *mexicano* bobbed his head, addressing her in the formal manner. He turned, clucking softly, and led the mare into the stables. Sallie followed him with her eyes, silent a moment. Then she looked around with a warm smile.

"Miguel believes horses are a superior race of people. He's been with Uncle John more than twenty years."

"No foolin'?" Morg sounded surprised. "That'd mean he came with Mr. Chisum from Texas."

"Yes," Sallie said wistfully. "A long time ago."

"How's your uncle gettin' along these days?"

"Not too well, I'm afraid. But he'll be delighted to see you. He thinks the sun rises and sets on your father."

Brad cleared his throat. "We don't want to be any bother, Miss Chisum. The bunkhouse would suit us just fine."

"Nonsense,' she protested. "We have plenty of room in the big house. And I insist you call me Sallie."

"Only if you call me Brad."

She laughed and led the way to the main house. Brad and Morg were shown to their rooms by one of the servants. Fresh water was fetched and they were allowed time to wash off the trail dust. A short while later supper was served in the large dining room. Four places were set, and when they entered, John Chisum was already seated at the head of the table. His general appearance left them both unsettled.

Chisum clearly belonged in bed. While he greeted them cordially enough, his ravaged face was that of a seriously ill man. His coloring was blotchy and his eyes were circled by bruised-looking brown rings. Throughout the meal, he picked at his food, eating hardly anything. From the other end of the table, Sallie watched him with a worried expression.

The conversation took an odd turn. Chisum spoke of long-ago cattle drives and the early days, when he'd first settled at South Spring. At one point he launched into a rambling, disconnected monologue on Cochise, the fearsome Apache war chief of a decade ago. His distant, preoccupied gaze was that of a man whose thoughts were forever fixed in the past. He talked as though there were no tomorrows, only yesterdays.

Listening to him, Brad was struck by a wayward thought. Dime novels, which were all the rage back East, had made household names of such stalwarts as Buffalo Bill Cody and Wild Bill Hickok. Yet the great majority of Americans had never heard of John Chisum or Charles Goodnight, much less Virgil Brannock. The men who'd actually won the West, defying a hostile land and the horseback tribes, were virtually unknown. It seemed somehow unjust, an inequitable wrong.

Brad suddenly thought himself fortunate. He was privileged to share a meal with a man who was already a legend among Westerners. John Chisum, who looked all too mortal tonight, was one of a dying breed. To Brad, the old cattleman seemed a mythical figure, at once wise and courageous. A symbol of a passing era.

He sat spellbound as John Chisum talked on.

The following day was hot and sticky. As Brad and Morg rode west along the Hondo, they saw thunderheads over the distant mountains. There was a close stillness in the air.

By noontime they were approaching the foothills. Sallie Chisum had packed them a lunch of cold chicken and bread and they stopped beside the river. There, under a leafy stand of cottonwoods, they ate in silence. Neither of them had much to say about their night at Jinglebob. The memory of the dying rancher was still too sharp.

After they had eaten, Morg seemed in better spirits. He'd been itching to try Brad's new six-gun and he suggested a round of target practice. A short distance upstream there was a dead cottonwood, and they walked in that direction. Brad used a jagged rock to edge a bull's-eye on the trunk of the tree.

Morg fired first. From the accustomed ten paces, he took a sideways stance. He brought the Colt to shoulder level and carefully aligned the sights. After each shot, he lowered his arm, studying the target. When he finished, he grunted coarsely to himself. Four shots were in the bull's-eye and one was just outside the ring.

"Should've done better," he said. "I jerked the trigger on that last shot."

"Still pretty good," Brad allowed. "Four out of five isn't nothin' to sneeze at."

"Well, it wasn't the gun's fault. You got yourself one that shoots dead center."

Brad reloaded without comment. His arm leveled and he snapped off three shots as fast as he could thumb the hammer. Then he holstered the Colt, squaring himself to the tree, and drew and fired. He repeated the drill, his draw somewhat smoother on the last shot. He was no gunslinger but he'd mastered the rudiments of close-range point shooting. All five shots were within the bull's-eye.

"Kee-rist!" Morg whooped. "You've been practicin'!"

"Yeah, I have," Brad acknowledged. "Burned up three boxes of shells comin' back from the trail drive."

"You boys ain't bad a'tall."

The voice jerked them around. A horseman loomed on the riverbank above them. Brad was suddenly aware that he'd holstered an empty gun. He sensed the horseman had waited for him to fire the last shot before speaking out. His concern took a sharp upturn when Morg whispered out of the corner of his mouth, "Billy the Kid."

Bonney stepped down out of the saddle. His eyes never left them as he worked his way down the riverbank. Brad was amazed by the young outlaw's slight build and short stature. He figured he was a full head taller and at least forty pounds heavier. Then, quickly, he reminded himself that looks were deceiving. The Kid, for all his size, was a stone-cold killer.

Morg plastered a grin on his face. "How you doing, Billy?"

"So-so," Bonney said, dead-eyed. "Who's your friend?"

"Oh, this here's my cousin, Brad Dawson."

Bonney made no offer to shake hands. He fixed Brad with a pale stare. "Where'd you learn to shoot, cousin?"

Brad ignored the sarcastic tone. "Here and there," he said quietly. "I've got a ways to go yet."

Morg shuffled uneasily. "We heard you were in Old Mexico, Billy. Everybody figured you was long gone."

"They figured wrong," Bonney said with a lopsided smile. "I hang my hat wherever it takes my fancy."

"Guess you know the sheriff's out to nail you?"

"Fat lotta good that'll do him! Pat Garrett couldn't find his ass with both hands."

"Well, I was just tellin' you," Morg added lamely. "There's a pretty hefty price on your head."

Bonney laughed a wild braying laugh. "Anybody comes huntin' me, they'll wind up in the boneyard. I won't be caught again."

Brad looked at him. "We know someone of the same opinion."

"Yeah, who's that?"

"A relative of ours . . . Clint Brannock."

Bonney gave him the fisheye. "You sayin' Clint's on my trail?"

"Nope," Brad answered. "Not that I've heard."

"Good," Bonney said, still staring at him. "You tell Clint I've got no bone to pick with the Brannocks. Leave be and let be, that's my motto."

Brad kept his gaze level. "I'll pass it along."

"Say, Billy," Morg cut in. "How about showin' us what you can do with a gun? We'd sure admire to see you shoot."

Bonney halfway lifted his pistol from the holster. Unlike most gunmen, he carried a double-action Colt Lightning, chambered for .41 caliber. His eyes took on a peculiar glitter and he grinned ferociously.

"Never show your tricks," he said in a soft, menacing lilt. "Otherwise you're liable to end up with an empty gun on your hip. Ain't that so, Cousin Brad?"

Brad merely stared at him. Bonney put two fingers to his mouth and let go a shrill whistle. His horse obediently moved down the bank and halted at his side. He stepped into the saddle, nodding to them, and forded the river. On the opposite side, he rode north.

Morg muttered an unintelligible oath. His eyes were still on the Kid. "Where you reckon he's headed?"

"To hell," Brad said. "He's got a one-way ticket."

Before they mounted, Brad took time to load his Colt. Their meeting with the young outlaw had been an instructive experience. As he swung aboard his horse, he made himself a promise.

He'd never again be caught with an empty gun.

20

Through the gathering dusk Clint rode into Jinglebob. The bunkhouses were ablaze with light and voices carried distinctly across the compound. He reined his buckskin toward the stables.

A dull and grinding weariness settled over him. For the past three weeks his watchword had been vigilance, wary caution. His nerves were gritty and raw, and he felt oddly unassured about the days ahead. He realized now there were damned few answers in life. Only tough questions.

The date was July 16. Almost a month ago, in Santa Fe, he'd uncovered a lead that took him south. An old and reliable source had tipped him that Claude Gentry, the former attorney general, might be found in the Seven Rivers country. Gentry, according to rumor, was accompanied by his onetime assistant, Fred Peterson.

Seven Rivers was a remote stretch of back country. Located east of the Guadalupe Mountains, it was watered by several streams that flowed into the Pecos. The area was a stronghold of small ranchers who had aligned themselves with the Santa Fe Ring during the Lincoln County War. They were avowed enemies of John Chisum, their principal sideline rustling Jinglebob livestock.

No better sanctuary existed for Gentry and Peterson. Hostility toward Chisum and the Brannocks still ran high. Clint rode there with the foreknowledge that lawmen were not welcome. A lawman named Brannock merely doubled the customary antagonism. One miscue, the slightest unguarded moment, and his life would have been forfeit. He never once relaxed his vigilance.

In the end, his search came to nothing After weeks of scouting the Seven Rivers country, he'd uncovered the worst possible news. Fred Peterson had been killed in a saloon shootout with a total stranger, a man who passed himself off as a saddle tramp. There was talk that Peterson had been goaded into an argument, and drunkenly pulled his gun. The saddle tramp had vanished within an hour of the shooting.

Clint was skeptical of the whole affair. He had a hunch the saddle tramp was a hired killer, sent there from Santa Fe. His suspicion was confirmed when he learned that Claude Gentry had made a run for Old Mexico. Hidden out at a ranch, Gentry had taken off upon hearing of Peterson's death. No fool, the former attorney general had realized it was only a matter of time. His name was next on the list.

From the vantage of hindsight Clint saw that a sequence of events had unfolded. Once he'd turned down Benton's offer of a truce, an alternative plan had been put into effect. The simplest solution was to remove the men who could bear witness, Claude Gentry and Fred Peterson. A gunman, posing as a drifter, had been dispatched to Seven Rivers. While he'd failed to kill both men, Gentry's disappearing act had served the same purpose. Any link to the Santa Fe Ring had now been severed.

For a brief moment Clint had considered crossing the border. But it was a passing idea, quickly shunted aside. Tracking Gentry across Old Mexico would have proved an exercise in futility. The country was too vast and the people there were leery of *gringo* lawmen. He figured it was better to bide his time, return to Santa Fe. His best hope now was to place Gentry's wife and family under surveillance. Sooner or later a fugitive always grew restless, and careless.

At the stables, the old *mexicano* took charge of his

buckskin. Clint walked up to the house and found Sallie seated on the porch swing. Her uncle had retired shortly after supper and she'd come outside for a breath of air. She seemed curiously unnerved by Clint's appearance.

"I've been thinking about you," she said. "You've been on my mind almost constantly since yesterday."

"What happened yesterday?"

"You haven't heard?"

"Heard what?"

"Billy . . ." She faltered, then went on. "William Bonney was killed night before last at Fort Sumner."

"I'll be damned," Clint said, clearly surprised. "Was it Pat Garrett that got him?"

"Yes."

The details were still sketchy. From news forwarded to her uncle, Sallie had only a general idea of what had occurred. It seemed Pat Garrett had traced the Kid to Fort Sumner, an abandoned army post on the northern Pecos. Pete Maxwell, a rancher, had established quarters in some of the old buildings. He was known to be a friend of the young outlaw.

Late at night, Garrett had slipped into Maxwell's bedroom. On the porch, two deputies were posted near the door. As he was questioning the rancher, Garrett heard the Kid's voice from outside, demanding that the deputies identify themselves. Before the deputies could reply, the Kid stepped through the door into Maxwell's bedroom. Garrett, with no warning whatever, shot him dead.

"It figures," Clint said when she finished. 'Garrett knew the Kid wouldn't come along without a fight. I reckon it was shoot first and ask questions later."

"Isn't that rather . . . coldblooded?"

"So's a hanging," Clint observed, "and the Kid was headed for the gallows. I suspect he would've preferred to get it quick."

"Perhaps you're right."

Sallie seemed oddly distracted. She led him into the

house and fixed him a cold supper. As he ate, she told him of the visit four days earlier by Morg and Brad. He then inquired after her uncle's health, listening without comment as she talked. She neither asked where he'd been nor did he volunteer any information. In all the time they'd known each other, he had never once spoken to her of his work.

Following supper, they strolled down to the river. In the dark, fireflies darted among the trees and the purl of the water was a low murmur. They paused under a willowy cottonwood, dimly visible beneath a moonless sky. She was close enough to touch, and her nearness seemed to him an invitation. He rolled himself a cigarette instead.

The soft glow of starlight shadowed her features. Her hair was drawn sleekly to the nape of her neck, tied with a ribbon, accentuating the smooth contours of her profile. She smelled sweet and alluring, and he was struck again by her loveliness. Yet, as in times past, he remained wary of involvement. She was not a woman to be trifled with or taken lightly. He kept his hands to himself.

Watching him, Sallie longed to feel his arms about her She was drawn to him in some way she couldn't define, and each time they were together the attraction became all the more compelling. Behind his hard exterior, she saw a man capable of gentleness and great sensitivity. She wanted him, but she'd decided she couldn't wait forever. He either felt the same way or he didn't, and tonight was the night to find out. She had no intention of ending up an old maid.

"You remember William Roberts, don't you?"

"Bill Roberts?" Clint asked. "Works at the mercantile in Lincoln?"

"Yes, that's the one."

"What about him?"

Her heart pounded and her throat went dry. She forced herself to say it quickly. "We've been seeing each other off and on. He's asked me to marry him."

There was a stark silence. Clint took a long drag on his

cigarette, uncomfortably aware that he was being put to
the test. He was genuinely fond of her, but he was not a
man who revealed his innermost feelings easily. Nor was
he able to explain that he was not ready for matrimony, an
end to a lifetime of wanderlust. He tried not to hurt her.

"I've always liked Roberts. He's a good man, steady."

She felt as if her insides had turned to stone. "Yes, he's
very dependable."

"Not like me," Clint said lightly. "A man in my line of
work, no tellin' where he'll wind up. You just never
know."

Her voice was husky, but she met his gaze steadily. "I
suppose that would never be a worry with Bill. A woman
could rely on him to always come home."

Clint managed a strained smile. "He'll make you a
good husband, Sallie. I wish you both the best."

"Thank you, Clint."

Her eyes misted and she smiled an upside-down smile.
She brushed his lips with a soft kiss, then turned and
walked back toward the house. Clint looked stolidly ahead,
staring out across the river.

He felt a strange sense of loss.

Early the next afternoon Clint topped the foothills guard-
ing Hondo Valley. He reined to a halt and sat for a time
studying the pastoral setting. At such moments, he experienced a feeling akin to homecoming.

All the way from the Jinglebob he'd been in a reflective
mood. But now, gazing down on the Hondo, he understood one of the reasons for his wanderlust. The concept of
"home" had long since become foreign to his nature. He
was reminded of an old rhyme, thought to have been
penned by a long-dead mountain man.

> My books are the brook,
> and my sermons the stones,
> My parson a wolf on a pulpit of bones.

Why he'd memorized it had never before been clear. Yet he saw now that the words aptly described the way he had chosen to live. He roamed the plains and mountains because the quiet solitude of the wilderness fed some need deep within himself. When he thought of home, it was always the place where Virgil and Elizabeth dwelled. He went there to visit because the pull of family was a powerful force. His stays were short because he forever heard the lure of a stronger call.

Elizabeth greeted him warmly. The boys were off working cattle and Jennifer had gone for a ride. After taking his hat, Elizabeth handed him an envelope sealed with wax. Her eyes sparkling with curiosity, she commented that a trooper from Fort Stanton had delivered it only yesterday. Clint tore open the envelope and quickly scanned a dispatch couched in concise military terms. He read it through again with a bemused expression.

"How about that," he said quizzically. "Mackenzie's at Fort Stanton. He wants to see me."

"Colonel Mackenzie?" Elizabeth inquired. "Your old commander?"

Clint tapped the dispatch. "According to the signature it's not 'colonel' anymore. He's been promoted to brigadier general."

"Does it say what he wants?"

"Not a clue," Clint remarked. "Hope to God it's nothin' about Lon. I'll ride over there tomorrow."

Elizabeth nodded absently. "Perhaps it's about your investigation. Were you able to learn anything at Seven Rivers?"

Clint briefly recounted the details of his manhunt. His tone was disgruntled, almost dour. "Benton's shrewd," he concluded. "So far, I've hit a blank wall."

Elizabeth appeared thoughtful. "One thing he can't hide is the land frauds. We're preparing a lawsuit against him right now."

"Has he got wind of it yet?"

"Until it's filed, there's no way for him to know. Why do you ask?"

"Just a hunch," Clint said in a dead monotone. "Be on the lookout the day the word leaks out. I'd wager that's the day Luis Varga drives his sheep across the Hondo."

She walked to the sofa and took a seat. Her face was lined with worry and she made no direct reply. At length Clint dropped into a chair opposite her. "What do you hear from Virgil?"

"His last letter was dated the second. By now he's on his way to Wyoming."

"Any idea when he'll be home?"

"I wouldn't think before the end of the month."

Her voice was troubled, vaguely upset. Clint sought to distract her onto other matters. He tried for a breezy tone. "Stopped by Jinglebob on the way here."

"Oh?" she said without much interest.

"Guess you haven't heard the news. Sallie Chisum and Bill Roberts are going to get hitched. She told me so herself."

Elizabeth suddenly sat straighter. She stared at him with shocked round eyes. "You're an absolute fool, Clint Brannock! You jilted her, didn't you?"

Clint winced. "How could I jilt her? We weren't keeping company."

"She would have married you in an instant! You know it very well, too."

"Who, me?" Clint mugged, hands outstretched. "You've got the wrong fellow, Beth. I'm not the marryin' kind."

"Tommyrot!" she fumed. "You're stuck in a rut, that's what you are!"

A thought tugged at the corner of Clint's mind. In a moment of insight, he realized he'd done Sallie Chisum an injustice. For years now, he had been comparing other women to Elizabeth, and they all suffered in the bargain. What he sought was a mirror image of the woman seated opposite him. Yet he'd never found one who even came close.

There was a twinge of guilt in the realization. She was, after all, his brother's wife. Still, on closer examination, he felt Virgil would not be offended. No man could help but admire Elizabeth. Nor was it possible to ignore her looks. She was beautiful as well as intelligent. And she had backbone, nerves like steel. A most uncommon combination.

"Well?" she demanded, interrupting his reverie. "Aren't you going to say anything?"

Clint knuckled his mustache. "What's to say? I guess I'll just have to keep lookin'."

"You're impossible!"

"That's what all the ladies tell me."

A faint simile curved the corners of her mouth. She gave him an affectionate look, and then, unable to contain herself, she laughed a low throaty laugh. Clint grinned like a tiger drunk on catnip.

He'd never before felt so close to a woman.

Sergeant Major Jack Quincannon ushered Clint into the office. The Fort Stanton garrison commander was notably absent. Ranald Mackenzie sat behind the desk.

The door closed and Clint halted before the desk. Mackenzie, with the single star of a brigadier general on his shoulder boards, rose from his chair. He extended his hand.

"I expected you yesterday, Mr. Brannock."

The formal tone alerted Clint to trouble. He shook hands with a sober expression. "I only got your message yesterday, General. Congratulations on the promotion."

"Thank you," Mackenzie said, motioning him to a chair. "Quite frankly, General Sherman feels the Apache campaign has been bungled. He's appointed me to take charge of all field operations."

"I knew it was bad," Clint said. "What's Victorio up to now?"

Mackenzie looked at him strangely. "Apparently you've been out of touch."

"Yeah, I have," Clint remarked. "Spent the last three weeks down in Seven Rivers country."

"Then I'm pleased to inform you that Victorio is dead."

Victorio was a Membreno Apache war chief. Some months before, he had led his band off the Warm Springs reservation. In a running fight with cavalry units, he had eluded capture and crossed the border into Old Mexico. From there, he and his warriors had raided across the Rio Grande with virtual impunity.

Mackenzie picked up the story at that point. A Mexican army detachment had recently trapped Victorio's band in the Tres Castillos Mountains. Victorio and sixty warriors, along with eighteen women and children, had perished in a savage battle. Only fifteen warriors, and perhaps twice that many women and children, had survived the fight. They were now led by a Membreno subchief, Nana.

A large topographical map was affixed to the wall. Mackenzie indicated a spot in Chihuahua, the northernmost Mexican province. There the Membrenos led by Nana had crossed the Rio Grande into New Mexico Territory. Headed north, they left in their wake the bloated corpses of several sheepherders and a party of prospectors. Three days past, a band of twenty-five Mescalero Apache had jumped the reservation and joined the Membrenos.

Turning west, Nana then led his strengthened war party into the Sacramento Mountains. Only two days ago, in Alamo Canyon, the Apache had ambushed a patrol of Ninth Cavalry troopers. Operating out of Fort Stanton, the patrol was caught in a withering crossfire and cut to ribbons. The grisly remains of the dead had been brought into the post just yesterday. Among the survivors was the regiment's chief of scouts.

"Needless to say," Mackenzie concluded, "I relieved him on the spot. I'm looking for a new chief of scouts."

"Hold on, General," Clint said quickly. "You know

damn well I'm involved in an investigation. So don't look
at me."

Mackenzie's headshake was slow and emphatic. "The
Santa Fe Ring can wait, Mr. Brannock. People are being
killed by the Apache *right now*."

"Yessir, I understand," Clint said in a carefully measured voice. "But there's a chance the Ring will move
against my family pretty quick. I figure I ought to hang
around."

"Correct me if I'm wrong," Mackenzie said crisply. "I
believe you are still under commission to the U.S. Army.
Am I mistaken or not?"

Clint looked him directly in the eyes. "I could always
resign, General."

"You could but you won't, Mr. Brannock. For if you
attempt it, I will have you thrown in the stockade."

Clint's jawline hardened. "I never knew you to play
dirty pool before."

Mackenzie's expression darkened. His hand balled into
a fist and his eyes turned metallic. He stared at Clint with
a cold, prophetic look.

"I intend to resolve the Apache problem for all time,
Mr. Brannock. You were of great service to me when we
drove the Comanche from the Staked Plains. I expect no
less of you now."

Clint remembered that ominous tone of voice. Mackenzie was a brilliant tactician and a ruthless fighter. The
Apache would be pursued and relentlessly attacked, whipped
into submission. No quarter would be granted, for Mackenzie never practiced mercy on the battlefield. Any Apache
who resisted would be killed.

The same attitude applied to Clint. His choice was to
serve as chief of scouts or sit out the campaign in the
guardhouse. Either way, the Santa Fe Ring, and Stephen
Benton, would have to wait. He finally nodded agreement
to Mackenzie.

"Sounds like I just volunteered. When do we start?"

"Today," Mackenzie said brusquely. "You will report to Captain Gilford, commander of D Troop. He already has his orders."

"One last thing, General."

"Yes?"

"You and me are quits the day the campaign ends. I'll give you my resignation in writing."

"Do as you see fit, Mr. Brannock."

Clint walked to the door. With his hand on the knob, he looked back. "How were things with Lon when you left Fort Sill?"

"No worse," Mackenzie commented dryly, 'and no better. Your nephew has all the makings of a renegade, Mr. Brannock. He thrives on trouble."

For a moment Clint seemed on the verge of another question. Then, with an abrupt nod, he went through the door. As the latch clicked, Mackenzie turned and stared at the large campaign map. His eyes were opaque, somehow stoic.

He estimated it would take ten days for Nana's raiding party. That left only one Apache war chief, a horseback barbarian with the mind of a strategist. His name was Geronimo.

21

Virgil arrived in Cheyenne toward the end of July. Outside town he rejoined the trail herd contracted to the Swan Land & Cattle Company. The ranch headquarters, located on the banks of the Chugwater, was a three-day drive north.

A war of words had delayed Virgil's departure from the Cherokee Outlet. As he'd originally predicted, the lease arrangement with the Cherokee Nation proved to be a short-lived secret. Once the news hit Washington, an uproar swept through the halls of government. Overnight, a campaign was orchestrated to oust the cattlemen from Indian lands.

There was a certain bureaucratic lunacy to the events of the past month. The Department of Interior at first issued a broadside of charges against the Cattlemen's Association. By law the Cherokee were forbidden to live in the Outlet, much less lease it to white men. While grazing permits might have been overlooked, there was no defensible excuse for the erection of permanent buildings. Clearly the Cherokee Nation had been hoodwinked by disreputable ranchers.

With the culprit firmly fixed in the public eye, the bureaucrats then went to work in earnest. The Secretary of Interior issued a directive ordering the cattlemen to remove their bunkhouses and line camps within twenty days. Should they refuse, he further requested that the War Department furnish troops to destroy all buildings erected in the Outlet. Everyone at Interior thought it a masterstroke, and sat back to await results.

A slight hitch developed. So far as the War Department was concerned, the military was being asked to pull Interior's chestnuts out of the fire. The Bureau of Indian Affairs had bollixed itself into another mess, and as usual, it was the army who would be required to do the fighting. Worse, there was disturbing news that some hothead named Brannock was all but daring the government to try moving the ranchers out. Ever conscious of their image, the generals cringed at the thought of taking the field against white men.

The Secretary of War bounced the problem back to Interior. In an artfully worded communiqué, he requested that the War Department be shown provisions of law which would protect the army from legal redress should it destroy private property within the Outlet. As an instrument of bureaucratic convolution, the request was without equal. Officials over at Interior were thunderstruck by the communiqué. As the army well knew, there were no such laws.

The Bureau of Indian Affairs found itself juggling a political bombshell. Without army troops to enforce its order, Interior was left in an untenable position. A new directive was quickly issued, instructing the Indian agent for the Nations to conduct an exhaustive investigation. In Washington circles it was rumored the agent had also been instructed to take his time. The best solution for all concerned was to let it quietly fade from the newspapers.

While the furor raged in Washington, Virgil put on a bold front. He stated publicly, and loudly, that nothing less than a full-scale campaign by the army could evict the cattlemen from their leased grazing lands. It was a monumental bluff, for the Association was, by law, a trespasser in the Outlet. His one hope was that the bureaucrats would muddy the water so badly that the main issue would become obscured. Their antics, in the end, far exceeded his expectations.

Never one to delude himself, Virgil knew he'd won

little more than a breathing spell. Of all politicians, none were more vindictive than petty bureaucrats made to appear the fool. The Interior Secretary and the Commissioner of Indian Affairs would neither forget nor forgive. They would bide their time, receptive to any skulduggery that might oust the Association from Cherokee lands. From a pragmatic standpoint, the fight had only just begun.

Wyoming was a pleasant respite. Once more with the trail drive, Virgil rode out front with the herd boss. Before them lay a shimmering sea of grass, lapping in unbroken waves as far as the eye could see. For cattlemen accustomed to the Southwest, where graze was sometimes sparse, the northern plains were an impressive sight. He'd heard it said that Wyoming had one month of spring, thirty days of summer, and ten feet of snow the rest of the year. Yet there was no denying the abundance of rich grazeland.

North of Cheyenne a carpet of emerald green swayed in the breeze. Over the grayish snarl of buffalo grass, the hardier bluestem grew thick and lush, tall enough to hide a suckling calf. Wildflowers of every description flourished alongside the grasses, as if an artist gone mad with color had daubed the landscape. The prairie had fattened millions of buffalo for untold centuries, and longhorns thrived on such graze. High Plains cattlemen looked upon it with biblical reverence. To them, it was the Promised Land.

Following the uprising of 1876, a peace treaty had been negotiated with the Sioux and the Northern Cheyenne. Except for reservation boundaries, a vast rangeland greater than all of Texas was transformed into public domain. Stockmen were at last free to graze their herds north of the Platte, and Texas cattle began funneling up the Goodnight-Loving Trail. Within the span of five years, more than a million longhorns were trailed onto the unsurveyed grasslands of Montana and Wyoming.

News of the beef bonanza quickly bridged the Atlantic. Lords and dukes, titled foreigners with funds to invest, were soon clamoring to join the boom. Absentee ownership shortly became commonplace, with English and Scots nobility widely represented. Cattlemen were also quick to recognize the advantages of entering into partnership with monied foreigners. One of the first to do so was a rancher who had contracted for two herds of Spur livestock. His name was Alexander Swan.

In 1873, Alex Swan had established a fledgling operation on the Big Laramie River. Though he prospered, he was a man who envisioned on a grand scale. Before long he joined forces with a Scottish syndicate which placed almost four million dollars at his disposal. The land he purchased outright lay along the Chugwater, a tributary of the Big Laramie, and amounted to less than ten square miles. From the Union Pacific Railroad, he then took an option to buy alternate sections totaling thirty-eight square miles. The interlocking grids were shrewdly located along rivers and streams.

By 1880, the Swan Land & Cattle Company stretched westward from Nebraska to Wyoming, and south from the Union Pacific tracks to the Platte River. All told, Alex Swan claimed twenty thousand square miles of rangeland, most of it public domain. Like other cattle barons, he kept his empire free of homesteaders by controlling access to the waterways. His Two Bar brand was to the High Plains what the Jinglebob was to the Southwest. A dominant force in territorial affairs, he was the founder of the Wyoming Stock Growers Association. Horse thieves and rustlers were known to steer wide of his headquarters on the Chugwater.

Some people accused Swan of high-handed tactics. To Virgil's way of thinking, it was a matter of a man holding, and protecting, what he'd carved from the wilderness. His situation on the Rio Hondo was little different from what Swan faced in Wyoming. There were those who coveted what others had built with the sweat of their labors. Whether it was land or cattle, or a herd of horses, nothing was secure unless a man was willing to draw the line. Having drawn it, he then had to prove he was a man of his word. Any transgressor must be made to pay a stiff penalty.

Three days out of Cheyenne the herd forded the Chugwater. Virgil rode ahead to the ranch headquarters, which was a mile or so upstream. He saw Alex Swan only once a year, but it was always a memorable meeting. Their attitude was one of mutual admiration, hard-won respect.

Neither of them ever went back on his word.

The plains swept onward like an amber ocean until, at the far horizon, the earth appeared to curl upward and join the molten sunset. A winged speck swooped low over the Chugwater and glided past on silent wings.

Virgil stood on the porch of the main house. He puffed his cigar, watching the nighthawk rise and soar gracefully into the sky. Whenever he visited, Margaret Swan always prepared a gargantuan supper in his honor. Tonight was no exception and he found himself pleasantly stuffed.

Alex Swan had suggested brandy on the porch. Virgil preceded him outside, pausing to light a cigar. As the nighthawk faded from sight, his thoughts unwittingly turned to the Hondo Valley. With the herd delivered, and his business completed, he was suddenly anxious to start for home. He'd been away too long and he sensed a quickening apprehension. It was time to return.

A letter from Elizabeth had been waiting for him in Cheyenne. Her tone was chatty and she'd written nothing to cause him alarm. Still, by reading between the lines, he gathered that she herself was concerned. She spoke of Clint being dragooned to scout against the Apache, off somewhere now with the Ninth Cavalry. That, more than anything else, put Virgil in a troubled mood. In his absence, he had relied on Clint to look after things at Spur. But Clint was gone and Elizabeth's letter was almost two weeks old. He told himself nothing had happened, and he halfway believed it. The other half left him worried, vaguely on edge.

"Here you go, Virgil."

Alex Swan appeared in the doorway. A ruddy-faced man with a walrus mustache, he had broad features topped by close-cropped hair. He extended a glass of brandy.

"Happy days," he said, lifting his own glass in a toast. "Always good to have you on the Two Bar."

Virgil clinked glasses. "Always good to be here, Alex."

Sipping their drinks, they stood by the porch banister. At supper, Virgil had regaled his hosts with stories of bureaucratic high jinks in the Outlet. But now Swan noted his old friend's somber attitude. He cocked one eye in a questioning look.

"Anything you want to talk about?"

"What do you mean?"

"C'mon, Virgil! I've known you too long. Why'd you get down-in-the-mouth so sudden?"

"Nothing sudden about it. I've been in a stew ever since I got to Cheyenne."

Virgil quickly recounted the situation on the Rio Hondo. Covering only the salient details, he stressed the sinister nature of the Santa Fe Ring. He went on to relate the gist of Elizabeth's letter.

"Tell you the truth," he concluded, "I damn near hopped a train in Cheyenne. I've got a feeling I should've headed home."

"Where'd you spend the night in Cheyenne?"

"The Drover's House," Virgil replied. "Where I always stay."

"There's your answer," Swan pointed out. "Any trouble brewing, I just suspect Beth would have wired you. Sounds like you're jumping at shadows."

"Maybe," Virgil conceded. "All the same, I'm a long ways from home."

Swan took a swig of brandy. "Want some advice?"

"Why not?" Virgil said, and chuckled. "You're gonna give it to me anyway."

"Forget the rules," Swan said with great relish. "Ben-

ton and his crowd don't stick to the straight and narrow.
Why should you?"

"What are you trying to say?"

Swan gave him a hard wise look. "Do unto others
before they do unto you. Don't wait for him to strike the
first blow."

"Wouldn't be easy," Virgil said after a moment. "Benton's hands are lily white. Somebody else always does his
dirty work."

"Why waste your time with hired hands? Your fight's
with the he-wolf."

"Alex, you ought to meet my brother sometime. You
two think an awful lot alike."

Swan nodded vigorously. "That just goes to prove my
point. Your own brother wouldn't steer you wrong, would
he?"

"No," Virgil said hesitantly. " 'Course, I've never
been one to go looking for trouble. It's just not my
style."

"Then maybe you ought to change your style—before
trouble finds you."

Virgil downed the last of his brandy. His eyes drifted
off and his expression became abstracted. Never before
had he called a man out, provoked a fight. Yet now the
idea had an undeniable logic.

Only a sucker waited for the other man to draw first
blood. He abruptly decided he'd wait no longer.

The moon cast a smoky light over the Rio Hondo. A
coyote's yipping howl sounded somewhere in the distance.
Then the night went still, stars scattered to the far horizon.

Along the banks of the Rio Bonito the first sheep appeared. Within minutes a few turned to hundreds and then
a long ghostly column of a thousand or more. On the
flanks, shepherds and their dogs drove the flock toward the
junction of the rivers. There the sheep spilled down the
embankment and splashed through the shallow waters of

the Hondo. Some moments later they waded ashore on Spur land.

Slim Atkins watched with disbelief. One of several cowhands assigned to guard the fording place, he'd drawn the midnight watch. For over a month he and his bunkmates had grumbled and grouched, dutifully taking their posts every night. At first, none of them questioned that the sheep would be driven across the Hondo. But then, after a matter of weeks, they began to have their doubts. Tonight Slim Atkins was a doubter no longer. He reined his horse about and galloped toward the compound.

Awakened from a dead sleep, Odell Slater was at first dumbstruck. He, too, had begun to believe it wouldn't happen. But now, with the sheep on Spur land, there was only one course of action. As foreman, he had his orders and he wouldn't flinch from a distasteful chore. He sent Atkins to roust out the men, but he saw no reason to disturb Mrs. Brannock. Ten minutes after being awakened, he had thirty cowhands armed and mounted. He led them west along the Hondo.

An hour before dawn Slater and his men struck. The moon had dropped beyond the mountains and the sheep were bedded down for the night. Slater's plan was direct and without frills, based largely on his knowledge of the river. Yelling and firing their six-guns, the cowhands rode forward in a thunderous wedge. They drove the sheep from the bedground, herding them westward along the Hondo. The *mexicano* shepherds scattered before the charge, running for their lives. None of them were armed and there was no thought of defending the flock.

A mile upstream the sheep were turned north. Shouting louder, their pistols roaring in the dark, the cowhands drove them over a steep embankment. The sheep stampeded, leaping blindly into the void, and landed heavily in a wide stretch of quicksand. There, first by the tens and then by the hundreds, they stuck in the thick muddy ooze. Their eyes wide with terror, bleating pitifully, those in the vanguard were quickly sucked under. Others, trapped and still struggling, formed a living bridge for those in the rear. Not one in ten made it safely to the opposite shore.

The dinge of false dawn brought the slaughter to a halt. Their horses arrayed along the riverbank, Slater and his men watched the quicksand perform its grisly work. The cowhands were strangely silent now, their eyes dulled by animals suffering a torturous death. None of them would forget what had occurred on the Hondo tonight. Nor would they voice any pride in what they'd done.

Odell Slater reined away from the river. His mouth was set in a grim line as he led the cowhands eastward. A golden shaft of light exploded over the distant foothills, full in his face. He felt oddly chilled by the oncoming sunrise.

"You fool!"

"Now, hold on, Miz Brannock."

Elizabeth stared at him, her face pale and furious. Slater stood, hat in hand, just inside the vestibule door. He'd reported to her only moments before, and her reaction left him thunderstruck. He darted an uneasy glance at John Taylor, who had accompanied him up to the main house. The Texican avoided his eyes, watching Elizabeth.

Her hair was still pinned up and she wore a housecoat over her nightgown. The shock of what she'd heard had now been replaced by seething anger. She struggled to control her temper.

"Have you any idea what you've done, Mr. Slater?"

"Yes, ma'am," Slater said, eyeing her warily. "I was just following orders—Mr. Brannock's orders."

"Were you?" Elizabeth said sharply. "I find that hard to believe."

"Well, it's the truth," Slater said in an aggrieved tone. "Why would I lie about a thing like that?"

Elizabeth gave him a reproachful look. "Are you saying my husband told you to drive those sheep into quicksand?"

"Not just exactly," Slater confessed. "The quicksand was my own idea."

"What were his orders—exactly?"

"Listen here, ma'am. I was with Mr. Brannock the day he told Luis Varga he'd kill them sheep. I heard him say it myself."

"Answer my question," Elizabeth persisted. "Did my husband directly order you to kill the sheep?"

Slater made an empty gesture with his hands. "What he told me was to keep 'em off Spur. It amounts to the same thing."

"No, Mr. Slater, it does not amount to the same thing. Had you chosen to do so, you could have driven those sheep back across the Hondo. Isn't that true?"

"Yeah," Slater growled, half under his breath. "But that ain't what Mr. Brannock wanted done."

Elizabeth flushed angrily. "If nothing else, I should fire you for stupidity. However, we'll wait until my husband returns. He can decide."

"Look here," Slater said indignantly. "You got no call to talk to me that way, Miz Brannock."

Elizabeth turned away. "Mr. Taylor, show him out. I've nothing more to say."

Taylor moved between them as Elizabeth went through the entryway to the parlor. Slater drew himself up stiffly, his features set in a scowl. When he was slow to move, Taylor took hold of his arm and walked him toward the door. He went along without argument.

In the parlor, Elizabeth stopped beside her desk. A cold premonition swept through her and she tried to steady herself. She realized with dark fatalism that some hours weigh against a whole lifetime. What had happened this morning on the Rio Hondo was one of those hours. She saw it now for what it was—a clever trap.

Suddenly, in that quicksilver splinter of time, she saw something more. She had no choice but to act before Virgil returned. To wait would be the worst thing, unthinkable and far too dangerous. For the trap was not meant for her. It was intended for Virgil.

A thought flashed through her mind. She opened the center drawer of her desk and removed a Colt pocket pistol. Short and stubby, the revolver was chambered for .41 caliber and suitable for a lady's pocketbook. Virgil had bought it for her years ago, a house gun for emergencies. Until now, she'd never considered using it.

Taylor halted in the doorway. She turned, the gun still in her hand, looking at him. Her voice was composed, strong.

"I know why those sheep were driven across the river."

"Some particular reason, you mean?"

She nodded. "Yesterday, Ira Hecht filed a lawsuit in federal district court. We've charged Stephen Benton with land fraud."

Taylor stared at her for a long moment. He read nothing in her eyes and his gaze slowly drifted down to her hand. "Why the gun?"

"Please have the buckboard brought around. We're leaving for Santa Fe."

She moved past him and through the vestibule. Taylor stood there listening to her footsteps, wondering about the gun. A lawsuit and a bunch of sheep seemed to him no answer.

No reason to shoot Stephen Benton.

22

The morning of August 6 was unusually hot. Santa Fe, because of its high altitude, generally enjoyed temperate summers. Today the sweltering heat seemed somehow oppressive.

John Taylor stepped off the passenger coach. He assisted Elizabeth down the steps and she walked to the edge of the depot platform. Hurriedly he hired a porter to run their bags over to the hotel. As he turned back, she was already rounding the corner of the stationhouse.

All the way from Lincoln she'd said practically nothing. Taylor's attempts at conversation were met with polite reserve. When he'd finally asked what she intended, she merely smiled. That cool smile worried him, even more than her silence. It seemed to him the calm before the storm.

Only after some thought had Taylor resolved the matter in his own mind. He was convinced that she meant to kill Stephen Benton upon their arrival in Santa Fe. Since she herself was in no personal danger, her reason had at first eluded him. Then, as though reading her mind, he understood. She was willing to commit murder to save her husband.

To Taylor, that was an honorable motive. He had killed men for far less, on occasion simply because the pay was right. So there was never any question that he would help her with Stephen Benton. Her husband's life was at stake and she meant to remove the source of danger. That seemed to Taylor not only prudent but also highly reasonable. Given the circumstances, he would have done the same himself.

One thing still puzzled Taylor. He'd never quite gotten a handle on the man who had hired him. Virgil Brannock was a faithful husband, and clearly worshiped his wife. Yet he was obsessed by ambition, flitting about the country from one project to another. In Taylor's view, it was a direct contradiction, and none too bright. Any man with a wife like Elizabeth Brannock would do well to stick around home. She was a woman other men might easily covet, and Taylor himself wasn't immune. Lately, he'd found it increasingly difficult to curb his tongue.

From the depot, they walked uptown. Elizabeth set the direction, skirting the plaza on the south side. There she rounded the corner onto Shelby Street and her pace seemed to quicken. Taylor sensed a change in her bearing, something different in her manner. Her chin was tilted and her eyes were slightly narrowed, as though she were gathering her composure. Halfway down the block, she turned into the door of a storefront office. A sign on the window was limned in bright sunlight.

STEPHEN E. BENTON
ATTORNEY-AT-LAW

The outer office was furnished with wooden armchairs and a desk. At the far end of the room the door to a private office was closed. Wilbur Latham was seated in one of the chairs and a male secretary was hunched over the desk, sorting through correspondence. As Elizabeth entered from the street, Latham pushed out of his chair. He moved to block her path.

"Don't," Taylor said from the doorway. "Just stand aside."

Latham bristled. "You're out of your league, Taylor."

"Think so?" Taylor said with a clenched smile. "Let's

suppose you're as good as me. Or maybe vicey-versa.
Where's that get us?''

Latham pondered it a moment. He saw that the Texan
had a point. From an even break, they would doubtless kill
one another. He finally nodded.

"Only the lady gets inside. You stay out here."

"Sounds reasonable," Taylor said, grinning. "We'll let
her and your boss have a little privacy.''

Elizabeth walked toward the rear of the room. As she
approached the desk, the male secretary started out of his
chair. He darted a glance at Taylor, then abruptly chose
discretion. With a weak smile, he sat down and folded his
hands on the desktop. Elizabeth marched past him.

Her pocketbook in her left hand, she opened the door to
the inner office. Benton looked up from a broad mahogany
desk littered with papers and rolled survey maps. His
expression turned from quick astonishment to guarded caution. She slammed the door behind her.

"It seems you were right after all, Mr. Benton."

"Oh?" Benton asked. "What about?"

"You said politics is a rough game."

"As I recall, you expressed indifference to the political
consequences. Or does memory serve me wrong?''

"I was mistaken," Elizabeth said. "I see now that we
are all affected by politics. Some to a greater degree than
others."

Benton was impressed by her composure. Her manner
was cool and deliberate, without a trace of animosity.
However strained their relationship, she never failed to
intrigue him. He indicated one of the leather wing-back
chairs before his desk.

"Won't you have a seat?"

"Thank you."

Elizabeth took a chair, placing her pocketbook in her
lap. Benton leaned forward, elbows on the desk, and
stared across at her. His gaze was one of curious cordiality.

"How may I help you, Mrs. Brannock?"

"You once offered to strike an accommodation."

"And you turned me down."

Elizabeth regarded him with great calmness. "I'm here today to make you an offer."

Benton smiled, as if sharing a private joke with himself. His manner was indulgent, faintly patronizing. "What sort of offer?"

"I'm willing to make restitution for the sheep."

"Sheep?" Benton echoed, clearly taken aback. "What sheep?"

"Luis Varga's sheep," Elizabeth said. "Killed night before last on the Rio Hondo."

Benton looked at her blandly. "Why would I be interested in Luis Varga's sheep? That's a matter between you and him."

"No," Elizabeth said firmly. "Varga is one of your *jefes políticos* in Lincoln County. I believe he's what's known as a stooge."

"I fail to see what Varga's sheep have to do with politics."

"Come now, Mr. Benton, there's no need to be devious about it. We both know Varga was acting on your orders."

Benton frowned. "Are you accusing me of something, Mrs. Brannock?"

"Of course," Elizabeth observed quietly. "At the very least, you're guilty of conspiracy."

"Harsh words," Benton said. "What would I have to gain from this incident?"

"You used Varga and his sheep as a provocation. I believe you mean to kill my husband."

"Nonsense!" Benton said in an orotund voice. "I'm not in the business of killing people, Mrs. Brannock."

"On the contrary," Elizabeth corrected him. "You hope to silence me by threatening my husband. I think politicians refer to it as quid pro quo."

Benton laughed, spread his hands. "We're back to talking accommodation. What sort of deal do you have in mind?"

"I will arrange to pay Varga for his sheep. In return, you will guarantee my husband's safety."

"That's it?" Benton demanded roughly. "How about the lawsuit Hecht filed against me? Will you have it withdrawn?"

"The lawsuit stands," Elizabeth said. "I'm talking about the sheep, nothing more."

Benton stabbed a blunt finger at her. "I'd advise you to change your tune. Luis Varga is known to have quite a temper."

"And you won't call him off?"

"Who, me?" Benton said, mocking her. "I have no control over a hotheaded *mexicano*."

"Is that your final word on it?"

"Here's my final word," Benton warned. "Your husband better watch his step, Mrs. Brannock. He's got a wife who won't listen to reason!"

Elizabeth fixed him with a strange, unsettling look. Her hand dipped into her pocketbook and reappeared with the stubby Colt. All in a motion, she rose, thumbing the hammer, and leaned across the desk. She placed the snout of the pistol on the exact center of his forehead.

Benton's eyes rolled upward at the gun. He sat immobilized, as though frozen in place, all the blood leeched out of his face. A thick silence settled in the room, the sound of their breathing unnaturally harsh. At last Elizabeth prodded him with the muzzle.

"Hear me," she said, her voice cold as ice. "Should any harm come to my husband, I will kill you myself. Nod your head if you understand."

Benton nodded. She stepped back, lowering the hammer, and dropped the pistol into her pocketbook. A sheen of perspiration beaded Benton's forehead and the color slowly returned to his face. She stared at him an instant longer.

"Don't underestimate me," she said. "I never make idle threats."

Benton merely looked at her. She turned and walked from the room. In the outer office, she found Taylor and Latham still locked in a standoff. She moved past them and emerged onto the street. Taylor followed her out the door.

For several moments they walked in silence. Then finally Taylor was overcome with curiosity. He glanced around at her.

"Why didn't you kill him?"

Elizabeth looked straight ahead. "I had no intention of killing him . . . not today."

"Not today?" Taylor repeated. "What the devil's that supposed to mean?"

"I offered him a quid pro quo instead."

"You'll have to spell that out."

Elizabeth smiled. "We made a deal. Or perhaps 'pact' would be the better word. I promised to shoot him if any harm comes to Virgil."

Taylor grunted. "You really think he'll stick to it?"

"I think he believes I'm serious. From the look on his face, there was little doubt of that."

"Showed him your popgun, did you?"

"Yes," Elizabeth said, laughing. "I gave him a very close look."

"Great God A'mighty! You're about the most unordinary lady I ever run across."

"Why, thank you, Mr. Taylor."

"Matter of fact . . ."

Taylor's voice dropped off in mid-sentence. Elizabeth noted a rather abrupt change in his manner. His expression was suddenly solemn and he averted his eyes. She couldn't imagine why he'd fallen silent.

"What is it?" she prompted. "Why did you stop?"

"Well—" Taylor actually looked bashful. "It's something I've been meanin' to say for quite a spell now."

"Yes," Elizabeth said curiously, "go on."

"I'm no saint, you understand. I've known lots of

women in my time. But you're . . .'' He faltered, groping
for words, then rushed on. "Well, I just admire you
more'n any woman I ever met."

Elizabeth had an uncanny gift of intuiting what people
left unsaid. Almost from the start, she'd sensed that
Taylor admired her, noted his hidden looks. But now she
heard something in his voice that disturbed her. He spoke
with the awkward hesitancy of a suitor.

"I'm flattered," she said slowly, "and I know you
meant it as a compliment. So please don't be offended—"

"No need to say it," Taylor interrupted. "You figure I
ought to button my lip and keep my place. What with me
being a hired hand and all."

"What I was about to day," Elizabeth went on, "is that
I consider you a friend. A good and loyal friend who
places my welfare before his own."

"But?—" Taylor pressed her. "What's the rest of it?"

"Simply put, I'm a married woman. Had anyone over-
heard what you just said, it would appear unseemly. People sometimes prefer to believe the worst."

"You know what?" Taylor said with a waggish grin.
"They might not be far off the mark. Leastways, where
I'm concerned."

Elizabeth stopped. They were nearing the corner of the
plaza and she waited until a passerby was out of earshot.
Then she looked straight at Taylor.

"I don't mean to be rude," she said, "but you're never
again to speak to me in that manner. I have a husband and
a family, and I will not be compromised, Mr. Taylor. Is
that clear?"

"Yes, ma'am, that's clear as a bell."

"And you're not offended?"

"No whichaway," Taylor said, smiling. " 'Course,
keepin' my mouth shut don't change nothing. I'm still
what you'd call an admirer."

Elizabeth looked exasperated. "Shall we agree that you'll
keep such thoughts to yourself?"

Taylor laughed. "I won't tell nobody if you don't."

"You have my promise on that, Mr. Taylor."

Elizabeth turned toward the plaza. As they crossed the street, she felt a mounting sense of concern. Once he'd started talking, Taylor had become emboldened, almost playful. She recognized the bantering tone of a man who would not be easily dissuaded. Worse, it was the tone that led men to take further liberties.

The whole thing infuriated her. She saw now that Taylor would ultimately have to be dismissed. Still, her annoyance was balanced against practical considerations. Until the matter of Stephen Benton was resolved, she could hardly afford to let Taylor go. After today, his services were more essential than ever.

She might yet have need of a hired gun.

Ira Hecht listened without interruption. Elizabeth started at the beginning and told the story to the end. She concluded on a note of cautious optimism.

"For the moment, I think we've discouraged further violence. Whatever else he is, Benton's no fool."

"Neither is he a coward," Hecht said. "I seriously doubt you've scared him off for good. At best, it's a temporary stalemate."

"Even so," Elizabeth countered, "we've bought time. Benton knows we're onto his scheme, and that's a deterrent in itself. He'll hold Varga in check for now."

They were seated in Hecht's office. Having heard Elizabeth out, he wasn't at all convinced that bloodshed had been averted. He glanced at Taylor, who was tilted back, his chair propped against the wall. The gunman shrugged with a look of skepticism.

"Well, one thing's for certain," Hecht commented. "Benton's preoccupied right now with our lawsuit. I'm convinced we'll prove fraudulent intent."

"Assuming we do," Elizabeth asked, "how long could he keep it in the appeals court?"

"Several months," Hecht said glumly. "Maybe as long as a year."

"And no crimincal charges could be brought until the appeals court issues a ruling."

"That's correct."

Elizabeth considered a moment. "Perhaps there's another way to get at Benton and the Santa Fe Ring. I'm referring to the elections in November."

A frown creased Hecht's brow. "Are you talking about a political challenge?"

"Yes, I am," Elizabeth affirmed. "I believe Benton and his crowd are vulnerable. I've thought it for some time."

"Vulnerable in what sense?"

"A groundswell reform movement. The people rather than the party."

Elizabeth quickly elaborated on her plan. Hecht was to contact the network of lawyers they had established throughout the territory. He would request an immediate investigation into the Ring's political influence at the county level. The objects of most intense scrutiny would be the Anglo bosses and the *jefes políticos*. The end result would be documented proof of the existence of a political machine. A corrupt and highly organized group of men working to subjugate New Mexico Territory.

When compiled, all the evidence would be turned over to Max Flagg. Elizabeth was confident that the publisher would jump at the chance for an exposé. Through his newspaper, the *New Mexican*, he could document the stranglehold on territorial politics. The effect would be to discredit the party machine and all the men associated with it. Finally, with the conspiracy exposed, a call would be sounded for reform. The appeal would be directed most specifically to the *mexicanos*, who comprised a voter majority. It would be a populist movement, a people's revolt.

No reform effort, Elizabeth observed, could succeed without offering an alternative. A slate of candidates would therefore be drawn from the network of attorneys and concerned *mexicanos*. In the general election, the reform candidates would then oppose the party hacks who now controlled the legislature. Hecht's job would be to coordinate the campaign and orchestrate a unified strategy among all candidates. Properly engineered, it would result in the downfall of Stephen Benton and the Santa Fe Ring.

When she stopped talking, Hecht appeared dumbfounded. He stared at her with a look of profound respect and a degree of awe. At length, he shook his head.

"Why do I get the feeling you didn't dream that up overnight?"

Elizabeth smiled. "Are you suggesting I have a devious mind?"

"Something like that," Hecht replied. "I think you had it planned from A to Z the first day you walked in here. Unless I'm badly mistaken, the legal-assistance service was your springboard into politics."

"Actually, it was more of a cornerstone. Our network of lawyers will enable us to build a whole new organization."

"All that to topple the Santa Fe Ring?"

"Along with Stephen Benton," Elizabeth confessed. "From the beginning, I wanted to bring his house of cards tumbling down. He's an evil man."

"And me?" Hecht inquired, smiling broadly. "Was I just your mouthpiece? A stalking horse?"

"Neither," Elizabeth said with conviction. "You are the standard-bearer, our rallying point. And one day soon, you'll be the voice of the people."

A sudden grin cracked Hecht's features. "And you'll be the ventriloquist, feeding me words. God, I can see it now!"

"Well, after all, Ira," Elizabeth said merrily, "a woman has no place in politics. It's still a man's world."

Hecht suddenly realized something that had eluded him until now. Elizabeth Brannock was no less a visionary than the trailblazers who had opened the frontier. Her compassion for the oppressed and her commitment to social change were the foundation of a political base. In time, her power would exceed that of Stephen Benton and John Chisum. Yet she would wisely remain in the background, content to let others attract the limelight. Her goal was reform, not personal power.

For the first time, Hecht fully appreciated the extent of her determination. There was a quiet strength about Elizabeth, an energy that touched something in other people. They were instinctively drawn to her, eager to do her bidding. She was an irresistible force, and for her, there were no immovable objects. She was indeed *La Mariposa de Hierro*—the Iron Butterfly.

"What about Max Flagg?" Hecht said after a long pause. "His newspaper's essential to the plan. Shouldn't we brief him?"

"No," Elizabeth said without hesitation. "Let's keep it to ourselves until we're ready to act. I want no premature leaks."

Hecht nodded approval. A strange inner look came over Elizabeth's face, and she seemed to stare past him. She was listening again to the words she'd just spoken, words more reflex than conscious thought. With sudden awareness she saw that she had mastered yet another tenet of the political craft: secrecy.

She was neither pleased nor saddened. Politics was, after all, a rough-and-tumble game. She would learn the rules as she went along.

23

Clouds dotted the cobalt sky. The landscape was dimly outlined in a haze of moonwash and pale starlight. A brittle silence enveloped the night.

Clint was stretched out on his belly. He lay atop a low ridge on the western slope of the San Mateo Mountains. The volcanic foothills were broken and rocky, studded with scrub brush. Directly below his position was a winding canyon unmarked on any map. He stared down at the Apache camp.

A lone cooking fire had been reduced to embers. Nana and his band were encamped around a spring-fed waterhole. The raiding party consisted of some forty warriors and perhaps half that many women and children. Their horse herd was bunched south of the waterhole, on a barren patch of graze. One night guard was posted along the western wall of the canyon.

For three days Clint and his scouts had tracked the raiding party through the mountains. The San Mateos were a brutal land of sawtoothed ridges slashed by deep, forbidding gorges. The range was roughly forty miles in length, dropping north to south toward the Rio Grande. Towering peaks, some ten thousand feet high, loomed against the moonlit sky.

Nana was a wily leader. He normally allowed no fires, and he selected campsites that provided excellent defensive cover. Tonight was one of those rare nights when he'd permitted a cooking fire to be kindled. A gaunt, trail-

weary horse had been killed and the band had feasted on
roasted meat. After the meal, they had bedded down around
the waterhole. Before sunrise, the raiding party would
once more be on the move.

The pursuit was now into its third week. D Troop,
commanded by Captain James Gilford, was part of the
Ninth Cavalry. The regiment, which comprised black enlisted men and white officers, had previously distinguished
itself in campaigns against the Comanche. Among Indians,
the troopers were universally known as the Buffalo Soldiers. Their short, matted hair resembled the wiry topknot
of a buffalo bull, and the name had followed them from
Indian Territory into New Mexico. Their reputation as
fierce, resourceful fighters was known to all the horseback
tribes.

On a normal day, Clint and his scouts ranged far ahead
of the troop. The Apache raiders had led them on a
grueling chase that began in the Sacramento Mountains.
From there the band had turned westerly, crossing the San
Andres range. A few days into the campaign, D Troop had
overtaken the raiding party, killing two warriors and capturing ten horses. Since then, they had never again come
within shooting distance of the band. The Apache avoided
another engagement, while still managing to raid outlying
ranches and steal fresh livestock. The pursuit rapidly evolved
into a contest of stamina.

From the slopes of the San Andres, Nana led his band
west into the *Jornada del Muerto*. A brooding stretch of
desert, the Journey of the Dead was almost fifty miles
wide. It was a land of mesquite and dust devils, with only
one known waterhole. To conserve their horses, the men
of D Troop crossed a good part of the Jornada on foot.
They lost ground on the Apache, even though Gilford
ordered a forced march that lasted a day and a night. Far to
the west, they kept their gaze fixed on mountains shrouded
in a murky haze.

Nana crossed the Rio Grande on July 30. For the next

several days his warriors cut a swath of death and destruction along the valley. Five *mexicanos* were slaughtered, and two prospectors were butchered outside the town of San Jose. Afterward, like shadowy wraiths, the Apache faded into the eastern foothills of the San Mateo range. By then Clint and his scouts were once more on the raiders' trail. The chase resumed in earnest through the desolate mountains.

A ring of army units was slowly encircling the Apache. By the first week in August, General Ranald Mackenzie had blanketed southwestern New Mexico with eighteen troops of cavalry. Operating independently, volunteer groups of Anglos were in the field as well. One self-organized militia, composed of thirty-six ranchers and cowhands, was ambushed deep in the mountains. The raiders killed one man, wounding several others, and stampeded all their horses. The survivors hobbled out of the San Mateos four days later.

D Troop, under Captain Gilford, was charged with maintaining unrelenting pressure on the Apache. Their mission was to drive the raiders out of the mountains and into the net of converging cavalry units. Yet Nana and his warriors were like will-o'-the-wisps, pausing only to steal fresh horses or pillage an isolated ranch. Some days, though handicapped by women and children, the raiders would cover seventy miles or more. The Buffalo Soldiers were forever a day behind, unable to strike a decisive blow.

Clint's scouts were Coyotero Apache. A band of the White Mountain Apache, they had been pacified by the army in 1875. The men were short and bowlegged, their features dark as obsidian. Their moccasins were the button-toed, knee-high footgear of the Apache, and their apronlike breechclouts flapped between their legs. They were tireless trackers, with superhuman endurance, and savage fighters. Clint, who had an ear for languages, won their respect from the first day he took charge. He told them in their own dialect that they would cover themselves with glory.

By capturing Nana, they would stand supreme above all Apache.

The statement was calculated to challenge the scouts. The Apache, who called themselves the *Tin-ne-ah*, were a proud people. The tribe was composed of five major groups, with many subgroups split into twenty or more bands. Whether Chiricahua, Jicarilla, or Mescalero, there was great rivalry, as well as great kinship, throughout the tribe. Yet nearly all the Apache looked upon the Coyoteros as renegades and traitors. For the past six years their allegiance had been to the army rather than the tribe.

The Coyoteros were therefore receptive to Clint's challenge. Their service under the white man's banner had made them outcasts, tribal lepers. By running Nana to ground, they saw a way to restore themselves, regain lost pride. Once again, they would prove themselves the equal of any Apache warrior. All the more important, by emerging victors over a bronco war leader, they would have served the cause of all the *Tin-ne-ah*. Their alliance with the bluecoats would at last bring peace to the People.

Clint reminded himself to sing their praises tonight. In the pale light of the moon, they had tracked Nana's band across the barren mountainous terrain. Their efforts had closed the gap and brought D Troop to within striking range. A dawn attack might well write an end to the campaign.

The encampment below was quiet and still. Clint inspected it one last time, fixing the layout in his mind. Then, careful of the slightest sound, he wormed his way down off the ridge. A short distance beyond the rimrock, he rose to his feet and gingerly made his way to the bottom of an arroyo. There, squatted beside their horses, the Coyoteros awaited his return.

Clint motioned them silent. His hands darted in a burst of sign language and the scouts bobbed their heads. Holding the reins, they walked their horses single file along the arroyo. A mile south of the encampment they finally mounted.

Ghostlike, they rode eastward into the mountains.

* * *

The Coyoteros rarely spoke on the trail. The lead scout set their course with an unerring sense of direction. Strung out behind, many of the others catnapped in their saddles. The only sound was the thud of unshod hooves striking stone.

Clint was favorably impressed by the Coyoteros. A lifetime spent in a harsh land had toughened them beyond the comprehension of most white men. They were able to subsist on little food and even less sleep, and their endurance never flagged. Their short, bandy-legged stature merely underscored their incredible hardiness.

A comparison with the Comanche was only natural. Clint thought the Comanche were better horsemen, unsurpassed as light cavalry. But the Apache were shrewder tacticians, far more disciplined as fighters. They were masters of the ambush, drawing an unsuspecting enemy into a murderous trap. Of greater significance, they invariably fought as a unit, concentrating their firepower on the opposing force. Their leaders exerted a control in battle that was curiously similar to the army's system of command.

Still another comparison was obvious to Clint. On the Staked Plains, he had taken part in subduing the Comanche. Now, as though reliving a past life, he was engaged in a campaign to suppress the Apache. For that, he placed the blame squarely on Ranald Mackenzie. Left to his own devices, he would have never again taken the field against Indians. The fact that he had been strong-armed into service as a scout still rankled. He no longer felt any obligation for Mackenzie's patronage of past years. Their accounts were now squared.

The prospect of ending the campaign preoccupied Clint's thoughts. A dawn attack, properly executed, would put a halt to Nana's bloody marauding. There was no question that the Apache would ultimately suffer the fate of all hostiles. With several regiments in the field, it was only a matter of time until the raiders were brought to bay. Yet

Clint preferred that it happen now, quickly ended with one
last fight. Whenever it happened, he'd already determined
his next course of action. He planned to resign his commission as special agent.

Out of touch for three weeks, Clint was nagged by a
sense of uncertainty. He'd had no word of the family or
the situation on Spur. Nor was there any way of knowing
whether or not Virgil had returned. Not once during the
campaign had he paused long enough to send a wire or
receive one. Still, he needed no communiqué to tell him
the state of things on the Hondo. There was only one
resolution to any dispute with a man such as Stephen
Benton. And his every instinct told him it wouldn't be
settled in a court of law.

Fear was an emotion with which he'd never been inti-
mate. While he was not a superstitious man, he nonetheless believed himself exempt from personal harm. Some
men were ordained to live out their natural lives, and for
him, a violent death simply wasn't in the cards. Yet he felt
no such assurances for members of his family, particularly
Virgil. He'd already seen one brother killed and the memory would haunt him all the days of his life. His dread that
it might happen again was with him constantly.

His thoughts never strayed far from the Rio Hondo.

D Troop was bivouacked beside a shallow stream. There
was ample water for the horses but none for coffee. No
fires were allowed tonight.

At sundown, Captain Gilford had ordered a halt. The
trail of the hostiles was scarcely three hours old, leading
west into the foothills. Fearful of betraying his position,
Gilford had decided on a cold camp. The scouts had gone
ahead, tracking through the oncoming dusk and into the
moonlit night. There was reason to believe that Nana's
weary band would have also halted at dark.

Clint and his scouts were passed through by the sentries.
On the edge of the camp, the Coyoteros dismounted and

walked their horses to the stream. Clint left his gelding with one of the scouts and proceeded to the center of the encampment. Troopers were scattered about on the ground, rolled in their blankets, hard asleep after a long day's ride. He eased through their ranks, heading toward the guidon staff, which was wedged into the sunbaked earth. The triangular pennant fluttered in a light breeze.

James Gilford was waiting for him. An austere man, the troop commander was in his late forties. His hair was streaked with gray and his features seemed chiseled from stone. He seldom bothered with the amenities, and he never smiled. Hands clasped behind his back, he nodded brusquely.

"What luck, Mr. Brannock?"

"We found them," Clint said. "Camped at a waterhole about five miles west of here. Even built themselves a fire."

"You don't say?" Gilford remarked. "Apparently Nana believes he's outrun us."

"Sort of looks that way."

"What's his position . . . the terrain?"

"Waterhole's down in a canyon. The sides drop off pretty sharp and it stretches north and south to hell and gone. No way to bottle them up."

Gilford frowned uncertainly. "Any chance of a mounted attack?"

"Nope," Clint said promptly. "Too steep a downgrade for horses. We'll have to do it on foot."

"Damn," Gilford swore. "I'd hoped for better."

"Nana knows his business. Hard spot to approach from any direction."

"How many in his band?"

"Same as before," Clint said. "No more than forty men. The rest are women and children."

"And the horse herd?"

"South of the camp," Clint noted. "I spotted one guard over on the west wall of the canyon."

Gilford hesitated, considering. Clint watched him a moment, then went on. "I've got an idea how it could be done."

"How might that be, Mr. Brannock?"

"We'll never make it down that slope without being spotted. The horse guard's certain to sound the alarm."

"What's your point?"

"No way we'll pull off a surprise attack. I'd suggest we ambush 'em instead."

Gilford squinted at him. "Where would this ambush take place?"

"There in the canyon," Clint said. "Put one bunch of troopers south of the camp and another bunch to the north. Then attack straight down that slope with a third bunch."

"Flush them out of camp," Gilford commented, "and force them into a trap. Is that it?"

"Pretty much," Clint allowed. "Whichever way they run, we'd have the canyon sealed off. The other two groups could box them off from the rear."

Gilford shook his head vigorously. "I make it a practice never to split my forces. You may recall the Battle of the Little Big Horn, Mr. Brannock. Custer learned the lesson the hard way."

Clint's eyes were impersonal. "A direct attack just won't work, Captain. You try it and you'll lose Nana."

"Not if you and your scouts stampede his horse herd. He would be forced to stand and fight, then."

"Guess nothin' I say would change your mind?"

"You worry about the horses, Mr. Brannock. Leave Nana to me."

Clint turned and walked off through the camp. He'd learned long ago when to stop wasting his breath. Some officers listened and others had a tin ear.

Captain James Gilford belonged in the latter category.

A smudge of light touched the eastern horizon. The moon dimmed beyond the foothills and the last stars flickered out. The sky turned the color of dirty pewter.

D Troop was dismounted behind the rimrock of the canyon. The men were formed on line as skirmishers, their Springfield carbines at the ready. Clint and the scouts were posted on the south, prepared to rush the horse herd. To the rear, at the bottom of the arroyo, every fourth man acted as a horse-holder.

Gilford raised his right arm. He hesitated a moment, waiting for the platoon leaders to acknowledge his signal. When he dropped his arm, the troop advanced over the rimrock and started down the steep incline. The men dug for footholds, struggling to keep their balance in the crumbling soil. A small avalanche of dirt and rocks went skittering toward the floor of the canyon.

A gunshot suddenly split the dawn stillness. On the western wall, the horse guard worked the lever of an old Henry carbine and sprayed the skirmishers with lead. Several of the men returned fire and sent him tumbling headlong off a flat-topped boulder. An instant later the Apache camp boiled to life, figures darting and bounding all around the waterhole. Gunfire abruptly became general as warriors below let go a ragged volley.

On Gilford's command, the troopers halted halfway down the slope. Ordered to fire at will, they braced themselves against the steep pitch and blasted away with their carbines. Accustomed to level ground, they misjudged the angle and most of their shots went high. Off to the south, the Coyoteros ignored Clint's guttural command to rush the horse herd. None of them seemed willing to advance into a buzzing hornet's nest.

Far below, the Apache warriors slowly retreated southward from the waterhole. The women and children were already mounted, hastily abandoning all their camp gear. Nana shouted over the drumming tattoo of gunfire, withdrawing his men in orderly relays. As the last of the rear guard approached the horse herd, the rest of the band clattered off down the canyon. The warriors unleashed a final volley, then scrambled aboard their ponies. Nana led them away at a full gallop.

Within seconds, the Apache rounded a distant bend. The troopers were ordered to cease fire and a deafening stillness fell over the canyon. Around the waterhole four warriors lay sprawled in death. One trooper had been killed and three others were wounded. The men of D Troop slowly lowered their carbines and stood immobilized on the slope. Their faces were streaked black with gunsmoke.

Captain James Gilford stared south along the canyon. His eyes were grim and his mouth was razored in a thin line. He looked as though he'd just seen victory crushed by the jaws of defeat.

On August 4 a pitched battle took place in the Black Mountains. There, in a place called Guerrillo Canyon, Nana and his warriors smashed head-on into a troop of cavalry. The troop commander, Lieutenant G. W. Smith, and five of his men were killed. The Apache, suffering only minor casualties, continued their flight southward.

D Troop passed through Guerrillo Canyon that afternoon. The six bodies, shrouded in rubber ponchos, were already draped across horses. A grizzled sergeant, as though recounting a bad dream, told them the tale of the fight. There was nothing to be done for the survivors, and Captain Gilford seemed impervious to any problems but his own. He ordered the pursuit of Nana resumed.

By the next day it became clear that the Apache had broken through the net of cavalry units. Nana and his band made a run for the border, outdistancing all pursuit. After crossing into Old Mexico, they took sanctuary in the Sierra Madre range. A short while later they were joined by Geronimo and a band of Chiricahua warriors. Their stronghold in the mountains was all but impregnable to attack.

The raid into New Mexico Territory had lasted almost two months. In that time, Nana and his warriors had

covered a thousand miles through land swarming with
cavalry patrols. Their guerrilla tactics enabled them to live
off the country while fighting off their pursuers. Forty
strong, they had killed more than fifty men and stolen
several hundred head of horses. By the end of the raid,
they had evaded a force of at least a thousand army troops.
Nana would be remembered as the Apache who outfoxed
and outfought an entire border command.

General Ranald Mackenzie took the brunt of the criti-
cism. Yet he was an old hand at Indian campaigns as well
as army politics. A resolute man, he'd taken three years to
subdue the Comanche. He had every confidence that the
Apache would eventually be whipped into submission.
Experience told him that Nana and Geronimo would grow
restive in their Sierra Madre lair. Content to bide his time,
he ordered the Fourth Cavalry Regiment to patrol the
border. He planned to be waiting when the hostiles once
more crossed over from Old Mexico.

Clint foresaw a long war. The conflict would be drawn
out by the very nature of the guerrilla tactics employed by
the Apache. One day, as with all the horseback tribes,
Nana and Geronimo would fall before the army juggernaut. But he saw their defeat in terms of years rather than
months, for the Apache would not easily return to the
reservation. Nor was he willing to fight them any longer.

He resigned as special agent on August 6.

24

Lon emerged from the cabin. Out of habit, he stood for a moment studying the wooded mountains. His gaze was sharp and he listened with a hunter's ear. The chatter of squirrels and the call of a kingfisher sounded through the forest. Nothing he heard disturbed him.

A quick glance at the sun told him it was midmorning. He walked to the corral and slipped the rawhide latch off the gate. His pinto and an old packhorse allowed themselves to be bridled. After saddling the pinto, he led the animals outside the corral. He left them tied to the fence.

Whistling under his breath, he returned to the cabin. Today was his birthday and Little Raven had invited him to spend the night. He had no doubt that she was planning a celebration in honor of the occasion. Among the Comanche, sixteen marked the passage of a boy into manhood.

The notion amused Lon. He'd been on his own almost a year now, answerable to no one but himself. That his sixteenth birthday magically transformed him into a man seemed somehow laughable. He had long since attained his manhood, as could be attested to by several hot-blooded Comanche girls. Still, he was in high spirits, pleased that Little Raven had remembered. She wasn't his natural mother, but the bond was close. He thought of himself as her adopted son.

From inside the cabin he brought two bales of hides. One was tightly packed with deerskins, which Little Raven would cure and tan. The other was a furry bale of pelts, muskrat and an occasional beaver he'd trapped in mountain streams. These he would sell to the white trader at the agency, where he now had an account of almost a hundred dollars. He lashed the bales onto the packhorse with stout rawhide thongs.

For Lon, the bales of hides represented independence. Over the past year he had enlightened himself in the ways of wild creatures. He had schooled himself in their habits and their quirks, what set one apart from the other. He knew where they fed, their favorite watering holes, the paths they used in flight and when unalarmed. Wild things, he'd found, were much like men. Their habits often got them killed.

Having mastered woodcraft, he was at one with the wild things. He'd learned to smear himself with scent from the toes of deer and stalk the great bucks at their watering holes and in their bedgrounds. Or he sometimes concealed himself at the scrapes where bucks would paw leaves and urinate in rutting season to attract the does. He ran a trap line as well, working ponds and distant streams. Wherever he roamed, there were now few mysteries in the wild.

An offshoot of his independence was freedom. He went where he pleased, when he pleased, and he was obligated to no man. His needs were simple, and what the wilderness failed to provide was easily obtained at the trader's store. As for his spiritual needs, he followed the old tribal ways, realized more fully now through peyote and deep inner visions. He subscribed to the Comanche belief that each man must be allowed to walk his own path. His was the freedom of a wild thing, alterable only by death.

Not that his life was without minor irritants. Whenever he left the mountain fastness, he entered the world of the *tahboy-boh*, the white man. His raid on the garrison horse pen had marked him as a troublemaker. After Mackenzie's departure for New Mexico, he'd come under closer scrutiny. The new post commander was a book soldier, with no patience for the work of pranksters. Worse, he believed Lon set a bad example for the other youngsters, fostering disrespect for authority. That, in the army scheme of things, was the cardinal sin.

Yet Lon was virtually immune to restraint. He was a white who by circumstance as well as choice lived among the Indians. To further compound matters, he was looked upon by the Comanche as one of their own. An added complication was his close relationship with Quanah, whose power within the tribe was all but absolute. Neither the army nor the agency knew how to restrict Lon without fueling unrest among his adopted people. The result was that he was largely untouchable by those who governed the reservation.

After attending to the packhorse, Lon went back inside the cabin. The most visible symbol of his freedom was hanging on a wall peg. He took down a gunbelt and holster, weighted with the bulk of a .44 Colt. Not quite a month ago, he'd bought the pistol from a whiskey smuggler who also dealt in illicit firearms. He wore it openly whenever he traveled to the agency, yet another act of defiance. The authorities, fearful of provoking an incident, pretended not to notice. The Comanche thought it a grand joke on the *tahboy-boh*.

Every evening after supper Lon walked off behind the cabin. There, on a fallen tree, he aligned various objects as targets. For the past several weeks he'd drilled himself in the rudiments of fast and fancy shooting. He had a hunter's natural eye and the reflexes of a lithe and springy bobcat. While speed was important, he set far more store on accuracy. Stalking deer, he had learned that a well-placed shot dropped the quarry in its tracks. He took the same approach to mastering the pistol.

By now, the rig was part of his normal attire. He buckled the wide gunbelt, seating the holstered Colt just over his right hipbone. On his way out the door, he collected a Winchester '73 that he'd bought from the same whiskey smuggler. He jammed the rifle into the saddleboot and swung aboard his spotted pony. Leading the packhorse, he turned away from the cabin.

The sun rose higher as he rode down out of the mountains. He was still whistling softly under his breath.

The trader's store was a half-mile east of the agency. The shelves were stocked with all manner of goods that the government saw no reason to provide. Prices were steep, but the Comanche had little choice in the matter. It was the only store on the reservation.

Lon arrived in the midafternoon. The day was muggy and hot, with no hint of a breeze. A shade tree outside the store was a gathering place for those who had come to trade. As the youngster dismounted, he waved to several men squatted beneath the tree. They nodded but went on talking among themselves.

Their reserved greeting was not unusual. Older men seldom exhibited any response to young people. A certain dignity of manner prevailed, even though their days as warriors were long past. Then, too, the Comanche thought it rude to stare. As a result, they rarely looked directly at a person. Their eyes were fixed instead on the middle distance.

The *tahboy-boh* was fooled completely by Comanche customs. The somber manner and distant look were interpreted as stoicism, lack of ordinary emotion. Yet, among immediate family, the Comanche were open and expressive, often quite demonstrative in their feelings. They were also given to bawdy good humor and elaborate practical jokes. Their gift for laughter simply wasn't displayed before the white man.

Entering the store, Lon was aware that the men outside now had a new topic of conversation. Their talk would turn to his horse-stealing raid and his mountain cabin. Among the Comanche, he was widely respected for holding to the old ways, living as a hunter. Even more, his notoriety as a prankster made him the object of considerable admiration. A laugh at the *tahboy-boh's* expense was the greatest joke of all.

Over and above all that was his defiance. The Comanche were humbled now, reduced to the squalor of blanket Indians. But at night, around the fires, they relived the glory of times past. Those days, not too long ago when they were lords of all they surveyed, a nation of horseback conquerors. Lon's rebellious acts were for them a small touch of vengeance. His defiance of the white man was a thing of pride, shared by all.

Edgar Smith, who owned the store, was of a different opinion. He considered Lon an arrogant young squirt, brash and cocky and sometimes insolent. Yet he was careful in his dealings with the youngster, offering a fair price in trade for the pelts. Beneath the insolence, Smith sensed a cold, impersonal anger. One day he thought it would explode in an outburst of violence. He took it as the worst possible sign that Lon had started wearing a gun.

Today, the trade was swiftly done. Smith fingered the pelts briefly and offered top dollar. Lon shrugged acceptance, then strolled through the store, looking for presents. He selected a bright-colored shawl for Little Raven and a pound of hard candy to satisfy Hank's sweet tooth. The balance of the money from the trade was credited to his store account. He now had a hundred and twelve dollars on the books.

Outside again, he walked to the hitch rack. As he was stowing the goods in his saddlebags, he heard his name called. He turned and saw Quanah with the men beneath the shade tree. The Quahadi chief was attired in a black broadcloth coat with gray-striped trousers and a collarless white shirt. His long hair was held back by a braided headband.

Quanah nodded to the men and moved toward the hitch rack. As he approached, Lon inspected his outfit, noting that he wore quilled moccasins. All Comanche were issued white man's clothing on annuity days. But it was univer-

sally altered to an Indian's idea of comfort. Until now
Lon had never seen a Comanche dressed in the *tahboy-boh*
manner. His interest quickened.

"*Hao*," he said, reverting to the old form of greeting.
"It is good to see you again, Father."

Quanah smiled. "You stay away too long, Strikes-Both-
Ways. How goes the hunting?"

"Some days good," Lon said modestly, "some days
not so good. A man works hard to outwit the wild things."

"Huh!" Quanah grunted. "Today you are both a hunter
and a man. Your mother told me she plans a celebration."

"She honors me too much. Wisdom seems a long road
to one of sixteen winters."

"Well spoken, Strikes-Both-Ways. Even the elders search
for greater wisdom."

Lon tried not to stare at the *tahboy-boh* clothing. But his
curiosity was apparent, and Quanah chuckled softly. "You
wonder why I am dressed like a white man. I see it on
your face."

"It is not my place to question."

"I will tell you anyway. For a time now, I have been
thinking on an idea. I leave tomorrow to discuss it with
Jonathan Doan."

Some three years past, Doan had operated the trade
store at the reservation. He'd sold out to Edgar Smith and
opened a similar establishment on the south bank of the
Red River. There, where the longhorn herds crossed over
into Indian Territory, he provisioned trail crews for the
drive ahead. His store was known to everyone as Doan's
Crossing.

Lon appeared puzzled. "We have a trader here. Why
not talk with him?"

"I seek advice," Quanah announced. "Doan knows the
ways of *tejano* cattlemen. I have it in my mind to do
business with them."

"Business?" Lon said, astonished. "With the *tejanos*?"

"The Texans are our enemies no longer. We must learn to profit from circumstance."

"I do not understand, Father."

Quanah looked thoughtful. "I am friends with the chief of the Cherokee. Lately, I heard he does business with a New Mexican named Brannock. Is that another of your kinsmen?"

"An uncle," Lon said blankly. "His full name is Virgil Brannock."

Quanah eyed him in silence for a moment. "I think perhaps you should ride with me to Doan's Crossing. We can talk along the way."

"Gladly, Father," Lon said. "I am honored."

Quanah returned to the men underneath the shade tree. Lon mounted, leading his packhorse, and rode south along Cache Creek. He thought himself fortunate and doubly honored. On the day of his manhood, he'd been singled out by the chief of the Quahadi. He swelled with pride, bursting to tell someone the news.

Little Raven welcomed him into her lodge. She made a fuss over the shawl and young Hank whooped with delight when he saw the rock candy. From a hidden spot, Little Raven then brought out a velvety buckskin shirt, elaborately beaded across the chest. She presented it to Lon with congratulations on his manhood.

Lon accepted the shirt with proper dignity. Then, unable to contain himself any longer, he told them about Quanah's invitation. Hank was at once envious and greatly impressed. Like most Comanche boys, he had never set foot off the reservation. A trip to the Texas side of the Red River seemed to him a grand adventure.

The reaction from Little Raven was somewhat pensive. She was happy for Lon, but she was concerned as well. For several months she'd been troubled by his defiant attitude. The horse raid, in her mind, had been the turning point. She viewed it in much the same way she looked upon the peyote ritual. His every act seemed designed to renounce his white blood. He considered himself, instead, one of the Quahadi. A Comanche.

All the more worrisome, she saw in Lon many of the traits she'd once seen in her husband. Earl Brannock had turned renegade, defying every authority when he became a *Comanchero*. The youngster, like his father, possessed that same ungovernable wild streak. What frightened her most was that he had now taken to wearing a gun on the reservation. He seemed determined to challenge the authorities.

The terrible part was the reason behind his defiance. While he'd never once spoken of it, Little Raven had a maternal instinct for the truth. His hatred of everything white was because he blamed the pony soldiers for his father's death. Some dark presentiment told her that he was bent on retribution, payment in kind for blood spilled. That, and the gun strapped around his hip, made her wary of the trip to Doan's Crossing. She thought it a mistake for him to venture out into the world of the *tahboy-boh*.

None of her fears were voiced. She knew him too well to think he would heed her counsel. She congratulated him instead on being honored by the great chief of the Quahadi. Then, as she'd planned all along, she prepared a feast to celebrate his birthday. The occasion was a festive one, and he preened at the attention. Once, when he laughed aloud, her heart stopped still.

He looked so much like the man she'd loved and lost.

Doan's Crossing was some forty miles southwest of Fort Sill. The Western Trail bisected the Red at that point and continued onward three hundred miles to the railhead at Dodge City. Since 1878, almost four million longhorns had splashed through the ford outside Jonathan Doan's store.

The Western Trail drove straight through the heart of the Comanche reservation. By treaty, the Indians were powerless to halt the flow of longhorns across their lands. Nor were they permitted to charge a head tax on the vast herds of cattle funneling up the trail. From that was born Quanah Parker's great scheme for the future of his people.

Late the next afternoon Quanah and Lon rode into Doan's Crossing. The main store was a frame structure flanked by several outbuildings and an open-sided warehouse. Chuck wagons were parked all around the warehouse, loading provisions for the drive northward. A dozen or more cowponies stood hip-shot at the hitch rack outside the store. For trailhands, it was the last chance at a drink of whiskey until Dodge City.

Jonathan Doan was a stocky bulldog of a man. Upon sighting Quanah he boomed out a jovial greeting, hurrying forward. A fast friendship had developed between them during his days as a reservation trader. He remembered Lon as well and held out a square, stubby-fingered hand. When he heard the purpose of their visit, he seemed flattered and perhaps a bit bemused. He listened attentively as Quanah outlined the idea.

What the Quahadi chief proposed was exactly what the Cherokee had done with their Outlet grant. A lease arrangement on reservation grazeland would benefit both the Texans and the Comanche. Furthermore, he explained, there was nothing in the Comanche treaty to prohibit such an agreement. He wanted Doan's advice on how the deal might be structured and on a reasonable leasing fee. He asked, as well, that Doan arrange an introduction to some of the larger ranchers.

"Helluva idea," Doan said when he finished. "And I know just the man to get things rolling. His name's Tom Oliver."

Quanah looked relieved. "You believe it can be arranged, then? The Texans will favor such a proposal?"

"Guaranteed," Doan assured him. "You're sittin' right astraddle the Western Trail. How could it miss?"

"Hey, Doan!"

A coarse shout broke into their conversation. Doan turned

and looked across the room. The bar was lined with trailhands and they were staring in Doan's direction. One of them, a wiry feist of a man, ducked his chin at Quanah and Lon. His mouth curled in a smirky grin.

"When'd you start hobnobbin' with gut eaters?"

"You dumb pissant," Doan growled. "This here's Quanah Parker, half Comanche and half Texican. Probably got more white blood than you do."

"That a fact?" the cowhand rasped. "Looks like any other red nigger to me. Stinks like one, too."

"Anybody stinks," Lon said abruptly, "it's you. Try wipin' the cowshit off your nose."

The smile froze on the cowhand's face. He shook his head as if a fly had buzzed his ear. "You're talkin' to me, boy?"

Doan moved to intercede, but Lon was faster. He took a step away from the counter where they were standing. There was something ominously quiet in his voice. "I'm not talkin' to you," he said. "I'm telling you to apologize—right now."

"Apologize!" The Texan let go a harsh bark of laughter. "Why the blue-billy hell would I do a thing like that?"

A cold tinsel glitter lighted Lon's eyes. " 'Cause if you don't, I'm gonna stop your clock."

"You talk mighty gawddamn big for a snot-nosed kid."

"Whyn't you try me, then?"

"Wait!" Doan shouted.

The cowhand clawed at the gun on his hip. Lon's arm dipped in a fast shadowy movement and the Colt appeared in his hand. He extended the pistol, thumbing the hammer, as the Texan got off a hurried snapshot. A slug whizzed past the youngster at the exact instant he feathered the trigger.

A bright red dot pocked the cowhand's shirtfront. His mouth dropped open and his jaw worked in a hoarse grunt. His gun clattered to the floor and he slowly corkscrewed to his knees. Then he slumped forward on his face, dead.

There was a moment of stunned silence. The men at the bar stared down at the cowhand with sullen disbelief. Doan suddenly pulled a sawed-off shotgun from beneath the counter, earing back both hammers. He wagged the muzzle in their direction.

"Don't nobody get any funny ideas."

The trailhands stood stock-still. Doan darted a sharp sidelong look at Quanah. "I'll hold 'em here till things cool down. You and the boy hightail it across the river and don't stop."

Quanah merely nodded, then walked straight to the door. Lon followed along a pace behind, still covering the Texans with his Colt. His face was void of any emotion.

Outside they mounted and turned their horses back across the Red. Neither of them spoke as they rode through the ford and gained the opposite shore.

There seemed nothing left to say.

25

A week later Clint rode into the agency. His eyes were bloodshot and he ached with fatigue. He had been in the saddle almost constantly for the last six days.

Word of the shootout had reached him in a roundabout manner. After the aborted Apache campaign, he had gone directly to Fort Stanton. He felt obligated to resign in person and he'd reported to Ranald Mackenzie. The general reluctantly agreed to forward the paperwork to Washington.

Mackenzie had then presented him with two telegraph messages. One was from the commander at Fort Sill, advising him that Lon had been involved in a killing. The details were sparse, but Quanah Parker was apparently a party in the affair. The shooting had taken place at Doan's Crossing.

The second wire was from the marshal of Fort Worth, Texas. As one lawman to another, he'd felt obliged to contact Clint. The shooting, because it involved Quanah Parker, had been widely reported. The dead trailhand's name was Emmett Jarrott and he had four brothers. There was talk that they intended to settle the score with Lon.

From Fort Stanton, Clint had proceeded on to Spur. There he'd learned of the slaughter of Luis Varga's sheep. Holding nothing back, Elizabeth had told him as well of her call on Stephen Benton. She felt she had the situation in hand, and she'd seen no reason to inform Virgil. She went on to say that Virgil's return had again been delayed.

273

While still in Wyoming, Virgil had received a wire from John Chisum. Influential stockmen from around the West had called an emergency meeting in Denver. Their purpose was to form a broad-based cattlemen's association, an organization of stockgrowers from every territory. Their goal was a cooperative effort in tracking down rustlers who skipped back and forth across boundary lines. John Chisum, who was now bedridden, had urged Virgil to attend the meeting. New Mexico ranchers needed a voice in the formation of the organization.

Clint had stopped overnight at Spur. Virgil's detour through Denver relieved him of one major concern. For the moment, the fight with Stephen Benton had been relegated to a back burner. As for Elizabeth, she seemed entirely capable of looking after affairs at the ranch. Clint's thoughts had therefore centered on the more immediate problem with Lon. The following morning he'd ridden toward Indian Territory.

Little Raven wasn't surprised to see him. When he rode up, she and Hank were working on a pile of deerskins. Neither of them had any doubt as to the purpose of his visit. Nor were they curious as to how he'd learned of the shooting. They simply stopped work, greeting him warmly, and led him inside the lodge. A galvanized coffeepot simmered over the remnants of the morning fire, and he gladly accepted a cup. Little Raven and the boy seated themselves opposite him.

Clint blew steam off the coffee. He took a sip, looking at Little Raven. "Lon up in the mountains?"

"Yes." Her eyes were like matched black pearls. "He hasn't come down since his return from Doan's Crossing."

"What the hell was he doing at Doan's, anyway?"

"He went there with Quanah."

"I know that," Clint said. "I'm asking why."

Little Raven briefly explained. She spoke of Quanah's plan to lease grazeland, as the Cherokee had done. Lon had been invited to accompany the chief, who sought advice from Jonathan Doan. She knew little more than that.

Clint studied her a moment. "What caused the shooting?"

Her voice echoed her dismay. "A drunken *tahboy-boh* insulted Quanah. Lon ordered him to apologize."

"And when he refused," Clint said heavily, "Lon shot him. Is that it?"

"There is talk that the *tejano* fired first."

"All the same, Lon goaded him into it. Isn't that how it happened?"

Her eyes were downcast. "Yes."

Clint rubbed the stubble along his jawline, reflective a moment. "How has he acted since he returned? Does he regret killing the Texan?"

"No," she said, her features shrouded with concern. "Lon believes the man deserved to be killed. He is proud of what he has done."

"He told you that himself?"

"Not in words," she said quietly. "But when he spoke of the killing, I was reminded of the old days. He was like a warrior home from a raid . . . very proud."

Clint drained the last of the coffee. He carefully placed the galvanized cup on the firestones, silent for a time. His eyes narrowed and he subjected her to a long, searching stare.

"What else?" he said. "There's something you're not telling me."

A troubled look came over her face. "The people honor him as they would a warrior. They say he risked his own life in defense of Quanah. At night, they sing his praises around the fires."

Clint watched her intently. "And he accepts their praise as his due. Is that what you're saying?"

She nodded. "The young men travel more often now to his cabin. He has become their leader, and more of them have joined his peyote band." She paused, slowly shook her head. "They say he has strong medicine."

"You're right," Clint said shortly. "Just like the old days."

"I fear for him, old friend. Were he to offer them the pipe, there are those who would smoke it."

"And he'd lead them off on some damnfool nonsense. Maybe even jump the reservation."

"Yes," she replied softly. "Or worse."

"No riddles between us," Clint demanded. "What are you trying to tell me?"

"A wolf cub no longer suckles once he has tasted blood. I fear Strikes-Both-Ways will kill again."

The frown lines around Clint's mouth deepened. He saw only one recourse, and while it was extreme, there seemed no alternative. At length, determined to save the youngster at any cost, he made the decision. He glanced up at Little Raven.

"We cannot allow him to run wild. Do you agree?"

"I love him as my own. How could I not agree?"

"Then it's settled," Clint said. "I'll take him to New Mexico and put him to work on the ranch. He has to be taught to behave himself."

There was a look of deep sadness in her eyes. "I wish there were another way. I cannot bear the thought of losing him."

"What other way is there?"

"None," she said hollowly. "I expected you to come for him. And now you have."

"Would you consider coming with us? I could probably work out something with the agency."

"Thank you, old friend," she said in a low voice. "Bull Calf and I belong here with the Quahadi. We would find no peace among the *tahboy-boh*."

"Neither will Lon," Clint said with a mirthless smile. "Not for a while, anyhow."

Little Raven was quiet, her gaze averted. "It will not be easy," she said after a moment. "Strikes-Both-Ways is ashamed of his white blood. He will resist leaving the People."

Clint's features set in a grim scowl. "He'll do what he's told, or wish he had. I won't take any argument."

"Perhaps you would take some advice."

"I would, and glad to get it. Nobody knows him better than you."

"Talk to him as a man," she cautioned. "Do not treat him like a boy. He obeys no one but himself now."

"Good advice," Clint said. "I'll keep it in mind."

"Uncle."

Hank spoke for the first time since they had entered the lodge. Clint looked across at him. "What is it?"

"When will you talk with my brother?"

"Today," Clint said. "No reason to put it off."

Hank held his gaze. "Will you take me along?"

"Why do you ask?"

"Because . . ." The boy halted, uncertain what he wanted to say. "What would it hurt if I were there? I wouldn't be in the way."

"No, I reckon you wouldn't."

"Then you'll let me go?"

Clint hesitated, flicking a glance at Little Raven. She caught the look and moved her head in a barely perceptible nod. His eyes swung back to the boy.

"How quick could you be ready to leave?"

"I'll get my pony!"

Hank bounded to his feet and disappeared through the doorhole. The lodge was suddenly quiet, the silence somehow strained. On impulse, Clint leaned forward and took Little Raven's hand. He squeezed it gently.

"You've raised a fine son in Bull Calf. Earl would have been proud."

She lowered her head. Tears were unseemly, a thing to be hidden except in mourning. She forced herself to hold it within, saying nothing of her other son. There would be time to grieve later.

When Strikes-Both-Ways was gone.

*   *   *

West of Fort Sill there was a fork in the military road. One branch split off toward the northwest and the other continued on westward. Cottony clouds stood motionless over the distant mountains.

Clint and Hank took the western fork. Some four miles ahead they would turn north, off the road. There, along the banks of a creek, a faint trail led deeper into the mountains. The wilderness trace ended at Lon's cabin.

A rider approached them, headed eastward. Out of the corner of his eye Clint caught some change in the boy. Hank seemed to tense, his bearing suddenly rigid. He shot a hidden glance at his uncle, and then looked straight ahead. He said nothing, though he'd recognized the rider.

Quanah halted his horse in the road. He no longer wore the black broadcloth coat and gray-striped trousers. He was dressed instead in buckskin pants and a loose-fitting linsey shirt. Even so, he was an imposing figure, somehow dignified. His broad features registered nothing.

"*Hao*, scout."

The greeting was directed to Clint. Quanah thought of him as a cavalry scout and still addressed him in that fashion. Clint's expression was equally stolid.

"*Hao*, Quanah."

The Quahadi chief heard something in Clint's tone. He sensed restrained anger, a note of resentment. His gaze shifted to the boy.

"You ride in good company, Bull Calf. Your uncle is a man of great respect."

Hank ducked his head shyly. He was unaccustomed to being addressed in so familiar a manner by the Comanche leader. Quanah smiled indulgently and looked back at Clint. He kept his voice neutral.

"I have just come from your other nephew, Strikes-Both-Ways. I spent the night at his camp."

Clint looped the reins around his saddle horn. He pulled out the makings and began rolling himself a smoke. "Another peyote session?" he asked dryly. "Or maybe a prayer for the dead *tejano*?"

Quanah didn't answer for a moment. "We are not men to badger words. Have you some quarrel with me, scout?"

Clint popped a sulfurhead on his thumbnail. He eyed Quanah over the flare of the match. "Tell me something," he said, lighting his cigarette. "Why did you take the boy to Doan's Crossing?"

"Your brother leases land from the Cherokee. I plan to make a similar arrangement for my own people. The Comanche are poor and need money."

"So?" Clint persisted. "What's that got to do with the boy?"

Quanah shrugged. "Strikes-Both-Ways should know of these things. One day he will be a leader among our people."

"Not likely," Clint said, exhaling smoke. "I'm taking him back to New Mexico."

"You do this because he killed the *tejano*?"

"What better reason?"

"You judge him too harshly, scout. As one of his blood, you should be proud of him. He fought to defend his honor."

"His honor," Clint said bluntly, "or yours?"

Quanah looked uncomfortable. "An insult to one Comanche is an insult to all the Comanche. He acted in good faith."

Clint flicked an ash off his cigarette. "What he did was kill a man for nothing. You could have walked away without a fight."

"From you," Quanah muttered aloud, "those are strange words. How many men have you killed in your time? Do you remember the number?"

"I remember," Clint said with a half-smile. "But I never killed in the name of honor. That seems a feeble excuse to take a man's life."

Quanah let his gaze drift off. He got a faraway look, as

though studying some matter of profound substance. At length, he gave Clint a sideways glance. He smiled stiffly.

"For winters beyond memory, the Comanche ruled wherever they rode. Now we are people who have nothing left but our honor. Perhaps it is a good reason to kill."

Clint fixed him with a piercing look. "Your honor is a personal matter, no one else's. Do your own killing."

"I could not have stopped Strikes-Both-Ways."

"Did you try?"

"Hear me, scout," Quanah replied formally. "You still think of him as a boy and all that is past. He is now a man."

"Man or boy," Clint sid tightly, "he's through here. I'm taking him home."

Quanah nodded wisely. "You misjudge him again, scout. Strikes-Both-Ways *is* home. He knows no other."

"Then it's high time for a change."

Clint gigged his horse. He rode past Quanah with a terse nod, his mouth clamped in a dour line. Hank darted the Quahadi chief a helpless look, then booted his pony into a trot. A short distance up the road, he fell in alongside his uncle.

Quanah sat motionless for a moment. He respected the scout and he regretted their harsh words. Yet he longed for those days now past, when there was no shame to killing. A time of simple truths and uncluttered ways.

The white man's road was hard to keep.

The sun slowly retreated westward. Beneath the late-afternoon heat, the mountains were still and quiet. A warm breeze listlessly stirred the treetops.

Clint rode in the lead. The trail was narrow and rocky, skirting a swift-running brook. For the past hour, with Hank bringing up the rear they had climbed steadily higher through the wilderness. Neither of them had spoken in a long while.

The cabin was less than a half-mile ahead. Clint remembered landmarks from his last visit and knew there wasn't far to go. For an instant, as he brooded on the task before him, his instincts were momentarily lulled. Then, abruptly, he got a prickly sensation and listened harder. All the bird calls had stopped.

Lon stepped out of the woods. The Winchester was cradled across his arms and the holstered Colt was strapped around his waist. He wore greasy buckskins and his hair shone like burnished wheat in the sun. He halted at the side of the trail.

"Uncle Clint," he said, grinning. "You make a lot of noise for an old cavalry scout. Heard you coming a long ways off."

"Save your wisecracks," Clint said sternly. "I want to talk to you."

Lon glanced past him to the boy. "*Hao*, little brother. How are things below?"

"Our mother is well," Hank said. "She wants you to know you are in her thoughts."

"And she in mine," Lon remarked. "I will come to see her soon."

Clint kneed his horse into a walk. Lon swung up behind Hank and they rode forward on the trail. At the clearing, they unsaddled their mounts and turned them into the corral. A stiff silence held as they moved to a patch of shade in front of the cabin.

Lon propped his rifle against the log wall. He exchanged a look with Hank, then folded his arms, waiting. Clint stood for a moment staring off into the forest, his eyes grim. At last, with a tight grip on himself, he turned back to the boys. He nodded to Lon.

"No need to waste words," he said evenly. "The man you killed has a whole slew of kinfolk. The word's out they aim to come lookin' for you."

"Let 'em," Lon said with a devil-may-care grin. "Nobody finds me unless I want to be found."

"You're wrong there," Clint told him. "Anybody can

be tracked down by someone who's determined enough. Texans believe in an eye for an eye."

Lon's mouth curled. "I'd know it before they got within ten miles of here. White men tend to draw attention on a reservation."

"Whether they do or don't doesn't matter. You've overstayed your welcome around here."

"What d'you mean?"

"I mean it's time you moved on. You're going back to New Mexico with me."

"Says you!" Lon hooted. "I'm not going anywhere."

"Yeah, you are," Clint said gruffly. "And I don't want any back talk. We leave tomorrow."

Lon laughed out loud. He pushed away from the cabin and his hand dropped to the holstered Colt. His eyes turned a searing blue. "You sure you wanna try it?"

Clint reacted with blind fury. He closed the distance between them and backhanded the youngster across the mouth. Lon bounced off the cabin wall, blood spurting from a split lip. Before he could recover himself, Clint reached down and jerked the Colt from his holster. Hefting the gun, he shook it in his face.

"Live and learn," Clint growled. 'Don't threaten a man unless you're ready to go whole hog."

"What the hell," Lon mumbled, wiping blood off his mouth. "You knew I wouldn't draw . . . not on you."

"Why all the tough talk, then?"

"I dunno," Lon said sheepishly. "Guess I couldn't think of nothin' else to do."

"Next time think a little longer. You'll save yourself some wear and tear."

"What you got in mind still won't work."

"Why not?"

Lon met his stare. "Because you'd have to lock me up night and day. One way or another, I'd get away and come back here." He hesitated, motioning around the clearing. "This is where I belong."

"We've got mountains in New Mexico."

"You know I'm not talkin' about mountains. I was raised a Comanche and that's what I'll always be. They're my people."

"We're your people too," Clint said. "For God's sake, we're not *tahboy-boh*! We're Brannocks."

"No argument there," Lon conceded. "It's just that I'd sooner be who I am."

"And who's that?"

"Strikes-Both-Ways."

The name somehow rocked Clint. He took a step back, as though he'd been struck a hard blow. His jaws clenched, and without thinking, he handed the gun to the youngster. Then he turned and walked off several paces.

For a long while, he stood lost in thought. His sudden fury—actually striking the youngster—had dulled the edge of his anger. Yet, even more telling, was how Lon saw himself. A Comanche in everything but blood.

Hard as it was to accept, Clint understood now what Quanah had said earlier. The youngster considered Little Raven and Bull Calf to be his family. He called himself Strikes-Both-Ways and he answered to no other name. His place was here and he refused to leave for the best of reasons. It was the only home he'd ever known.

Clint walked back to the cabin. He fixed Lon with a hard look. "Here's the deal," he said. "Come hell or high water, you won't leave the reservation. Not till I give you the say so."

"Fine by me," Lon said agreeably. "I've got no yen to go anywhere, anyhow."

"And you'll stay the hell away from Doan's Crossing. I want your word on it."

"You've got it. I'll stick close to home."

"Well then, it's settled," Clint said with a sudden grin. "So let's talk about something important. What's for supper?"

The boys stared at him blankly. Then, as his grin broadened, they all burst out laughing. Clint draped an arm around their shoulders and walked them toward the cabin door. A thought occurred and he halfway nodded to himself.

He had a notion Little Raven would approve.

26

The stagecoach bounced and swayed. Off to the left, the Rio Bonito sparkled under a midday sun. The driver popped his whip, urging the six-horse hitch onward. Lincoln lay beyond a far bend in the roadway.

Virgil was seated beside one of the coach windows. The other passengers, four men and a woman, had long since lapsed into silence. The heat, mixed with the dust and the jounce of the stage, discouraged conversation. Even the whiskey drummer, seated opposite Virgil, had stopped telling jokes.

From Denver, Virgil had traveled by train to Socorro. There he'd wired ahead, requesting that the Lincoln telegrapher get word to someone at the ranch. His instructions were to have a buckboard waiting when the stage arrived. The long trip to the Outlet and Wyoming, with a stopover in Denver, had kept him away too long. He was anxious to get home.

The meeting in Denver had taken longer than expected. Originally scheduled to last a week, it had dragged on for ten days. The leaders from every cattlemen's association throughout the West were in attendance. Their principal interest was the loss of livestock at the hands of horse thieves and rustlers. Some spoke of an Outlaw Trail that reportedly began on the High Plains and zigzagged through the Rockies. There were rumors that it extended all the way to Old Mexico.

By voice vote, the ranchers agreed on a name the first

285

day. The organization would be called the International Cattlemen's Association, though its most distant member was from southern Texas. After that the meeting degenerated into squabbling among the various cliques. One faction advocated a war of extermination against the outlaws. Another group supported government intervention, reliance on U.S. marshals and federal courts. None of them seemed willing to compromise.

On the sixth day, Virgil finally took the floor. He argued persuasively for large contributions from each of the member associations. His purpose was to create a war chest to be used on the political front. He believed a lobbying effort should be mounted with each of the state and territorial legislatures. Once the politicians were in their pockets, they could do as they pleased with the rustlers. Summary justice, he noted, was illegal as hell. Hanging thieves required the support of friends in high places.

The members were impressed. They knew of Virgil's work in New Mexico and his bold invasion of the Cherokee Outlet. Enterprising rogues themselves, they admired a man who mixed pragmatism with guile. By unanimous vote, they levied adequate funds to establish a war kitty. Then, at Charlie Goodnight's suggestion, they voted Virgil onto the board of directors. His job would be to allocate funds where needed and coordinate the lobbying effort. Which everyone accepted as the polite term for bribing politicians.

The next four days were spent hammering out an accord. The hard-line faction finally browbeat their opponents into a declaration of war. A comittee was formed to locate and hire what would be entered in the association records as "regulators." Essentially hired gunmen, the regulators would travel wherever needed, unhindered by territorial boundaries. Their job would be to track down and eradicate the outlaw gangs. Summary justice, dispensed at the end of a rope, would be their stock in trade.

Upon leaving Denver, Virgil felt he had accomplished something of far-reaching substance. He'd been accepted as a member of a club comprising the West's most powerful stockgrowers. His election to the board of directors was a high honor, one that carried immense prestige. The connections he had made were of incalculable value where business affairs were concerned. He foresaw the day when Spur would rival the Jinglebob or Alexander Swan's Two Bar spread. The future suddenly looked limitless.

Out the coach window, Virgil saw a familiar landmark roll past. He realized they were within a mile of Lincoln and his jubilation quickened. All the way from Denver his thoughts had been on Elizabeth. He wanted to share his triumph with her, watch her eyes brighten with excitement. She alone understood the extent of his ambition, the importance of creating a legacy for those to come. A legacy to mark the Brannock bloodline.

Unbidden, his thoughts turned to Clint. The papers in Denver had headlined the inconclusive Apache campaign. A letter from Elizabeth informed him of Clint's break with the army and his subsequent trip to Indian Territory. She alluded to problems with Lon, without detailing the specifics. From the tone of her letter, Virgil assumed that all was well at Spur. She had made only passing mention of the lawsuit against Stephen Benton. The court hearing was set for September 9, some three weeks off. She was confident of the final verdict.

Virgil was relieved but puzzled. He knew Stephen Benton to be a vindictive man, capable of the vilest act. The lawsuit could only have fueled what already amounted to a vendetta. At the very least, he'd expected another probe onto Spur lands by Luis Varga's sheep. Yet, according to Elizabeth's letter, Benton had made no effort at retaliation. All that seemed out of character, at odds with Benton's past methods. There was a touch of the enigma about it, and that worried Virgil. He prided himself on knowing his enemies.

The stage rolled to a halt outside the express office. When Virgil climbed down, he found Morg and Brad waiting for him. The boys greeted him with wide grins and arm-pumping handshakes. His wire had arrived yesterday and Elizabeth had asked them to meet the stage. Their orders were to put him in the buckboard and drive him straight home. Elizabeth was planning a family celebration to mark his return.

Something in their manner rang false. Virgil halted beside the buckboard and demanded an explanation. Hesitant at first, they finally broke under his sharp stare. The riddle of Stephen Benton was shortly revealed as the boys tried to outtalk one another. Brad recounted the night of what the hands jokingly referred to as the "sheep massacre." Morg followed with the story of his mother's mysterious trip to Santa Fe. She'd confided in no one, with the possible exception of Clint. Still, it seemed unnatural that Benton hadn't retaliated in some fashion.

"One more thing," Morg concluded. "Mom wanted to tell you herself, but we've already spilled the beans anyway. Odell Slater quit last Saturday."

"Quit?" Virgil rumbled. "Why the hell would he quit?"

" 'Cause of Mom," Morg said, lowering his eyes. "She rode him hard for killing Varga's sheep. He finally got a bellyful and asked for his wages."

"Christ!" Virgil fumed. "I warned Varga what would happen. Slater was just following orders."

"Well, he's long gone now."

"Who'd your mother take on as foreman?"

Morg laughed. "You're not gonna believe it, but she's runnin' things herself. Every morning, the *segundos* report up to the main house. She's got 'em jumpin' like crickets on a hot stove."

"I'll be damned," Virgil said, astounded. "Your mother never ceases to amaze me. How's she managed?"

"Tough as nails, that's how! They don't call her the Iron Butterfly for nothin'."

"No, they certainly don't. She's got more starch than most men."

"Speakin' of which," Brad interjected, "here comes our fearless sheriff."

The remark denoted a mood spreading throughout Lincoln County. Pat Garrett had emerged oddly tarnished from the death of Billy the Kid. Townspeople and large ranchers tended to approve his methods. But there was an altogether different attitude among cowhands and *mexicanos*. Their feeling was that he had shot William Bonney in cold blood, without warning. Some called it an execution.

Garrett crossed the street from the courthouse. His expression was glum and his slouch-shouldered manner lacked the vitality of days past. Virgil thought he looked curiously dispirited, like a kicked dog. The lawman barely nodded to the boys and gave Virgil a limp handshake. His eyes were jaundiced, without fire.

"Figured I better warn you," he said. "Luis Varga's been making threats against you."

Virgil appeared unsurprised. "I take it you're talking about his sheep?"

Garrett nodded. "Odell Slater showed up here after he quit your outfit. He got drunk as a hoot owl and ran off at the mouth. Claimed you ordered him to kill Varga's sheep."

"That a fact?" Virgil said, avoiding a direct reply. "Have you got some idea of arresting me?"

"Nope," Garrett said frankly. "Varga come to see me and wanted to swear out a warrant. I told him to stuff it."

"And that's when he started making threats?"

"Yeah, it was. He's sayin' the law only works for *gringos*. The word's around he aims to square accounts himself."

Virgil thought for a moment. "Has he actually said he intends to kill me?"

"Not just exactly," Garrett observed. "He's telling everybody there's no justice for *mexicanos*. Says it's between you and him now, a matter of honor."

Outwardly Virgil appeared calm and impassive. Yet he was all too aware that he'd been marked for death. At Stephen Benton's orders, Varga had turned the sheep incident into a personal affront. Worse, Varga had shrewdly raised the specter of racial injustice.

Virgil felt a grudging admiration. The groundwork had been laid for a showdown, with public sentiment favoring Varga. A personal insult, tinged with racial overtones, entitled any man to confront his adversary. The law took a "hands-off" policy toward such affairs, for it fell under an unwritten code. The aggrieved party had a right to demand satisfaction.

"Offhand," Virgil said in a remote, musing tone, "I'd say they've snookered me pretty good. I'm wrong whatever I do."

"Keep a sharp eye," Garrett cautioned. "You won't get a helluva lot of warning."

A puzzled frown knotted Virgil's features. "Any idea where I might find Odell Slater?"

"After he sobered up, he took off. Nobody's seen him in a couple of days."

"Figures," Virgil said. "If I was him, I would've left town too."

"Gettin' to be a regular epidemic. I'm not long for Lincoln myself."

"What do you mean?"

"Guess you haven't heard," Garrett said, clearly disgruntled. "I won't be renominated for sheriff. I'm on my way out."

"News to me," Virgil said. "What happened?"

"Billy the Kid, that's what happened! Folks are sayin' I could've taken him alive. Wish't I'd never heard of the sorry bastard."

"What about Chisum?" Virgil asked. "Won't he support you?"

"Wouldn't matter," Garrett said. "The party regulars want a candidate that can win. They've cut me loose."

"What'll you do now?"

"Haven't decided just yet. Hell, who knows, maybe I'll try my hand at ranchin'. People gotta eat."

"One thing's for sure. It'd beat wearing a badge."

"You just said a mouthful."

There was a strained silence. They shook hands and Garrett started to turn away. Then, from upstreet, a voice was raised in an angry shout. "Brannock!"

Virgil swung around at the sound of his name. Outside the saloon, he saw Luis Varga step off the boardwalk into the street. The *mexicano* sheepman had a pistol in hand, holding it at his side. *"Hijo de puta!"* he cursed. "Defend yourself."

Garrett ducked behind the buckboard. Virgil shoved Morg aside and went for his own gun. As he swept his coattail back, Varga drew a bead on him. Virgil cleared leather at the exact instant the *mexicano* fired.

The slug struck Virgil just above the belt line. He stumbled forward, clutching his stomach, and suddenly sagged at the knees. He sat down heavily in the dirt, supporting himself upright with his left arm. His vision blurred and he tried to focus on Varga. His hand shook unsteadily as he raised the pistol.

Upstreet, Varga thumbed the hammer for a second shot. He sighted carefully, amazed that the *gringo* was still upright. As his finger touched the trigger, he caught movement off to one side. His eyes shifted and he saw Brad with a Colt six-gun extended at arm's length. Too late, he tried to swing his pistol onto the younger man. Brad shot him in the chest.

A bloodburst splattered across Varga's shirt pocket. His mouth opened in a gashlike cry of pain and his face went chalky. Another slug dusted him front and rear as Brad fired again. His hands splayed at empty air and he vomited a great gout of blood down over his chest. His eyeballs rolled back in his head, the sockets ghostly white, and his legs buckled. He fell dead in the street.

Virgil collapsed, still attempting to raise his pistol. He slumped forward and dropped facedown in the dirt. Morg was abruptly galvanized, pushing away from the buckboard as his father went down. He fell to his knees and rolled Virgil over on his back. A trickle of blood leaked out of Virgil's mouth.

"Get your mother," he said weakly. "Hurry."

Brad put a hand on the boy's shoulder. "You stay with your pa. I'll get her."

Morg nodded, holding his father in his arms. Brad pushed past Garrett, who was moving forward, and jumped into the buckboard. He backed it into the street and lashed out with the reins. The team bolted into a headlong gallop.

Garrett leaned down, about to check Virgil's wound. Morg batted his hand away with a protective blow. His face twisted in a grimace and he looked up at the lawman. "Fetch the doc. Go on . . . get him!"

Ugly lines strained the youngster's face, and Garrett simply nodded. He hurried off down the street.

The flesh around the bullet wound was puffy and discolored. Virgil lay stretched out on the operating table, his features waxen. He was naked, the lower half of his body covered with a sheet.

Dr. Wood carefully cleaned the wound with a carbolic solution. He had shooed Morg into the waiting room after the boy helped him undress Virgil. Working swiftly, he'd then put Virgil under with ether and gathered a tray of instruments. He was now prepared to operate.

The position of the wound looked bad. Having operated on dozens of gunshot victims, Wood knew there was no time to waste with a stomach wound. Unless the operation was performed within an hour, the patient invariably died from massive internal hemorrhage. Nor was he encouraged by Virgil's irregular pulse and shallow breathing. He selected a scalpel from the tray.

Blood spurted as his incision opened the abdominal wall. He quickly applied sterilized wadding and stemmed the flow with clamps. Bending closer, he examined the cavity and found none of the major vessels severed. His hopes were momentarily lifted and he explored further. The bullet had entered slightly above and to the right of the bellybutton. The wound channel appeared to drop downward at an acute angle.

Wood probed deeper, then suddenly stopped. His features paled and he cursed savagely to himself. Gingerly working his way through the ropy intestines, he counted five perforations along the track of the bullet. All hope vanished, for he'd never known a patient to recover from extensive damage of the lower bowels. He probed deeper still and found the slug lodged at the base of the spine. His face beaded with sweat.

Stepping back, Wood mentally cataloged the injuries. Nothing in his experience, and certainly nothing in the medical journals, offered a solution. The bullet itself, which he dared not remove, would result in paralysis of the lower limbs. As for the perforated intestines, the prognosis was even graver. At best, he gave Virgil twelve hours. Anything more would be a miracle.

From the tray, Wood took a suturing needle and a spool of catgut. Slowly, with meticulous stitches, he began repairing the shredded intestines. In the end, however carefully he sewed, he knew it was nothing more than a stopgap measure. His skill could stop the hemorrhaging and prolong life for a short while. The man on the table would still die.

Dr. Chester Wood was an agnostic. Yet, as he sutured, he uttered a small prayer. He hoped Elizabeth would hurry.

*   *   *

Early that evening the buckboard slid to a stop outside the clinic. A fresh team of horses, lathered with sweat, stood hooked in the traces. Brad had pushed them at a lope all the way from Spur.

Elizabeth hopped from the buckboard. Her skirts lifted high, she ran up the pathway. Jennifer was only a step behind, followed closely by Brad and John Taylor. They found Morg alone in the waiting room. His features were grim.

The door to the inner office opened. Wood closed it behind him and moved into the waiting room. The others turned in his direction, suddenly enveloped in a thick silence. His expression was stony, revealing nothing.

Elizabeth searched his eyes. "Virgil . . ." she said in a shaky voice. "Is he . . . ?"

"Holding on," Wood said gently. "I've got him dosed with laudanum."

"Will he . . . ?" Elizabeth stopped, drew a deep, unsteady breath. "How bad is it?"

Wood's eyes appeared to turn inward on something too terrible for speech. He slowly shook his head, staring at her with a dark empty look. Elizabeth put a hand to her throat, all the color drained from her face. Her voice failed her.

"No!" Jennifer cried, watching him with wide-eyed horror. "You mustn't let him—"

She choked on the word, unable to finish. Wood lifted his hands in a hopeless shrug. "I'm sorry," he said. "I've done all I can."

"Oh—my—God . . ."

A strangled scream rose from Jennifer's throat. She began to weep in an odd whimpering way, like a hurt child. For a moment it appeared she might slump to the floor, and then she turned toward Brad. He enfolded her in his arms.

Morg lowered his head, no longer able to watch. An hour or so earlier, Wood had told him the worst. His father had begun to hemorrhage, apparently the result of sutures tearing loose. Virgil's limbs were cold to the touch and his pulse rate was dropping. The physician dared not attempt another operation.

"Elizabeth . . ." Wood said now. "There's not much time. I suggest you go in alone."

Elizabeth took hold of herself. She put on a brave face, summoning some inner reserve, and nodded. Wood walked her to the door, holding it open as she entered the office. He closed it softly behind her.

The room was bathed in the cider glow of a lamp. Virgil's features were ashen, his breathing labored. Elizabeth moved to the operating table, took his hand in hers. His skin was cold and clammy, and she recognized the signs. She wanted not to believe, but her medical training overrode emotion. She knew she'd arrived barely in time.

Tears sprang to her eyes. Her mind reeled with the impossibility of his death. She recalled so vividly the day of their marriage, their weekend honeymoon. His wonder that their firstborn was a girl, and his pride that she'd given him a son. A lifetime of shared dreams and unimaginable triumphs and love. There seemed so much left to do, all their plans for the future.

She brushed away the tears. Bending down, she ran her hand over his hair and kissed him tenderly on the mouth. He stirred, as though waiting for her touch, and broke through the hold of the sedative. His eyes opened and he stared at her groggily. A slow smile warmed his face.

"Beth . . ."

"Yes, sweetheart," she whispered, her lips trembling. "I'm here now."

"I—"

His voice cracked. She leaned closer, her eyes shining moistly. "Yes," she said huskily, "I hear you. What is it?"

"I . . ."

For what seemed a sliver of eternity, he tried to speak.

His eyes glazed over and a pulse throbbed one last time in his neck. Then, as though extinguished on a shallow intake of breath, the light went out of his eyes. The last sound he heard was Elizabeth's voice.

"I love you too," she said. "I always will."

27

The casket was borne along by six cowhands. A few steps behind the pallbearers were Elizabeth and Clint, followed by the rest of the family. Funeral guests, and the balance of the ranch hands, were strung out in a long column.

The procession entered the family cemetery. The plot was located beneath a tall shade tree, looking westward toward the mountains. Some years ago, shortly after settling on the Rio Hondo, Virgil had selected the site himself. He was the first of the Brannocks to be buried there.

The cowhands lowered the coffin onto planks laid across the open grave. Then they removed their hats and stepped back. Elizabeth walked to the side of the grave, supporting herself on Clint's arm. Jennifer and Morg, along with Brad and the housekeeper, Mrs. Murphy, stopped behind them. There was a moment of leaden silence.

The mourners were packed row upon row around the small cemetery. Sallie Chisum was there, representing her uncle, who was too ill to travel. Beside her stood John Taylor and Dr. Chester Wood and several ranchers from distant outfits. Altogether, including the cowhands, more than a hundred people had gathered to pay homage to the founder of Spur.

For Clint, there was a sense of the unreal about the burial. Late that morning, he had ridden in from Indian Territory. Upon entering the house, he'd learned that Virgil had been killed day before yesterday. The shock had barely registered before guests began arriving for the graveside services. Grimy from the trail, he'd just had time for a quick bath and a shave.

Even now, with the casket before him, he found it difficult to accept. Yet, despite the unreality, he was overwhelmed by a mixture of grief and guilt. What he'd feared most had happened, and in large measure, he blamed himself. Had he stayed closer to Spur, he might somehow have prevented Virgil's death. His trip to the reservation seemed not just ill-timed, but miserably shortsighted. He felt it had cost him his last brother.

A preacher from town had agreed to perform the services. He moved to the head of the grave, dressed in his black funeral suit, and opened his Bible. The mourners bowed their heads as he began to read.

"The Lord is my shepherd; I shall not want. He maketh me to lie down in green pastures; he leadeth me beside the still waters. He restoreth my . . ."

Elizabeth scarcely heard the words. She stared at the coffin, her eyes like glazed alabaster, and saw nothing. Instead, revealed in her mind's eye was the image of all that had once been and would never be again. Her thoughts were suspended in the emptiness of unexpired emotions, and within the darkness of her torment she sought meaning. She found only the realization that nothing remains constant.

Still, she grieved for what seemed to her a senseless death. She was haunted by the belief that Virgil's life had been extinguished to no purpose. As though she had closed her eyes for only a moment, she awoke to find that the order of all about her had changed. Deep inside, she felt somehow cheated and yet oddly aware that there was constancy even in the midst of change. Although Virgil was gone, he would never really cease to exist. A part of him would forever be . . .

". . . with the certainty that we shall all meet again at the Resurrection, through Jesus Christ our Lord. Amen."

The preacher closed his Bible. Then the sound of ropes

sawing on wood jarred Elizabeth back to the present. She blinked and saw the pallbearers gently lowering the casket into the ground. She took hold of herself, fought the sudden rush of tears, and looked away from the grave. Her thoughts hardened to indrawn bleakness, focusing on the task ahead. A life for a life . . .

Jennifer broke down. Wracked by sobs, she tried to muffle her grief with a handkerchief. Brad put an arm around her shoulders as the top of the coffin disappeared into the ground. When Eizabeth turned away from the gravesite, they fell in beside her. Morg and Mrs. Murphy, who was crying loudly, brought up the rear. Of the family members, only Clint remained behind. He watched without expression as several cowhands moved forward with shovels.

The crowd parted before Elizabeth. She paused here and there to accept condolences and exchange a word with old friends. Chester Wood appeared particularly sorrowful, and the cowhands nodded respectfully as she moved past. She led the way from the cemetery and walked toward the center of the compound. Some of the ranchers had a long way to travel and custom required that they be fed before departing. A large meal, prepared by the bunkhouse cooks, was already spread on outdoor tables.

Sallie Chisum halted beside Clint. He stared into the open grave, his eyes vacant. The men with shovels had delayed, waiting at a respectful distance. She touched his arm.

"I'm so terribly sorry," she said softly. "I know how close you and Virgil were."

"Yeah, we were," Clint said, still staring down at the coffin. "Hard to believe he's gone."

"Uncle John asked to be remembered. He thought the world of Virgil."

"Tell him I'm obliged. He was about the best friend Virge ever had."

"I know he'll appreciate the sentiment. All the more so since it comes from you."

Clint merely nodded, his features abstracted. After a moment, she lightly touched his arm again, then turned toward the compound. He seemed only vaguely aware that she had walked away, that he was once more alone. His gaze was still fixed on the grave.

He was thinking of Stephen Benton.

The guests began departing late that afternoon. Some would camp beside the trail that night on their homeward journey. Others would travel through the night and on into the next day.

A pall fell over the compound. When the last of the guests rode out, everything seemed abnormally quiet. All work chores had been suspended for the funeral and the cowhands loafed around outside the bunkhouse. Yet there was none of the bantering and laughter common to a gathering of rough men.

To them, Virgil had always seemed larger than life. They spoke of him in the same vein as John Chisum and Charlie Goodnight. On the Rio Hondo, he was already a legend and the stories would soon grow to mythical proportions. The cowhands had thought him beyond the frailties of ordinary men, somehow indestructible. His death sobered them, made them aware of their own mortality.

Jennifer retreated to her room. As for many young girls, her father had been a compelling force in her life. The image of him laid out in his coffin left her unstrung and inconsolable. She wanted nothing more than to cloister herself and be alone with her heartbreak. Morg and Brad, who were equally grief-stricken, wandered off down by the river. Their bereavement was inward, for convention dictated that grown men never showed emotion. The sudden emptiness in their lives was shared in silence.

Some while later Elizabeth entered the parlor. She found Clint slumped in an overstuffed chair, smoking a cigarette.

His features were drawn and he looked up with a glassy smile. Her own face was tortured with anguish, but she'd cried herself out. She felt drained of tears, curiously numb.

Clint waited while she seated herself on the sofa. "How's Jen?" he asked. "Any better?"

"Not really," Elizabeth said with a dazed smile. "She can't accept the fact that her father is gone."

"Know the feeling," Clint said dully. "Things won't be the same without him."

"Yes," she said in a hushed voice. "Never the same again."

"How are you holding up?"

"Oh, I'll get through it somehow. As the minister so tactfully put it—life goes on."

Clint grunted sharply. "Preachers are full of cheery advice. Guess it helps to wear rose-colored glasses."

When she didn't respond, Clint took a long drag on his cigarette. He exhaled smoke, watching her. "Will you be able to manage things by yourself?"

"Yes, I can manage," she said. "Of course, I was hoping you might stay on. Virgil always wanted you to be a part of Spur."

"You don't need me," Clint said vaguely. "Morg's got cattle in his blood, and he's near full-grown. From what I've seen, Brad's no slouch either. He'll help take up the slack."

"What if I said I do need you? Would that change your mind?"

Clint avoided her gaze. His feelings about her whipsawed from one extreme to the other. What he felt for her was unlike anything he'd ever known for another woman. Yet he was uncomfortable with the emotion, and only too aware that she thought of him as a brother. To stay on at Spur would spoil it, and somehow dishonor the memory of Virgil. He told himself it was time to move on.

"You know me"—he laughed, spread his hands—"I'm

the original fiddle-foot. Always got an itch to see what's over the next hill.''

Her face was serious. "What will you do?"

"What comes natural," Clint said with an odd smile. "There's always work for an old law dog."

"Aren't we the pair," she murmured. "We talk all around it without ever saying his name."

"Whose name?"

"Stephen Benton."

Clint's expression was unreadable. "What about Benton?"

"One of us," she said in a low, intense whisper, "will have to kill him. Had you planned to flip a coin for the privilege?"

Clint stood abruptly. He tossed his cigarette into the fireplace and moved to the parlor window. Outside, he saw Brad appear on the riverbank and walk toward the house. At length, he scrubbed his face with his palms and turned back to Elizabeth. His voice was hard and determined.

"I'm leaving for Santa Fe," he said. "I don't want any foolish talk about you coming along."

She leaned forward, her face clouded by concern. "If you kill Benton, you'll be an outlaw all the rest of your life. You'll never wear a badge again. Is that what you want?"

Clint uttered a broken laugh. "You intended to kill him yourself. Where's the difference?"

"I'm the widow." Her gaze didn't waver. "I'd never be prosecuted for killing my husband's murderer. It simply wouldn't come to trial."

"What proof do you have that he's behind Virgil's murder?"

"Well, none—" she said doubtfully. "But everyone knows he's responsible."

"Huh-uh," Clint said, shaking his head. "That won't hold water and you know it. You'd be branded a murderess yourself."

"And you?" She entreated him with her eyes. "I can't bear the thought of you in prison—or worse."

Clint waved his hand as though dusting away the problem. "Don't forget, I know all the tricks of getting lost and staying lost. They won't catch me."

"Perhaps not," she said, lowering her eyes. "But even then, I'd never see you again. I would have lost Virgil and you."

Clint studied her a moment, his face masked by conflict. Then his eyes went cold and vengeful. His voice was barely audible.

"Benton has to be killed," he said. "Otherwise he'll walk away clean. The law can't touch him."

She nodded, then smiled a little. "So nothing I say will dissuade you."

"No," Clint said calmly. "But I don't want any argument where you're concerned. Just stay put and leave it to me—all right?"

She struggled to keep her voice under control. "All right," she promised, "on one condition. Should anything happen to you . . ."

"Nothing will," Clint assured her. "I'm an old hand at this sort of thing."

"Will I see you again?"

"Why, sure you will. Nobody keeps us Brannocks apart for long."

Clint crossed to the sofa. He bent down and kissed her lightly on the cheek. Her hand touched his face, lingering there a moment. A terrible sense of loss came over her and tears welled up in her eyes. He stepped back, looking at her as though fixing her forever in memory. Then he walked from the parlor.

Outside, he found Brad seated on the veranda. The young man uncoiled from the porch swing and got to his feet. Clint nodded, moving toward him. "Where's Morg?"

"Down by the river," Brad said. "I figured he needed some time alone. He's pretty busted up."

"Only natural," Clint observed. "Him and his dad were two of a kind."

"Yeah, they sure were."

Clint paused, cleared his throat. "I wanted to thank you for what you did. You bought Virge some extra time."

"Only wish't I'd acted sooner. I might've stopped Varga before he got started."

"Nobody could've done more. I'm proud of the way you handled yourself."

"Look here," Brad said suddenly. "I know where you're headed and what you aim to do. I'd like to come along."

Clint stared at him. "Come along for what?"

"You're fixin' to kill Benton. Way I hear it, he don't travel alone. Another gun might come in handy."

"I appreciate the offer, but I'd prefer you stick close to Elizabeth. She'll need your help running Spur."

Brad ducked his head. "That sounds like you won't be back this way."

"Life's funny," Clint said, smiling. "Things don't always work out the way you figure."

They shook hands with a firm grasp. A short while later Clint rode out on the buckskin gelding. The sun was dropping lower by the time he gained the western foothills. There he paused, twisting around in the saddle, and looked back at the valley. Some inner voice told him it was a last look.

His days on the Rio Hondo were done.

The gathering forenoon heat beat down on Santa Fe. Few people were on the streets and the plaza itself was virtually empty. A mangy dog lay sprawled in the shade of the bandstand.

Clint was posted on the west side of the plaza. He'd been on the road for three days and his jawline was dark with stubble. Shortly before eleven that morning, he had circled town and left his horse hitched behind the train station. Hat tugged low, he had then walked uptown.

So far, no one had recognized him. He stood beneath the portico of a notions store, partially hidden by the shade. His gaze was fixed on the opposite side of the plaza, the southeast corner. He was waiting for the noon hour, confident that all men were creatures of habit. Stephen Benton took his midday meal in a café down from the notions store. Ever punctual, he crossed the plaza on the stroke of twelve.

From where Clint was standing, the U.S. marshal's office was across the street. He stiffened as Ned Holt, the territory's chief lawman, stepped through the door. Holt happened to glance in his direction and Clint moved deeper into the shade of the portico. The marshal took a hitch at his gunbelt and crossed to the opposite corner.

Holt was a stocky, broad-shouldered man with watchful eyes and a dark mustache. He halted a pace away from Clint, frowning heavily. "Hullo, Clint," he said. "Sorry to hear about your brother."

"One of those things," Clint said, no timbre in his voice. "Happens to the best of us."

Holt hesitated, considering. "Word's out you resigned your army commission. Guess that makes you a civilian now."

"Appears that way," Clint said equably. "You driving at something, Ned?"

"Well, I reckon that changes the shape of things. What with you not wearin' a badge anymore."

"I don't take your point."

"Yeah, you do," Holt said deliberately. "You're here to settle accounts with Benton. Hell, it's written all over you."

Clint's eyes narrowed. "Whatever I'm here for, it's a private matter. Has nothing to do with you, Ned."

Holt grunted sourly. "You know better than that, Clint. I can't let you shoot a man down in cold blood. Not even a sorry sonovabitch like Benton."

"Suppose I told you it wouldn't work like that?"

"What d'you mean?"

"You forgot about Benton's watchdog."

"Wilbur Latham?"

Clint nodded. "Benton will get a helluva lot better shake than he gave Virgil."

"Even so," Holt said, "I can't let you do it. No man's got the right to take the law into his own hands."

"Don't try to stop me, Ned."

"What would you do," Holt demanded, "kill me too?"

"I'd rather not."

Clint stared him straight in the eye. Holt knew the look and he understood that it was no idle threat. Any attempt to intervene would almost certainly result in his own death. He'd seen Clint in action too many times to doubt the outcome.

"Jesus," he muttered. "Why'd you have to turn in your badge? That would've give me an easy out."

"Next time I'll—"

Clint abruptly stopped. He saw Benton, accompanied by Wilbur Latham, round the southeast corner. They crossed the street and entered the parklike plaza behind the bandstand. For a moment they were hidden from view.

"Stay out of it, Ned."

With a last warning, Clint stepped off the boardwalk. He crossed from the notions store to an entrance at the west side of the plaza. The pathway he took intersected other pathways at the base of the Civil War monument. He walked forward at an unhurried pace.

Benton and Lathan spotted him at almost the same instant. As they cleared the monument on the far side, they halted, staring at him. Benton's face went slack with fear and he seemed rooted in place. Latham brushed past him, moving forward a step. He positioned himself to block Clint.

"Forget it," he said with a lazy smile. "You're liable to stretch your luck."

Clint's eyes were stoned with rage. "Time to earn your pay, Wilbur. Get to it."

"Let's talk about—"

Hoping for an edge, Latham tried an old ruse. As he spoke, his hand swept upward toward his pistol. Clint saw it coming and beat him to the draw by a split second. The first slug jolted Latham, sent him windmilling backward a couple of steps. Clint shot him again and the bullet punched through the gunman's skull. He dropped dead in the pathway.

Benton scurried around behind the monument. The tall granite column was broad at the base and effectively screened him for a moment. When he popped back into view, he had a bulldog pistol extended at arm's length. His eyes were maddened with fear and his hand shook violently. He fired twice, quick snap shots scarcely a heartbeat apart.

One slug plucked at Clint's sleeve. The other sizzled past like an angry wasp. He sighted over the top of his Colt, taking deliberate aim, and touched the trigger. A starburst of blood exploded across Benton's breastbone. His jaw worked in soundless amazement and the bulldog pistol fell from his hand. Shuffling forward, his legs gave way and he crumpled against the base of the monument. He lay perfectly still.

All around the plaza passersby were frozen in an attitude of stunned disbelief. Clint stood there, thumb hooked over the six-gun's hammer, staring at the body. A footstep on the path behind him alerted him too late. Ned Holt rapped out a sharp command.

"Drop it, Clint. Don't make me shoot you."

A swift beat of time slipped past. Clint debated whether to fight and end it there or take his chances with a judge. Then, not yet ready to die, he dropped the Colt on the ground. There was no need to await the lawman's next command. He raised his hands overhead.

Ned Holt marched him off to the territorial prison.

28

The engineer cut the throttle and set the brakes. Steam hissed and the train rolled to a stop outside the depot. At the rear, the conductor stepped off the passenger coach.

General Ranald Mackenzie emerged onto the platform. He turned extending his hand, and assisted Elizabeth from the coach. John Taylor was next out the door, his arms weighted down with luggage. They walked toward the end of the depot.

Three days past Elizabeth had received a wire from the U.S. marshal. The message advised her that Clint had been charged with two counts of manslaughter. He was being held in the territorial prison, awaiting a court hearing. The proceedings would determine whether he should be bound over for trial.

Elizabeth immediately telegraphed Ira Hecht. She authorized him to act on Clint's behalf and request that bail bond be set by the court. Whatever the amount, she agreed to pledge Spur as surety against Clint's release. Some hours later, Hecht wired back with sobering news. The court refused to set bond pending the hearing.

Late that same evening Elizabeth appeared unannounced at Fort Stanton. John Taylor escorted her into post headquarters, where she demanded to see the commanding general. Summoned from his private quarters, Mackenzie greeted her with cordial deference. She informed him of the situation and outlined how she intended to proceed. No great persuasion was required to enlist Mackenzie's support.

The following morning they departed for Santa Fe. On the stagecoach, and later aboard the train, Elizabeth and Mackenzie plotted strategy. He had wired ahead, requesting a personal interview with Governor Lew Wallace. No mention was made regarding the purpose of his visit or the urgency behind his request. Nor was it stated that he would be accompanied by the widow of Virgil Brannock. Forewarned was forearmed, and their plan was to take the governor off guard.

From the train depot, they proceeded directly to the Exchange Hotel. While they were being shown to their rooms, Taylor went off to collect Ira Hecht. For the next hour they huddled in a final strategy session with the young lawyer. He informed them that the political establishment had been thrown into disarray by Benton's death. Nonetheless, the dead man's former cronies were pressing for a quick arraignment and a speedy trial. Their object was to smear the Brannock name with a manslaughter conviction.

Hecht went on to explain. The November elections were less than three months away. Among the members of the Santa Fe Ring, there was widespread concern for the outcome. With Benton dead, the source of their leadership had been removed at a critical time. Worse, they were all too aware that the reform movement was attracting groundswell support from *mexicanos*. By convicting Clint, they hoped to tar Elizabeth by association and thereby undercut the reform candidates.

A rumor was already circulating regarding the killings. Clint's motive, according to the grapevine, was not revenge alone. As the brother-in-law of Elizabeth Brannock, he had acted as well to eliminate the opposition leader. Stephen Benton's murder, people were whispering, was motivated as much by politics as by personal matters. No one questioned that the rumor had been started by cronies of the former ringleader. Yet people loved nothing quite so much as a juicy scandal. Whether truth or lie, the gossips were working overtime.

Hecht concluded on a somber note. Where Clint was concerned, the political situation was a double-edged sword. Should his case go to trial, the jurors might easily perceive him as a pawn in the struggle for power. On the other hand, they might just as easily brand him a cold and calculating killer, the tool of his sister-in-law. All things considered, the simplest solution was to avoid the risk of a formal court hearing. An appeal to the governor seemed the next logical step.

Elizabeth's reaction somewhat mystified the young attorney. Far from being upset, she positively radiated confidence. Yet, when he questioned her, she sidestepped a direct reply. She simply smiled an enigmatic smile and told him not to worry.

Outside the hotel, they parted company. Hecht returned to his office, thoroughly baffled. Elizabeth and Mackenzie, trailed by John Taylor, crossed the plaza to the Governor's Palace. While Taylor waited in the anteroom, an aide ushered them into the governor's private office. Elizabeth swept through the door like a grande dame at a society gala.

"Governor," she trilled, extending her hand. "How nice of you to see us on such short notice."

Lew Wallace appeared befuddled. He looked from Elizabeth to Mackenzie and back again. He accepted her hand by the fingertips and stopped himself just short of bowing. After asking them to be seated, he dropped into the chair behind his desk. His gaze shifted to Mackenzie.

"To be frank," he said, "I'm somewhat at a loss, General. Your wire led me to believe you wished to discuss an official matter."

"And so I do," Mackenzie assured him earnestly. "Mrs. Brannock and I are here regarding a court hearing of the most critical nature. I believe you're familiar with the case involving Clint Brannock."

"Indeed, I am," Wallace grumbled. "No disrespect, Mrs. Brannock, but your brother-in-law might have picked a better spot. I dislike the sound of gunfire outside the territorial capitol."

Elizabeth returned his gaze steadily. "We had gunfire in Lincoln last week, Governor. You may have heard that my husband was killed."

"Most unfortunate." Wallace pursed his lips, nodded solemnly. "I admired your husband greatly, Mrs. Brannock. Please accept my condolences."

"Thank you," Elizabeth said, smiling faintly. "Of course, all that has a direct bearing on why we're here today. You see, Stephen Benton ordered my husband's death."

"Have you any proof of his involvement?"

"Have you any doubt of it, Governor?"

"Certainly I'm aware of the antagonism that existed. At best, however, we're talking conjecture and supposition. Not hard evidence."

Elizabeth tilted her chin. "Stephen Benton threatened my husband in an effort to stop my investigations into land fraud. Wilbur Latham, in Benton's name, made similar threats to Clint." She paused, staring across the desk. "Do you call that conjecture?"

"No," Wallace said in a precise voice. "I call it circumstantial evidence, hardly more than hearsay. As such, it is inadmissible in a court of law."

Mackenzie flipped a hand back and forth. "Governor, we're not interested in legal mumbo jumbo, the technicalities. Circumstantial or not, there is a direct link between Stephen Benton and the murder of Virgil Brannock."

Wallace lifted an eyebrow in question. "Your presence here leaves me puzzled, General. What interest does the military have in a civil matter?"

"For almost eight years," Mackenzie pointed out, "Clint Brannock served his country honorably and faithfully. I will not sit idly by and see him railroaded into prison."

"Strong words," Wallace said. "So far as I can determine, Mr. Brannock acted with considerable premeditation. Do you deny that he came here with the express purpose of killing Benton?"

"Come now, Governor," Mackenzie said with a knowing look. "Clint was on the verge of connecting Benton and the Santa Fe Ring to the *Comanchero* trade. On three separate occasions, their assassins attempted to kill him. And they finally killed his brother."

Mackenzie paused, leaning forward. He rapped the edge of the desk with his knuckles and fixed Wallace with a hard look. "Let's not forget who the cutthroats are in this matter. Graft and corruption—and assassinations—are a way of life in New Mexico. Clint was wholly justified in killing Stephen Benton."

Wallace's face was dispassionate. "No man can place himself above the law. A case could be made that William Bonney was justified in killing those who tried to kill him. Would you exonerate him as well?"

Mackenzie laughed without humor. "I recall you once offered amnesty to Billy the Kid and his entire gang. Aren't you being somewhat selective with the law, Governor?"

"On the contrary," Wallace countered. "I was attempting to halt the bloodshed in Lincoln County. Extreme circumstances sometimes require expedient means."

"Precisely!" Mackenzie said, slapping the desktop. "President Hayes ordered you to stop the violence and your neck was on the line. So in that instance, the end justified the means. Don't you think that sounds a bit self-serving?"

"How dare you!" Wallace flared. "I will not be lectured on morals and ethics, not by anyone. You presume too much, sir."

"Gentlemen, please," Elizabeth interjected hastily. "Harsh words and recriminations will get us nowhere. I suggest we look at this from a practical standpoint."

Wallace glowered at Mackenzie a moment longer. Then, regaining his composure, he directed his attention to Elizabeth. "Above all else, I'm a resonable man, Mrs. Brannock. What is it you propose?"

"I believe your tenure as governor expires this year."

"Yes, that's correct," Wallace affirmed. "The President has assured me a successor will be appointed sometime this fall."

"Would you agree that your mission here has not been fully realized?"

"I would," Wallace confessed. "One of my major goals was to achieve political stability. I regret to say I've failed."

Elizabeth gave him a cool look of appraisal. "How would you like to depart New Mexico a hero?"

"I beg your pardon."

"Let's suppose I could rout the Santa Fe Ring. And in the process, make a first step toward political stability. Wouldn't that be a feather in your cap?"

Wallace shook his head. "You'll pardon my saying so, but that appears rather unlikely."

Elizabeth smiled. "Are you aware I put together the reform movement?"

"I've heard rumors to that effect."

"What if I told you I could substantiate the corruption of the Santa Fe Ring?"

"No offense," Wallace said, "but I would have to see that with my own eyes."

"You will," Elizabeth informed him. "We have documented proof of conspiracy and widespread graft. Max Flagg will publish it as an exposé in the *New Mexican*."

"You're serious, aren't you?"

"Of course," Elizabeth said lightly. "Virgil taught me never to brag before the fact. We now have the proof in hand."

Wallace leaned back in his chair, steepling his hands, and tapped his index fingers together. He studied her intently. "I presume there's a quid pro quo involved. Are we talking about your brother-in-law?"

"Yes," Elizabeth said firmly. "I want all charges against Clint dropped."

"Why would I consider such a step?"

"Three reasons," Elizabeth observed. "First, it would not be politically expedient to bring Clint to trial. The Santa Fe Ring would attempt to smear me—and the reform movement—by association. That might very well cost us the election."

Wallace nodded owlishly. "And the second reason?"

"No jury would convict Clint."

"Indeed?"

Elizabeth batted her eyelashes. "Imagine me on the witness stand, Governor. A widow, still in mourning, testifying against her husband's murderer. The jury would probably award Clint a medal."

Wallace strummed the tip of his nose. "I see your point."

"Now, as to the third reason," Elizabeth went on, "In exchange for Clint's release, I will instruct Max Flagg to credit you with the downfall of the Santa Fe Ring. Think of it, Governor"—she paused, looked him squarely in the eye—"the man who brought political stability to New Mexico. Has a nice ring, doesn't it?"

"Hmmm." Wallace considered a moment. "I think you'll do well in politics, Mrs. Brannock. You have an unusually devious mind."

"So I've been told."

There was an instant of calculation while Wallace stared at her. "Very well," he said, "I'll arrange to have the charges dropped. However, there's a condition attached."

"What kind of condition?"

"I want Clint Brannock out of New Mexico. In fact, I insist that he leave today."

Elizabeth sounded troubled. "How long would he have to stay away?"

"A year," Wallace said emphatically. "We need time

for tempers to cool over Benton's death. Otherwise, there'll be no end to the bloodshed.''

"What if Clint refuses?''

"The matter is not negotiable, Mrs. Brannock. Either he leaves the territory or he stands trial. I want the killing ended.''

Elizabeth exchanged a glance with Mackenzie. He arched one eyebrow and slowly nodded his head. She sighed inwardly, aware that she'd been forced into a corner. Then, marking yet another lesson learned, she reminded herself that politics was grounded in compromise. She really had no choice.

"If I agree,'' she said hesitantly, "how soon could you have him released?''

"Within the hour,'' Wallace replied. "On your guarantee that he'll leave Santa Fe this afternoon.''

"Governor, I believe I've just made my first political deal.''

"I daresay it won't be your last, Mrs. Brannock.''

"Neither the last nor the best. I intend to get better as I go along.''

Wallace recalled a scrap of gossip he'd heard from an acquaintance in Lincoln County. The *mexicanos* had coined their own name for Elizabeth Brannock. *La Mariposa de Hierro.*

He thought it a fitting tribute to the lady. New Mexico was the perfect setting for an Iron Butterfly.

"I will like hell!''

"Clint, listen to reason.''

"Thanks, but no thanks. I won't be run out of the territory. And that's final.''

Elizabeth looked at him with a wounded expression. Not ten minutes past, Clint had been brought under armed guard from the prison lockup. He'd listened with mounting anger as she outlined the condition placed on his release. Her pleas, thus far, had been bluntly rejected.

Mackenzie stood by the window. They were sequestered in a conference room down the hall from the governor's office. Outside was a flagstone patio shaded by tall trees. Staring up at the sky, Mackenzie toyed with the germ of an idea. He hadn't yet broached it to Clint.

"General Mackenzie," Elizabeth said now, "would you talk to him? I can't seem to make him understand."

"Understand what?" Clint demanded. "You and Wallace struck a deal without my say so. That's the long and the short of it."

Mackenzie turned from the window. "Mrs. Brannock was acting in your own best interests. Why be bullheaded about it?"

"Why not?" Clint said stubbornly. "I won't be posted into limbo because I killed Benton. Hell, I did everybody a favor."

Mackenzie shrugged, eyebrows raised. "A jury might not see it that way. Would you prefer to stand trial?"

Clint leaned forward in his chair, arms across his knees. He stared down at the floor. "I suppose you're right," he said at length. "It just sticks in my craw, that's all."

"Perhaps it's not as bad as it sounds. In fact, I have something in mind that seems made to order."

"What's that?"

"You're an excellent scout," Mackenzie said with a wry smile. "but you're an even better lawman. I happen to know someone who could use a man of your talents."

Clint looked inquisitive. "Where?"

"The U.S. marshal at Fort Smith owes me a favor. While I was commanding Fort Sill, I provided him with assistance on occasion. I'm confident he would take you on as a deputy marshal."

Clint examined the notion. "I recollect the Fort Smith marshals have jurisdiction over the Nations. Way I heard it, lots of white outlaws hole up there."

"That's correct," Mackenzie remarked. "They take sanctuary among the Five Civilized Tribes. A lawman rides into the Nations at his own peril."

"Sounds like you're trying to sell me on the job."

"For the most part, you'd be operating on your own. Isn't that what you prefer?"

"Something else," Elizabeth added quickly. "Working there would put you nearer Lon and Hank. You could see them whenever you wished."

"Lord love us," Clint said with a ghost of a grin. "You're determined to pack me off, aren't you?"

Elizabeth laughed. "As the general said, it's made to order. You'd feel lost without a badge of some sort."

"Hell, why not?" Clint's smile broadened. "I need a change of scenery anyway."

A short time later Elizabeth and Clint emerged from the building. Clint once more wore his Colt six-gun, and his buckskin gelding waited at the hitch rack. There was a bittersweet moment as they halted beneath the portico. Neither of them knew quite what to say, how to frame it in words. Nor were they comfortable with the thought of parting.

"Write me," Clint said awkwardly. "I'll want to know how you're getting along."

"Don't worry," she murmured. "I'll do just fine."

"All the same, I'd like to hear. It's liable to be a while before I see the Hondo again."

She smiled brightly. "A year isn't forever. We'll all be together before you know it."

Clint nodded. "Look after yourself, Beth."

Her eyes suddenly misted. She went up on tiptoe and brushed his cheek with a soft kiss. Clint squeezed her arm and turned away, walking to his horse. He stood there a moment, his hand on the pommel, then stepped into the saddle. A slow smile tugged at the corner of his mouth. He looked at her.

"Give 'em hell in the elections."

"I will," she promised. "Holy hell from the Brannocks."

Clint laughed and reined the gelding about. From the opposite side of the plaza he waved one last time, then turned south onto the Santa Fe Trail. Outside town he stopped on a knoll and twisted around in the saddle. Sunset cast a ruddy glow across the mountains and he fixed the sight in mind. As though from a distance, he heard her voice again and nodded to himself. A year wasn't all that long.

He rode toward Indian Territory.

About the Author

Matt Braun is the author of over thirty novels, and the winner of the Golden Spur Award from the Western Writers of America for his novel *The Kincaids*. A true Westerner, he was born in Oklahoma and descends from a long line of ranchers. He writes with a passion for historical accuracy and detail that has earned him a reputation as the most authentic portrayer of the American West.